DEATH AT THE DOUBLE R

ROBIN T. POPP

LARKSPUR LANE PUBLISHING, LLC

Contents

CHAPTER ONE

THE PIERCING BLARE OF the alarm jolted Elise Richardson out of her deep slumber. She reluctantly opened one eye, only to be met with darkness enveloping her room. With a groan, she reached out to silence the shrill sound emanating from her phone. It took several fumbling swipes at her phone screen before she was successful, but the resulting silence was like music to her ears.

She had stayed up way too late the night before, pouring over today's presentation until the wee hours of the morning. Now, all she wanted was to sink back into the welcoming embrace of sleep. But as her heavy eyelids drooped closed again, she jolted herself awake. Today was not a day for giving in to temptation. She had worked hard to climb the ladder at *Tinslow and McNeal, Inc.*, and sleeping in was not part of her path to success.

With a determined sigh, Elise climbed out of bed, quickly showered, and then selected an outfit that radiated success and professionalism. After dressing, she headed to the kitchen to brew her morning coffee and review her presentation one last time.

As she sipped on her strong espresso, she mentally rehearsed her pitch until it was ingrained in her mind. Then, with a sense of purpose and determination, she left her modest apartment and joined the sea of commuters on the bustling streets of New York City. Arriving at the office precisely at 7:45 a.m., she felt a flutter of excitement in her stomach. Today could be a very good day—if everything went well.

Maddie's singsong voice filled the air as she entered Elise's office. "Today's the big day," she announced with a hint of excitement, her steps light and quick on the plush carpet.

"Fingers crossed," Elise replied, joining in on Maddie's excitement. "Oh, before I forget." Reaching down, she pulled out a medium-sized gift bag from beneath her desk and eagerly handed it to Maddie. "I got you something."

Maddie's eyes widened in surprise. "Me? What for? It's not even my birthday."

"Just open it," Elise urged with a grin.

She watched as Maddie reached into the bag and pulled out a box with a picture of an Apple iPad Mini on the front.

"Elise. What did you do? These things are expensive."

"You've been spending all your extra money helping your mom with her medical bills. I wanted to do something nice for you, to thank you for being the world's best administrative assistant."

"Thank you," Maddie said, clutching the box to her chest. She loved new technology like other women loved Tiffany's jewelry. "You shouldn't have. It's way too expensive, but I love it. Next time, though, try spending some of your hard-earned money on yourself."

Elise brushed off Maddie's comment with a dismissive wave. "Plenty of time for that later—after I make vice president. Speaking of, I'd better get set up." Gathering up her laptop and notes, she headed down the hall.

She was nearly giddy as she stood in the conference room twenty minutes later. Through the room's glass wall, she watched Bob, the President of *Tinslow and McNeal*, escorting the Johnston Corporation's chief officers to the conference room. Following behind them were *Tinslow and McNeal* executives—and Sean. He would no doubt try to take more credit for the presentation than he deserved.

Don't jinx it by thinking about him.

Refocusing her thoughts on the matter at hand, she waited for everyone to take their seats. Once they had, she greeted them with a smile and waited until everyone fell silent.

Show time!

"Johnston Corporation is currently the fifth largest manufacturer of home exercise equipment," Elise began in a clear voice, "and that is a highly respectable position; however, it won't last. In today's economy, consumers have less discretionary income to spend and exercise equipment isn't high on the list of priority purchases, especially high-end equipment, such as yours. What you need—and what I'm going to present to you today—is an ad campaign that changes the perception of J-Corp's equipment and moves it from a like-to-have to a must-have."

From their rapt expressions, she knew she had their attention. Pressing a button to kill the overhead lights, she launched the video she'd spent the past three months putting together. As images played across the projector screen, Elise's attention remained on the client's faces. They weren't looking away. That was a good sign.

The muted sound of her cell phone vibrating against the notebook where it rested was an unwelcome distraction. She glanced at the caller ID as she hurriedly tapped the ignore button to quiet it.

Diego Juarez.

The brother I never had.

As the only two children living full-time on the Double R Ranch—Elise being the owner's daughter and Diego being the ranch foreman's son—they had spent most of their time together and, at one time, had been close.

That was a long time ago, though. She hadn't talked to him in years.

I wonder what he wants?

Vowing to call him back later, she turned her attention back to the video and saw that the ad spot was ending. As the last notes of music faded, the screen went black, leaving the room dark and silent.

She waited, letting the impact of the ad settle in before turning up the lights.

As all eyes turned to her, she felt a rush of excitement at their expressions. She didn't need them to say anything to know they'd liked the video. They'd taken the bait. All she had to do now was set the hook.

"We showed that same video to a consumer test group," she continued her presentation. "In an audience made up of—"

The slight noise of her vibrating phone momentarily distracted her and her gaze flew to her phone screen.

Diego Juarez. Again?

Didn't he realize she had a job? Hell, didn't he have a job? Shouldn't he be entertaining guests? Showing them the ropes, literally. After all, it was a dude ranch.

She quickly recovered and continued with her report, spitting out the words by rote, thanks to hours of practice.

"As you can see," she continued, shoving thoughts of Diego from her mind, "seventy-three percent of the men and eighty-two percent of the women responded favorably to the ad's messaging. Let me break this down for you."

She brought up the next slide in her presentation and let the group have a moment of silence to study the numbers.

This time when her phone started vibrating, its buzzing seemed inordinately loud, drawing everyone's attention.

She glanced around, embarrassed. "Sorry," she muttered, once again hitting the ignore button.

Diego, what the hell?

He never called her.

The thought sent a frisson of uneasiness through her as she picked up the phone and slipped it into her jacket pocket. She struggled to pick up the presentation where she'd left off and, after a few minutes, she once again forgot about the phone.

Then Maddie appeared in the hallway outside the conference room.

"I'm sorry to interrupt," she said after quietly opening the door. "Ms. Richardson, there's an emergency phone call for you." She paused. "Your father's been in an accident."

"What?" She was sure she'd heard wrong. Now Diego's incessant phone calls made more sense.

"I'm sorry," she apologized to the group. "I should take this."

"You go ahead," Sean said magnanimously, standing. "I've got this." He held his hand out for the remote control.

Every fiber of her being screamed not to give it to him, but she felt the gazes of the others in the room staring at her; waiting for her to comply.

Don't make a scene, she told herself as she forced herself to surrender the remote. "Thank you." She bit out the words. Don't screw me over was the message she tried to convey with her eyes.

She left the room with as much dignity as she could muster.

"Did Diego say what happened?" She asked Maddie as, together, they hurried down the hallway.

"No. I tried to tell him you were in an important meeting, but he insisted I interrupt."

"It's okay. Thank you for getting me."

By now, they'd reached Elise's office. She went immediately to her desk and picked up the phone, pushing the button that would take Diego off hold.

"Diego?"

"Elise, thank God." His voice sounded harried and much deeper than she remembered it. "There's been an accident. Your father's been hurt. He was out riding and fell off his horse. Or maybe he was thrown; we don't know exactly what happened." He paused, and she braced, knowing there was more. He'd pulled her from a meeting, after all. "When he landed, he hit his head on a rock. Hard. Cracked his skull. The doctors have done all they can, but..." He paused. "He's dying, Elise."

"What?" Her mind struggled to process words she never expected to hear. "No. That can't be right."

"I'm sorry. God, I'm so sorry. I know it's tough to get the news like this, but I thought you'd want to get here before..."

Before he died.

The words hung out there, unspoken.

"How long does he have?" Tears choked her voice, and she had to clear her throat before trying to speak again. "Days? Weeks?"

"Hours. Maybe."

No.

"Is he in pain? Is he...suffering?"

"I don't know. I don't think so. He's not conscious and the doctors don't expect him to wake up. His body is shutting down."

"What hospital?" she asked.

"South Texas in McAllen."

"Okay." Slowly, her mind started working. "I'll leave as soon as I finish this presentation."

"Are you fucking kidding me?" Diego growled at her. "Your father is dying and you're going back to work?"

"I'm in the middle of something really important," she tried to explain, "and you said he wouldn't wake up, so—"

He cut her off. "Just stop. I thought that maybe you'd like the chance to make your peace with your father *before* he died. Sorry to have bothered you."

He disconnected the call before she could say another word. Replacing the receiver in its cradle, she rubbed her forehead, trying to relieve the stress.

He was right, of course, but if the first flight didn't leave for another four hours, she could finish the presentation. On the other hand, if she left before finishing the presentation, there was a chance she'd lose the promotion.

It wasn't fair.

"Is everything all right?"

Elise looked up to find Maddie standing in the doorway, looking concerned.

"No." She quickly explained the situation. "I need to get home right away," she finished.

"There's a car waiting downstairs to take you to the airport," Maddie said, holding out several pieces of paper. "Here is your itinerary. Your flight out of LaGuardia leaves in two hours. That's enough time to get there and go through security, but not enough time for you to run home first and pack. Buy clothes when you get there. Lord knows it wouldn't hurt you to have one casual outfit. In Dallas, you'll have to change planes." Seeing Elise's incredulous expression, she added, "I could tell from his voice and what little I heard on your end that the situation was critical, so I booked your travel. When you reach McAllen, there will be a driver and car waiting to take you wherever you need to go."

"But the presentation—"

"Let Sean handle it. Bob knows who did the heavy-lifting."

Elise hoped she was right.

"I'll make your excuses to the others," Maddie continued. Coming all the way into the office, she opened the bottom desk drawer and retrieved Elise's purse, which held her small laptop. She held it out to her. "Go." When Elise would have protested, Maddie stopped her. "Elise. I might complain about taking care of my mother, but I wouldn't trade it for the world. Family is more important than any job; it has to come first. Now go." She made a shooing gesture with her hand. "And don't forget to call me later and let me know how things are going."

Maddie was right. "Thank you so much." She gave the other woman a quick hug and then headed to the elevators, walking as quickly as she dared in four-inch heels.

Three hours later, sitting on the plane, en route to Dallas, thoughts of her father consumed Elise. The harsh words they'd last spoken echoed in her mind, making her cringe at the memory.

"You never come home to visit anymore," he had complained.

"I'm working on my career," she'd countered. "I only get a little time off."

"Come work for me," he'd suggested. "We could use your marketing skills. I'd pay you, of course."

She hadn't taken the suggestion seriously. "Move back to Las Palomas? I'd suffocate."

"What do you mean? You used to love it here. Maybe if you visited more often, you'd remember that."

"Or maybe I'm more like Mom and prefer the big city."

It was a low blow, and she'd regretted the words as soon as they'd left her lips, but she'd been so angry with her father for pressuring her, she hadn't apologized.

Her mother, who hated small towns and the ranching life, had given Las Palomas five years before she'd swallowed a handful of tranquilizers and washed them down with a glass or two of whiskey.

While her mother lay dying, eleven-year-old Elise and nine-year-old Diego had been out riding the ranch's back pastures with their fathers. Elise used to love riding. She loved the openness of the sprawling pastures and the sense of freedom that came with being on horseback.

They'd found a Longhorn skull on their ride and upon returning to the house, Elise had rushed inside to tell her mother about it.

At first, she'd thought her mother was only sleeping, but no matter how hard she'd tried, she couldn't wake her. She'd run from the room, barreling into Diego, who was coming in to find her.

"It's Momma," she'd told him, trying hard to hold back the tears. "I think she's sick...or something."

It was the "or something" that had terrified her. Diego, seeing her fear, had left Elise to go see for himself.

His expression when he returned was unreadable. In silence, he'd taken her by the hand and together they'd run to the barn.

Their expressions must have alarmed their fathers because the men stopped rubbing down the horses and moved to meet them.

Elise hadn't known what to say, but Diego had pulled his own father down low enough to whisper into his ear.

Elise didn't know what Diego said, but she would always remember that his father never questioned or doubted his son. Such was their relationship. He'd simply told Diego to find his mother and ask her to call for the doctor.

Then, shouting for one of the ranch hands to come tend the horses, he'd grabbed Elise's father by the arm and they'd hurried to the main house, speaking in tones too soft for Elise to hear.

Diego and his parents lived in the ranch foreman's house, located close to the barn. When they arrived, Diego had told his mother what was happening.

She called Doc Parker and though he arrived in minutes, it was still too late.

Elise knew her mother had hated living in Las Palomas; hated living on the ranch. What she couldn't understand was why her mother would rather kill herself than continue living there with her husband and child. Because she couldn't understand, she blamed herself for not being a better daughter and for leaving her mother alone so often while she went riding with her father. She also blamed her father for not helping her mother.

Elise stopped riding horses and focused on her schoolwork. As for her father, maybe it was because he missed his wife, or maybe it was because he also felt guilty, but whatever the reason, more of his time and attention started going to the ranch, leaving less of it for his daughter, which became yet another bone of contention for Elise.

She thought back to that last exchange. It was hard to realize it had been almost a year ago. He'd flown to New York City because she'd been too busy to fly down. The argument had happened on their first night together. After that, the visit had been so strained, her father had changed his plans and flown back early. She'd intended to call him to apologize but had gotten busy with work and put it off. The longer she'd waited to call, the more difficult it became. A phone call wouldn't have been enough anyway, so she'd been planning to go home for a visit as soon as her schedule allowed. Only things never seemed to slow down, and she always thought there'd be time to go later.

What if she'd been wrong? What if her father died before she had time to apologize?

She turned her head to stare blindly out the window as tears filled her eyes and then spilled down her cheeks.

Chapter Two

Thanks to flight cancelations and delays, it was late when Elise finally landed in McAllen, Texas, the nearest big city to Las Palomas.

Fortunately, the driver Maddie had hired had waited for her and she was now sitting in the back of a town car, heading to the hospital.

Taking out her cell phone, she took a couple of deep breaths to steady her nerves. The sandwich she'd eaten while waiting in the Dallas airport now felt like a lead weight, sitting in the pit of her stomach. She placed the call to Diego and waited for him to answer, which he did after the second ring.

"How is he?" she asked without preamble.

"No change." He sounded weary. "Where are you?"

"In town. Finally. My Dallas connection was canceled and the next flight to McAllen departed late, but I'm headed to the hospital now and should be there in about fifteen minutes."

"Good. I'll meet you in the lobby."

They disconnected, and Elise thought about seeing Diego again. How long had it been? Her last visit home had been nearly five years ago, but Diego had been away at college. She remembered his parents, Jorge and Nina, had regaled her with stories of Diego's success in computer programming. She remembered being surprised later when she learned that he'd returned to the ranch to work rather than head to one of the big cities to work in IT.

So, continuing her train of thought, that meant the last time she'd seen him in person had been his high school graduation. How much had he changed in the past seven years? Would she even recognize him?

At eighteen and having worked on the ranch his entire life, he'd been lean but muscular, and attractive in a rough sort of way. The girls in high school had thrown themselves at him, hoping to get his attention. According to his mother, college had been the same and while he'd dated some, there had been no serious relationships. She wondered if he was dating anyone now.

A new thought hit her. Was Diego married? The thought was unsettling, and she didn't want to think about why that was.

She was here for her father; nothing more.

The fifteen-minute drive to the hospital seemed to take forever, but eventually, her car pulled up to the hospital's main entrance and stopped. Elise dug in her purse for a credit card and paid the driver before getting out.

Inside, even at this late hour, the hospital reception area had people waiting. She scanned the faces of the men in the lobby and was surprised to find that none of them looked familiar. Deciding that Diego hadn't yet arrived, she started for the receptionist's desk, intending to get directions to her father's room.

As she crossed the area, her attention was immediately drawn to the man leaning against the column. He was casually dressed, wearing a pair of well-fitted jeans and a blue linen button-down shirt that accentuated his muscular physique. The sleeves were rolled up, revealing tanned, muscular arms. His short, dark hair was tousled, as if he had been running his fingers through it. It made him look disheveled but attractive.

All this, she took in at a glance, not wanting to be caught staring. Diego had taken his father's position as ranch foreman, so she needed to be looking for someone who looked like they worked around horses and cattle all day, not this polished stranger.

She walked past the man without looking at him and continued to the receptionist's desk.

"Elise?"

The sound of her name made her turn around. Immediately, her gaze fell on a young Hispanic man standing off to the side that she hadn't noticed in her earlier search of the lobby. His boyish features were more in keeping with the image of Diego as she remembered him, including the stained work shirt and jeans. Even his boots looked dusty and well-worn.

The last of her doubts fled when he waved and started walking toward her. Returning his smile, she changed directions and headed toward him. As they got closer, though, she noticed he wasn't meeting her gaze.

Was he still mad at her?

She grudgingly admitted that his anger was justified, but she hadn't stayed in New York, had she? He could cut her a little slack.

Instead of stopping when he reached her, he brushed past her without saying a word.

Stunned, she turned and saw him approach a group of people just coming into the hospital.

"I don't know if I should be hurt or amused that you thought that boy was me," a deep, familiar voice said from just behind her.

Elise whirled around and stared at a blue linen button-down shirt covering a very broad, male chest. Tilting her head back, she looked up into the face of the handsome man who, moments ago, had been leaning against the column. Now he was smiling down at her.

"I did not," she automatically denied, feeling her face redden in embarrassment.

Holy crap. This is Diego?

He arched one eyebrow as he gave her a knowing look.

"Oh, all right. You win. I didn't recognize you, but in my defense, you've changed a lot in the last seven years. I don't remember you being this tall, for starters."

"I had a late growth spurt in college." His gaze ran over her. "Nice outfit."

She was impeccably dressed, for work. Now she felt decidedly over-dressed. "There wasn't time to change before going to the airport."

"Relax, you look nice. Shall we go see your father?"

He didn't wait for her reply, but placed his hand against the small of her back and guided her through the lobby.

"How is he?" she asked, not sure she was ready to hear the answer. "What are the doctors saying?"

"He's the same." His tone was bleak, and she knew he was suffering. With her in New York and Diego's folks in Florida, her father and Diego had grown close. "The doctors are doing what they can to make him comfortable, but they say his injuries are too severe."

"Tell me again what happened?"

"I don't know exactly. I had to go out of town and didn't get back until late. The first thing I did was take a shower. Then I went to find Roy, to let him know I was back, but he wasn't anywhere in the main house. I thought he might still be on the back deck, but he wasn't there either. When I checked the barn, I found his horse missing, so I knew he'd gone for a ride. I decided to go look for him. I was in the back pasture when I saw—" Diego looked around and lowered his voice. "*El Muerto.*"

Elise gave him a "so what" look. She'd grown up on the ranch and had seen the ghost riding across the pasture more times than she could count.

"No, this was different," he said, correctly interpreting her look. "He rode right up to me, close enough I could see right through him. And the air got icy. It's the middle of summer, hot as hell, but when I exhaled, my breath turned white. Then *El Muerto* raised his arm and pointed a bony finger at me. Scared the shit out of me. I thought he was coming for me." He paused, visibly shaken. "But that wasn't the worst part."

They'd reached the elevators, and when the doors opened, they stepped inside. Because they weren't the only passengers, he didn't continue his story until they'd reached the third floor and stepped off.

"The worst part was seeing Roy's horse behind *El Muerto*—without Roy sitting in the saddle. That's when I knew something was wrong. When *El Muerto* rode off, I didn't stop to think about it. I just rode after him. We ended up in the middle of the back pasture where I found Roy, bloodied and unconscious. The best I can figure is that his horse spooked, and he fell off, hitting his head on a rock when he landed. I called Doc Niven right away to come out. I was too afraid to move your dad; afraid I'd make the situation worse. Then, I called Rodrigo. Told him to meet Doc at the main house and bring him back to the south pasture. Doc examined your dad and immediately called for a helicopter to transport Roy here to South Texas. I caught a ride with them. That was the longest ride of my life." He paused before adding, "I never should have left town. None of this would've happened if I'd stayed."

"You can't know that, Diego," she said. "Accidents happen."

Elise wasn't sure what more she could say, so she reached out to lay a comforting hand on his arm. He smiled down at her as he briefly covered her hand with his much larger one.

They reached the doors of the intensive care unit and after Diego pressed the intercom button, a disembodied voice spoke through the speaker, requesting his name. The sound was slightly muffled, giving it an eerie quality.

"It's Diego Juarez, here to see Roy Richardson. I've got Roy's daughter with me," he replied.

"Sure thing, hon," the voice responded warmly. After a moment of static, the doors to the ICU slowly opened.

"Hon?" Elise gave him a curious look.

He shrugged. "Friendly staff. Shall we?" He gestured for her to enter first and she stepped cautiously through the doors.

As soon as they crossed the threshold, she was greeted by the steady beeping of patient monitoring equipment and hushed conversations among medical staff at the nursing station in the center of the large room. The smell of antiseptic was overpowering, and despite it being late at night, the room was illuminated by bright fluorescent lights.

The unit consisted of patient rooms with curtained glass walls and doorways that lined three walls. As they walked past, Elise caught glimpses through the curtains of patients hooked up to IVs and machines monitoring their vitals. The gravity of it all gave the atmosphere a somber and sobering feeling.

Her heart sank as she realized that all the patients in this area were seriously ill or injured. Some may not survive. The reality of why she was there suddenly hit her like a ton of bricks.

Diego guided her to a room, and they entered. A nurse stood by the bed checking an IV pump, but Elise's eyes were fixed on her father lying in the hospital bed.

Beneath the bruises and swollen features, she barely recognized him. His skin had taken on a sickly gray hue, making him appear much older and frailer than she remembered. Never in her entire life had she thought of her father as anything less than strong and formidable.

Now, seeing him so weak and vulnerable, Elise couldn't help but feel a surge of emotions she hadn't anticipated.

"Sue, this is Roy's daughter, Elise." Diego introduced her to the nurse standing beside the bed. Her soft smile was filled with sympathy as she greeted them.

"How is he doing?" Elise inquired, her voice trembling slightly.

"The same, I'm afraid. Now that you're here, I'll call the doctor," Sue responded, giving her a reassuring pat on the shoulder before hurrying out of the room. Elise took a moment to gather herself before setting her purse down on the cool tile floor beneath the window.

A few minutes later, a young woman in a crisp white coat entered the room and extended her hand with a warm smile.

"Hello, I'm Dr. Lott."

Elise shook her hand and braced herself for what was to come. For the next ten minutes, Dr. Lott carefully explained her father's condition—severe head trauma resulting in brain damage similar to a massive stroke, plus internal bleeding from being trampled by his horse after being thrown. The prognosis was grim, and tears began to well up in Elise's eyes as the doctor urged her to prepare for the worst.

As they spoke, Diego stood by stoically, absorbing every word from the doctor. When Elise ran out of questions, Dr. Lott left the room after reassuring them that she was just a call away if needed.

"You both must be exhausted," Sue said kindly, entering the room once again after the doctor had left. "Can I get you some coffee or anything else to drink?"

Both Elise and Diego politely declined her offer.

"Well, I'll leave you alone then. Call me if you need anything," Sue said before exiting with a gentle smile.

After Sue left, Elise wiped away tears that had gathered in her eyes and went to stand by her father's bedside. "Do you think he can hear us?" she asked Diego.

"I don't know," he admitted, joining her on the opposite side of the bed. He gently took Roy's hand in his own, a gesture that filled Elise with envy. "Roy, Elise is here."

Diego met her gaze and gave a slight nod, encouraging her to say something; anything to her father.

With a hesitant breath, Elise mirrored Diego's action, slowly taking the hand that lay closest to her. This hand had guided her through childhood and adolescence with its gentle touch and unwavering support. Now, it felt foreign and fragile in hers.

"Hey, Dad," she started, her voice catching in her throat as she struggled to find the words. A wave of emotion overwhelmed her—remorse for his injury, regret for not returning home sooner, and the old familiar anger at her father for her mother's death. Amidst all these conflicting feelings, one stood out starkly: desolation. Her father was dying; too soon and before they could mend the rift that had grown between them.

Diego must have sensed her turmoil because he gently laid her father's hand back on the bed before coming to stand beside her. Wrapping his arm around her shoulders, he pulled her close, offering his silent support. She leaned into him, feeling emotionally drained and weak, hoping some of his solid strength would seep into her.

After a moment, he released her. "I'm going to step out briefly."

"What? No, where are you going?" she protested, not wanting to be left alone.

"Elise, talk to him. He's never stopped loving you. He talked about you all the time," Diego insisted. "So even if he can't understand what you're telling him, he needs to hear your voice—and I know there are things you want to say to him before you don't have the opportunity anymore."

Then he was gone, leaving Elise alone with her thoughts and her father's fading presence. With trembling hands, she let go of his hand and pulled the bedside chair closer. Sitting down, she reached for his hand again; cool to the touch compared to the warm solidity she remembered from years past. Tears welled up in her eyes as she struggled to find the right words.

"Hey, Dad." She cleared her throat, trying to sound braver than she felt. "You didn't have to go to all this trouble to get me here."

Her attempt at dry humor fell flat in the somber atmosphere and she recognized her use of it as a defense mechanism; a shield behind which to hide her true feelings. If ever there was a time to be honest, it was now. Elise took a deep breath.

"I'm sorry I didn't come home to visit. I'm doing important things in New York...and I thought we'd have more time." As soon as the words left her mouth, she regretted them.

Stop it. He's dying. He doesn't care about your rationalizations. All he wanted was to see his daughter, and you were too busy.

"I love you, Dad," she said softly, tears welling up in her eyes. "I never meant to hurt you. Please don't leave me. I'll miss you so much." The guilt of not visiting him sooner weighed heavy on her heart.

"When you get better, maybe we can go riding?" she suggested, trying to keep the conversation light. "I miss riding with you—only this time, you need to be careful." She smiled through her tears. "Maybe we should put you on old Snowflake. He's so old—"

She stopped; sure her father had just squeezed her hand.

"Dad? Can you hear me?" She looked at him expectantly. And then he did it again, he squeezed her hand. This time, she was sure of it. Had the doctor been wrong? Could he be waking up?

"Dad, can you hear me?" she repeated, her voice cracking with emotion. "You had an accident. You're in the hospital. I'm here with you, and so is Diego."

Diego! She needed to get him.

"Hang on, Dad. I'm going to get Diego and call the nurse." Reluctantly letting go of his hand, she ran to the doorway. Diego was standing at the nurse's station talking to Sue, but he looked up as soon as he saw Elise.

"What's wrong?" His face filled with concern as he rushed towards her.

"I think he's waking up." The possibility had Elise wound so tight, her whole body trembled with anticipation. She looked past Diego to Sue, her eyes pleading for urgency. "Come quickly."

They hurried back to the room, their footsteps echoing against the sterile white walls. Elise took her father's hand once again, hoping for another response. Sue stood across from her on the other side of the bed, exchanging words with Diego in hushed tones. Words Elise couldn't understand over the deafening ringing in her ears.

Then several nurses came rushing into the room with Dr. Lott following closely after them. Diego went to Elise and gently guided her away from the bed as the newcomers crowded around it.

There was a flurry of activity and shouting, like a chaotic symphony playing out before her very eyes. Elise watched it all in a daze, feeling detached and surreal as if she were watching a movie instead of living through this moment. Then reality hit hard as she realized that the loud ringing wasn't inside her head; it was the sound of the heart monitor alerting them to a stopped heartbeat.

CHAPTER THREE

As the flat line on the heart monitor slowly registered in her mind, Elise's body leaned heavily against Diego, seeking his strength and support. She felt as though time itself had slowed or come to a stop—the bustling hospital staff and their frantic efforts to revive her father seemed like distant, muted background noise.

Despite their efforts, at 11:42 p.m., Roy Richardson was pronounced dead. In that instant, Elise was left alone in the world.

The hospital gave her a moment to grieve, but that was all. There were questions to answer and seemingly endless hours of paperwork to complete. Feeling overwhelmed, Elise was grateful for Diego's presence. Despite the exhaustion that must have been weighing heavily on him, he stayed by her side, helping her to answer questions about her father's insurance and funeral arrangements, which, she realized, she knew nothing about. In a daze, she listened as Diego provided the necessary information and made arrangements for her father's body to be sent to the funeral home in Las Palomas. His personal belongings were placed in a bag and given to Elise to take with her.

By the time they finished, it was well past two in the morning and Elise felt numb with grief and fatigue. Turning to Diego, she suggested finding a place to stay for the night.

"You must be exhausted," she said softly.

"I am," he admitted with a weary sigh, running his fingers through his hair. "But I also need to get back to the ranch. Rodrigo is taking care of things with the guests."

"Does the bus route still run through Las Palomas?"

"Yes, but I've got a better idea."

They'd reached the first of the waiting taxis, and Diego bent low, speaking to the driver through the open passenger window. "You just start your shift?"

"No, man." The driver replied. "I'm coming off. You'll be my last fare."

Diego thanked him and continued to the next cab. He asked the same question of the next two cabs before finding a driver who'd just started his shift.

"How much to take us to Las Palomas?" Diego asked him.

The driver looked aghast. "Are you kidding? That's over a hundred miles. It'd be cheaper to rent a car or take the bus."

"True," Diego admitted, "but if I rented a car, one of us," he gestured to Elise and then himself, "would have to drive and we're both exhausted. And the bus won't head out for another three hours. I don't want to wait."

Diego reached into his wallet and pulled out a wad of hundred-dollar bills, holding them up for the driver to inspect.

The man's eyes widened at the sight of the money and he grinned. "You've got yourself a ride," he said with a nod.

"Good." Diego opened the door for Elise, who climbed into the backseat without hesitation.

"Do me a favor," Diego said to the driver as he settled into the seat beside Elise and gave him their destination. "Keep the radio volume low."

Elise felt herself sinking deeper into the soft leather seat, her energy draining out of her body. She was struggling to process everything that had happened in such a short amount of time.

"You okay?" Diego asked, his voice filled with concern.

She shrugged, not wanting to burden him with her thoughts. "I don't know. Right now, I just feel...numb."

He nodded understandingly. "I know. Try to get some rest. We'll figure everything out later."

Grateful for his comfort, she turned to stare out the window at the city lights passing by in a blur. Soon, she heard Diego's deep breathing next to her and envied his ability to fall asleep so easily.

The cabbie switched on the radio, filling the air with lively Spanish voices discussing sports. Although she couldn't understand most of it, she found the cadence of their speech melodic and soothing. The steady vibrations of the cab on the road made her drowsy and she began to shiver in the cool air-conditioning. Seeking warmth, she scooted closer to Diego and, resting her head against his arm, closed her eyes. She felt safe and protected in his presence, the sound of his steady breathing lulling her into a peaceful slumber.

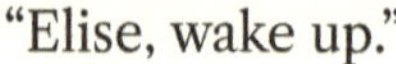

"Elise, wake up."

The sound of Diego's voice brought Elise out of her slumber. Feeling like she'd been run over by a bulldozer, she groggily opened her eyes. Every part of her body ached from the long day of travel, hours at the hospital, and then the car ride to Las Palomas. To her embarrassment, she realized that her head was resting against Diego's chest, his arm wrapped protectively around her shoulders as she'd slept.

Quickly pulling away and sitting upright, she mumbled an apology. "I got cold," she explained.

Diego gave her a wry smile but simply said, "We're home."

Not my home, she silently reminded herself. This was her father's home, but...

My father is dead.

She tested the words in her head, picking at the wound to see how tender it was.

Diego opened the door and, after climbing out, reached back for her hand to help her out. She wanted to refuse, but her stiff legs protested. Gratefully accepting his offer, she climbed out of the car with his assistance.

As Diego paid the driver, Elise couldn't help but notice the sun peeking over the horizon—a new day dawning. While she recognized the symbolism, she was too tired to fully appreciate it.

Turning, she studied her old home. It hadn't changed much over the years. From the front, it looked deceptively small. In truth, it had started out small—just two bedrooms, a kitchen, dining room and a family room. The additions had come a few years later when her father had turned their home into a working dude ranch. They had replaced the garage with a commercial kitchen, attached to which were added a dining hall and a guest recreation room. Then a new garage had been added to complete the project.

They had also built a bunkhouse past the barn, and this was where the ranch hands stayed. The ranch foreman's house was on the other side of that. Between the main house and the barn were nine small guest bungalows.

The sound of the cab's tires on the gravel as it drove away brought her attention back to the moment.

"Shall we go inside?" Diego suggested, moving towards the front door and using his key to unlock it.

Elise entered the foyer, which opened up into a spacious great room. She paused, her eyes widening in surprise as she took in her surroundings. "Wow," she gasped.

Apparently, the outside of the house was the only thing that hadn't changed since she was last there. The walls had been repainted using a technique that left them looking like painted stone. New saddle-colored leather couches stood where the old fabric ones had been. The floor had been re-tiled and tanned cow hides, rather than area rugs, lay strategically about. The fireplace had been enlarged to run nearly the width of the far wall and redone in white stone. A polished, gnarled wood mantelpiece ran the length of it. Mounted above it was a set of Longhorn cattle horns. To the right, standing in the corner facing out into the room, was a large screen TV.

The separate formal dining room, which was located to the left of the foyer, had years ago been remade into a study, but now it had French doors, which were standing open. Her father's modest desk had been replaced with a larger one of dark oak. Behind it was a black desk chair and in front stood two burgundy guest chairs, all made of leather.

"When did all of this happen?" Elise asked, still in disbelief at how different, yet stunningly beautiful, the place looked.

"Last February," Diego replied with a small chuckle. "So, what's that? Fifteen months ago? We closed down the ranch and brought in some crews to help with the renovations. By the end of the month, it was all done. Looks pretty nice, don't you think?"

"It's fantastic," Elise said in amazement, "but it must have cost a fortune."

Diego shrugged nonchalantly, the corners of his mouth turning up in a half-smile. "What's the adage? You've got to spend money to make money." He waved his hands around in a gesture that encompassed their surroundings. "The place needed a facelift."

He pulled out his phone, glancing at the time. "The staff will be up and starting their chores soon. They'll need to be told about Roy."

Elise nodded. "They'll have questions," she reasoned aloud. "They'll want to know if they still have jobs." She hadn't even had time to process her father's passing, let alone think about the responsibilities that were now hers. "What do I tell them?"

Diego stepped close, placing a comforting hand on her shoulder. "We tell them that Roy passed quietly with you by his side. As far as we know, he didn't suffer." He paused before adding, "For now, things continue as normal. The rest, we'll figure out later. And remember, you're not alone in this."

With a grateful nod, Elise set her purse down on the floor beside the couch and followed him to the large commercial kitchen.

"Diego, you're back." A young woman in her early twenties, who looked vaguely familiar, greeted them with a warm smile, wiping her hands on a towel draped around her neck. Behind her, three other women Elise didn't recognize were busy chopping vegetables at the kitchen island.

"How is he?" the young woman asked with concern etched into her features.

Diego shook his head sadly. "He didn't make it."

The room fell quiet as the young woman's expression turned to one of grief.

"*Madre de Dios*," she whispered, her voice cracking as she wiped away tears threatening to fall. Behind her, the three women set down their knives and began to softly weep.

The young woman turned towards Elise with sorrowful eyes. "*Lo siento*."

Elise placed a hand on her shoulder in a gesture of comfort. "It's Carmen, isn't it?" she asked, finally recognizing Diego's younger cousin.

"Carmen took over mother's position as head cook," Diego explained. He gestured to the other three women, left to right. "And I don't think you've met Cindi Gates, Maria Hernandez and Denise Gonzales."

Elise's heart raced as she tried to commit their names to memory. They stood in front of her, expressions somber and sympathetic, their eyes filled with unspoken sorrow. She could feel their warmth and kindness radiating toward her, despite the heavy weight of grief that hung over them all.

"It's nice to meet you all," Elise managed to say, her voice soft and shaky. "I wish it could be under different circumstances." Guilt washed over her at the thought that this meeting could have been under different circumstances if she had just bothered to come home sooner.

Carmen took Elise's hands gently in hers. "Your father, he was a good man. We'll miss him terribly."

Tears threatened to spill from Elise's eyes again as she nodded gratefully. "Thank you."

Sensing Elise's discomfort, Carmen gave her hands a final squeeze before releasing them. "Let us know if there's anything we can do."

Diego spoke up then, breaking the emotional moment. "We're going out to tell Rodrigo and the boys. As for the guests, they'll have to be informed as well, but let's try to keep things as normal as possible for them."

Elise's heart fluttered with alarm at the mention of guests. She had no idea how to run a dude ranch; it was never something she had planned on inheriting.

"Don't worry," Diego said reassuringly, as if sensing her inner turmoil. "Everyone knows what to do. The ranch practically runs itself these days."

Grateful for his support and guidance, Elise allowed Diego to take the lead. It was clear he was used to running things around here, and for now, she would have to trust in his experience.

When his hand came to rest at the small of her back, guiding her out of the kitchen, she let him. They made their way through the dining hall and recreation room, before finally reaching the back door.

As Elise stepped into the garage, she took in the array of vehicles—her father's old red Ford F-150, two ATVs, and three electric golf carts. It was a reminder of the hard work that went into running this ranch.

The bunkhouse was about two hundred yards from the house. On the occasional days when the weather wasn't blistering hot, or it wasn't raining, it made for a pleasant walk from the main house. Since those days were the exception and not the rule, electric golf carts were used to get around.

"How many ranch hands do you have?" Elise asked as they climbed into the first cart, Diego taking his place behind the wheel.

"Ten. The men who used to work here while we were growing up have retired, but you'll recognize most of the current staff from high school."

He listed off their names, but Elise's mind was elsewhere, lost in memories of summers spent on the ranch.

The sun was above the horizon now, casting a warm yellow glow over the vast landscape. She knew that soon enough, the guests would be waking up and heading to the dining hall for a hot breakfast buffet and coffee prepared by Carmen and her team in the kitchen. Meanwhile, the ranch hands would be busy tending to chores.

"Are you okay?" Diego's voice brought Elise back to reality as they pulled up to the bunkhouse. "I can handle this if you want to wait here."

Shaking her head, she climbed out of the cart. "No, I need to do this." She took a deep breath before continuing. "Besides, I know it can't be easy for you either."

Diego nodded, his expression sympathetic. "Alright, then. Let's get this over with."

The bunkhouse stood as a modest, yet sturdy, wooden structure on the ranch. A large door opened into a spacious common room that boasted a television and an array of couches and chairs, enough to comfortably seat a dozen people. At the far end of the room, a dining area with a fully functioning kitchen beckoned, though the ranch hands typically took their meals in the larger dining hall with the guests. Two doors on either side of the common room led to narrow hallways lined with bedrooms. Each hallway held three bedrooms on one side and two bedrooms and a bathroom on the other.

As Elise and Diego entered through the front door, they were met with the sight of the ten ranch hands sitting in the common room, drinking coffee. The group turned collectively at their arrival, their expressions grim. One of them, who appeared to be four or five years older than the rest, spoke up.

"Roy?" he asked.

Diego shook his head. "He didn't make it."

"Damn," he muttered, getting to his feet. He went to Diego and gave his shoulder an affectionate squeeze. "I'm sorry, man." Then he turned to Elise and introduced himself. "Hi.

I'm Rodrigo Salander. Your father was a good man. We're all going to miss him."

The rest of the men offered their condolences in hushed tones. Elise recognized most of them from high school, though there were a couple of new faces.

"Thank you," she said softly, noticing how some of them discreetly wiped away tears.

"Don't worry about the guests," Rodrigo reassured Diego and Elise. "We'll take care of them. I know you'll have your hands full sorting out your dad's affairs," he added to Elise.

"Thanks," Diego replied gratefully. "We appreciate it."

They bid farewell shortly after, returned to the cart, and made their way back to the main house.

"I know you're exhausted, but we should talk," Diego said as he parked the cart in the garage, his expression serious.

"I know," she agreed. "But not now." Her head was pounding and her body ached with exhaustion as she climbed out of the cart, leaving him no choice but to do the same. She could feel his eyes on her as she stumbled towards the house, trying to ignore the sharp pain in her temples.

As she reached the back door, she turned to face him. "I have a horrible headache and I'm exhausted," she admitted. "You must be just as tired as I am."

He hesitated before nodding in agreement. "Yes, you're right. We should both get some rest."

Relief washed over her and she let out a sigh. "Thank you."

She headed inside, not caring whether or not he followed her. Only the knowledge that her old comfortable bed waited a few yards away gave her the energy to keep walking.

"Elise, wait."

She ignored him and continued through the family room, grabbing her purse along the way. The hallway past the foyer was dark because all the doors were closed. Elise's bedroom door was the second door on the right, with the first door leading to the guest bathroom. Her father's room was at the end of the hall.

Pushing open her own bedroom door, she stepped inside.

Something wasn't right.

The room that greeted her was not her bedroom. A rustic queen-sized bed made of rough-hewn cedar stood in place of her elegant white canopy bed. The once vibrant pink and purple comforter was gone, replaced by a tan and black one. Instead of posters of her teenage heartthrobs adorning the walls, there were now Native American artworks. Worst of all, someone had left a pile of dirty men's clothes in the corner.

Elise felt a surge of panic rise up within her as she looked around in confusion. "What happened to my room?"

"That's what I wanted to tell you," Diego said, coming up to stand beside her. "It's been...repurposed."

"What?"

"Roy packed up your belongings and gave away the furniture because you said you weren't coming back."

"What?" It seemed to be the only word she could utter.

"Yeah. I'm really sorry, but he said he asked you if you wanted any of it and you said no."

Elise thought back and remembered the conversation. "I thought he meant did I want the furniture shipped to my apartment in New York. I didn't realize he was giving my room away. Whose room is it now?"

"Mine," he admitted.

"I thought you lived in the foreman's house?" She sounded shrewish but damn it, she was tired and that had been her bedroom.

"I was, but your dad asked me to move in with him. I guess he was lonely and neither of us needed as much space as we had. So, I moved into your old bedroom and Rodrigo and his wife and kids moved into the foreman's house."

What she wouldn't give to pretend not to understand, stomp her feet in indignation and yell about the injustice of it all. Only she understood, so instead she heaved a sigh and considered her options.

Biting her lip, she glanced down the hall toward her father's room. "I don't think I can sleep in his bed," she said. "What about one of the guest bungalows? Are any of them open?" It might even work out better if she wasn't in the main house surrounded by all the memories of her father and their past.

"We have guests in all of them except the one currently being renovated."

"Great. I can stay there."

"No. I don't think you'd be comfortable there."

She heaved a sigh. "Fine. I guess I can stay at Ruby Mae's. Do you know where Dad kept the keys to his truck?"

He was shaking his head before she finished speaking. "It's summer. Tourists are in town. Every room in her bed-and-breakfast is filled."

She wondered if any of her friends would let her stay with them and then realized she hadn't kept in touch with any of them.

Damn.

She looked toward her father's room and muttered, mostly to herself. "I really don't think I can sleep in his bed."

"No need. You can sleep here," Diego said, gesturing to his bed.

She stared at it, then turned to Diego. "I'm not sharing a bed with you."

"Good to know, but I wasn't offering," he said without smiling.

Ouch! She felt her face flush and hoped the dim hall lighting would hide it from his gaze.

"You can take my room and I'll stay in the bungalow being renovated," he clarified before she could think how to reply. "It's not a problem."

"I could take the couch—"

"Elise! I'm not arguing about this. I can see in your face—you're exhausted. Don't make a big deal out of it. Just let me grab a change of clothes and I'll get out of your way."

He walked into the room to the open closet and pulled out a shirt. From the chest of drawers, he removed underwear, socks, and jeans.

"There are clean towels in the bathroom," he told her. "Help yourself to shampoo and whatever else you need."

"Thank you."

He started to leave, but stopped when he reached the doorway. "You'll want a change of clothes."

True. She could wash her panties in the sink and hope they dried in a couple of hours. Still, the only outfit she had was the one she was wearing and a business skirt with high heels was not practical attire on the ranch.

"T-shirts are in the second drawer," he said, as if reading her thoughts. "I don't think my jeans will fit you, but some of my shorts might. They're in the third drawer. Help yourself."

"Thanks," she said again.

He nodded. "Get some sleep."

Elise watched him step out and pull the door closed. Its click sounded like the closing of another chapter in her life, bringing a sense of finality and loneliness to it.

Hoping she'd feel better after some rest, she closed the curtains to block out the sun. Next, she grabbed one of Diego's clean T-shirts and a pair of Nylon shorts. Exhaustion swept over her until she thought she might pass out standing up.

She headed into the bathroom, needing to wash away the effects of the day. This room, too, was strangely alien to her. The color of the walls, the floor and tile had all changed.

She tried not to dwell on it because she was already feeling like a stranger in her childhood home; she didn't need to feel any worse.

Careful to fold her clothes neatly as she removed them, she started the shower. While she waited for the water to heat, she located a clean towel.

Then she stepped into the shower.

Beneath the rain of hot water, she felt her body relax and the wall she'd erected to buffer her emotions crumbled. With the sound of the shower to mask the sound of her crying, Elise wept as she'd only done once before in her life—when her mother died. At least back then, she'd had her father to comfort her. Now she had no one.

Time passed. She had no idea how much, but probably not much since the shower water was still hot when she finally pulled herself together. Feeling drained, she finished her shower and a few minutes later, wearing the borrowed T-shirt and shorts, Elise opened the bathroom door.

As soon as she stepped into the room, she spotted a box sitting just inside the door. It hadn't been there before, so Diego must have brought it in while she was showering.

It irritated her that he'd come into the room without knocking. Then, a more embarrassing thought occurred to her. Had he heard her crying?

Moving to the box, she opened it. A quick search revealed some of her old clothes, including jeans, shirts, lingerie, and a couple of pairs of old shoes. Her earlier embarrassment turned into gratitude. Her father must have kept some of her things and Diego, despite his own exhaustion, had looked for and found them. At least she wouldn't have to wear Diego's clothes the entire time.

Making a mental note to thank him, she crawled into the bed, savoring the feel of cool sheets against her skin, still warm from the shower. The plump pillow cradled her head much in the same way the soft bed enveloped her body. The sheets carried the scent of the same soap she'd used in the shower and something more; something masculine but not unpleasant.

Diego.

Maybe she should have felt awkward sleeping in his bed. After all these years, they were practically strangers. Instead, surrounded by his scent, she felt cocooned and safe. With a final, exhausted sigh, she fell asleep.

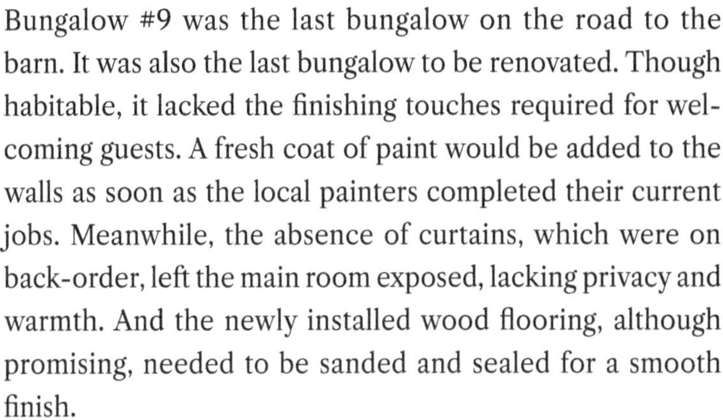

Bungalow #9 was the last bungalow on the road to the barn. It was also the last bungalow to be renovated. Though habitable, it lacked the finishing touches required for welcoming guests. A fresh coat of paint would be added to the walls as soon as the local painters completed their current jobs. Meanwhile, the absence of curtains, which were on back-order, left the main room exposed, lacking privacy and warmth. And the newly installed wood flooring, although promising, needed to be sanded and sealed for a smooth finish.

Diego didn't care about any of that. So long as the air conditioning and plumbing both worked and he had a bed in which to sleep, he was fine.

Stretching out on the queen-sized bed, he should have been unconscious the instant he closed his eyes, but sleep eluded him as thoughts of Elise filled his head.

As soon as he'd seen her, he'd known he was in trouble. She'd walked into the hospital lobby looking frazzled and travel worn, with her wrinkled skirt and strands of blonde hair pulled free from a once neat bun. She'd looked so damned sexy he'd nearly groaned aloud.

He'd actually gotten excited for the ten seconds it took for her to walk toward him, allowing himself to fantasize about greeting her with a warm hug; maybe even a chaste kiss. She'd dashed those dreams when she'd walked past him toward the day laborer she'd assumed was him.

Anger bubbled up inside him. It was like they were back in high school, when he'd worshipped the ground she walked on, and she didn't remember he was alive. She'd been head cheerleader, dating JD Drake, the football team's star quarterback. The fact that he and Elise had once been best friends didn't seem to matter. He was the foreman's kid and she couldn't afford to be seen with him.

Well, he wasn't that high school kid anymore. He was a grown ass man who refused to get involved with anyone who couldn't respect him for himself. Besides, what would be the point? She wasn't planning on staying. No, it was best to keep things casual; for the safety of his pride and his heart.

It was the perfect strategy, in theory.

In actual practice, though, it had proved impossible to corral his emotions. He'd tried. God knows, he'd tried. Hadn't he faked falling asleep in the cab so they wouldn't have to talk? So what if he'd waited until the sound of her steady breathing told him she'd fallen asleep before slipping his arm around her? He'd only done it to keep her warm. It had nothing to do with wanting to hold her in his arms, to feel her body pressed against his.

Yeah, right. Who was he kidding?

Now, with Roy's passing, she'd inherited the ranch. To say he was worried about her plans for the ranch was an understatement. There was so much at stake. So many people depended on the Double R for their livelihood.

Diego sighed and shifted, hoping to find a more comfortable position. He tried not to imagine Elise sleeping in his bed. The sound of her sobs coming from the shower had roused every protective instinct in him, and he'd wanted to stick around and offer comfort. He'd left, understanding the humiliation she would feel if she knew he had accidentally eavesdropped on her.

Before leaving the main house, he'd given last-minute instructions to Carmen not to wake Elise so she could sleep as late as she wanted. In his bed. Wrapped in his sheets.

He stifled another groan and shifted his position again. If he fell asleep at all, it would be a miracle—and Diego had given up believing in miracles a long time ago. Still, he closed his eyes and started counting down from one hundred; then changed his mind and started over from one thousand.

CHAPTER FOUR

"BILL, I KNOW THEY'RE an odd bunch," Chief of Police Samantha "Sam" Hunter said into her phone, glancing at the time on her watch to see it was pushing 3:00 p.m. "But you're talking about a group of old ladies who like to drink wine and dance around in the woods. Are they really hurting anyone?"

Bill Murphy was the owner of the Murphy RV and travel trailer park where most of the visitors to Las Palomas stayed. The reason they frequented his park was two-fold. First, the Rio Maldito, which was a favorite haunt of *La Llorona*, ran through Bill's RV park. Guests staying there would almost assuredly see the ghost of the wailing woman walking along the river on a moonlit night. Second, it was the only RV park in town.

Of course, on the other side of the river was the Las Palomas Game Preserve—or the "woods," as the locals referred to it—where the town's wiccan group liked to hold their midnight ceremonies.

"Sam, if it was just the dancing and drinking, I might get people to ignore them, but last night, they were beating drums and smoking pot."

Sam rubbed her forehead with her free hand, feeling a headache coming on. "Okay, Bill. I'll talk to them."

"Thank you."

After hanging up the phone, she debated on whether she should go now to the new age bookstore up the block to talk to the wiccan group's leader. She had a pretty good idea how the conversation would go and heaved a heavy sigh.

Not for the first time, she wondered how she got here; back in Las Palomas serving as the chief of police.

Sam was a native of Las Palomas and eight years ago, like most high school graduates, she'd been eager to leave the small town. It had only taken one year of college, though, to realize that wasn't for her. True crime and forensic stories had been her secret, guilty pleasure, so, in a surprise move to her family, she'd applied to the Houston police academy.

After she'd graduated from the academy, she'd worked the next four years as an officer with the Houston PD. Then her mother had become ill and Sam had returned home. Needing a job, she had joined the Las Palomas police department.

By the time her mother made a full recovery, Sam knew she'd never go back to Houston. Las Palomas was her home; it was where she wanted to live and work.

A year ago, when the then-current chief of police had retired, the mayor had asked Sam to fill the position, ironically because she had more "big city" police experience than the other Las Palomas officers.

Twenty-six years old and already chief of police. At first, she was thrilled, but then quickly discovered that being in charge wasn't nearly as exciting as it sounded. She spent most of her time listening to complaints and reviewing paperwork.

She stared at the documents piled on her desk and wondered how the policing of one small, relatively quiet town resulted in so much paperwork.

A knock at her door came as a welcomed distraction.

"Come in," she called.

The door opened, and a woman poked her head inside. "Are you busy?"

This was fortuitous, Sam thought, gesturing for her visitor to come in and sit in one of her guest chairs. The woman was in her fifties, though she looked younger. She wore her long blond hair parted in the middle, so it hung in straight curtains on either side of her attractive face. Today, she wore a sage colored cotton peasant blouse and skirt with a leather belt at her waist. Long feathered earrings fell from her earlobes and dozens of slender bangles jangled around both wrists. Sam knew that if she could see them, the woman would have ugly brown Earth sandals on her feet.

This woman owned the new age book shop up the street and was the leader of the wiccan group.

"What brings you here this morning?" Sam asked.

"I can't drop in and say hello to my only daughter?" Katherine Hunter asked.

"I got a call from Bill. He says you and your followers," she used her fingers to make air quotes, "were beating drums and smoking weed last night."

Her mother waved her hand in the air dismissively. "Bill's an old fuddy-duddy. What does he know, anyway? We were protecting the town from evil spirits." Her mother's face remained passive as she refused to acknowledge the complaint.

"There's a sound ordinance in town. No loud noises after midnight. And smoking weed is against the law—for everyone—but most especially for the mother of the chief of police." She sighed. "Why can't you be like everyone else and smoke your weed in the privacy of your home?"

"It wasn't weed, dear. We were drinking wine and burning sage, to cleanse our ceremonial site."

Sam shook her head; she was not so naïve that she believed her mother. This was an old argument and not one Sam cared to have again. "Just so you know, if any of my officers or I catch you smoking weed, we're going to arrest you. It doesn't matter who you're related to." Her mother cocked her head to the side and Sam knew it was all the acknowledgment she'd get. It was time to change the subject. Sam gestured to the thermos in her mother's hands. "What's that?"

"Coffee." She set the thermos on Sam's desk. "It's Nana's newest blend. I want you to try it and let me know what you think."

"Okay." She took the thermos and, unscrewing the top, smelled her grandmother's brew. "This better not have any legally questionable herbs in it."

"It doesn't." She shrugged. "At least, not as far as I know."

"Okay, well thanks." She screwed the cap back on, thinking her mother would leave now. Instead, her mother continued to sit in the chair and look at her expectantly. "Was there something else?"

"Yes. I need to warn you. Something bad is coming."

"What are you talking about?"

"I did a reading for you this morning."

Sam didn't have to ask what kind of reading. Her mother always carried around a deck of tarot cards. "Okay. Any chance you saw something specific?"

"Death was in your present and The Hanged Man was in your future."

Sam sighed—again. "Mother, I don't know what that means."

"Well, it could mean there's been a literal death, or it could be a figurative death; like the end of a relationship, for instance, or a major change in your life."

Sam simply nodded, taking it in. "And The Hanged Man?"

"That represents criminal activity."

"Okay." She wanted to point out to her mother that dealing with criminal activity was pretty much all she did. "I don't suppose you got a name or description of the illegal activity?"

Her mother scoffed. "It doesn't work that way."

She sighed. "Okay, well, thanks for the heads up."

"Sam, don't blow off this warning," her mother snapped. "I want you to promise me you'll be careful."

Knowing her mother loved her and only wanted to see her safe, Sam softened her tone. "I promise."

There was another knock at her door and Bev, the department secretary and part-time dispatcher, opened the door and stuck her head inside. "Doc Niven is here to see you. He says it's important."

"Okay, thanks," Sam said. "You can send him in." Then, turning to her mother, "Thanks for dropping by, Mom." Her mother nodded and rose from her seat. "I'll call you later—and thanks for the coffee."

As her mother left, she passed a distinguished-looking man in his early forties. They exchanged greetings and then her mother was gone and the man stepped into Sam's office.

"Hey, Doc," Sam greeted Las Palomas' primary physician and, as needed, medical examiner. "What brings you by this morning?"

He gestured to the door. "Mind if I close this?"

"Of course. Go ahead and then have a seat." She gestured to one of her guest chairs while surreptitiously glancing at the time on her office phone display. Now it was almost 3:30 p.m. "You want some coffee?"

"No. Thanks."

He took a seat, and Sam waited for him to speak.

"There was an accident last night at the Richardson ranch."

"There was?" It was the first she'd heard of it. "Anyone hurt?"

"Yeah," Doc nodded. "I was called out there a little after two in the morning. Roy Richardson was thrown from his horse and hit his head on a rock hard enough to render him unconscious. Diego found him and called me." He paused. "It was serious. I had to call for medical transport to South Texas."

Doc paused there and Sam didn't know if that was the end of the story or not. "How's he doing now?" She asked.

"He died last night."

"Oh, no," Sam gasped, the news coming as a shock. She knew Roy Richardson, of course. Las Palomas was not a big town, so everyone knew everyone. Sam and Elise, Roy's daughter, had gone to high school together. "Does Elise know? If not, I can call her."

"Diego called her. I learned she made it to South Texas before Roy passed, but he never regained consciousness."

Sam shook her head. "That's a damn shame." Had this been the death her mother warned her about? "Thanks for stopping by and letting me know."

She expected him to leave then, but he didn't. "There's more."

"Okay." She waited patiently for him to continue, sensing he needed a moment to gather his thoughts.

"Because Roy was my patient, I followed up with the physician at South Texas who treated him. She emailed me copies of the medical record and X-rays taken at the hospital. After examining them, I called her back. I was concerned about what I was seeing and wanted a second opinion." He paused again, clearly concerned.

"What is it, Doc?"

He cleared his throat and met her gaze. "I think Roy Richardson was murdered."

The announcement surprised her. "That's a serious allegation. What are you basing this on?"

He stood and, pulling out his phone, came to stand beside Sam so they could look at his phone screen together. What

Sam saw was a picture of Roy Richardson's body laid out on a gurney with a sheet draped over his hips and legs, leaving his upper torso bare. The dark bruises covering his chest were in stark contrast to the pallor of his skin.

"Roy's right shoulder was dislocated, which likely happened when he fell from his horse. The bruising you see here," he pointed to the screen, "was likely made by horse hooves. The other bruises, you see here?" He pointed them out in the picture. "A fist made these." He swiped the screen to show Sam the next two pictures, which showed the back of Roy's hands. "Abrasions along the knuckles."

"So Roy got into a fight," Sam said, drawing the obvious conclusion. "But that doesn't mean he was murdered."

"True, but here's where it gets really suspicious," he told her, swiping to yet another picture. This one showed the left side of Roy's head, where there was obvious trauma; there were two separate wounds and blood matting the hair. "Here and here," he pointed to two separate places, "X-rays show his skull was fractured in two places."

That got her attention. "From falling?"

Doc straightened, shutting off his phone and putting it back into his jeans pocket before returning to his seat. "What are the chances that Roy fell, hitting his head against two rocks with enough force to fracture his skull? Remember, he landed on his right shoulder when he fell, so his shoulder hit the ground first, taking the brunt of the impact. Plus, the fractures are on the front, left side of his head."

Sam tried to visualize a sequence of events that would explain Roy's injuries. "You think someone was out there with him and either spooked his horse, so it threw him, or pulled him from his horse hard enough to dislocate his shoulder? Then, while he was on the ground, the two of them fought. Roy's assailant grabbed a rock and bashed him in the head twice, hard enough to fracture his skull and render him unconscious."

Doc nodded. "That's what I think. I can't prove it, of course."

No, proving it would be her responsibility. "It would be interesting to take a look at the rock—or rocks—that caused those injuries," she mused out loud.

Across from her, Doc nodded. Only moments ago, had she really been thinking her life was boring? Well, that had certainly changed.

Grabbing the truck keys off her desk, she stood. "Thanks for dropping by, Doc. I think it's time for me to head over to the Double R and look around."

CHAPTER FIVE

Elise came awake suddenly, without knowing what woke her. The room was dark but a crack between the curtains revealed it was light outside. She wondered if it was later the same day or was it the next morning?

When she heard a buzzing sound, she recognized it as the noise that woke her and scrambled out of bed to retrieve her cell phone from her purse where it sat on the floor beside a chest of drawers.

She glanced at the caller ID as she swiped the open bar. It was Bob, her boss.

"This is Elise," she answered.

"Elise, it's Bob. Maddie told me as much as she knew. Is everything ok?"

Elise rubbed her forehead as everything came rushing back. "No, it's not. My father was in an accident. He... he passed away last night."

What time was it? She pulled her phone away from her ear to glance at the screen.

3:00 p.m. That would make it 4:00 p.m. in New York.

She put the phone back to her ear.

"...anything we can do?"

"I need to take a few days off, if that's all right. I was an only child and my mother died years ago, so I'll have to make funeral arrangements. My father owned and operated a dude ranch. It's an actual working ranch and I'll need to find someone who can run it while I'm in New York. At least until I figure out what to do with it."

"Of course, I understand. We'll manage without you for a few days, but it's important you come back as soon as possible. As our new Vice-President of Marketing, you'll have a lot going on here, now that Johnston Corporation has signed with us."

Elise's brain, still fogged over with fatigue, struggled to process the news. "We got the account? Wait, did you say vice-president?"

He chuckled. "We did, and I did. Congratulations on your promotion. You deserve it. Your presentation blew the Johnston group away and they want you to be personally in charge of their account."

There it was. The promotion she had worked tirelessly to achieve. Now it was hers and the timing of it sucked.

"Thank you so much." She couldn't even feel happy about it because she had no one with whom to share the news. Her father was dead.

"You might not be thanking me after you've worked with Johnston Corporation," Bob joked, unaware of her feelings. "Now take a couple of days for bereavement and we'll see you next week."

He clicked off the line before she could say anything more.

Sitting on the edge of the bed, she tried to get a handle on her emotions. She'd slept a good six hours, but rather than feeling rested, she felt like a Mac truck had hit her.

Going into the bathroom, she splashed cold water on her face, hoping it might help her wake up. Seeing the dark circles under her eyes had her pulling open her make-up drawer before remembering the bathroom was no longer hers and the only make-up she had with her was a tube of lip gloss and some face powder.

Fortunately, no one expected her to look her best. Then an image of Diego leaning against the column in the hospital lobby, looking like he'd stepped out of the pages of GQ Magazine, flashed through her head.

Well, damn. She splashed more cold water on her face, hoping to give it some color, then did what she could with the lip gloss and powder, mentally adding make-up to her growing list of things to buy in town.

The jeans and T-shirt she'd pulled from the box earlier were lying on the chair, so she quickly changed into them, amazed that they still fit. Well, the jeans might have been snug in the hip area, but not so much she had to worry that seams would split if she bent over.

After using Diego's brush to work the tangles from her hair, she pulled it back in a ponytail, which she secured with a rubber band she found around a doorknob. Another search through the box of clothes revealed a pair of flip-flops which she slipped onto her feet.

Time to face the world, she told herself.

Leaving the bedroom, it surprised her to find a dozen or more flower arrangements sitting on every surface of the family room. The news of her father's death had apparently reached the town and people were sending their condolences. It warmed her heart to know her father had so many friends who cared about him.

"I'll tell her you came by," a woman said from nearby.

"Thank you, Carmen."

The man's familiar voice had Elise rushing to the foyer. "JD?"

Elise hadn't seen Joe Drake (aka "JD") since they'd both gone off to college, but her high school sweetheart stood there looking as handsome as ever. His full head of blond hair had darkened over the years and he'd put on a little weight, but he was still in great shape.

"Elise, you look good." He came forward and swept her into his arms for a hug. "How are you doing?" There was genuine concern in his tone.

"I'm okay," she told him, stepping back to put some distance between them. "It's nice of you to stop by. Do you have time to sit and talk?"

"I do," he said, giving her a warm smile.

She turned to Carmen. "Thank you for answering the door and letting me sleep. It looks like you've been busy." She gestured to all the flowers.

"I didn't mind," Carmen said. "Your father had many friends. By the way, I just made a fresh pitcher of tea. Can I bring you both a glass?"

The tea would be refreshing and would have the caffeine she craved. "That would be terrific, thanks."

Carmen nodded and walked off.

"Damn, it's good to see you again," JD exclaimed as they walked into the family room and sat on the couch, facing each other like they had so many times before.

"How long are you in town?" She remembered he'd moved to Dallas.

"Actually, I live here now."

"No. Since when?"

"Almost two years now. Dad needed help running the place, so I came home."

"Aren't you the wonderful son?" she teased. "How are your folks?"

"Well, to be honest, it's been rough. Dad ran off about six months ago with another woman. We've not heard from or seen him since. He and Mom had been fighting a lot and I think the only reason he didn't take off earlier was he felt too guilty. When I moved back home, he knew I'd help Mom with the ranch, so there was no reason for him to stick around."

"Oh, that's horrible. I'm so sorry."

He shrugged dismissively. "Mom took it hard, of course. She doesn't go out much anymore. She prefers staying at home."

Carmen appeared at that moment with their glasses of tea.

"Thank you." Elise accepted her glass and immediately took a sip. The cold liquid slid down her throat and tasted divine. "Wow, this is great." She gave Carmen an appreciative smile, which was acknowledged with a slight nod.

"Here you go, JD," Carmen said, handing him the other glass. "How'd the science project turn out?" JD's eyes furrowed in confusion. "It's been a while, but I ran into you at the hardware store. You said you were helping your nephew with a project. I thought you said it was a science project but maybe it was an art project. I remember you had a lot of paint in your basket."

JD's face relaxed into a smile. "Sure, I remember now. Art project and it turned out great. Thanks for asking."

Carmen smiled. "Y'all want anything else? I have some cookies coming out of the oven soon."

Elise turned to JD and raised an eyebrow in question.

He chuckled, patting his stomach as if suggesting he carried a few too many pounds. "While I'd love a cookie, I'd better not. Thanks."

Elise declined as well, and Carmen left them to return to the kitchen.

After Elise was sure the woman was out of earshot, she gave JD a raised eyebrow look. "Your nephew? How long have I been gone?" As far as Elise knew, JD was an only child.

"Andy. He's the son of one of my ranch hands," he explained. "I was in a hurry and saying 'nephew' seemed easier than trying to explain my relationship to the boy."

She smiled. "I see your point. Well, gosh, you look good. I guess the ranching life agrees with you."

"Actually, I'm training horses, not ranching."

"Really?" She tried to remember the last time she'd seen JD ride a horse, but couldn't. "And you like it?"

"Sure. It pays the bills and lets me stay on the ranch to take care of Mom. Enough about me, though. What about you? You look as pretty as you did back in high school. Tell me what you've been doing these past couple of years." He took a drink of his tea, then set the glass on the coffee table.

"Well, there's not much to tell. After college, I took a marketing position with *Tinslow and McNeal* in New York City. I've been there ever since."

"What's it like living in the Big Apple?"

She smiled. "Exciting. The city never sleeps. There's always something going on."

"Sounds like a big change from our sleepy little town." His brows furrowed. "I guess you're going to hate giving it up."

"What do you mean?"

"I was assuming you'd move back to run the Double R now that your dad's gone. But maybe you're planning to work remotely? I mean, if COVID proved anything, it's that most jobs can be done remotely."

She smiled, considering the possibility, and quickly dismissed it. "Most of what I do is customer facing, especially now. If I moved here, I'd have to spend most of my time traveling back and forth to New York City. That could get expensive, and I don't think the company would foot the bill, even for their new VP of Marketing."

"Vice president? I'm impressed."

She smiled. "I was just promoted. In fact, you're the first person I've told."

"I'm honored. Congratulations." JD smiled.

"Thanks." His words warmed her, reminding her why she'd been so fond of him in high school. He was easy to get along with and was as proud of her achievements as his own, which had been many. She always thought he'd go far in life.

"Listen, Elise." His tone was somber. "My timing is going to be great or horrible, but I'm just going to put this out there and hope you don't take offense."

"Okay... " she said slowly, waiting for him to continue.

"It doesn't sound like you want to give up your job and life in New York City, so I might have a solution. I've been doing pretty well with my business and now I'm looking to expand. Since your property is next to mine, I'd like to buy it."

Elise stared at him, stunned. This could be the answer to her problems. "Seriously?"

He smiled. "Absolutely."

Then she frowned. "What about the staff? Ranch hands? And Diego? And we have guests staying here and more booked over the summer. We'd have to refund their money if we closed the ranch."

"I'm sorry," he said, smiling. "I should have been clearer. I don't want to close the ranch. It would complement my horse-training business nicely. So, I'd keep the staff and operate the ranch the same as your dad did."

"Wow. JD, I don't know what to say. That's very generous of you. I wouldn't even know what to ask for this place."

"We can worry about the details later. I just wanted you to know I was interested in buying the place. I think it might be nicer if you sold it to someone who grew up here rather than to an outsider."

"Outsider?"

He nodded. "Like Tom Kobbel. You might not have met him yet, but he's an investment banker who's looking to buy up property so he can build a hotel or resort or some such thing."

Else frowned. "I wouldn't think Las Palomas had enough tourists to justify the expense of a hotel."

"We don't, at least, not yet. I think a big commercial hotel might draw more people here than we want. Or, the opposite could happen and the tourist traffic stays the same and Kobbel's new hotel closes down, leaving us with an abandoned eyesore sitting on this beautiful piece of property."

Elise couldn't disagree with him, so she nodded.

"Look, Elise. I've had a couple of run-ins with Kobbel. He's persistent. I don't care if you listen to what he says, but promise me you won't sell this place to him without first letting me see if I can match his offer."

She smiled. "Of course. I promise. I'd much rather have this place go to someone who's practically like family to me."

"Thanks. We can work out the details whenever you're ready."

"It might be a couple of weeks," she warned him. "While my father had a will, it will need to go through probate. I'm not sure how long that will take, but calling my dad's attorney is on my list of things to do today, so I can let you know."

"Works for me." He stood. "I should go now, but it was sure great to see you again after all these years."

"I agree," she said, also rising so she could walk him to the door.

"Maybe we could do dinner one night while you're still in town?" He suggested.

She nodded. "Thanks. I'd like that."

She walked him outside and watched him drive off, feeling slightly less overwhelmed. JD buying the ranch wouldn't bring her father back, but it would solve the most current problem of figuring out what to do with the ranch.

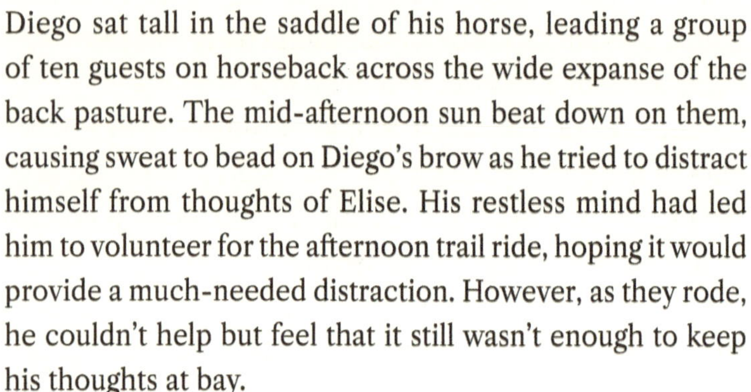

Diego sat tall in the saddle of his horse, leading a group of ten guests on horseback across the wide expanse of the back pasture. The mid-afternoon sun beat down on them, causing sweat to bead on Diego's brow as he tried to distract himself from thoughts of Elise. His restless mind had led him to volunteer for the afternoon trail ride, hoping it would provide a much-needed distraction. However, as they rode, he couldn't help but feel that it still wasn't enough to keep his thoughts at bay.

He was so consumed by his own inner turmoil that he didn't even notice when his mount stopped walking.

"Is something wrong?" one of the guests asked, breaking through Diego's foggy thoughts.

"Sorry," he apologized. He'd taken them the long way around the pasture, purposely avoiding the spot where he had found Roy lying unconscious. Turning to the group, he couldn't help but feel a shiver run down his spine. This land held a dark history that still lingered in the air.

"This pasture is haunted," he said, deliberately capturing the attention of the guests. "In 1850, a notorious rustler by the name of Vidal and his two partners stole horses belonging to Texas Ranger Creed Taylor. Back then, horse and cattle theft was considered a more serious crime than murder."

Diego's voice lowered as he continued with the story, recounting how Taylor and fellow ranger William "Big Foot" Wallace had tracked down and captured Vidal and his accomplices. After killing them, Wallace had decapitated Vidal and secured his headless body to the saddle of a wild mustang as a warning to other criminals.

"Even now, on clear nights, it's said that *El Muerto*—the headless horseman—can be seen galloping along that very rise over there," he pointed to the ridge of land off to their right, "as a grim reminder to criminals that justice can be swift and brutal." He paused, allowing the guests to absorb the story.

When he felt enough time had passed, he resumed the ride. Once they reached the barn, the guests hurried off to freshen up and relax before dinner while Diego and a few of the ranch hands unsaddled and brushed down each horse.

After completing his duties, Diego headed to the main house where he found the kitchen alive with the smell of spices and sizzling meats and his cousin hard at work. Carmen looked up from her cutting board as he entered.

"Good ride?" she asked, wiping her hands on her apron.

"Yeah, thanks. Is Elise awake?"

"She's in the family room, entertaining company."

Diego's steps faltered at the mention of company. "Who?"

"JD."

His heart sank at the mention of their neighbor. JD was not someone he particularly liked, but he still wanted to see Elise. Bracing himself, he continued through the kitchen and headed for the family room. Just as he reached the doorway, he saw Elise closing the front door.

"JD was here?" he asked, planting himself in front of her with his arms crossed.

She smiled softly. "Yes. You just missed him."

"What did he want?" he demanded.

Her brow furrowed. "To offer his condolences."

He snorted in disbelief. "Yeah, right. What else did he want?"

"If you must know," she began, her voice taking on a serious tone, "he offered to buy the ranch."

Diego's jaw clenched. "Well, it's not for sale."

Elise raised an eyebrow at his outburst. "I don't think that's your decision."

Her words hit him like a punch to the gut. Was she serious? "Elise?"

"Now, don't get upset," she said calmly, reaching out to place a hand on his arm. "It's the perfect solution. You know I can't stay here. Besides, I don't know the first thing about running a dude ranch."

"But—"

"No, let me finish," she interrupted. "If you're worried about him shutting down the ranch, he said he wouldn't do that. He wants to run it with you as foreman and keep everyone else in their positions as well."

He felt a surge of anger but forced himself to speak calmly. "You know he's lying, right? JD has no intention of running a dude ranch. As soon as he gets the chance, he'll fire everyone except for maybe one or two of the ranch hands to help with his horse business."

Diego saw a spark of disapproval in her eyes, causing them to harden into a steely glare. "I'm sorry you don't approve," she said curtly, her posture stiff. "But there's no way I'm staying here to run the ranch."

"Then let me run it," he offered, his voice calm but pleading.

Elise let out an exasperated sigh, her frustration palpable. "Is the ranch even financially sustainable?" she asked, her tone bordering on accusatory. "Because my job doesn't pay enough for me to support the ranch and my apartment in New York City." The truth hung heavy in the air as he stayed silent. "It's not, is it?"

He sighed heavily and stalled by rubbing his face with one hand. "The ranch is just managing to cover its expenses at the moment," he admitted begrudgingly. "We've had some unexpected issues recently that have been quite costly to resolve."

"Like what?"

"Like the tank in the south pasture, for instance. We found a dead deer floating in it, contaminating the water supply. Not only did we have to dispose of the carcass, but we also had to drain the tank and rent a bulldozer to dig a new one."

He saw her eyes widen in surprise. "It drowned?" she asked incredulously.

He didn't want to tell her the truth—that someone had purposely shot and dumped the deer in the tank as an act of sabotage. If she knew that there were people trying to harm the ranch, she'd likely want to sell it even faster.

She continued staring at him intently, waiting for an answer. Just as Diego was about to respond, there was a knock at the front door, providing a welcome interruption.

He quickly made his way over to answer it, with Elise following closely behind. When he opened the door, he was surprised to see a slightly overweight man in his fifties standing on the doorstep. The man had a ring of salt-and-pepper hair surrounding his otherwise bald head, and a trim dark mustache above his lips.

"Edmundo," Diego greeted him warmly, extending a hand for a handshake. "What brings you by?"

"I heard you were back, and I was eager to speak with you both," the man said, his voice rich and smooth like a fine wine. Diego cast a glance back at Elise, who listened but seemed slightly bewildered. He realized that she had never met Roy's attorney, as Edmundo had moved to Las Palomas after she had left for college.

Diego welcomed the man inside, introducing him to Elise. "Edmundo, may I present Elise Richardson? Roy's daughter. Elise, this is Edmundo Barientos, your father's attorney."

"It's a pleasure to meet you," Elise said politely, extending her hand for a shake.

"Your father spoke highly of you," Edmundo replied with a warm smile. "I am deeply sorry for your loss. Roy was not just my client; he was also a dear friend. He will be greatly missed."

"Thank you," Elise acknowledged, gesturing for them to move into the family room. "Mr. Barientos, would you care for something to drink?"

"No, thank you," he declined graciously before settling into one of the plush side chairs. "The news of Roy's passing came as quite a shock earlier today. It is a tremendous loss for us all."

Elise nodded in agreement. "Your timing is fortuitous. Diego and I were just discussing what to do with the ranch. I am considering selling it." She glanced at Mr. Barientos for approval.

The attorney remained silent for a moment, his gaze lingering on the two of them. "Is that so?" he finally spoke up. "Well then, I can certainly arrange for that if it is what you both decide." His tone held confidence.

"Both?" Diego interjected curiously.

Mr. Barientos nodded, gesturing first towards Elise and then towards Diego. "The two of you, of course."

Diego glanced at Elise and saw she looked as confused as he felt.

"I don't understand," she finally said.

Edmundo cleared his throat. "I'm sorry. I thought you both knew. Roy placed all of his assets, including this ranch and everything associated with it, into a living trust several years ago."

"A living trust?" That was clearly news to Elise. "What does that mean, exactly?"

"Well, it means your father didn't own the ranch. The Richardson Trust does. Roy was the sole trustee in charge. Upon his death, you and Diego become co-trustees, which means the two of you manage the trust and, subsequently, the ranch. Now, if you want to sell the ranch, the terms of the trust stipulate that you can only sell it if both co-trustees agree. Upon the sale of the ranch, profits will be disbursed evenly between the trustees and the trust will be dissolved."

"What if one of us doesn't want to sell the ranch?" Diego asked. He glanced at Elise. "Elise already has a job and life in New York City, but I would like to keep the ranch."

"Well, neither of you has to accept the position of a co-trustee," Edmundo told them. "If one of you refuses the position, then the remaining trustee becomes the sole trustee responsible for the ranch. It's important to note, however, that refusing the position does not entitle you to compensation. Technically, neither of you owns the ranch. The Richardson Trust does. If one trustee steps down, then the remaining trustee becomes the sole trustee. After that, if the sole trustee sells the ranch, then he or she is entitled to 100% of the proceeds. So, it's really in your best interests to both remain co-trustees until you both mutually agree to either keep or sell the ranch."

Diego's mind was a flurry of emotions as he processed the news. Beside him, Elise was equally stunned and speechless. The air in the room felt heavy, charged with tension.

"I'll need to send you both some papers to sign," Edmundo finally spoke up after a moment, breaking the silence. He cleared his throat before continuing. "As trustees, it's important to have your signatures on file. I can also provide you with a form to terminate your position as trustee, if you wish." He paused again, his eyes scanning their faces. "There are other matters concerning the operation of the ranch that we should discuss, but perhaps it's best to give you some time to process this news first."

He stood, signaling the conversation was over for now. Mutely, Elise and Diego also rose and followed him to the door where they said their goodbyes.

Elise looked like she had been hit by a truck when Diego closed the door behind Edmundo and turned to her.

"Well, Dad certainly complicated things, didn't he?" she said, her voice sounding hollow.

"Actually, it's pretty simple. Tell JD the ranch isn't for sale." He started walking away, with her trailing behind him.

"Can't we at least talk about it?" she pleaded.

"There's nothing left to say. I want us to run this ranch together. If that's not what you want, then simply terminate your position as co-trustee." His tone brooked no argument.

He felt her gaze burning into his back as they made their way through the house, but he didn't waver. Roy had entrusted him with the responsibility of protecting and preserving the ranch, and he would do whatever it took to fulfill that duty.

The sudden sound of the doorbell made them both stop in their tracks.

CHAPTER SIX

ELISE OPENED THE DOOR to find a young woman standing there.

"Sam Hunter?"

"Hey, Elise."

"Come on in," Elise invited her, stepping back so she could come into the house.

Sam Hunter had changed little since high school, Elise thought. With her lean, athletic build, piercing blue eyes and long blond hair caught up in a ponytail, she was as beautiful as ever. The police uniform, however, was unexpected.

"It's good to see you again," Elise said, closing the door.

"I'm sorry about your dad," Sam told her, then turned to acknowledge Diego, who'd stepped forward to join them. "Diego."

"Chief," he greeted her. "Is this a social call?"

Sam shot Elise what seemed like an apologetic look. "No, actually it isn't."

"What's going on?" Elise asked. "Did he just call you chief?"

The other woman nodded. "Chief of the Las Palomas PD," Sam said.

"Since when?"

"Since about a year ago."

Elise was stunned. She didn't feel like she'd been away that long and yet so many things had changed.

"I'm sorry I'm catching you all at a bad time," Sam continued. "Doc dropped by to tell me about Roy. Diego, I understand you're the one who found him out in the pasture?"

"That's right."

"I'd like you to show me where you found him."

"Sure," Diego said, casting a quick, bewildered glance at Elise, who was just as clueless as him about why Sam wanted to see where her father was injured.

"Why?" she asked.

"Just routine, when someone dies under..." She wobbled her head back and forth like she was searching for the right word. "Mysterious? Circumstances."

"My father was thrown from his horse," Elise protested.

"Was he?" Sam countered. "You have the name of someone who witnessed the event?"

Elise remained silent because, of course, she knew of no such witness.

"We can take one of the golf carts," Diego offered, gesturing for Sam to follow him past the family room, toward the kitchen. When Elise started to follow, Sam held up a hand to stop her.

"Would you mind waiting here for Zelda? I called her on my way over and asked her to join me," Sam said.

"Um, sure," Elise agreed, another memory from high school hitting her. Zelda Zahn was not only Sam's best friend, but she had some kind of paranormal ability, which had set her apart from Elise and her friends, who had considered themselves to be "normal." Shaking off the thought, she turned to Diego. "How will I know where to find you?"

Both he and Sam smiled at her, but it was Sam who spoke. "Zelda will know the way." Then she turned to Diego. "Shall we go?"

<hr>

Elise stood in the family room for several minutes after Sam and Diego left, wondering if it was her imagination that Sam was acting strange. Why would the police need to see where her father fell off his horse?

Not knowing the answer was making her antsy. She needed a distraction. Her gaze fell on the bag of her father's personal effects the hospital had given her.

Picking it up, she carried it to her father's room, hesitating only briefly before opening the bedroom door.

She stopped just inside to look around and smiled when she saw the unmade bed.

"I like it that way," her father used to say. "And I'm just going to unmake it again so why waste time in the morning making it up?"

His pajamas lay at the foot of the bed with his slippers on the floor nearby. On his bedside table, the book he'd been reading lay with a bookmark poking out. Elise knew she'd find a picture of her mother in the nightstand drawer. To the right, against the wall, stood the small familiar desk that used to be in the study. In the desk chair sat a laundry basket of folded clothes. On the left side of the room sat his dresser. Loose change lay scattered across the top on one side and on the other sat framed pictures of Elise and her parents taken during happier times. Everything about the room looked lived in, like the occupant had merely stepped away and would return at any moment.

The realization that he was gone struck her and she, again, had to fight the lump growing in her throat. She practically threw the bag of clothes on the chair sitting between the dresser and the doorway in her haste to leave the room.

Hurrying into her own bedroom, Elise sat on the edge of the bed, taking deep breaths to collect herself. She was nearly back to normal when a knock at the front door signaled Zelda's arrival.

The stunningly attractive woman Elise opened the door to, however, looked nothing like the gangly girl she'd known in high school. The woman standing before her had thick black hair that hung in ringlets half-way down her back and large silver hooped earrings. Her peasant blouse was loosely belted with several shiny metal chains, the dangling tails of which disappeared into the folds of her full, ankle-length gathered skirt. Rings adorned her fingers, including her thumbs. Elise half expected to see toe rings on carefully pedicured feet. Instead, she spotted canvas sneakers peeking out from under the hem of the skirt.

"Zelda?" Elise asked, looking for any resemblance between this woman and the girl she remembered from high school.

The woman gave her a friendly smile. "Hi, Elise. It's good to see you again. I'm very sorry for your loss."

"Thank you." She stepped back. "Please come in." She waited for Zelda to step inside and then closed the door. "Wow, I hardly recognized you. Please don't take this the wrong way, but you look fantastic."

"Thanks," she said. "I guess you could say I was a late bloomer. You haven't changed. You were beautiful back in high school and you still are."

Elise smiled to acknowledge the compliment. "Sam asked me to take you out to the south pasture." She gestured toward the kitchen. "We can go through the kitchen. There's a golf cart in the garage."

They walked together through the kitchen, then through the guest dining room until they reached the garage where the other golf carts sat. They climbed into one and Elise started the engine.

"I can get us to the south pasture," she said before driving off. "After that, I'm not sure where they are."

"That's okay. I can tell you."

"That's what Sam and Diego said, but I don't understand how you can know."

"I'll follow their auras."

"Auras?"

Zelda didn't seem offended by the question and Elise guessed she'd heard it before a couple hundred times. "Everyone has an aura, or energy pattern, and each person's aura is unique, like fingerprints. Everywhere we go, we leave behind traces of our aura. Think of it like carrying a bag of uniquely colored flour that has a small hole in it, leaving behind a trail of that flour as you move through life. Anyone who comes across your trail knows you were there because the color of the flour is unique to you. Auras are like that flour."

"Wow. I had no idea. That's... it's... " She struggled to find the right word.

"Freaky?"

Elise shrugged. "Maybe." They left the garage, taking the road that led past the bungalows.

"You want to know what's really freaky?" Zelda asked as they drove past the barn. "The living are not the only ones who have these energy auras. Ghosts have them, too, because, like the living, they are made up of energy. Although the trace energy left behind by ghosts isn't as vibrant."

"You're right. That's really freaky." She smiled to take any sting out of her words. "So, you'll be able to find Sam and Diego by following their auras."

Zelda smiled and nodded.

"Wow! That could be a really handy ability, but with all those aura trails, one on top of another, how do you know if they're coming or going?"

"One end of the trail will be brighter than the other. The brighter end is more recent, so it tells me where the person or ghost was heading."

"Doesn't that get confusing after a while, with so many trails?"

"They don't last long. A couple of days or weeks, depending on the weather. Wind currents will disperse the trace energy and each new person or ghost who crosses a space, leaves behind their own trail, which eventually obliterates any trails that were already there."

Elise, who thought she finally understood, couldn't think of an intelligent reply. "Freaky."

Reaching the gate to the south pasture, she stopped the golf cart long enough for Zelda to get out and open the gate so she could drive through.

"Which way?" Elise asked after Zelda had closed the gate and rejoined her in the cart.

Zelda looked around and then pointed off to the left. It took about ten minutes with Elise following Zelda's directions before they found Sam and Diego. Elise pulled the golf cart next to the other one, and they got out. Diego was waiting by the golf cart while Sam was some distance away, bent down, examining something on the ground.

"Hi, Zelda," Diego greeted them. "Sam asked you to join her when you got here." He turned to Elise. "She invited us to return to the house and wait for her."

Elise wanted to protest, but as Zelda walked off, Diego started steering her back to the golf cart.

"Wait," she protested. "I want to look around."

"Bad idea," he told her, taking hold of her elbow to keep her from walking away. "Let's go."

This time, she got in on the passenger side and let him drive the cart.

"What's going on, Diego?" She asked him as they headed back.

"I'm not sure, but she's acting like it's a crime scene."

"A crime scene? I thought Dad fell off his horse."

"Me, too." He glanced over at her. "Let's not jump to conclusions. Sam said she'd come back and explain. Let's see what she has to say."

CHAPTER SEVEN

SAM TURNED AS ZELDA walked toward her. "Careful where you step," she advised, satisfied to note that Diego and Elise had taken one of the golf carts and were returning to the main house.

"Have you found anything?" Zelda asked. The women had talked earlier, and Sam had shared her suspicions with Zelda.

"I see signs of a struggle," Sam said. "What about you? Whose auras do you see out here?"

"There are a lot of different auras here. I recognize some of them, like Roy, Diego and a few of the stable hands, but there are definitely some here that I don't recognize. Which, if you think about it, makes sense, considering this is a dude ranch and the guests ride out here."

"I was afraid of that. Come look at this," Sam directed her, pointing to the ground close to where she was standing. "This is where I see signs of a struggle. See these large smudges? Horse and cattle hooves don't leave that kind of pattern. A couple of men fighting would." She sighed, examining the ground. "And I found traces of blood on top of the dirt, so I'm pretty sure this is where Roy fought his attacker. Tell me what you see."

Zelda moved forward, her gaze growing distant. Sam knew she was using her special sight as she walked around, being careful not to step on the smudged areas.

"There are several overlapping auras in this area. The ones I recognize belong to Roy, Diego, Doc Niven and Rodrigo."

"That makes sense," Sam told her. "What about the others?"

Zelda shook her head. "None I can recognize. There's too much overlap to make out individual patterns. Sorry."

Sam sighed. "That's okay. Every piece of information helps." She gazed around the area. "I don't suppose Roy's ghost is here?" Sam knew it was possible but thought Zelda would have mentioned it already.

"No."

"Yeah, that would have been too easy," Sam muttered as she started moving around the area, occasionally using the toe of her boot to turn over a rock or move aside scrub brush.

"We could ask Sylvia to reach out to Roy," Zelda suggested, referring to the leader of the Saturday Seance Circle. "If Roy hasn't completely crossed over, it's possible she can summon him."

In any other city, the suggestion would be ludicrous, and it struck Sam again just how different Las Palomas was from other places.

"That's actually not a bad idea." She continued moving in an ever-widening circle, and then stopped. "Hello. What's this?" She pulled out her cell phone and snapped several pictures of the rock.

"What is it?" Zelda asked, coming closer.

"Maybe nothing." Sam put the camera away and pulled a pair of latex gloves and a baggie from her pocket. After pulling on the gloves, she picked up the rock and dropped it into the baggie. "Then again, maybe it's the murder weapon." She held up the baggie for a closer look at the dark reddish-brown substance covering one side of the rock. "Does this look like dried blood to you?"

"Are you sure it's not mud? Or manure?" Zelda asked, peering at the rock.

"I'll give it to Doc for testing, but I think it's too dark to be mud, and it's definitely not manure."

"It's kind of far from where his body was found," Zelda observed.

"I suspect Roy's attacker tossed it over here, hoping it wouldn't be found."

"Is it possible that Roy's horse threw him over here, he hit his head on the rock and crawled over to where his body was found before losing consciousness?"

Sam shook her head. "I don't think so. I found this rock bloody side down. If Roy fell and hit his head, the rock should have been bloody side up. No, I think this might be our murder weapon." The two exchanged looks.

"I found something, too," Zelda told her. "It might be nothing, but—"

"Show me."

Zelda led her over to a mesquite bush growing only a couple of feet from where Sam found the rock.

"Don't touch it," Sam warned as she bent to take a closer look.

The partially uprooted bush had a scrap of yellowish-white fabric stuck on one of its branches. Again, she used her phone to take pictures before pulling another baggie from her pocket into which she placed the scrap of cloth.

"You think it's important?" Zelda asked.

"It could be. This bush is close enough to where we found signs of a fight. You see how the bush is uprooted? I'm guessing one or both of them fell against this bush during the fight and their clothing caught on the branch. The question is, whose clothing? Roy's? Or his attacker's?"

They continued searching the area but found nothing else.

"We can head back to the house now," Sam told Zelda.

They rode in silence and, reaching the garage, Sam parked inside.

"What now?" Zelda asked.

"Now I'll let you get back to your shop while I go inside and talk to Elise and Diego. I want to know where they were the night Roy was killed."

"You can't possibly think either of them had anything to do with it," Zelda protested.

"It doesn't matter what I think," she said. "I have to investigate every possibility. I owe it to Roy to find the truth and, if Elise and Diego are innocent—which, like you, I hope they are—then I owe it to them as well."

Chapter Eight

"Knock, knock."

Sam's voice came from the direction of the kitchen.

"We're in the family room," Diego shouted back.

Casting Diego a worried look, Elise rose from the couch, waiting for Sam to appear.

"Can you tell us what's going on?" Diego asked Sam.

"Yes." She gestured to the couch. "Let's sit, shall we?"

Elise sat back down, and Diego walked over to join her. Sam took the chair nearest the couch and sat. "I wasn't sure before, but after examining the scene, I believe Roy's death was not an accident."

"What?" Elise felt the shock of Sam's words throughout her body.

"What are you talking about?" Diego asked.

"Doc Niven talked to the physician who treated Roy at South Texas. Roy's right shoulder was dislocated." Diego opened his mouth, but Sam held up her hand to silence him. "A fall off his horse might explain the shoulder, but it doesn't explain the abrasions on his knuckles or the skull fractures on the front, left side of his head." She paused, giving them time to absorb the information, before continuing. "I also found evidence of a struggle in the pasture."

"What kind of evidence?" Elise asked.

"Places where the dirt is flattened, consistent with bodies rolling on the ground. About fifteen feet from where Roy's body was found, I found a baseball-sized rock with blood on it. According to the physician, the blows to Roy's head rendered him unconscious. It would have been impossible for him to crawl any distance after hitting his head. That suggests a second person used the rock to hit Roy in the head and then tossed the rock away, probably hoping no one would find it."

"Oh, my God," Elise moaned, her hand going up automatically to cover her mouth. Suddenly, she was finding it hard to breathe. She wasn't aware that Diego had slipped his arm around her until he pulled her close and she felt the warmth and strength of his body against hers. "Who would have done that?"

"I don't know," Sam admitted. "But I intend to find out." She frowned and looked thoughtful for a moment. "Either of you hear what happened to Boyd Hanger?" Elise, who did not know who Boyd Hanger might be, glanced at Diego.

"Rancher on the other side of town," he told her, before turning to Sam. "I heard he passed recently."

"But you didn't hear how, right?" Diego shook his head and Sam continued, "We've been keeping that quiet and I'm going to ask that you not tell anyone what I'm about to tell you." She waited for them to nod their agreement before continuing. "He was killed. Stabbed through the chest. We suspect by transients." She sighed. "It's been a problem for us lately. Undocumented immigrants sneaking into the country and setting up camp wherever they can. We believe Boyd came across illegals camping on his land and confronted them. There was a fight and Boyd lost. Maybe he was stabbed in self-defense; maybe he wasn't. We may never know. The reason I'm telling you this is because it's possible the same thing happened to Roy. I didn't see signs of a camp out there, but maybe he confronted them before they had time to set up." She shrugged. "It's just one theory."

Elise tried to wrap her thoughts around this new information but felt like she was failing. "You'll keep us posted on what you discover?" she asked.

"Of course."

Elise rose, intending to walk Sam to the door, but Sam remained seated. "Was there something else?"

Sam nodded. "That Roy was killed by illegal immigrants is one theory. Another is that someone he knew killed him." She pulled a notebook and pen from her shirt pocket. "I need to ask you both some questions."

Elise gasped. "Surely you don't think I killed my father."

"Standard procedure. Most murder victims are killed by someone they know, so it's important to rule out as many of your father's family and friends as I can. The smaller my pool of suspects, the better."

Elise slowly sank back down onto the couch. "What questions?"

"First, I need to know where each of you was the night before last, when Roy was attacked. I'll also need to talk to the ranch employees and guests here that night." She flipped the notebook open to a clean page and, with pen poised above paper, turned to Elise. "Elise, let's start with you. Where were you that night?"

"In New York City."

"Can anyone vouch for you?"

Elise nodded. "My executive admin, my boss and several co-workers were with me in the office until I left around six-fifteen that evening. We have to swipe our badges entering and exiting the building, so security should have a record of when I badged out. From work, I went home. I was there the entire evening, working on a presentation. I was back in the office the next morning by seven forty-five. Again, security and my admin can validate that."

"And do you live alone?"

"Yes."

"No boyfriend? Anyone who can verify you were at home?" Sam questioned.

Elise didn't like the implication. "Do you really think I had time to fly to Texas, sneak out to the back pasture, attack my father and then fly back to New York in time to be at work early the next morning?" Sam didn't respond, but simply kept looking at her. "Fine. No, boyfriend. I was home alone, but I logged into work, so there's likely a record of my sign-in and the URL address should prove it was from my home Wi-Fi."

Sam reached into her front pocket again and pulled out a business card. She handed it to Elise. "If you'll email me with the names and contact info of your co-workers and your company, I'd appreciate it."

"Sure." Elise leaned forward and took the card from her. She knew Sam was only doing her job, but at the moment, she wasn't feeling particularly hospitable.

"Thank you," Sam said, scratching notes into her note-book. Then she turned to Diego. "Where were you?"

"Somewhere between Houston and here."

"Care to be more specific?"

"Sure. I was on Highway 59, halfway between Goliad and Berclair."

She frowned. "What were you doing there?"

"That's where I was when my water hose sprung a leak."

Sam heaved a heavy sigh. "Come on, Diego. You know what I'm asking. Don't make me drag it out of you."

Beside her, Elise heard Diego take a breath. "Okay. I left early that morning to drive to Houston—"

"Why?" Sam interrupted him.

"I had a job interview."

"What?" Elise gasped. Had Diego been planning to quit? Her father would have been heartbroken.

"What time was your interview?" Sam asked.

"Eleven o'clock."

"And it ended...?"

"We were done by noon."

"I'll need names and contact information but go on."

"I was driving back from the interview and was some-where between Goliad and Berclair, when my water hose sprung a leak. Of course, it was the one spot where I had no cell phone service. Anyway, I had to pull my truck over and I sat there for several hours waiting for someone to stop and give me a lift—to Berclair. The service station there wasn't equipped to replace my water hose, so I bought duct tape. Then I had to wait around a couple more hours until the gas station attendant got off duty and could give me a ride back to my truck."

"What time was that?"

He shrugged. "I don't know – seven or eight, maybe?"

Sam pulled out her phone and tapped the screen several times. Finally, she slipped it back into her pocket. "Berclair is less than four hours from Las Palomas. Where'd you go when you got back?"

"The trip back took me closer to five hours since I had to drive slow and keep adding water," Diego told her. "As soon as I got into town, I dropped my truck off at Dwayne's Service Shop. That was around one in the morning. I walked to the ranch from there."

"Okay. What then?"

"I went straight to my room to shower. After being out in the heat all day, I needed one. Then, I went to the kitchen and drank a beer. I needed that, too. I'd noticed earlier that Roy's bedroom door was open, so I checked the back deck for him. It's not like him to be out at that hour, so I got..." Diego hesitated, "worried isn't really the right word. I was more curious about what he was doing still up."

"Is that when you called Rodrigo?" Sam asked.

"No," Diego said. "Rodrigo was asleep and, like I said, I wasn't exactly worried about Roy. Not yet. When I couldn't find him, I went out to the barn, on the chance he was there. That's when I noticed his horse was gone. That's when I got worried. It's not like Roy to ride after dark, so if that's what he did, there'd have to be a reason for it."

"Why do you think he did?"

Diego gave her a skeptical look. "You're asking me to speculate."

She nodded. "I am. You probably knew him best."

Elise felt the sting of the comment, but knew Sam was right.

Diego drew in a deep breath and then let it out slowly. "Okay. My first thought was that he encountered whoever put that deer in the tank. You remember we called you about it?" She nodded. "Another thought was that he just needed to get away from the ranch for a bit and clear his head. This morning, Rodrigo told me there was a problem earlier that night. A couple of nights ago, Mrs. McNamara got drunk and started flirting with Roy. He wasn't interested and tried to get away from her by going into the house. She followed him. When her husband caught up to her, she was all over Roy. They had some words. Then Monday evening, Rodrigo said that when the wife disappeared, the husband, once again, accused Roy of messing around with her. I think he even took a swing at Roy. Anyway, Rodrigo said Roy told them they should plan to check out the next day, but Rodrigo said they left that same night."

"Did Roy hit him back?" Sam asked, reminding Elise that they found abrasions on her father's knuckles.

"I don't know," Diego replied. "Again, you'll need to ask Rodrigo."

"You have this guest's contact information?"

"Yeah, in our records. I can get it for you," he told her.

"So, tell me about finding Roy," Sam encouraged.

"Well, when I realized his horse was gone, I went out to look for him."

"It must have been hard to find him in the dark. That pasture's pretty big."

"Yeah, well, I had help."

Sam's head snapped up as her attention moved from her notes to Diego's face. "Go on."

"*El Muerto* appeared."

"*El Muerto*?" Sam challenged.

"Yeah, you know. The headless horseman."

She huffed. "I know who it is. So he was making his ride? I thought he usually did that at midnight."

"He wasn't making his ride," Diego said. "He just appeared out of nowhere. Scared the bejeezus out of me. And he had Roy's horse with him. At that point, I knew something bad had happened. When the ghost turned and headed off down the back side of the ridge, I followed him. He led me to where Roy was lying. He was unconscious when I found him. That's when I called Doc Niven and woke him up. Doc told me not to move him, since we didn't know the extent of his injuries. I also called Rodrigo and asked him to wait for Doc at the main house and then bring him to where I was waiting with Roy. Doc got there, examined Roy and called for the helicopter to take him to South Texas hospital."

"You rode with them?" Diego nodded. "Did Roy regain consciousness while you were with him?"

Elise thought Diego looked like he wished to God that her father had but shook his head. "No."

"Okay." Sam closed her notebook and put it and the pen back in her front shirt pocket. "I'll need that list of guests," she reminded them. "And I'd like to talk to both Carmen and Rodrigo before I leave. Preferably not together."

"I'll call them and ask them to come up to the house. Elise and I can make ourselves scarce while you talk to them."

"Thanks. I actually want to talk to all of the staff, but I'll start with those two for now."

Diego quickly made the two calls. After disconnecting from the last one, he turned to Sam. "They're on their way up. Elise and I will be in the study, with the door closed." Then he turned to Elise. "Shall we?" He gave her no time to protest before pulling her to a standing position and then placing a hand at the small of her back to steer her toward the front of the house.

"Would you mind closing the door?" Diego asked her as soon as they reached the study. He was already crossing the room to the desk. When he reached it, he opened the laptop sitting on top and powered it on.

Elise was still in shock as she dropped into the chair facing the desk. "Who would murder Dad?"

She was speaking mostly to herself, so hadn't expected Diego to answer, but he did.

"I don't know, but I sure as hell plan to find out." Deigo typed on the keyboard.

"How? Sam's not going to let you go poking around an active investigation."

"I'm not planning to ask permission. She," he pointed toward the family room, "thinks I murdered your father. If she's busy trying to pin this on me, she won't be looking for the actual murderer."

Elise scoffed. "She doesn't think you killed Dad."

"Maybe she didn't say it in so many words, but she's thinking it. Why wouldn't she? I don't have an alibi."

She thought he was overreacting but kept that thought to herself. Her gaze slid toward the family room where Sam waited for either Carmen or Rodrigo. "I wish we could hear what they were saying."

Diego met her gaze over the top of the computer, a gleam in his eye. "Then maybe you'd like to join me on this side of the desk?"

Curious, she got up and moved around to sit in the desk chair he'd just vacated for her. To her surprise, there on the laptop screen was a live feed of the family room. Sam was sitting in the same chair, still waiting for Carmen or Rodrigo.

"I installed security cameras around the house last year after one of our guests sneaked in here and stole some stuff."

"You're kidding." She was aghast that a guest would do such a thing.

"That time, it was only small stuff. A set of stone coasters with the ranch's brand on them and a set of highball glasses, also with the ranch's brand engraved on them. I told Roy at the time that we ought to open a small gift shop and sell that stuff. Maybe folks would buy it instead of stealing it."

She glanced up at him. "That's actually a great idea."

He scowled at her. "You sound surprised. It's an obvious solution. It doesn't require a special marketing degree to think of it."

"Sorry, you're right, of course. I didn't mean to sound insulting." She turned her attention back to the computer screen. "Where is the camera?" Judging from the angle of the picture, the camera had to be installed on the wall between the sliding glass door and the fireplace, but she didn't remember seeing a camera there.

"You know the mirror hanging by the fireplace?"

"Yeah."

"It's a two-way mirror. I built a shelf into the wall behind it, ran electricity to an outlet at the back of the shelf and that's where the camera sits."

"That's..." He raised an eyebrow like he was waiting for her to insult him. "Kind of ingenious," she finished.

At that moment, Carmen walked in from the kitchen and they saw Sam gesture for Carmen to sit on the couch.

He smiled. "Thanks. So, want to hear what they're saying?"

"Won't we get in trouble for this?"

He winked at her. "Only if we get caught." He reached out, about to click a button on the computer, but Elise put out a hand to stop him.

"Will they be able to hear us?"

"No. The microphone is off."

He clicked a button on the laptop keyboard and suddenly they could hear the conversation taking place in the other room.

"...reason to believe Roy's death wasn't an accident," Sam was saying. "So, I'm talking to everyone. Where were you the night Roy had his accident?"

Carmen's eyebrows rose in surprise. "You think I killed him?"

"It's a routine question," Sam explained. "I'm asking everyone." She stopped and waited for Carmen to respond.

"Oh, okay. Well, I was here earlier that evening. I'm the head chef and the meal service for the guests is my responsibility. The kitchen staff—that's Cindi Gates, Maria Hernandez and Denise Gonzales—served dinner at about seven that evening. Do you need to know what was on the menu?"

Elise couldn't tell if Carmen was being pithy, or it was a legitimate question.

"That's okay," Sam answered patiently. "Anything unusual happen at dinner?"

Carmen suddenly looked uncomfortable. "There was one incident. It involved a guest and his wife. It happened after we served appetizers. I was in the kitchen prepping the next course when I heard yelling out on the deck. When I went outside, Mr. McNamara—that was the guest's name—was up in Roy's face. He was yelling about Roy messing around with his wife—which, of course, he wasn't."

"How can you be sure Roy wasn't sneaking around with her?"

Carmen looked indignant. "First, Roy isn't that way. And second, Roy was with me in the kitchen from the time the husband said his wife went missing. We had some delivery issues with the food and were having to make some last-minute menu changes."

"Maybe the wife was hiding in Roy's bedroom, waiting for him."

Carmen shrugged. "I don't see how she'd get back there without us knowing, but even if she did, why? Roy spent the evening helping me in the kitchen. He wasn't with her in the bedroom. And when he finished helping me, he went out to entertain his guests."

"Okay." Sam made a note in her notebook before looking again at Carmen. "Go on. You heard loud voices and went outside. Mr. McNamara was threatening Roy. Did he hit Roy?"

"He sure did. That's when Rodrigo and Elliot stepped in to help. They got between McNamara and Roy, not that Roy was trying to hit him back or anything. Roy told him he didn't know where his wife was, but he would send some people out to locate her and then they both needed to check out the next morning."

"What happened then?"

"Mr. McNamara shouted that he'd kill any man messing around with his wife. That's when Rodrigo and Elliott escorted him off the deck. When I saw Rodrigo later, he said they were gone, so I guess they found his wife, although I don't know where."

Sam made a few more notes before asking, "Were you here for the entire meal?"

"And then some." When Sam gave her a quizzical look, she elaborated. "I don't get to go home until the guests have retired."

"What time was that?"

She cocked her head in thought. "Probably about twelve-thirty or twelve-forty."

It was hard to read Sam's expression, but her tone reflected her surprise. "Isn't that kind of late?"

Carmen smiled. "Not around here. Guests want to see *El Muerto*, so they stay out on the deck, drinking and socializing until late. He normally appears around midnight or shortly after that. The guests watch the entire ride and then head off to their bungalows afterward."

"And did *El Muerto* ride that night?"

"Sure did," Carmen replied. "Oh. I just remembered. That was unusual, too. *El Muerto*'s ride. Usually, he rides all the way across the back ridge, but that night, he only made it half-way before he disappeared." She quirked her lips. "The guests were a little disappointed, but it's not like we can control what a ghost does. Anyway, by the time he finished his ride, the guys had put the sound system and alcohol away, so there was no reason for the guests to stick around. They started heading off to their bungalows. The girls and I finished up in the kitchen and headed home."

"What time was that?"

"I don't know. Maybe one?"

"Can anyone validate you were at home?"

"Sal, my husband."

Sam made a few more notes in her book before setting it in her lap.

"Thank you, Carmen. I think that's all the questions I have for now. Would you mind sending Rodrigo in?"

Elise and Diego watched Carmen leave the room.

"What do you think?" Elise asked Diego. "Do you think the McNamaras came back, followed Dad out to the back pasture, and attacked him?"

"I don't know," Diego said, sounding somber. "I can't see a rational person doing that, but I guess we're not dealing with a rational person. Still, I don't see McNamara being the type to sneak around in a dark pasture to get his revenge. Using social media to bad-mouth the ranch seems more his style."

At that moment, Rodrigo appeared on the screen.

"Afternoon, Chief," he said, greeting Sam. "I understand you wanted to talk to me?"

"Yes, thanks for making the time."

"Sure."

Sam gestured to the couch and, as she'd done before, waited for him to sit before she began.

"I don't know how much Carmen might have mentioned to you..." she started, letting him answer the implied question.

A frown creased his brows. "She said Roy was murdered."

"That's what the evidence strongly suggests," she said. "Did she also tell you I'm trying to confirm people's whereabouts that night?" He nodded. "Good, then can you tell me where you were that night, starting when dinner was served?"

"We—the hands, that is—rotate working the dinner shift. That night, Elliot and I were working."

"What does it mean to work the dinner shift?"

"We help carry food out from the kitchen, set up the sound system, tap the keg and make sure dinner runs smoothly."

Sam nodded. "Tell me about McNamara."

Rodrigo's lips pursed with disdain. "That guy was nuts, thinking Roy was fooling around with his wife. Pardon me saying so, but his wife was a skanky ho. She was always coming down to the bunkhouse and flirting with the guys."

"Was she sleeping with one of the guys?"

"It's against the rules." He sighed, "but yeah. I'm pretty sure one or two of them had sex with her, but not Roy."

Sam made a note on her pad. "You and Elliott ran interference when McNamara attacked Roy at the dinner, didn't you?"

"Yeah, but not before he punched Roy. Roy didn't hit him back, though. He asked me and Elliott to escort McNamara away from the house and see if someone could locate his wife. I sent Elliott to the bunkhouse to find the wife while I waited with McNamara. While we stood there waiting, McNamara seemed to calm down."

"And you stayed with him until his wife returned to their bungalow? What time was that?" Rodrigo dropped his head and looked uncomfortable. "Rodrigo?"

"Wyatt Henshaw showed up looking for Roy. He was drunk and you know how Wyatt gets when he's like that." Sam nodded. "Roy fired him the week before and I didn't think it was going to help Wyatt get his job back if he talked to Roy in that state. I called Wyatt's father to come get him. McNamara was still with me and the two of us tried to keep Wyatt from going in the back to find Roy. But then Elliott showed up with McNamara's wife and things got a little chaotic."

"What do you mean?"

"Well, McNamara started yelling at the wife and she started hitting him. It took both me and Elliott to separate them. Meanwhile, Wyatt took that as his chance to slip away. We had just gotten the McNamaras quieted down when Cindi came running out front to say Roy needed help with Wyatt. Elliott and I left the McNamaras out front and hurried around back."

"What were Roy and Wyatt doing when you got there?"

"They were yelling at each other. Roy was telling Wyatt how he'd screwed up and Wyatt was demanding Roy give him another chance. The thing is, he'd already used up his second chance. He was just too drunk to realize it.

"What do you mean?"

"Roy fired Wyatt three months ago but because he and Wyatt's father are friends, he agreed to hire him back."

"Do you know why Roy fired him?"

"Sure. Same reason both times. He was late getting to work and about half the time, showed up drunk. One of the guests fell off her horse because he didn't cinch the saddle tight enough. She only sprained her wrist, but it could have been worse." He shook his head. "Wyatt didn't care. He was belligerent to the male guests and flirted with the female guests. And I think he hated kids. I can't tell you how many times Roy and I took him aside to counsel him but he wouldn't listen."

"Did Matt come pick up his son?"

Rodrigo sighed. "He showed up, but by the time he got here, Wyatt had driven off."

"And the McNamaras?"

"They were gone, as well. We thought they'd gone back to their bungalow, but when we checked, they were gone. So was their car and all their luggage."

"Do you remember what time this was?

"Maybe nine-thirty? Dinner was almost over, and Elliott and I had to set up the bar and start pouring drinks."

"How long did you play bartender?"

"We waited until we saw *El Muerto* start his ride. That's when we shut down the sound system and took the alcohol inside."

"Did you stick around to watch *El Muerto*'s ride?"

He shook his head. "No. My days are pretty long, and this had been a tough one. Elliot and I made sure the alcohol was locked up and then I headed to my house. Elliott he went to the bunkhouse. I was probably in bed by one. Fell asleep right away. Then I got Diego's call about two telling me Roy'd been hurt and go up to the main house and wait for Doc Niven, so I could take him out to the back pasture."

"What did Diego say about finding Roy?" she asked.

"Not much. He said Roy was badly hurt and I remember he was pretty upset. He and Roy; they were really close, you know?"

"What happened after Doc got here?"

"I took him out to the back pasture. He examined Roy and then called for the air lift to South Texas. The copter set down in the middle of the pasture and they loaded Roy into the back. Diego refused to be left behind, so he jumped into the copter. After they took off, Doc drove the golf cart back to the main house and left. I took Roy's and Diego's horses back to the barn and took care of them. Then I went back to bed for another hour or so."

"Thanks, Rodrigo," Sam said. "I think that's all for now."

The interview was over. Elise watched Rodrigo get up from the couch and walk off. Diego reached past her to the keyboard, clicked a button and shut the lid of the laptop. Then he picked up a nearby file folder and dropped it on top of the laptop before opening it. Then he bent over her and pointed to a random spot on the page.

Elise had just enough time to notice the print on the pages was upside down before Sam appeared on the other side of the French doors. She made sure they saw her before she opened them.

"I think I'm done here for now," she told them. "I'd appreciate it if you would send me that list of names and contact info soon."

"Sure thing," Diego told her, dropping his hand to his side as he straightened.

"I'll see myself out." She started for the door but then looked back. "Might be best if you both stayed in town for the next couple of days." Then she left.

Elise looked over at Diego. "Is she serious? She's treating us like suspects. We have to do something." The feeling of being helpless was both foreign and disconcerting. She didn't like it one bit.

Diego, perhaps sensing her unease, placed a reassuring hand on her shoulder. "We will."

"Like what?"

He shook his head. "I don't know. Yet. For now, though, we keep our eyes and ears open, agreed?" She nodded. "I'm going to head out to the barn and see what I can learn from the hands."

"What should I do?"

"Maybe look through your father's stuff. Talk to Barientos. Let's find out if your father had any enemies." He gave her shoulder a final squeeze. "Not tonight, though. You've been through enough. We'll be starting dinner service in an hour so I can have Carmen bring you a plate if you don't feel like mingling with the guests tonight."

Until he'd made the offer, she hadn't realized how much she wanted to be alone. "Thank you. I'd appreciate that."

"You bet. The guests might gather on the back deck after dinner, but they won't come inside and bother you. Maybe you can relax, watch a little TV before going to bed."

"Thank you, Diego. You're being really nice to me and I appreciate it."

"Don't worry, Elise." He gave her shoulder another gentle squeeze. "We're going to figure all of this out—together.

CHAPTER NINE

THE NEXT MORNING, ELISE went into the main house's small kitchen and made coffee. She knew she could have gone into the commercial kitchen, where Carmen likely had coffee already made, but she didn't feel like facing other people this early in the morning.

A quick search of the pantry and refrigerator yielded cereal and milk, so she poured herself a bowl of cereal to eat. She ate in minutes and then washed and put away her dishes.

Carrying a freshly poured cup of coffee and her purse containing her laptop into the study, Elise sat at the desk and prepared to do some work.

She spent the first hour responding to emails. When the last of her coffee turned cold, Elise took a break and called the funeral home. She talked to them about the type of service she wanted for her father, but when it came time to schedule the date, she learned that she'd have to wait until Sam released the body. That wouldn't happen until after

Doc Niven had performed an autopsy which, conveniently, he could perform using a room specifically set up for that purpose at the funeral home.

Before ending the call, she got from them a list of what they needed from her: clothes for her father, pictures for the memorial video and music choices for the service.

A wave of despair washed over her as she thought about everything. Her father was dead; maybe even murdered. The police had no clue as to the identity of his killer. She still had to bury her father, once the body was released and who knew when that would be. She had no idea what to do about the ranch and, despite all this, the clock was ticking because Bob wanted her back in New York City ASAP.

"Everything okay?" Diego's deep voice rumbled through the room.

She looked over to see him standing in the open doorway.

She shrugged and gave him a wan smile. "Okay is kind of relative these days, you know?"

He nodded.

"What do you have there?" She asked, gesturing to the stack of thick cardboard he had tucked under one arm.

"Boxes. Or at least they will be once you tape the bottoms closed. For Roy's stuff."

"Oh, thank you. I guess I need to go through his things; decide what to keep and what to throw away."

"I'd be glad to help, if you want the company."

She studied his face as she considered his offer.

"Thanks," she finally said. "I'm not looking forward to going through his things, you know?"

"Yeah, I do." His tone was sympathetic. "I think there's a roll of packing tape in the bottom drawer of that desk. Would you mind getting it?"

She found the tape and followed him to her father's room, stopping when she reached the doorway.

"You okay?" he asked, looking back at her.

"Yeah. It's hard, you know? It's like he just stepped out of the room and will be back any second."

"I know. I'm sorry, Elise. It's a hell of a thing to have happened. If you'd rather, tell me what you want done and I'll take care of it. I can get Carmen, or one of the others, to help me."

"Thanks. I'll be okay." As if needing to prove her point, she stepped into the room and joined him at the foot of the bed where he'd set the stack of folded boxes. Taking turns with the tape, they put together four medium-sized boxes.

"All right," he said. "Where do you want to start?"

"Closet." It would be the easiest, she thought, because she had no desire to keep any of his clothes.

Opening the doors to the modest walk-in closet, she studied the contents. Hanging from the rod across the back were mostly work shirts, with a couple of nicer dress shirts mixed in. She also found five sports jackets and two suits. He'd given up most of his "city" clothes after they'd moved to Las Palomas because he'd had no need for them anymore.

Elise grabbed the two suits and held them up. "What do you think?" She asked Diego. "The brown? Or the blue?"

He frowned at them before turning his gaze on her. "Roy would hate to be buried in a suit."

His statement startled a laugh out of her. "He would, wouldn't he?"

Sighing, she took the suits off their hangers and started folding them. "You think any of the ranch hands or their families might want some of these clothes?" She stopped, having thought of something else. "Is there anything of his you'd like to keep?"

He gave her a speculative look. "Maybe. To be honest, I hadn't really thought about it, but now that I am, there are a couple of his hats I'd like and if you don't want to keep his gold and silver Texas belt buckle for yourself, I always liked that."

She smiled. "Absolutely, keep it. He'd like that you had it." She turned back to the closet. "Okay, so what outfit do you think he'd like to wear for all eternity?"

They worked together for another hour and by the time they were done, her father's socks and underwear had been thrown away, along with those clothes too stained or ratty to be donated. She'd kept one of his flannel shirts for herself. It was something she could wear with a pair of leggings, but mostly she wanted it because the smell reminded her of him. The rest of the clothes went into the boxes. Diego promised to send a couple of hands to the house later to pick them up and take them to the bunkhouse where the men could take what they wanted. If there were any items left, they would be donated to a church, which would ensure they reached those in need of clothes.

Then Diego left Elise to return to the barn, where guests waited for him to teach them how to rope a wooden cow.

Once more alone, in the silence of her father's room, Elise's gaze fell upon his desk. It was made of dark, polished wood and scattered with an array of papers, pens, and old photographs, but what caught her eye were the series of black, leather-bound books neatly lined up along the top.

Curiosity getting the better of her, she sat in the desk chair and took the nearest book from its place, laying it on the desktop with care. Carefully, she opened it, revealing thick, creamy pages filled with her father's bold and familiar script.

She hadn't realized her father kept a personal journal. Maybe she would have known that about him, if she'd bothered to visit. The sense of guilt that washed over her was becoming all too familiar.

Feeling like an intruder in his private thoughts, she started to close the book, but curiosity stopped her. What if Sam was right and her father's death wasn't an accident? What if he was murdered? Could the killer be someone he knew? Someone he had written about in his journal?

With determination, she leaned back in the chair and began to read, searching for any clues that could lead to the truth.

—◆O◆—

"Good job," Diego told the eight-year-old girl struggling to control the rope; a job that was almost bigger than her. She and her thirteen-year-old brother had been his only two roping students this morning and, while the children had a genuine interest in learning to rope a cow, even the wooden one standing a short distance in front of them, Diego recognized the roping session for what it was—a babysitting gig while the children's parents ran into town to shop and maybe take in a ghost-sighting.

"Is it true there are ghosts in town?" the little girl asked, not sounding excited at the prospect.

"Mom and Dad went to see the courthouse and the hanging tree, but they wouldn't take us," her brother grumbled. "I think it'd be cool to see a ghost. I heard the hanging tree is haunted by the ghosts of the men who were hanged and they grab people who get too close.

As he said this last part, he reached out and grabbed his sister, making her jump as she screamed in terror.

Diego shot the boy a stern look as he laid a comforting hand on the girl's shoulder. "It's true that the tree is haunted," he admitted. "And while the ghosts do make the tree limbs shake, they can't grab you."

"I heard Momma talking to Daddy about a pink lady in the courthouse," the little girl said.

"That's right." Diego gently took the rope from her fingers and coiled it into a smaller size that would better fit her hand. He thought about sharing the story of Yolanda Glossop, the young woman who died when a prisoner found a gun and used it to attempt his escape. He decided against it.

"She's not really pink," he said instead. "They call her that because she's wearing a pink outfit."

"Does she try to grab you?" the girl asked, her voice sounding small from fear. "I don't want Mommy and Daddy to get hurt."

"No," Diego reassured her. "The only thing the Pink Lady does is sit at her typewriter and type."

"That doesn't sound too scary," the girl said. "But I don't want to see any ghosts."

"There are ghosts here, too," her brother told her before Diego could stop him.

The little girl's eyes went wide with terror, and she started looking around like a ghost might jump out at her any second.

"It's true that we have a ghost," Diego said. "A cowboy who rides his horse across the back pasture at night."

"Oh. That doesn't sound too bad," she said, growing calmer.

"Yeah, but he doesn't have a head!" Her brother announced.

Again, her eyes grew wide and when she turned to him, Diego saw her lower lip quiver.

"*El Muerto*—that's the name of our cowboy ghost—is looking for bad people; people who broke the law or did something wrong." He shot the boy a hard look, not wanting to terrify the child, but he was okay scaring him a little. "If you haven't done anything bad, the ghost won't come looking for you."

This time, it was the boy's eyes that grew wider, and Diego hoped that maybe now he'd stop teasing his sister.

Just then, Diego caught sight of Elliott through the open doorway of the barn. Putting his finger to his lips, he whistled loud enough to get the hand's attention and then, when he turned, Diego gestured for him to come over.

"I think that's enough roping practice for one day," he told the kids.

"Hey, Boss-man," Elliott greeted him before tipping his hat to the kids.

"Have you checked the fence today?"

Elliott shook his head. "Not yet."

"You have time to do it now?"

"Sure thing." He started to walk away, but Diego stopped him with a quick gesture, then turned to the kids.

"How would you like to ride with Elliott in the ATV to check the fences? It takes excellent eyesight to spot where the wires might be cut. Do you think you can do that?"

Both kids nodded vigorously.

Diego turned to Elliott, who gave a quick nod, letting Diego know he didn't mind taking the kids.

"Thanks," Diego said. "I left Elise going through Roy's stuff at the house and I feel like I should get back and help her."

"No worries," Elliott said, turning to the kids. "We got this, don't we?"

They both nodded.

"Lunch should be ready by the time you get back," Diego added. "You can leave them with Carmen if their parents aren't back by then."

He watched the small group head off, then paused at the barn to rehang the practice ropes before making his way to the big house. As he entered, he noticed the familiar smell of wood and polish that always seemed to permeate through the rooms.

Elise was still in her father's bedroom, sitting at his antique oak desk, lost in a thick black leather-bound book. She looked up as he entered, and he noticed her eyes were slightly red and glassy, as if she had been crying.

"Are you okay?" Diego asked softly, his heart aching to hold her and comfort her, though he remained by the doorway, unsure of how to approach her.

"Did you know Dad kept personal journals?" Her voice was quiet and distant, as if she were still absorbed in the words on the page.

"No, I didn't," he replied gently.

"He didn't write every day, but he was consistent." She gestured to several identical-looking books stacked neatly in a box by her feet. "Look at all of them. They go back years." She flipped back through the pages, stopping at one in particular. "Listen to this entry. It's from five years ago.

> *Today Diego graduated from UT. I don't know who was prouder of him, me or his folks. I feel blessed that he's allowed me to remain a part of his life. That boy is going to go far. He graduated a year early and already there are companies trying to recruit him for his IT skills. Jorge can't figure out how to work the TV remote, so Diego didn't get his talent from him but there's no prouder father in the audience today.*

She stopped reading and looked up at him, her eyes filled with emotion. "He loved you, you know."

Diego felt a lump forming in his throat and blinked back the tears threatening to spill. "I loved him, too. He was like a second father to me." His voice cracked on the last words. "I didn't kill him."

"Of course you didn't." She seemed surprised by his confession, but then her features softened, and she smiled, understanding passing between them. "For Sam to even suggest such a thing is absurd."

The swell of gratitude in Diego's chest was almost overwhelming. "Thank you." He gestured to the room. "What can I help you with in here?"

She stood and took a slow look around the room, her expression heavy with memories. "I don't think I can handle going through any more of his belongings today. It all feels like an invasion of privacy—sifting through his clothes and personal items, reading his private journals." She let out a weary sigh and shrugged. "I don't know. Maybe he wouldn't care that I was reading his journals, especially since reading them makes me feel a little closer to him." After a moment of thought, she turned to Diego with a small smile. "I don't think he'd mind if you wanted to read them, too."

"Okay. Maybe." With a sheepish smile, he entered the room as she bent over to pick up the box. His eyes traced the graceful curve of her back and the gentle sway of her hips before focusing on the item in her hands. "Here, let me get that," he said, stepping closer to take the box from her.

"Thanks." She stepped out of his way, giving him room to carry the box.

"Where do you want it?" he asked, glancing around the room.

"In my—well, your—room, for now," she replied with a small laugh, following him down the hall to his old room.

Stepping inside, he couldn't help but notice how Elise's presence seemed to fill every inch of the room. The box of clothes he had left for her the night before was now sitting on the bed, clothes spilling out over the sides. It was clear that she had already gone through it. Setting down the box of journals just inside the doorway, he joined her in the hallway.

"By the way, thank you for the box of my old clothes," she said.

"You're welcome. As I was leaving yesterday, I remembered Roy kept some of your stuff. I found that box in his closet. I thought maybe you could use some clothes while you're here," he said.

"It was thoughtful of you. So, did you finish up what you needed to do outside?" she asked.

"For now. Roping class today was more a babysitting class. My students were a couple of kids whose parents left them here while they went into town."

"Kids? When did the Double R start allowing kids?"

"About a year ago, I guess. There just weren't enough bookings with businesses wanting team-building experiences or adults wanting an exclusive adults-only cowboy experience, so we had to expand our client pool. Opening up to families seemed the most expedient way of doing that."

"Is the ranch set up to deal with kids?" She sounded dubious.

He shrugged. "We do okay, I guess."

They fell silent, and it felt awkward to Diego. Conversation no longer came as easily to them; their worlds had drifted apart and Diego worried that the distance might be too far to bridge, but he'd be damned if he didn't try.

"I know it's early, but are you hungry?" he asked. "We don't have to eat here with the guests. We could run into town and eat at Kathy's Café. Or, if you feel like a beer or something stronger, we could go to The Waterin' Hole."

He remembered to breathe again when she smiled and said, "that actually sounds pretty perfect. Do you think we could stop off at one or two stores so I can pick up a couple of things? I could use a couple new outfits and I'm sure you don't want me to keep pilfering your shampoo and toothpaste. Plus, I really need some make-up." She smiled.

"You're beautiful without make-up," he told her truthfully, "but I don't mind stopping."

"Then just give me a minute to... " She paused. "Nope, I guess I don't need a minute. No make-up to fix or clothes to change into. I guess I'm ready to go when you are."

Feeling happier than he should have the day after the death of his mentor and partner, Diego took Elise to lunch.

CHAPTER TEN

ACROSS TOWN, SAM STEPPED into their only interrogation room, where Wyatt Henshaw sat waiting for her. He looked up when she stepped into the room, and she noted his red eyes and disheveled appearance. It surprised her he was awake and functioning this early in the morning.

She took a seat across the table from him and then set the pad and pen she'd been holding on top. Wyatt watched her, but said nothing.

"I've asked Dane to join us," she informed him. She'd wanted Dane Wolfe, her top officer, present as a witness, as much as for his help, should Wyatt's famous temper surface and she needed help to subdue him.

Wyatt only shrugged at her announcement.

"Can I get you something to drink? Coffee? Or water?"

"I'd take a whiskey," he replied, and she ignored him.

Dane walked in then and took a seat beside her.

"I want to ask you about the last time you talked to Roy Richardson," Sam began.

"I'm not talking without a lawyer present," he informed them.

"You're not under arrest," Dane said.

"Don't care." He crossed his arms and stared at them belligerently.

"Fine," Sam said. "Who's your lawyer?"

"Don't have one."

Sam nodded her head slowly, then turned to Dane. "Let's call Matt. Let him know we're holding Wyatt on suspicion of murder." To Wyatt, she said, "we can hold you for forty-eight hours without charging you with anything. That will give your dad time to secure an attorney for you. How's that?"

"I don't want to stay here," he protested.

"Well, you wouldn't have to if you talk to us, but it's your choice."

Wyatt glared at them and then rubbed a dirty hand across his face. "Fine. What do you want to know?"

"To be clear," Sam said. "You're waiving your right to an attorney?"

"Yeah, yeah."

"Okay." Sam opened her notebook and picked up her pen. "I understand you went out to the Double R the night Roy was killed."

He nodded. "That's right. I wanted my job back."

She made a note in the notebook. "He tell you why he fired you?"

"Said I was slacking off." He made a sound of disgust. "I wasn't. I worked just as hard as them other guys. If I'm a slacker, then they are, too."

"What happened when you talked to Roy?" Sam asked.

He pursed his lips and frowned. "I don't exactly remember." He held his hands up, anticipating their protest. "God's honest truth. If I drink too much, I brown-out."

Sam wondered if that was a convenient excuse to not answer a question? Or had he really consumed so much alcohol that he'd lost part of his memory? "I understand you and Roy had a heated exchange," she said, hoping to jog his memory.

"Probably," Wyatt said. "When he fired me, he said I wouldn't get another chance, but I had to try. I didn't want to have to tell Dad I got fired again."

"Where'd you go after you left the ranch?" Dane asked.

Wyatt shook his head. "Don't remember. Dog House, maybe."

"How long were you there?"

"Don't know. I remember leaving the Double R, but everything after that is..." He waved his hand in the air like he was clearing away smoke. "Anyways, I woke up in my truck the next morning. It was parked in the street in front of my house." He grimaced and rubbed the base of his neck.

Noticing, Sam thought there might be more. "Anything else?"

He gave a slight shrug. "I don't know if it's important, but when I woke up, I couldn't find my keys. Thought maybe I'd dropped them on the truck floor, but I looked. I ended up letting myself into my house using the key I have hidden in the—" He stopped and glanced at them both suspiciously, cleared his throat and then continued. "Using my extra key. I thought I'd shower first, then look again. Anyway, when I opened the front screen door, there were my truck keys, laying on the threshold between the front door and the screen door."

"How'd they get there?" Sam wondered out loud.

Wyatt rubbed the back of his neck again and gave a sheepish laugh. "I must have gone home and then went back out to my truck because I forgot something. When I didn't have my keys on me, I must have thought I'd lost them, so I slept in the front seat of my truck."

Sam wasn't convinced Wyatt was their killer. Glancing over at Dane, she saw him subtly shake his head and sighed, knowing they had to let Wyatt go.

"Okay, Wyatt," she said. "If Dane or I catch you driving drunk, we'll throw your ass in jail for sure, got it?"

"Got it," he grumbled. "Can I go?"

Sam gestured toward the door and watched him walk out.

"So, what'd we learn?" Dane asked her.

"Not much," she admitted. "Just that we can add another name to our growing list of suspects without alibis for the night Roy was killed."

They watched Wyatt leave the station and Sam wondered if they were making a mistake.

"You think he's telling the truth?" Dane asked as he followed her into her office.

"You mean about passing out and not remembering what he did that night? Probably."

"I want to run over to Dwayne's and confirm that Diego dropped off his truck that night like he claims."

"What do you think the chances are that he'll have working security cameras that can confirm the time?" Sam asked.

"Probably not good. I've been on him for months to install cameras around his property, but he keeps coming up with excuses not to."

Sam shook her head in disgust. "Does he understand the cameras aren't that expensive and he can monitor them from his phone?"

"Yeah. I explained all of that, but you know Dwayne. He knows everything there is to know about motor vehicles, but knows jack about most everything else."

Sam slowly nodded, her thoughts churning like a whirlpool in her mind. She detested this part of an investigation—the endless possibilities and the unknowns that could lead them down any path, good or bad.

"I'll let you know what I find out," Dane told her, stepping out of her office with confident strides and leaving her alone to confront the silence that surrounded her. As she made her way around the desk, intending to sit down and delve into the case, she passed through a sudden icy spot in the air and stopped, feeling the hairs on her arms prickle in response.

"George? Is that you?"

The late George Crowley had been police chief thirty years ago and was one of the smartest officers of his time. His untimely death from a heart attack while working late had left many believing he still haunted the station.

As she stepped past the sudden chill in the air and stood behind her desk, she couldn't help but feel a tinge of uncertainty. She wasn't afraid of ghosts, but she couldn't deny the presence of something inexplicable in this room.

"George, if you're here, I'm open to any suggestions on how to proceed with this case."

Feeling foolish for talking out loud to an invisible entity, Sam was about to brush off the whole incident when suddenly the papers on her desk began to shake and vibrate with a force that felt like an isolated earthquake. As she watched in fascination, one sheet separated from the others and floated gently to the floor. Then, just as suddenly as it started, everything fell silent once more.

Curiosity getting the better of her, Sam cautiously picked up the sheet from the floor and held it up to read it. It was a list of employees and guests from the Double R Ranch.

"Thanks for nothing," she muttered, feeling disappointed. She'd been hoping for something less obvious than talking to the employees and guests, but maybe that was George's point. There was no way to fast-track the investigation.

Snapping a picture of the list with her phone, she left the office and caught up to Dane outside just as he was getting into his truck.

"I'll go with you to the service shop," she told him, going around to the passenger side of his truck. "When we're done there, I want to run out to the ranch and start interviewing the employees."

Dane shrugged and got into his truck. A few minutes later, they were at Dwayne's where they learned Diego had, in fact, dropped his truck off the night Roy was killed. Dwayne also confirmed that when he'd opened the hood of Diego's truck, he'd found a busted water hose being held together with duct tape. As far as what time Diego had dropped off his truck, they still didn't know. While Dwayne had finally purchased cameras, they sat boxed on a shelf, waiting to be installed.

Fifteen minutes after they'd left the police station, Sam and Dane were headed to the Double R Ranch.

When they arrived, Sam directed Dane to take the small road that led past the guest bungalows to the barn and park there.

Elliott Peterson was mucking out a stall when they entered the barn. Seeing them, he stepped out to greet them.

"Hey, Sam. Dane. What brings you out?"

"We were hoping to talk to the ranch hands," Dane told him as they moved further into the barn, closing the gap so they wouldn't have to shout.

"Is this about who murdered Roy?" He asked them. They nodded. "Well, it's just me and Leo out here right now." He gestured to a stall further into the barn where Leo was presumably working. "Everyone is either on the trail ride or in town. We take the guests out into the back pasture to ride around for a bit. Diego took Elise into town to buy some things and then he said something about grabbing lunch before heading back."

"I've already talked to Diego and Elise." She glanced at her watch and saw it was almost 11:00 a.m. "When will the others be back?"

Elliott shrugged. "They're usually gone for a couple of hours, but they'll be back by noon, for sure."

Sam glanced over at Dane, who gave a subtle shrug. They'd talk to Elliot and Leo now and catch up with the others later.

"Where were you the night Roy was killed?" she asked.

"Here. I was helping Rodrigo work the dinner service. You know, serving food, making sure the guests have what they need. That kind of thing."

"I understand there was trouble with some of the guests," Dane said.

"That's right," he said, nodding. "That would be the Mc-Namaras. He came up to Roy that night during dinner and accused him of fooling around with his wife. Caused quite a scene."

"Was Roy fooling around with his wife?"

"Oh, hell, no." His tone was adamant. "Roy wouldn't mess around with the guests."

"But someone other than her husband was sleeping with her," Dane said, making the statement sound more like an obvious conclusion rather than a question.

"I'd rather not say. There are rules about sleeping with the guests. I don't want to get anyone fired."

Especially himself, Sam thought. "It's important we know everything, but if what you tell us turns out not to be relevant to the case, then I don't see any reason it needs to get out. It'll stay between us." She glanced at Dane and saw him nod his agreement.

Elliott sighed. "Okay, well. The truth is, we all slept with Evie. It's not like we went out looking for it, but damn it, what was I supposed to do? I came off duty one night and found her in my bed! Naked!"

"Yeah, I'm sure you couldn't help yourself." Sam's sarcasm was lost on him. "Go on."

"Well, that night, the husband didn't believe Roy when he said he hadn't fooled around with the man's wife. Mc-

Namara punched Roy in the jaw. Not hard, but he knocked Roy back a couple of steps. Looked like he wanted to hit him again, so that's when Rodrigo and I stepped in. Roy told Rodrigo to escort McNamara to his bungalow while I went to find his wife."

"Where was she?" Dane asked.

"Bunkhouse." He glanced toward the back of the barn and lowered his tone. "With Leo. I told her it was time to leave and gave her a lift to where her husband was waiting."

"What happened then?" Sam asked.

He made a face. "Wyatt was arguing with Rodrigo and McNamara when we got there. As soon as she saw her husband, Mrs. McNamara starting yelling and hitting him with her fists. Me and Rodrigo separated them and got them calmed down, but by then, Wyatt had taken off. So we left the McNamaras and went to find him. After Wyatt left, we went to check on the McNamaras and found they were gone, too."

A movement further back in the barn caught her attention and when Sam looked up, she noticed Leo had come out of the stall in which he'd been working and was now standing in the doorway, listening.

"Tell us about the incident with Wyatt," she said to Elliot.

The story he told was the same as Rodrigo's. Wyatt had arrived, drunk, and demanded Roy give him back his job. Roy refused and they exchanged words. Then Wyatt stormed off and drove away.

"Did you see *El Muerto* ride that night?" Dane asked.

"Yeah, sure did. I was up at the guest house, cleaning up, when he rode across the pasture."

"Anything unusual about his ride?" Sam asked, causing Elliott's brows to furrow.

"Like what?"

"I don't know. You tell me."

He seemed to think back to that night. "No. Seemed the same as usual."

"Okay. Anything else?" Sam noticed his gaze momentarily shifted away. "Elliott?"

He shook his head. "It's not important."

"Why don't you let us be the judge," Dane prodded him.

He drew in a heavy breath before letting it out. "I worked the morning shift the day Roy got hurt, so I was up early. I was hungry and there wasn't anything at the bunkhouse to eat, so I went up to the main kitchen about five that morning to find something. Anyway, the kitchen was empty and while I was rummaging around for food, I heard raised voices coming from the main house. I know I shouldn't have eavesdropped, but...," he shrugged. "I was curious. I went over to the door and opened it a crack. It was Roy and Diego. They were arguing about the ranch, and I overheard Roy laugh and say that the only way Diego would get any part of the ranch was over his dead body."

Sam considered the information. Taken out of context, it certainly looked bad for Diego. She wondered how it would look once the comment was given context. She'd have to ask Diego about it.

"How did Diego respond?" Dane asked.

"He was mad. Said something in Mexican. *Roy es de mala leche*." Elliott screwed up his expression. "I looked it up, it means Roy is bad milk. Didn't make no sense to me."

Sam nodded, inwardly smiling at the literal translation of the Spanish idiom for being in a foul mood. "Was there any more to the conversation?"

"Not that I heard. I didn't want them to catch me listening, so I closed the door, grabbed some muffins and got the hell out of there." He paused. "Wait. You don't think Diego killed Roy, do you?" He swore, suddenly seeming very upset. "No way. That'd be messed up."

"Diego said he didn't get back to the ranch until after one the next morning. Any chance you saw him when he got back?"

Elliott shook his head. "No. I didn't see him again until Wednesday morning, when he told us Roy was dead."

"Thanks, Elliott. Last question. Do you know if Roy had any enemies?" Dane asked.

"No. He was a good guy and a fair boss. As far as I know, everyone liked him."

"Okay. Thanks for your time," she said. "If you think of anything else, please let me know."

"Will do."

He glanced back at Leo, who was still standing in the open stall door, watching them. Sam and Dane went over to talk to him.

"You're Leo Stoddart?" Sam asked, remembering his last name from the list Diego had sent her.

"Yeah, that's me." His eyes narrowed as he studied them, clearly uneasy in their presence.

"Do you mind if we ask you some questions about the night Roy Richardson was killed?" Dane asked him.

"I didn't do it."

"No one's accusing you," Sam said. The guy was on edge, but a lot of people got nervous around cops. It didn't mean he was guilty of anything.

"Tell us about Monday night, starting with where you were," Dane said.

"I was here. Well, in the bunkhouse. Monday was my night off."

"You spent your night off in the bunkhouse?"

Leo glowered at them. "Don't act like you ain't already been told. I was entertaining a guest."

"Evelyn McNamara," Dane supplied.

"Yeah. That's right."

"Until when?"

He glanced off into the distance for a moment while he thought. "I guess it was about eight-thirty."

"What did you do after she left?" Dane asked.

"Took a shower and went to bed because I was working the morning shift. Have to get up early and feed the horses and give them time to digest their food before the guests show up, wanting to ride."

"Can you think of anyone who might have wanted to hurt Roy?"

Sam thought it looked like he wanted to answer her question, but then he shook his head, so they thanked him for his time and returned to Sam's truck.

"What do you make of it?" Dane asked, buckling his seatbelt.

"*Curiouser and curiouser*," she said as they drove away, quoting Alice's line from *Alice in Wonderland*.

CHAPTER ELEVEN

ACROSS TOWN, ELISE SAT in the front seat beside Diego as he pulled the truck into an open parking spot in front of The Waterin' Hole. The history of the bar and grill dated back to the mid-1800's when it had once been the only saloon in town. It had been owned and operated by the Stepanik family for all its recorded history. Over the years, the saloon had undergone needed renovations to bring it up to electrical and plumbing codes. There'd been the occasional structural shoring up, but great care had been taken to keep the original look and feel of the saloon. If one looked closely at the ceiling, one could still see the bullet holes from the occasional gunfights that broke out in those early days.

Elise smiled to herself when Diego shut off the engine, exited the truck and hurried around to the passenger side in time to open the door for her. After so many years in New York City, she'd forgotten the chivalrous nature of southern men.

When he offered her a hand down, she laid her hand in his, appreciating the feel of his warm, roughened skin against her palm.

She slid down the seat until her flip-flop clad feet hit the pavement. Then, because Diego still held her hand, she tilted her head back to look up at him. He was standing too close, mere inches separating them. She hadn't remembered him being so tall. Or so well built. Today, he wore a T-shirt and it stretched tightly across his well-muscled chest. The short sleeves seemed barely able to contain his biceps.

Elise swallowed as her entire body reacted to his nearness. Gone was her childhood friend, and in his place was this man who exuded raw masculinity in his every look and action. It left her feeling aroused and unsettled.

She slipped her hand from his, reminding herself that these were not the feelings she needed to be having around Diego. Other than sharing a joint interest in who killed her father and being co-trustees of the Richardson Trust, they had nothing in common.

If Diego was upset that she'd pulled her hand away, he didn't show it. Instead, he closed the truck door and, with a hand resting gently against her lower back, guided her to the door of the bar and grill.

"Thanks again for stopping at the boutique. I appreciate it," she told him once they were sitting in a booth against the side wall.

"You were in and out of there pretty fast. You sure you got what you needed?"

"I bought a couple changes of clothes. That should be enough, for now." She looked around the room, feeling a little awkward. She recognized several faces but couldn't remember names. Had she really been gone that long?

An older woman with well-coiffed gray hair and wearing a Mrs. Cleaver dress with a pearl necklace approached their booth.

"Elise Richardson, it is so good to see you again," she said. "I'm so sorry about your father. He was a dear boy. As I was telling Henri," she pronounced it *awn-ree*, "this is such a tragedy. I will, of course, be trying to contact him. Perhaps you'd like to join me?" She glanced at Diego. "And you, too, Diego. I think it would comfort Roy to have you both there. Shall we try this Saturday evening? My house at nine?"

It took Elise a full minute before she realized the woman was talking about holding a séance—and then, of course, she recognized her. "Thank you, Mrs. Winters. That's very kind of you."

Sylvia Winters was the head of the Saturday Seance Circle. "Say you'll come."

"We will," Diego told her. That seemed to satisfy Mrs. Winters and after gifting them with a smile, she left them to join three other people sitting at a nearby table.

"I almost didn't recognize her," Elise told Diego. "And who is Henri?"

Diego chuckled. "Henri is Sylvia's spirit guide."

"What happened to Patrice? I thought he was her spirit guide."

"Patrice finally moved on. Passed beyond the veil," he said solemnly, hand going to his heart, before giving her a quick wink.

"Do you think that only French men are qualified to be spirit guides?" she asked, smiling. "Or is it that Sylvia has a thing for French spirit guides?"

Diego gave a soft laugh. "I think some things are better kept a mystery."

"Why'd you tell her we'd go to her séance?"

He shrugged. "Why not?"

Anywhere else in the world, this conversation might have sounded ridiculous. The real possibility of talking to her father again made Elise glad she was in Las Palomas.

While they had been talking to Sylvia, the waitress had come back with their drinks. Elise reached for her Southern-n- Seven and took a drink.

"Do you think it's possible? That we could talk to Dad again?" she asked Diego.

To her relief, he turned thoughtful rather than scoff at her. "I know you've been gone a while and so maybe you don't remember just how..." He looked like he was struggling to find the correct word. Finally, he settled for, "not normal this town is, so yeah, I think it might be possible."

What would it be like to talk to her father? She was still trying to imagine it when the waitress appeared with their lunch order and for the next few minutes, Elise focused on eating her salad. Grief, as it turned out, made her hungry.

"Is this place still owned by the Stepaniks?" Elise asked, after a while.

He nodded. "It is. Kevin took over after his father retired. Do you remember Kevin? He would have been a freshman when you were a senior."

She furrowed her brow in concentration before nodding slowly. "I think I do." She took a sip of her drink before continuing. "You know, I remember so much about this town and yet, it feels like I've been gone forever."

"You have been gone forever, Elise," Diego said kindly. "And I, for one, have missed you." His hand twitched on the table, wanting to reach out and touch hers but he was afraid of rejection, again.

Instead, he changed the subject. "So, what's it like living in New York City?"

A brighter smile crossed her face as she talked about her new life. "It's amazing. The energy and excitement are unlike anything I've experienced before. There's always something going on—art museums to explore, Broadway plays to see, and endless choices for food that I never even knew existed." She paused thoughtfully before adding with a laugh, "It truly is the city that never sleeps."

His heart sank listening to her go on and on about the merits of The Big Apple. "What about your job?" He asked when she finally paused. "What is it you do again?"

"I'm in marketing. I do a lot of film, online and print advertising," she said, "but what I like to do most is branding. There's something about creating a brand that perfectly reflects the product or service." She shrugged. "I don't know. I enjoy the work. In fact, I just recently signed a huge account."

She paused when someone stopped by their table. When Diego looked up to see who it was, he wanted to groan out loud.

"JD!" Elise exclaimed.

"Elise. It's great to see you getting out," JD said, giving Diego a passing glance. "I hope we're still on for that date before you head back to New York?"

Diego silently seethed at the thought of Elise going out with this asshat, but kept his expression neutral, waiting for Elise to respond.

"Of course," she said. "I'd like that."

"Good. And congrats again on the promotion. Vice President of Marketing. That's quite an achievement, don't you think, Juarez?"

"Indeed," Diego agreed, acting as if her promotion to vice president wasn't news to him, all the while, secretly hurting because she'd shared this news with JD, but not with him or her father. Like they weren't really part of her life. It was high school all over again.

"I'll call you later, Elise," JD was saying. "Enjoy your lunch."

Diego stared after him, hate and if he was honest, jealousy, filling him. "Vice President of Marketing, huh?"

"Yeah. I was just about to tell you."

"But you told JD first," he bit out, not bothering to soften his tone. There was a time when she came to him first; told him everything first. Then JD came into her life and replaced him. Maybe he was a fool to think that anything had changed with Roy's death. "I didn't realize you two were still so close."

"That's not fair," she shot back. "JD came over to visit right after I was told of the promotion."

"I guess he was in the right place at the right time," he snarled, unable to stem the flow of hurt and anger. Knowing he needed to leave before he made the situation worse, he folded his napkin and tossed it across his plate before downing the rest of his beer. "I'll pay the bill and meet you outside." Without giving her a chance to respond, he turned and headed toward the bar.

Elise watched Diego leave, feeling close to tears. He acted like she'd slighted him when she had done no such thing. Worse, he'd made a scene, and it was hard not to feel like everyone in the bar was now staring at her.

With the food in her stomach turning into a nauseous mass, she took her time folding her napkin and laying it on the table beside her plate. Mimicking Diego, she finished the rest of her drink and was about to leave when a man slid into the booth opposite her.

"Excuse me for interrupting your lunch, Ms. Richardson," he said, holding out his hand to her. "I wanted to introduce myself to you. I'm Tom Kobbel."

Elise stared at the offered hand for a long moment before reluctantly shaking it. She developed an instant dislike for the rude man whose name sounded familiar but whom she couldn't place. The last thing she wanted was to remain at the table, but something told her that if she left, this man would follow her outside. It would be better to deal with him now.

"What can I do for you, Mr. Kobbel?" If he noticed the frost in her tone, he didn't react to it.

"Elise—may I call you Elise? I'm an investment banker from New York City. I have a client who is interested in turning Las Palomas into a vacation destination. This client has sent me here to research properties suitable for building a resort."

Although she thought she knew where this conversation was headed, she still asked the question. "What does that have to do with me?"

He had the decency to look abashed. "I was sorry to hear about your father's passing." Elise seriously doubted that but said nothing. "I spoke to him a few weeks before he passed to ask if he was interested in selling the ranch. Now that he's gone, I thought I would see if you're interested in selling. I understand you live and work in New York City, so operating a ranch like this could be quite a hardship. My client is interested in buying it. We would buy the place as is. Just name your price."

Elise considered telling the man he was mistaken in his assumption that she had inherited the ranch but didn't feel like going into details that were none of his business.

"Mr. Kobbel, do you have a card?" she asked instead.

With a grin, he reached into his shirt pocket and, pulling one out, handed it to her.

She made a show of looking at it and then offered him a polite smile. "Thank you. Should we decide to sell the ranch, I will let you know." Not that she had any intention of calling him.

Without giving him a chance to engage her in further conversation, she rose and headed for the door. Outside, she found Diego leaning against the front of his truck, waiting for her. The truck was already running and when he spotted her, he pushed away and walked to the passenger door, opening it for her. This time, he didn't offer her a hand, and she mourned its absence. She felt a need to talk; to clear the air between them but sensed that now was not the time. Diego wasn't ready to listen. She half expected him to take her directly home, but he took her to the drug store as originally planned, though he didn't go into the store with her. Rather, he waited for her in the truck as she ran inside and bought make-up and other toiletries.

Chapter Twelve

Dane was about to drop Sam off at The Waterin' Hole, where she was to meet Zelda for lunch, when Zelda texted to tell her Debra was there and Sam might want to be a few minutes late. Since Sam had a pretty good idea that meant Debra was upset and Sam wasn't in the mood to deal with her tears, she asked Dane to drop her off at her mother's store, instead.

As Sam stood in front of the store, she thought, not for the first time, that the quaint, old-English facade was one of her favorites of all the store fronts in town. Her mother's store was located just off the main downtown square, and the quaint appearance helped draw foot traffic to the shops on that block.

Walking inside, Sam listened for the chime that sounded every time the door opened.

"Hello, Samantha," her mother called to her from where she stood behind the front counter.

"Hi, Mom. How's it going?"

"The goddess has blessed us with another beautiful day." Today, her mother wore a dark purple broom-skirt covered in astrological signs stenciled in gold. Her light gold peasant blouse was belted with decorative leather straps and her large purple feathered earrings peeked out from behind her hair.

"Is that Samantha?" An older woman asked, appearing at the mouth of the short hallway that led to the store's breakroom.

"Nanna? I didn't know you'd be here," Sam greeted her grandmother, who was a seventy-eight-year-old clone of Sam's mother, only instead of wearing gold and purple, her grandmother wore a cream-colored blouse over a dark brown skirt. Nanna wore her long gray hair in a braid down her back and she shared her daughter's taste in footwear, which Sam thought was unfortunate. Those brown sandals were hideous. Really, what was wrong with tennis shoes or flip-flops?

"I'm helping today," Nanna informed her. "We have another book club meeting tonight."

Sam mentally shook her head. Her mother and grandmother were die-hard, sun-worshiping, earth-loving, wine-guzzling, pot-smoking hippies and "book club" was code for the wiccan gatherings that were the bane of Sam's existence.

"You know that if you get caught smoking weed out in the park, my officers will arrest you." Even to herself, she was sounding like a broken record, but she had yet to feel like her mother or grandmother took her seriously.

As if to confirm her fear, Katherine made a chuffing noise as she waved Sam's comment aside, clearly unperturbed.

"I'm serious, Mom. As chief of police, I have a responsibility to uphold the law. No exceptions."

"You would arrest your own grandmother?" Nanna protested.

"No. Exceptions." Sam reiterated, enunciating each word separately.

"Well, you don't need to worry. We ran out of pot this morning and I won't be able to get more until tomorrow."

Sam slapped her hands over her ears and looked aghast at her mother. "Please! I don't want to hear this. Haven't you heard of plausible deniability?"

Her mother chuckled and, fortunately, changed the subject. "Did you just stop by to say hi? Or did you need something?"

Sam strolled up to the "L" shaped front counter and sat on one of the stools running along the long side. Nanna came over and sat beside her.

"You heard that Roy Richardson died, right?" Sam asked.

"Didn't I tell you Death was in your present?" Her mother reminded her. "Such a tragic accident."

"I'm not so sure it was an accident."

"What are you saying?" Her mother looked shocked. Sam couldn't bring herself to say the word out loud, but her mother had no such compunction. "Murder? Oh my, goddess." She pinned Sam with a look. "The Hanged Man."

Sam wanted to argue it was only coincidence but didn't. Her mother wouldn't believe it, anyway.

"Who would do such a thing?" Nanna asked. "And why?"

Sam shook her head. "The problem is almost anything can become a motive for murder. According to Mr. Barientos, the only two people who benefit from Roy's death are Diego and Elise."

"No!" her mother exclaimed. "You can't believe either of them would do such a thing."

"I don't want to believe it," Sam admitted, "but I don't have the luxury of being subjective about this. They both had motive, but only Diego had opportunity. Plus, he has no alibi for the evening of Roy's murder." She paused, momentarily lost in thought. "There had to have been signs of trouble leading up to the murder, so someone knows something. I just have to figure out who that someone is." Easier said than done, she thought.

"What can we do to help?" Her mother looked thoughtful. "There might be a spell we can cast to show us the guilty party," she began.

Sam hid her smile. "Thank you, but I'll let you know if I need any spells." Sam tried to imagine how that would go over in court. *Your honor, I know the accused party is guilty of murder because my mother's spell identified him.* Yeah, that would go over well.

"Maybe you could ask Roy who killed him?" Nanna suggested.

Sam laughed at the joke until she realized her grandmother wasn't joking. "Come again?"

"Have a seance."

The suggestion should have been laughable, but not in Las Palomas. "I'll think about it," she promised. "In the meantime, maybe you could keep your ears and eyes open and let me know if you learn anything? I've got to go. Are we still on for dinner tonight?"

"Yes, we'll be there," Katherine assured her. "What time again?"

"I should be off work by seven," Sam said. "So, let's say dinner at seven-thirty? Is that too late for you?"

"No, dear. That will be fine," Nanna assured her, resting a hand on Sam's forearm. "So long as we're finished by ten. That's when our book club meets."

Two meetings in one week? That was a lot of partying for a group of old ladies, Sam thought, even as she assured them they would be done with dinner in time. Then she gave each woman a quick hug and kiss goodbye before heading for the door. She stopped with her hand on the door handle and turned back to them.

"Just a heads up. Dane is patrolling tonight. You don't intimidate him like you do the others, so if he catches you doing something illegal, you won't be able to talk him into letting you go. Like you did with Chad. Or Steve. You'll go to jail and have to spend the night there."

"Don't worry, dear. We wouldn't dream of trying to talk Dane out of arresting us," her mother assured her with a smile, which was not exactly the assurance Sam had been hoping for.

Nanna clapped her hands together in glee. "How exciting. I can't remember the last time we spent a night in the hoosegow."

"Yes, you do, Mother. It was four months ago when Sam caught us stealing the crawfish from St. Mary's crawfish boil."

"You ruined their fundraiser by releasing the main dish into the river."

"All God's creatures deserve a chance to live," her mother intoned.

"Tell that to the cow that died so you could wear those nasty sandals," Sam muttered under her breath.

"What's that, dear?" Nanna called.

"Nothing." Sam pulled open the door. "Love you both," she hollered as she left the store.

It took her only a couple of minutes to reach The Waterin' Hole, two blocks from her mother's store. As expected, Zelda was already sitting at a table. Sitting beside her was their friend, Debra Pecoraro.

Zelda had her arm around Debra's shoulders and, from the way the other woman's shoulder shook, Debra was crying. Again.

Which explained why Zelda had suggested Sam be late. Sam liked Debra, but she was tired of the woman's dramatics. She wondered if that was what finally drove Jerry, Debra's husband, away?

It didn't require deductive reasoning to understand that Jerry, by words, deeds, or the lack thereof, was responsible for Debra's current state of upset. It wasn't that he was abusive; maybe it would have been easier if he was, because then Sam could arrest him and lock him away. The truth was that Jerry was a decent guy who was no longer in love with his wife and wanted out of his marriage. Sadly, Debra was still in love with her husband and refused to consider divorce.

The more Debra fought to keep Jerry, the more Jerry fought to get away. The operative word being "fought."

Sam slid into the booth across from her friends and exchanged looks with Zelda. "What happened?" she asked.

"Jerry packed a bag last night and left. This morning, before she left the house, Debra got served divorce papers," Zelda told her.

"I didn't think he was serious," Debra cried, tears streaming down her cheeks.

They'd been down this road before. Too many times. "Debra, Jerry's been talking about divorce for six months now. Getting the divorce papers really shouldn't come as a surprise," Sam said, earning a scowl from Zelda. She shrugged her shoulders, as much as saying "whatever."

"But he agreed counseling was a good idea," Debra whined.

"Were those his exact words?" Sam asked.

The tears momentarily stopped as Debra thought back. Then, a moment later, they started up again. "Oh, God. That ass. He said counseling was a good idea and I should set up an appointment to talk to someone. I thought that meant he wanted me to set up an appointment for the both of us, but that's not what he meant, is it?"

"No, I don't think so," Sam told her as gently as she could. It was time for some tough love, and she knew Zelda wouldn't be the one to dole it out. "Debra. I think it's time to accept that Jerry no longer wants to be married. It doesn't mean you failed at marriage; it just means he's not the one you should be married to. There's someone out there for you, though. Someone who wants to be with you as much as you want to be with him."

"Sam's right," Zelda chipped in. "There's a whole new life just waiting for you, but you can't start it until you let this one go." She sighed out loud, giving it a dreamy quality. "Think of the fun we can have together? Three single women on the prowl." Zelda wiggled her eyebrows suggestively. "As soon as your divorce is final, we should go on a singles cruise. Wouldn't that be fun?"

"We could go to Alaska," Debra suggested. "See the whales."

"No, girl," Zelda said. "We're going someplace hot, where the men walk around in nothing but their swimming trunks. Know what I'm saying?"

At her wink, Debra smiled, and the waterworks dried up. For now. Sam knew there would be more before everything was said and done, but change was coming, and the sooner Debra accepted it, the better.

Drying the last of her tears, Debra picked up her phone. "Crap. It's already after twelve-forty-five," she said. "I've got to run. Mrs. Petrie is coming at one for a cut and color."

Before she could gather her purse, a waitress appeared at their table carrying a small to-go box. "I put your sandwich in here. You can pay for it next time you come in."

"Thanks, Irene. I appreciate it." As the waitress walked off, Debra stuffed the to-go box into her over-sized purse. Then, giving Sam and Zelda each a quick hug, she left the cafe to head across Town Park square to the salon where she worked as a beautician.

"How's the investigation into Roy's murder going?" Zelda asked a few minutes later, after she and Sam had given their order to the waitress.

"Not as well as I'd like," Sam admitted. "I've been trying to interview everyone who works at the ranch, but it's hard for them to get away and come into the station. I've not forced the issue yet, but it might come to that. Dane and I ran out there earlier to see if we could talk to them, but only Elliott and Leo were around. Plus, I have a list of the guests I'm working through. The few I've talked to know nothing. So, I've got zilch." She paused. "Mom suggested we hold a seance."

"Oh!" Zelda's eyes lit up. "So, you can talk to Roy. That's a great idea." She sounded enthused. "And there's no time like the present to ask about it." She gestured and Sam turned to see Sylvia Winters sitting at a table not far away.

The older woman was an enigma. She dressed like the pastor's wife on Sunday morning, but rumor had it she saw more action than a two-bit hooker on dollar night.

"Go on," Zelda urged. "Maybe she can devote the next seance to contacting Roy."

"Yeah, sure. Why not? I'll be right back."

She slid out of the booth and headed across the room, finally stopping beside the table Sylvia shared with JoAnn Bolland, a local seamstress, Nita Garcia, the mayor's wife, and Parker Woodruff, a retired teacher who now helped at the hardware store.

"Hey," she greeted them. "I'm so sorry to interrupt your meal, but I wondered if I might have a quick word with Sylvia?"

"Of course, dear," Sylvia said, folding her napkin and laying it on the table beside her plate before getting to her feet. "Why don't we step over here for a minute?" She gestured they move to the back hall that led to the restrooms. Once there, Sylvia, who was only about five feet four inches, looked up at Sam expectantly.

"If possible, I'd like to try to contact Roy Richardson." Sam had decided not to mince words. "To ask him about the night he was killed. I was hoping you might be able to help?" She realized again how ludicrous such a request would have sounded outside of Las Palomas.

"Of course, dear. Is this Saturday too soon? My Circle members and I had already planned to reach out to Roy." At Sam's surprised expression, she explained. "Sometimes, troubled spirits need our help to move on by giving them a chance to communicate one last time with the living. I just spoke with Diego and Elise—they were here earlier—and they are coming. If you come, then I'll ask JoAnn and Nita if they can complete our six seats."

"Thanks, Sylvia. I'll be there. Um. Do you mind if I bring Zelda? She was looking forward to attending a seance." Sam had no idea if that was true, but there was no way she was attending this gathering by herself. Not that she doubted Sylvia's ability to contact the dead. Well, not exactly. It's just that Zelda, because of her ability to see auras, was better at handling all this "woo-woo" stuff, not that Sam ever let herself be heard referring to the town's paranormal activities as "woo-woo." On the paranormal continuum of believer to non-believer, Sam was just off center-bubble in a position of heavy skepticism.

"Excellent," Sylvia said, unaware of Sam's doubt. "Come to my house Saturday night, nine o'clock sharp. I can't promise we'll be able to contact him, but if we do, it would be helpful if you knew what questions you want to ask."

"Great. We'll be there."

They parted ways and, as Sam returned to her table, she felt just the slightest bit optimistic. Maybe Saturday night she'd get a break in the case.

CHAPTER THIRTEEN

RETURNING TO THE RANCH, Diego dropped Elise off at the main house.

"I have to run to McAllen this afternoon and won't get back until late." His tone was clipped. *Just the facts, ma'am.*

"Okay." She wanted to ask about his errand but knew it wasn't any of her business. She hated this awkwardness between them and searched for a way to fix it. "Do you want to join me for breakfast tomorrow?" she asked before she could talk herself out of it.

He studied her for so long she expected him to turn her down.

"Yeah. I'd like that," he finally said.

She smiled. "Good. I'll see you then. Is seven too late?"

"No, that'll be fine. I'll see you then." He waved and drove off, leaving her feeling bereft.

She mentally shook herself. *Get over it.*

Left alone, Elise went inside to put away the clothes and toiletries she'd purchased. She took a few minutes to put on make-up. Not a lot, but enough so she no longer looked like an extra on the set of *The Walking Dead.* Then she grabbed her laptop and headed into the front study.

While her computer booted up, she called Maddie.

"Sean's moping around the office," she said. "He's not happy you got the promotion, and he's telling anyone who'll listen that you stole his idea for the Johnston account."

"That's a damn lie," Elise protested, outraged.

"Relax," Maddie said soothingly. "No one believes him. You earned that promotion, fair and square."

Elise sighed, knowing it did no good to remain upset.

"How are things there?" Maddie continued.

"Not good," she admitted. "They think my father was murdered."

"What?" Maddie's shock was obvious. "Seriously?"

"Yeah."

"Oh, Elise. How horrible. I'm so sorry. Do they know who killed him?"

"No. The police chief here has started an investigation."

"Are you planning to stay down there, then?"

"I can't. Who knows how long it will take to find the killer? That's if they ever do. No, I'm planning to fly back to New York after the funeral, but I don't know when that's going to be. Now that they've ruled it homicide, an autopsy is required, so I can't bury my father until the police have released his body."

"I understand. Do you want me to update Bob?"

"No. I'll do it, as soon as I know something definite."

"Okay. Is there anything I can do?"

"Text me if you see important emails come in?" Elise requested. She'd given Maddie view-access to her inbox after learning that Maddie, unlike her two predecessors, could maintain confidentiality. "I'm going to do as much work as I can from here, but I don't know how timely I can be and I don't want to miss anything urgent."

"Sure thing."

They spent a few minutes talking about current accounts and Elise asked Maddie to follow up on a few things.

"Okay," Elise said when they were done. "I guess I'll call you later." She was about to disconnect the call when Maddie stopped her.

"Elise, before you go, there is one thing."

"Yes?"

"Bob asked me to set up interviews with you to speak to the candidates for your executive admin position."

Elise heard the words, but they didn't make sense. "Are you quitting?"

"No, but I'm a Level Two Executive Admin. Only Level Three Executive Admins can work for vice-presidents."

Elise mentally heaved a sigh. "Seriously?"

"Apparently so."

For Elise, the solution to the problem was easy. She wasn't likely to find another admin as good as Maddie. "I don't want another admin, so congratulations on your promotion to Level Three. I'm going to sign into Workday right now and put your promotion through, effective next pay period." Over the phone, she heard Maddie's sigh of relief.

"Thank you, Elise."

They disconnected, and Elise immediately logged into their Workday app. When she finished submitting the position change, she followed up with emails to the VP of Human Resources and Bob, explaining why Maddie was deserving of the promotion and why she wanted to keep Maddie as her personal admin. Then she spent the next couple of hours answering the emails that had accumulated in her inbox.

By 4:00 p.m., she was tired of working and needed a break. Wandering into the commercial kitchen in search of a glass of sweet tea and something to snack on, she found Carmen working at the counter. When she asked about that night's meal, Carmen told her they were planning to have smoked salmon with risotto and bacon-wrapped asparagus.

"Do you always prepare such," she paused, "*posh* dishes for the guests?" She couldn't help thinking that BBQ sandwiches or hamburgers would have been a better choice. And a less expensive one.

"We do now. A couple of years ago, your father and Diego decided a stay at the ranch should be a high-end experience for their guests and we should serve the food they would find at a four-star restaurant. They argued their guests could get a burger and fries in town, if that's what they wanted."

"Interesting," she said, absently patting her stomach.

"Hungry?" Carmen asked, noticing her gesture.

"A little. I didn't get to finish my salad at lunch. Do you have anything I can snack on?"

"How about some macaroni and cheese?"

Elise jumped on it. "Yes, please."

Carmen retrieved a container from the refrigerator and handed it to her. "I made it earlier today."

"Great. Thanks."

Elise dished some into a bowl, which she then put in the microwave for heating. When the microwave dinged, she took out the bowl and tasted the macaroni to check if it was hot enough. The first swallow had her closing her eyes.

"Oh, my God. This is delicious!"

"Thanks." Carmen beamed at her from across the kitchen. "It's my own original recipe."

"This is what you should feed the guests." Maybe they did. "Is this ever on the menu?"

Carmen shook her head. "Not posh enough," she said, using Elise's term.

"That's crazy. I love it." She put the bowl back in the microwave to warm it a little more, wondering if she'd look like a glutton if she got more of the macaroni now.

Better to wait until later, she thought, but if she couldn't sleep tonight, she knew what she was getting for a midnight snack.

Carrying the food back to the study, she sat in front of her computer. Curiosity had her pulling up the Double R Ranch's website. What she saw made her cringe. The Double R logo appeared in the upper left corner, along with the ranch's address. Two horizontal bars were beneath that, with menu options appearing between them.

She flipped through the pages and found they were all about the same in that they were all—she searched for the right word. Mundane. Pages of boring black text on a pale green background.

What the website needed was color. And branding. And pictures!

Feeling suddenly inspired, she grabbed her phone and went outside. Claiming one of the golf carts, she drove out to the barn. Inside, several hands were brushing horses. Two more were working horses in the outer ring. In the tack room, saddles sat on stands with the bridles hanging on front-mounted hooks. She took pictures of all of it.

Then she let herself into the back pasture and drove across the hard, bumpy ground until she reached the top of the rise. In the distance, a small herd of cattle grazed. Using the camera's zoom function, she took several pictures of the herd.

About to head back to the barn, she spotted Rodrigo riding his horse. Targeting him with her camera lens, she snapped several pictures of him. When she finished, she swiped through the pictures she'd taken, pleased with what she had.

Heading back to the house, she stopped when she drew close enough to see the two children sitting on the back deck, playing cards. She raised her phone to take their picture but decided against it. They looked bored out of their minds.

Of course they were, she thought, continuing to the garage. What was there for kids to do at the ranch? It was all geared toward adults.

Kids wanted to play, have fun. She thought back to when she and Diego had been kids and what they'd done for fun, aside from riding horses.

It gave her an idea.

She scanned the shelves along the side of the garage until she spotted a roll of industrial plastic sheeting. She got it down and then searched for where her father had stored the camping gear. Finding it, she pulled the stakes out of the tent box. Next, she grabbed the long garden hose hanging on the wall and one of the sprinkler heads off the shelf. Then, armed with it all, she took it inside and set it on the kitchen table.

She needed to cut the sheeting, so she searched the drawers until she found a pair of scissors. Then she went to the laundry room to retrieve a bottle of laundry detergent.

Not wanting to get the clothes she was wearing wet, she went to her room and dug through the box of old clothes, hoping to find a bathing suit but had to settle for a T-shirt and shorts.

Returning to the kitchen, she gathered up the supplies and went out on the deck. The children were still there, looking hot and bored.

Elise set her supplies down at the edge of the deck and looked over at the kids. "Are you guests here at the ranch?"

They nodded.

"I'm Elise," she introduced herself. "My father owns -" She swallowed the sudden lump in her throat and tried again. "My father owned the ranch."

"I'm Bill," the boy said. "But everyone calls me Bubbie." He looked like he was in his early teens. "This is my sister, Mary, but she goes by Sissy."

"Well, it's nice to meet you both. Are your parents about?"

"No. They went out to the back pasture to help put up fences," Bubbie said. "Sissy and I didn't want to go, so they left us here to watch movies on our iPad, but it died, and we got tired of waiting for it to charge."

"I see. It's kind of hot out here on the deck," she commented. "Makes me want to cool off. We don't have a pool, but I bet we could make our own slip-n-slide. Does that sound like fun?"

The kids' expressions turned from bored to excited. "Yes!"

"Could Paul and Jonah play, too?" Sissy asked.

"Who are Paul and Jonah?"

"They're our cousins. We all came here together. They didn't want to watch movies with us, so they went to their bungalow," Bubbie explained.

"All right," Elise said, coming up with a plan. "You go change into your bathing suits and tell Paul and Jonah to change as well. Then come back here and you can help me set up."

Elise smiled as they raced off and made a mental note to talk to Diego about having more kid-appropriate activities at the dude ranch if they were going to target families.

It didn't take long for the kids to change clothes and come back to help her. Elise had already cut a length of plastic sheeting and the four kids held it down on the back lawn while she used the tent stakes to secure it in place. Next, she set up the sprinkler to keep the plastic wet and poured a thin line of detergent down the length of the sheet. In no time, the kids were taking turns running and sliding on the plastic. Peals of laughter filled the air, bringing Elise a rare feeling of joy. This had been a good idea.

At one point, she took a turn, getting a running start and then flopping onto the plastic. The ground was a little harder than she remembered it being as a kid, but her momentum carried her most of the length of plastic.

The kids cheered and then lined up to take their turns. After a while, Elise let the kids continue without her and went back to the deck to watch.

That's where Carmen found her a short time later.

"Are you okay?" Elise thought she looked upset.

"I'm kind of freaking out," Carmen admitted. "I really need to talk to Diego. Do you know how I can reach him?"

"He drove to McAllen this afternoon and said he wouldn't be back until late. Is there a problem?"

Carmen huffed out a breath. "The salmon for tonight's dinner? It was supposed to be delivered by three o'clock. It's almost five. I called the delivery guy, and he's stuck somewhere between Corpus and here. With our salmon sitting in the back of his truck." Another sigh. "I don't have a backup meal because tomorrow the guests are supposed to eat on their own and then most of them are checking out the day after. I need Diego to tell me what he wants to do, but he's not answering his phone. Dinner is supposed to be in two hours, and I'm running out of time to prep."

Elise thought she might have an idea. "I'm sure those fancy meals are nice, but I'm not sure that's really what the guests expect. Let's serve burgers and hot dogs, cooked on the grill. And some of that fantastic mac-n-cheese you made. With cookies or brownies for dessert? We could use paper plates and plastic flatware," she continued, warming to the idea. "And red-and-white checkered tablecloths? We could get some of the guys to carry the tables from the big dining room and set them up on the lawn. Just make it one big picnic. And, to save time, I bet if you called ahead to the grocery store and told them what you need and how much, they could pull it together so all you have to do is pick it up. They might even deliver it."

She watched Carmen's face and could almost see her thinking it through.

"I think it'll work," Carmen agreed. "You don't think the dinner will be too simple?"

Elise shook her head. "No, I really don't think so."

"What about the asparagus and risotto?"

Carmen had been wrapping the asparagus when Elise had gone into the kitchen for a snack. She didn't remember seeing risotto but thought that might be something that had to be cooked last minute. "Serve the asparagus. It'll be a nice side dish, along with some fries. Save the risotto for another time."

"Do you think it will disappoint the guests when they don't get the salmon?"

"Maybe, but it's not like we have much choice." If the guests had their hearts set on salmon, then changing the meal was a risk, but as co-trustee of the ranch, it was a risk she was willing to take. "If anyone complains, we can simply explain the delivery issue. Maybe, to be safe, in addition to soft drinks for the kids, we have an assortment of liquor and wines and a keg of beer available?"

Carmen smiled. "Sounds like fun. I'll leave Diego a message that we worked it out and then I'll call the store before running into town. Thanks so much. I appreciate it."

"Of course. I'm glad I could help."

Carmen started to go back inside but stopped to watch the children playing. "That slip-n-slide was a great idea," she told Elise, gesturing to it. "I worry that when families come here, the kids don't have a good time. That won't be the case this time. Those kids are having a blast."

"Oh, speaking of kids having a blast, do you think you could pick up the makings for s'mores? I can give you money."

"Good idea, but I don't need money. The ranch has an account with the grocery store. See you soon."

She gave Elise a quick wave and headed back inside the house, leaving Elise to worry about Diego's reaction when he learned about the menu change.

Well, if he didn't like it, too bad. She was his new partner and had every right to make operational changes.

Another peel of laughter distracted her from her worries, and she went back to watching the kids. It made her happy to see them having fun. Feeling inspired, she took several pictures of them.

They were still at it an hour later, when the adult guests started returning from the pasture. Elise knew the work they'd been doing was hard, and they'd be hot, sweaty, and dirty. She figured they'd stop at their bungalows before coming to the main house for refreshments and dinner. It surprised her then, when the adults, alerted by the children's peals of laughter, changed direction and headed across the back lawn to see what was going on.

"Look, Dad!" Sissy shouted to one man as he reached them. "Elise made us a slip-n-slide. Watch me!" She ran and dove for the ground, sliding to the very end.

"That looks like fun," he told his daughter. Then he looked over at Elise. "Thank you. This was a great idea."

She smiled, acknowledging his thanks, then gestured to the slip-n-slide. "That's heavy-duty plastic. If you felt so inclined, I don't think you'll hurt it." He looked at her like the idea had not occurred to him to join the kids, but now a gleam came into his eyes. "Might be refreshing," she added.

That seemed to be the push he needed. Backing up a few steps, he ran forward and belly flopped onto the slide. Bubbie had, moments before, poured a fresh line of detergent along the plastic, which helped his father slide nearly the entire distance.

The kids jumped up and down with excitement.

"What's going on here?" a woman asked. Elise hadn't noticed her until she spoke.

"Hey, Mom," Bubbie shouted. "Want to play?"

She looked dubious at first, but when her husband stood up, wiping the water from his face and laughing, she seemed to make up her mind.

"Stand back," she warned them. Then she, too, made a running start and dove for the ground. By the time she reached the end of the slide, laughing, they'd drawn the attention of the other adults.

Feeling encouraged, Elise slipped inside and asked Cindi, one of the kitchen staff, to prepare refreshments for everyone. By the time they were done, and she helped Cindi carry them outside, several more adults had joined in the fun.

Elise wished they had a pool for the guests to enjoy. Building one would take time, but this was not only Texas, but it was the country. There were other options. When she saw Rodrigo later that night at dinner, she asked him to let her know the next time one of the hands went into town. There was something she wanted them to pick up for her.

Hours later, Elise left the party still taking place on the back lawn and went inside. The simple meal had been a big hit with adults and kids alike, especially Carmen's mac-n-cheese. The atmosphere of dinner had been relaxed and Elise had enjoyed visiting with the guests as they dined, drank beer, and listened to music.

She snapped a few more pictures before saying goodnight.

Inside, she headed to her room. After changing into night-clothes – that is, one of Diego's worn T-shirts and loose shorts—she sat on the side of the bed and looked through the pictures on her phone. With each swipe of the screen, she grew more excited about adding them to the website. Soon, she was too excited to sleep, so she made her way to the study and booted up her laptop.

She created her webpage ideas using PowerPoint and, after a few false starts while she experimented with colors and font styles, she eventually settled on a theme and went to work.

She developed a new brand for the ranch which she then used on the web pages. With the help of an artificial intelli-gence app, she came up with text, which she hoped would ramp up the ranch's appeal. She included several of the new pictures she'd taken on the web pages and the rest went into the website's photo gallery.

Satisfied with the website, she carried her laptop into the dining room to start working on brochures. It would be a late night, but she didn't care. Working late at night like this reminded her of her college days, when she would work late, drink coffee and let her creativity take free rein.

It was several hours later, when she took a break to make another cup of coffee, that she finally noticed the time. It was almost two o'clock. She hadn't noticed the passage of time because she'd been having too much fun. When was the last time that had happened?

Sadly, she couldn't remember.

She was having fun now, though, so when the coffee maker burbled to signal her coffee was ready, she poured herself a cup and continued working on a brochure. As new ideas came to her, she once again lost track of time.

Hours later, now too tired to keep her eyes open, she saved her work and shoved her laptop to the side. She lay her head down on the table, intending only to rest her eyes for a moment before heading off to bed. That was as far as she got before falling fast asleep.

Chapter Fourteen

After the lunch fiasco with Elise the day before, Diego had been glad he'd had that errand to run in McAllen. It had given him an excuse to avoid seeing her. It still stung that she'd shared her good news with JD before sharing it with him. Had he really thought they'd bonded over Roy's death?

He was a fool.

And yet, upon rising early this morning, his first thought had been of Elise, and he was glad he'd accepted her invitation to breakfast. He wanted to see her, wanted to spend more time with her, even if all she did was stomp on his heart.

God help me.

"Morning," Carmen greeted him when he entered the main kitchen. "You missed a party last night."

"I heard." He went over to where she had a pot of coffee waiting and poured himself a cup. "From what Rodrigo and the guys told me, the burgers and hot dogs were a big hit."

"They were," she agreed. "So was my mac-n-cheese, and we made s'mores cooked over the fire pit for dessert."

Not exactly the type of meal he and Roy usually served. "And the guests didn't mind we didn't serve a nicer meal?"

"Mind? Are you kidding? They loved it. I even got several requests to do it again. I can't take credit for it, though. It was all Elise's idea. She deserves all the credit." She hesitated. "There's something else you should know."

He braced himself for bad news even as he studied her face for a hint of what she was about to tell him. "What?"

"Elise spent time with the kids yesterday afternoon."

"What kids?"

She scowled at him. "The guests' kids, of course. She made a slip-n-slide out of plastic sheeting, the water hose and laundry detergent." Warm memories of when he and Elise had done that as kids came rushing back. "The kids had a blast and when the adults got back from working in the pasture, they joined in. Diego," she waited until he met her gaze. "I've never seen the guests have so much fun."

He and Roy had opened the ranch up to include families but hadn't changed their menu or activities to be more kid-friendly. Elise, who claimed to not want any part of running the ranch, had not only recognized their mistake, but addressed it.

Feeling chagrined, he said goodbye to Carmen and continued to the main house. When he reached the small dining area, he found Elise sitting slumped over the dining room table—fast asleep!

She'd obviously been working on her laptop, as it was now pushed to the center of the table, allowing her room to lay her head down on top of her crossed arms.

He stopped in the archway, loathe to wake her. Or maybe he just wanted to gaze upon her without feeling her rejection.

He indulged himself for a full minute before going back to the commercial kitchen where Carmen had breakfast ready. He made up two plates and carried them into the house, where he stuck them in the oven to stay warm. Fixing a second mug of coffee for Elise, he set it down near her on the table, but not so close she might accidentally hit it. He fanned the air above her mug, wafting the aroma of coffee towards her, then sat in the chair beside her and waited.

It only took a couple of minutes before he saw one eyelid crack open enough for her to peer through it. Whether she saw him sitting there, he wasn't sure because she gave no sign, but without lifting her head, she reached one hand toward the coffee and pulled the mug closer.

Then, with great effort, it seemed, she raised her head enough to bring the mug to her lips and take a drink before letting her head fall back down to rest on the table.

It happened twice before she struggled to a sitting position.

"Thank you," she said, finally turning to peer over at him.

"You were up pretty late, I guess," he said.

She nodded.

He gestured to her laptop. "Working?"

"Yeah. I only meant to rest my eyes for a moment. Guess I fell asleep. What time is it?" She found her phone resting face down on the table and turned it over, bringing the screen to life. Seven-twenty. "Damn. I meant to get up and make us breakfast."

"No worries. I grabbed a couple of plates from the kitchen, but instead of eating, maybe you'd rather go to bed? Catch up on some sleep."

She shook her head. "Later." She took another drink of coffee.

"I heard dinner was a big success last night," he said. "I'm sorry I missed it."

"I'm sorry if I overstepped. I know you and Dad wanted special menus, but the guests seemed to really enjoy what we served."

"Are you kidding? It's all anyone can talk about this morning. Your ideas were a big hit."

"It was a good time," she admitted.

"I'm sorry if handling the guests kept you from getting your work done, though, and that's why you were up all night. I should have been here to deal with the problems."

She waved his comment aside. "It was no trouble. I kind of enjoyed it. And I wasn't doing office work last night. I was actually working on something for the ranch."

He noted the excitement in her tone and watched as she pulled her laptop forward and woke the screen.

At that moment, her stomach growled, and she slapped a hand over her belly.

"Maybe we should eat first," he suggested.

"Good idea," she agreed.

"I'll grab our plates." His gaze dipped long enough that she wondered if she'd spilled coffee down her shirt. "Do me a favor. While I grab the plates, go get dressed?"

She was trying to decide if she was offended when he cleared his throat. "Go on," he suggested. "I think I'll sit here for a minute."

Feeling confused, she watched him shift in his seat. She wanted to tell him she was perfectly comfortable eating in her nightshirt and gym shorts—after all, he'd seen her in less when they used to swim at the community pool, but all the coffee she'd had the night before caught up to her, so she excused herself and went to her room.

Stepping into the bathroom, she studied her appearance in the mirror. No bed head hair since she hadn't slept in a bed last night and her mascara hadn't smudged too badly. Her gaze lowered to her shirt to make sure she hadn't spilled coffee down her front, and what she saw made her face heat. The T-shirt was so old and the cotton fabric so thin that it covered her like a second skin, doing nothing to hide the swell of her breasts or the way her nipples had pebbled beneath the fabric's soft caress.

Diego was being chivalrous, again, by suggesting she change clothes, but that didn't explain his obvious discomfort. Had he been embarrassed for her? Or had his discomfort meant something else?

Did he find her attractive?

She hardly dared consider the possibility. They had a long history. They'd practically grown up as brother and sister, yet that hadn't stopped her from noticing that he'd grown into an extremely sexy man. Dare she even hope that he also found her attractive?

Lord, with thoughts like these, sleeping in his bed was going to take on a whole new challenge.

Pushing the uncertainty aside for now, she quickly changed into less revealing clothes and, because she was there, brushed her hair and applied make-up because, well, vanity—thy name is Elise, she thought with some derision. What did she hope to gain by making herself more attractive to him? The last thing either of them needed was to get romantically involved with the other. And yet, here she was, trying to look her best for him. Trying to tempt him.

And what would she do if it worked? If he kissed her?

With an inward sigh, she knew she wouldn't even try to resist.

Returning to the dining room, she found a plate of scrambled eggs, bacon, and a buttered English muffin waiting for her. Diego had even refilled her mug of coffee.

"This looks great," she said, taking her seat. When Diego didn't immediately answer, she realized he was busy looking at something on her computer screen.

"What's this?" He asked her, turning the laptop so she could see the PowerPoint presentation of her sample web pages. She must not have closed the program before falling asleep, so when the computer screen woke up, there it was.

"That's what I wanted to show you," she said, trying not to sound too excited. "It's just an idea I was playing around with. Designing websites and brochures, ad campaigns—it's kind of what I do."

He studied the screen some more while Elise held her breath.

"This is fantastic work, Elise. I never would have thought about using those colors. The pictures are a nice touch. We're usually so busy, we never stop to take pictures."

"I think it gives the website more of the look and feel of a Dude Ranch, and you want your target audience to see pictures of people having fun."

He was nodding. "Yeah. Absolutely. Is it okay if I use your ideas?" He shrugged. "I could pay you for the work you did."

She waved the suggestion aside. "You're welcome to use any of these ideas and no, you may not pay me. If any of those suggestions help make the ranch more profitable, then it's benefiting me as much as it's benefiting you. I'll email you those files and the pictures. You can forward them to your web designer. I might have a copy of a release form you can use. You'll need to get the people in those pictures to sign it before you post their picture on the Internet."

"Actually, I'm the web designer."

She stared at him, feeling stunned. "Really?" Then it occurred to her that he might think she was criticizing his work. "I'm sorry," she quickly added, suddenly embarrassed. "It's not that the current website is bad. I just thought it could use a facelift."

"No, don't apologize. You're right. I'm better at coding than designing, and I think the changes you made look great."

"Well, if you're sure you don't mind, I had a couple of additional ideas on using pop-ups I'd like to share with you, if the coding isn't too complicated."

He smiled. "Don't let the current website fool you. I might lack creativity, but I'm no slouch when it comes to coding. I'm pretty sure I can code any idea you come up with."

That he might be able to deliver a website that looked and performed exactly as she envisioned made her smile. How often had she come up with the perfect website design only to scale it back because her client's IT resources weren't up to the task? "In that case, let me show you some of those ideas."

For the next twenty minutes, she shared her ideas for the ranch and the website with him. She was both surprised and grateful that he listened to all of them. There were, of course, a few ideas he wasn't crazy about, but he was respectful when he voiced his opinion, telling her precisely what he liked and what he didn't, and why.

At one point in their discussion, Diego took charge of her laptop and started typing. A few minutes later, he turned the laptop around to show her what was on the screen. At first, she thought she was looking at her PowerPoint mock-up in presentation mode, but when she looked closer, she realized the PowerPoint app wasn't even open. Diego had implemented her suggestions and created a new website page.

"This is amazing," she told him. "I've never seen anyone code on the fly like that."

"This is just a beta site for now. I want to get the entire website revised before I upload it to the Internet—and I need to get those release forms signed. I uploaded the PowerPoint website file and the digital pictures you'd saved in that folder to our website storage folder, so you don't need to email them to me, but I do still need that release form so I can print copies for the guests to sign." He reached into his back pocket to remove his wallet, opened it and withdrew a business card, which he handed to her. "My email address is on this."

She studied the plain white card: *Diego Juarez, IT Consultant.*

Below his name was his email address and cell phone number. Her thoughts immediately turned to ways to make the card more appealing. Maybe she'd do a couple of mock-ups to share with him.

She was a little surprised at how excited she felt. She'd been up all night and, a few minutes ago, was dead on her feet, but now felt energized. Her work in New York had been challenging and rewarding, but it had been a long time since it had been exhilarating.

"I like the ideas you have for our guests," Diego said, interrupting her thoughts. "Though I have to admit, I have no clue how to host some of these. Wine tasting? Murder mystery weekend? Writer's retreat? Corporate team building?"

"It's not a problem. There are people who specialize in these things that we can hire to help. The corporate team building could be as simple as dividing the guests into different teams charged with performing a task or activity that forces them to work together. Writer's retreat would be fairly easy. Mostly what writers want are quiet places where they can write or read when they aren't socializing with other writers. Oh, and plenty of snacks, wine, and mixed drinks. Maybe an activity or two if they're interested. For the murder mystery weekend," she paused, thinking Diego looked a little overwhelmed. "Don't worry about it," she told him. "There are plenty of resources available if we want to pursue any of these ideas."

"I'm floored. Really." His expression grew somber. "I wish Roy could've been here. He always said you had talent. Did he know about your promotion?"

She tensed at the question, remembering how mad he'd gotten yesterday. "No. I'd only just learned about the promotion a few minutes before JD showed up at the house to offer his condolences. He asked about my job and I was still so buzzed over it I told him about it. I was going to share the news with you, but then Sam showed up and said Dad had been murdered. I kind of forgot all about it."

"I was out of line yesterday. I'm sorry," he said, offering a sincere apology. He placed a gentle hand on her forearm, and the tension she'd been feeling slowly dissipated. She felt the warmth radiating from his touch and it was sending tingles up her arm. "I'm very happy for you. Your dad would have been so proud of you."

A relieved sigh escaped her lips as he offered his apology. "Thank you," she replied, looking into his eyes with a mixture of gratitude and fondness.

Their gazes held for a moment longer than necessary, both caught up in the intensity of the moment. Then, suddenly looking self-conscious, Diego cleared his throat. "Okay, show me the rest of your ideas," he said, leaning closer towards her so they could both see the screen.

As they discussed the ranch's website, they unconsciously moved their chairs closer together, creating a sense of intimacy between them. At one point, when she'd turned to look at him, she was drawn to the deep brown pools of his eyes, feeling an inexplicable pull towards him. It was as if there was a magnetic force guiding her movements towards him. The space between them seemed to shrink as they leaned in even closer, their faces mere inches apart. She felt her heart racing, wondering if he could hear it thumping loudly in her chest. Nervously moistening her lips with her tongue, she caught her breath as she saw his gaze darken with desire.

Their closeness was palpable now, and she could almost feel his warm breath on her face as he exhaled. A part of her wanted him to kiss her, but another part hesitated.

Before anything could happen, Carmen appeared in the open archway and came to an abrupt stop as both Elise and Diego jerked apart, no doubt looking like two teenagers who nearly got caught by their parents while making out on the couch.

"Sorry. I didn't mean to interrupt."

"It's okay, " Diego said, his voice sounding husky. "We were working on the ranch's website. What is it you need?"

"I can come back," she offered.

"No, it's fine. I was just leaving," Elise said, pushing away from the table. "I have calls to make." Grabbing up her laptop and mouse, she hurried from the room, unable to escape fast enough.

CHAPTER FIFTEEN

AFTER FINISHING A FEW business calls, Elise shut her laptop and, returning to the kitchen, quickly washed the breakfast dishes. She hesitated before returning the plates and flatware to the commercial kitchen, afraid of the knowing look Carmen and possibly the rest of the kitchen staff might direct at her, but she needn't have worried. They were busy feeding the guests, and she was able to put away the plates and flatware and slip back into the main house without being noticed.

Then she headed to the bedroom. Despite breakfast and coffee, she had a headache due to fatigue, so she decided to lie down and take a nap.

Usually, as soon as she tried to relax, her brain would kick into high gear, keeping her awake. She expected that to happen this time, especially considering everything she had to worry about with her father's death and funeral, the ranch, work and...Diego. Even in her mind, his name was spoken with a sigh.

There was no future for them. She knew that. Kept telling herself that. Yet, this once, she allowed herself to entertain the possibility and when she drifted off to sleep, images of a smiling Diego filled her thoughts.

She awoke hours later, feeling noticeably better. The fatigue headache was gone. Checking her phone, she saw that she'd slept the morning away, and it was now early afternoon. She climbed out of bed and thought about logging into work, but then decided against it. She wasn't in the mood.

She stepped outside her bedroom and stared down the long hall at the doorway at the end. Her father's bedroom. She had the rest of his desk to go through, and there was no reason to put it off any longer.

As a feeling of depression washed over her, she headed down the dim hallway, not even bothering to flip on the lights. They wouldn't lighten her mood.

With her hand resting on the doorknob, she hesitated before entering the dark room. The blackout curtains were doing their job well; not even a sliver of light seeped through. She took a step inside and felt her way along the wall, searching for the light switch. Suddenly, a strange glow appeared in front of her legs.

What in the world?

Her fingers finally found the switch, and with a flick upwards, the room was illuminated. And there, right in front of her, was the bag of her father's clothes that she had brought home from the hospital. Intrigued by the mysterious light, she inspected each piece of clothing but couldn't find its source. Wondering if she was imagining things, she turned off the overhead light once more.

To her surprise, the glowing specks reappeared. Confused and slightly exasperated, she repeated turning on and off the lights until she located one of the specks and pressed her finger against it. Flipping on the lights again revealed that her finger was touching a button on her father's shirt.

Curiosity now fully piqued, she grabbed her phone from her back pocket and activated the flashlight app. As the beam shone on the button, she noticed a strand of yellow-ish-white thread wrapped around it. The realization hit her like a ton of bricks—his thread did not belong to her father's deep navy-blue shirt.

Could it be evidence left behind by his attacker?

Had their struggle resulted in some piece of clothing tearing off and leaving this trace behind? It seemed improbable, considering that such evidence would have likely been lost or removed during her father's transport and treatment at the hospital.

A sudden memory flooded her mind, of the kind nurse who had placed the bag in her trembling hands. The nurse had explained that the EMTs had to cut off her father's clothes during transport to quickly assess and treat his injuries.

Her mind raced with questions as she considered the possibility that the thread she found came from his attackers' clothing.

Remembering that she'd forgotten to call Sam about the clothes, she immediately called the police station. Sam was out but Dane took her call. With a quiver in her voice, she explained what she had discovered and waited anxiously for his response. Dane instructed her to carefully handle the bag and not let anyone else touch it. He promised to send someone out to get it. Then, they'd send the contents of the bag to the lab for analysis and find out more about the potential evidence.

Feeling satisfied that she had contributed in some small way to her father's investigation, she ended the call and mentally shifted gears. It was time to delve into her father's desk.

As the first drawer slid open, she couldn't help but be surprised by its contents. Her old sketch pad? She carefully lifted it out and noticed something beneath it—her set of charcoal pencils.

Why did he still have these?

A sudden realization hit her like a ton of bricks—he must have missed her. And with that realization came a flood of regret for all the time she had wasted not spending it with him, all because of a petty argument that no longer seemed important.

She felt a lump forming in her throat but forced herself to swallow it down. Flipping open the sketch pad, she gazed at the drawings within.

The first few were simple sketches from her high school art class—a bowl of fruit and a cornucopia. Turning the pages, she saw they were filled with landscapes from around the ranch, each one capturing a different perspective.

Then there was a portrait of Diego. As a young man on the cusp of adulthood, he had been breathtakingly handsome. She couldn't help but smile as she looked upon the familiar smile and sparkling eyes she had so accurately captured in her drawing. With a tinge of reluctance, she turned to the next page to see what other memories lay in store for her.

The next page held a sketch of her mother and father. With trembling hands, she traced the faded images, the weight of grief heavy on her shoulders. Both of her parents were gone, leaving behind a void that could never be filled. Unable to hold back the overwhelming sense of loss that consumed her, tears pricked at the corners of her eyes.

Frustration and anger welled up inside of her as she thought about how unfair life—and death—could be. In an attempt to regain control of her emotions, she closed the pad lying in front of her. Picking it up, she grabbed the set of charcoal pencils from the drawer and left the room, making her way out to the back deck.

Sitting down at one of the tables overlooking the pastures and barn, she sharpened her pencils while scanning her surroundings for inspiration. The first sketch she made was a simple one—a large black bull grazing in the side pasture. All too soon, though, her thoughts turned to Diego, and she flipped to a clean page.

The pencil moved swiftly across the page as she captured every detail of his handsome face. Over the years, he had grown more chiseled and leaner, but his eyes remained just as striking as they were in high school. She wished she had pastels so she could accurately depict the rich chocolate brown hue of his irises, framed by long, envy-inducing lashes that any woman would covet.

The warm sun beat down on her as she focused intently on capturing the details of his face. The soft sound of a child's voice broke through her concentration, and she nearly ruined her drawing with a sudden start.

"That's Diego."

Looking up, she recognized Sissy from the day before. "That's right."

"He taught me and Bubbie how to rope cows." Then she turned and yelled to her brother, just coming up the deck steps. "Hey Bubbie, come here. Look at this picture she's drawing."

Bubbie sauntered over to them, his hands shoved deep into his pockets. Elise held the sketchpad at an angle so he could see it better. All pretense left his face as he looked at the picture.

"Wow. That's really good," he exclaimed. "It almost looks like a photograph." He gave Elise a genuine smile.

"Do either of you draw?" she asked.

Bubbie shrugged nonchalantly.

"Not as good as you," Sissy admitted.

"Would you like me to draw your picture?" Elise offered kindly.

They both nodded eagerly, their eyes shining with excitement.

"Why don't you sit together at that table?" Elise suggested, gesturing towards a small table nearby. Excitedly, they scurried over to it and sat down, side-by-side. With practiced ease, Elise quickly sketched a rough outline of the pair, capturing their youthful energy and sibling bond. She used her phone to snap a quick photo, knowing it would help her add details and finish the sketch later.

"Okay," she told them. "I still need to fine-tune it, but here's a quick preview." They eagerly leaned in to get a closer look, and Elise couldn't help but smile when she saw their delighted expressions.

"That's really good," Sissy exclaimed with admiration.

"How'd you learn to do that?" Bubbie asked, genuinely curious.

"I took art classes in school, but I've also practiced a lot on my own." She paused, thinking for a moment before adding, "Would you like to give it a try?" As soon as she saw their eyes light up, she knew that was exactly what they wanted to do all along.

Elise pulled a couple of clean pages out of her sketch pad and handed them to the kids. "Why don't we sit together at the table, so we can share the pencils."

As the children drew pictures of horses and cows, Elise continued working on the drawing of them.

She lost all track of time, so she was startled when one of the hands appeared on the back deck sometime later, walking toward her.

"Boss says you wanted to see me?"

She looked at him, feeling confused. She wasn't even sure she knew his name. "I'm sorry?"

He gestured vaguely toward the barn. "Rodrigo. He said if I was going into town, I should come see you first." He cocked his head to the side. "Well, I'm headed into town, so here I am."

Now she remembered. "Yes. Thank you so much. I'm afraid I don't remember your name."

"It's Leo, ma'am."

She smiled. "Well, Leo, this is asking a lot, but I would like you to purchase the largest round, metal water trough you can find. Hopefully, at least six feet in diameter, but larger if they have it. You might need to hook up the flatbed trailer and take that."

He gave her a confused look. "Ma'am, we have extra water troughs at the barn."

"How big are they?"

He shrugged. "The usual size, I guess. 'Bout three feet across. Plus, the horses have water in their stalls and the cattle can drink from the pond."

Elise smiled. "This isn't for the animals. It's for the guests. To play in, or sit in. It won't be deep enough to swim in, but it'll give them a fun place to escape the hot sun."

He nodded as a knowing look came into his eyes. "Like a hot tub, only with cool water."

"Exactly."

"Got it," he said, pulling a pen and small but thick bound notebook from his front shirt pocket. Holding the notebook in his right hand, he opened it and flipped past the first several pages before starting to write. "Round, metal trough. Six feet in diameter." When he looked up and caught her watching him, he gave a sheepish smile. "I have ADHD. I take meds for it, but I still have trouble remembering stuff, so I write everything down." He smiled. "That way, all I have to remember is to check this book."

Elise smiled. "I understand. Thank you for doing this. When you come back, I'd appreciate it if you and a couple of the guys could put it over there." She pointed to a spot a short distance from the slip-n-slide, where the trough could sit under the one tree in the backyard and take advantage of the afternoon shade. The trough would kill the grass sitting under it but would be worth it if the guests enjoyed it. If they didn't use it, then she'd have it taken up and use it elsewhere. The grass would grow back.

"I like your drawing," Leo told her, gesturing to her open sketchpad where she was working on the picture of the kids. "You're really good."

"Thank you."

"I like to draw, too." He shrugged. "It's mostly doodles. You want to see?"

"Sure."

He bent down and flipped the thick notebook over so they were looking at the back cover and then he fanned the pages in the lower left corner. As he did, the drawing of a small hula dancer swung her hips back and forth.

"That's remarkable. It's like a stop-action movie. Can I see it again?"

"Sure," he said, smiling at her as he fanned the pages once more.

"That's really amazing. May I look at your drawings?"

He nodded once more and handed her the notebook. Inside, on the back side of every page, in the lower left corner, he had drawn the hula dancer, each page showing the figure in a slightly altered position. When Elise fanned the pages like he'd done earlier, the hula dancer danced before her eyes. She did it a second and third time, charmed by the small stop action movie.

"You're very talented." She handed the notebook back to him.

"Like I said, I'd be lost without my notebook, but if you really like my drawing—" He tore a page out from the middle of it, scrawled his name across the top of the page and handed it to her with a smile and a wink. "Your very own autographed original."

She laughed. "Thank you so much."

"My pleasure. Now, I'd best be going. I'll get that trough set up for you soon as I can," he told her, slipping the notebook back into his shirt pocket. Then he touched his fingers to his forehead in a goodbye salute and left.

Taking inspiration from Leo, Elise told the kids she'd be right back and went inside to her father's study. There, she cut pages of printer paper into fourths and then stapled several small stacks together, making small notebooks. She took them outside to where the kids were still drawing at the table.

"Want to see something cool?"

When they nodded, she made several quick drawings on the lower corners of one of the "notebooks" and then fanned the pages so the kids could see her stop-action movie. It was crude, but effective. The kids could hardly wait to get started and spent the next hour creating and then sharing their own stop-action movies.

Chapter Sixteen

THE NEXT MORNING, ELISE awoke, realizing it was Saturday. She and Diego would join the Saturday Seance Circle that evening in their attempt to contact her father.

She didn't know how to feel about that. On the one hand, she'd grown up in Las Palomas, watching *El Muerto* ride across her back pasture. She'd visited Murphy's RV park to watch *Llorona* walk along the Rio Maldito riverbank. She'd sat at Kathy's Cafe and witnessed dishes float across the room, carried by long-dead wait staff. None of that meant she believed a group of people sitting around a Ouija board could summon her dead father.

But what if they could? She felt like the police weren't having any luck finding her father's murderer. It had been four days! The more time that went by, the less likely it was they'd ever find the person. Perhaps it was unfair of her to think that way. After all, they hadn't promised to keep her apprised of their investigation, but the lack of any information left her feeling despondent and restless.

She needed to do something. Anything.

An idea came to her, galvanizing her into action. She quickly dressed and made her way to the garage, where she confiscated a golf cart.

Minutes later, she was driving the golf cart through the gate of the south pasture. After securing the gate behind her, she drove the cart across the pasture, feeling the warm breeze on her face and across her bare arms. The humidity was low today, so it was possible to go outside and not feel like she was being water-boarded, which was how it normally felt when the humidity was in its normal 70-90% range.

She continued driving toward the spot where her father's body was found. She held little hope that she'd find something that Sam had missed on her earlier inspection of the site, but she wanted to examine the site for herself.

As she reached the spot, Elise slowed the cart to a stop in the same place she had parked the day she drove Zelda out. She took in the sight before her, unsure of what to expect. Would she feel her father's presence here? Or would the ground be tainted by death and evil?

As she stood in the bright sunlight, she felt and sensed nothing. Stretched out before her was simply a patch of unremarkable earth.

With a sigh of relief, she began walking around the area, her eyes scanning the ground for any signs of foul play. After thirty minutes of fruitless searching, feeling hot and frustrated, she gave up. Either she was too inexperienced to find anything, or there was nothing here to find.

Returning to the cart, Elise sat for a moment, surveying the sprawling seventy-five acres of flat land before her. Sparse patches of dry grass, prickly cactus plants, and stunted mesquite bushes dotted the arid landscape. The only sound was the faint lowing of cattle grazing down by the pond. In this vast expanse of emptiness, one could almost feel completely alone.

She briefly considered driving further back into the pasture to look for campsites undocumented immigrants had made on their property, but while the temperature wasn't brutally hot, it was still warmer than she liked.

Heading back toward the house, she pressed down harder on the accelerator, wanting to create a breeze. Feeling the cart pick up speed, a rush of exhilaration filled her body. With each bump and dip, her mood became lighter until laughter bubbled forth. When she spied a cactus in the shape of Buddy Christ from the movie *Dogma*, she couldn't take her eyes off it.

The two large stems growing forward from the side looked like outstretched arms, and misshapen red flowers blooming at the end of the stems looked like hands; one hand pointing forward while the other made a "thumbs up" gesture.

Surely it was a sign? Though what kind of portent was a Buddy Christ shaped cactus?

Still focused on the cactus, she lifted her foot off the accelerator, intending to take a closer look. The cart's speed slowed, which was the only reason she didn't fly through the front windshield when the cart hit the ditch.

The impact had Elise's butt lifting off the seat. She immediately crashed back down, landing sideways on the seat, and then nearly bounced to the floorboards before righting herself. Her jaw snapped shut with enough force, she worried she'd chipped a tooth.

With the cart now stopped, she took a moment to run a finger along the edges of her teeth. Miraculously, they seemed undamaged. She gave silent thanks that she hadn't bitten her tongue.

Then, with shaky hands holding onto the side rails of the windshield, she hauled herself out of the cart and stood for a moment, trying to catch her breath, and let her racing heart slow down.

She was afraid to walk to the front of the cart; afraid to see what damage she'd done because she'd definitely heard the crunch of plastic.

Knowing she couldn't put it off, she walked around to the front and blew out the breath she'd been holding.

The front shield was cracked down the middle and there was no telling what damage she'd done to the engine. Continuing around the front, she saw the right side—which made the initial contact with the other side of the ditch—was now bent at an angle with the corner of the wheel-well pressed against the front right tire. Even if the cart started, she wouldn't be able to drive it without risking a blowout.

She cast a rueful gaze at the cactus that no longer looked so friendly and started walking. She didn't know how she was going to break the news to Diego, but figured she had a fifteen-minute walk ahead of her to figure it out.

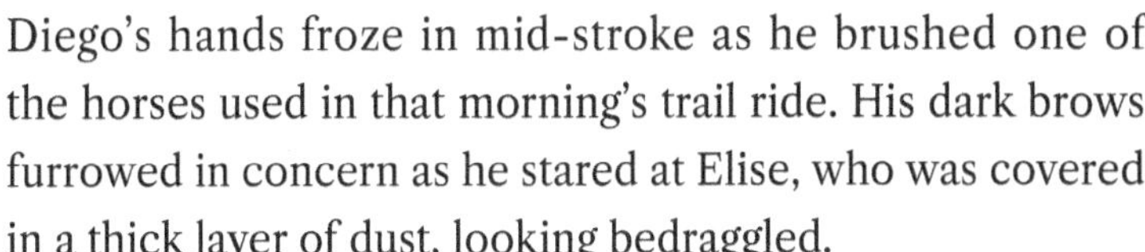

Diego's hands froze in mid-stroke as he brushed one of the horses used in that morning's trail ride. His dark brows furrowed in concern as he stared at Elise, who was covered in a thick layer of dust, looking bedraggled.

"Say again," he demanded, his voice low and serious.

Elise frowned back at him, not wanting to admit what had happened. "I may have... um... crashed one of the golf carts," she admitted reluctantly.

Diego turned away from her and placed the grooming brush on a shelf inside the tack room.

He grabbed a water bottle from inside the tack room and then, gently taking her arm, he led her to sit on a bale of hay.

"Are you hurt?" he asked, offering her the bottle.

She gratefully accepted it and took a long drink before answering. "No, just dusty and embarrassed."

"You look exhausted," he observed. "How far did you have to walk?"

"I'm not sure. Far enough," Elise replied, still catching her breath. "There's this ditch in the pasture that I didn't see until I hit it. This cactus distracted me and..." Her words trailed off as she realized how stupid she sounded. "I'll pay for the damages."

She avoided looking at him, not wanting to see any disappointment or disapproval in his gaze. She couldn't believe she had let one moment of distraction cause this much trouble and embarrassment.

"I don't give a damn about the golf cart, Elise," he said with a tinge of concern in his voice that caught her off guard. "I care about you. Are you sure you're not hurt? Those plastic windshields don't offer much protection. You could have been thrown out of the cart."

Her surprise only grew as he showed no signs of anger or disappointment. "Thank you."

"For what?"

"For not scolding me over this."

"Come on, Elise. Did you really think I would?"

"My father would have."

"Well, I'm not your father and while I am disappointed about losing the use of a golf cart around the ranch, it's just a golf cart. You, on the other hand, are irreplaceable."

As their gazes met, she noticed a shift in his expression. There was something more at play here; some underlying meaning that made her feel like she was standing on unsteady ground. The atmosphere shifted from casual to charged, and the ensuing silence became uncomfortable as she grew all too aware of him. She didn't know what to say or do to defuse the sudden tension; didn't know if she wanted to.

Diego was the one to break the spell that had fallen over them. "Why?"

She was confused. "Why did I crash the cart? I told you. I didn't mean to."

He shook his head. "No, I get that. Why were you distracted by a cactus?"

Oh. Now she wished she hadn't mentioned the cactus. "It's stupid, really." When he continued to stare at her, she knew she had to tell him. "It's just that from a certain angle, it looked like Buddy Christ."

A slow smile spread across his face as he pointed at her with one hand and made a thumbs up gesture with the other.

She rolled her eyes. "Yeah, that's the one."

He laughed and dropped his arms. "This I've got to see. When you're ready, we'll go back out there and take a look at the cart—and Buddy Christ. We can use the other golf cart." He paused and winked as he added, "I'll drive."

Leaving her to rest, he put the horse in its stall and then went up to the main house to get the other golf cart. After picking her up at the barn, they drove out to the south pasture.

A few minutes later, they stood on the other side of the two-foot-deep ditch, staring at the damaged cart.

"Yeah," Diego sighed, rubbing at the back of his neck. "You smashed the hell out of it, didn't you?"

Elise sighed. "Can it be fixed?"

He turned to her and gave a half-shrug. "Probably. I'll have one of the guys take it to Dwayne's. We still have two more we can use." Then he looked around until he spotted the cactus. As his face broke out into a smile, he walked over to it. "Good thing you didn't smash into this," he said, gesturing to the cactus. "No telling what kind of bad luck you'd have after plowing into Buddy Christ."

"Ha. Ha." She snarked back, but then grew serious. "It looks like him, right?"

He nodded. "It does." After studying the cactus for another moment or two, he looked around. "What the hell were you doing all the way out here?"

She briefly debated making up a story that sounded better than the truth but then decided against it. "I came out to look at where Dad was killed," she admitted. "And I thought about looking for campsites, but I got too hot."

He slowly nodded. "Tell you what. I don't have time today, but why don't I go with you to look for campsites. We can check out the pasture together first thing in the morning. Maybe go on horseback."

Elise was overwhelmed with gratitude. He hadn't tried to talk her out of looking and he hadn't suggested he go alone. "I'd really like that," she said truthfully. "Thanks."

"Okay. It's settled. We'll go tomorrow morning. Sun will be up by six. Think you'll be awake by then?"

"Sure, no problem."

He nodded. "Then I'll meet you in the barn at six tomorrow morning."

By unspoken agreement they started back to the cart. On the drive back to the main house, they discussed what time they wanted to leave for the seance and agreed that Diego would pick Elise up at 8:40 p.m.

"With any luck, we'll be done by ten-thirty or eleven," Diego said. When Elise looked at him, he explained. "Full moon tonight."

It took her a minute to understand but when she did, she wasn't sure she wanted to see *El Muerto* ride. The last time had ended in tragedy. Tonight, she would hope for a better outcome.

Chapter Seventeen

Diego and Elise arrived at Sylvia's house at 9:00 p.m. sharp, just as the older woman had instructed. He knocked on the door and was surprised when Zelda opened it.

"Hi. Come on in," she greeted them, stepping back to let them enter. "Sylvia's got everything set up here in the formal living room." She gestured to the large room to their right.

"I didn't know you were a member of the SSC," he commented, a little under his breath.

"I'm not," Zelda replied, equally soft. "Sam and I came tonight because we're hoping to talk to Roy. Same as you, I imagine."

Interesting, he thought, placing his hand gently against Elise's back and guiding her into the room.

In the middle of the room, a large round card table sat with six chairs positioned around it. Several lit candles sat in the center, their flickering light causing shadows to dance across the dimly lit room.

"Elise and Diego, welcome!" Sylvia greeted them. As per her usual attire, she wore a vintage royal blue dress with a simple strand of pearls around her neck. She gestured to the middle-aged woman standing beside her, whose outfit of worn jeans and pull-over blouse looked drab by comparison. "JoAnn has agreed to be our sixth for tonight."

"Hi, JoAnn," Diego greeted her. "Have you met Elise?" He didn't wait for her to respond because he remembered JoAnn and her mother had moved to Las Palomas after he'd graduated from high school. "Elise, this is JoAnn Bollard. She's not only our local seamstress, but she's the one who embroiders the ranch brand onto our work shirts. JoAnn, this is Elise Richardson. Roy's daughter. She lives and works in New York City."

Elise held out her hand to JoAnn and the women each mumbled, "nice to meet you." Then JoAnn turned to Diego.

"I know Leo said to call him when I finished the latest order for the ranch, but since you're here, I can just let you know. The order's ready for pickup."

"Thanks, JoAnn," Diego said, not understanding what she was talking about, but now was not the time to ask. Not when he was busy second-guessing the wisdom of coming tonight—and he wasn't the only one. One glance at Elise's tightly gripped hands, and he knew she was on edge. How could she not be? Whether or not they contacted Roy's spirit, it was going to be a traumatic evening for her.

He wanted nothing more than to take her into his arms and offer comfort. Sadly, he had to resist such temptation. Instead, he moved with her toward the table, to stand behind two of the chairs. Diego nodded in greeting to Sam, who stood on his other side behind a chair.

"Are there specific seats you'd like us to take?" he asked Sylvia.

By now, the others had joined them at the table, everyone standing behind a chair. Sylvia's gaze moved slowly around, like it made a difference to the spirit world in which chair they sat. Then, apparently satisfied with the current order, she nodded. "This will work. Please sit."

Trying not to scoff at what seemed like campy theatrics, Diego pulled out Elise's chair and held it while she sat. Being the only male at the table, he felt compelled to help the other women with their chairs. An image of him scurrying about filled his head.

He was relieved then, when he looked up from helping Elise, to see that the other women were settled in their chairs. JoAnn and Zelda sat to Sylvia's left and right, respectively. Sam sat next to Zelda and Elise was in the chair beside JoAnn, leaving Diego sitting between Elise and Sam, across from Sylvia. He quickly took his seat as Sylvia began to speak.

"Before we get started," she said, "I want to give you an idea of what to expect, since I don't believe any of you, other than JoAnn, has attended a seance before." She looked at each of them before continuing. "We will hold hands, creating a circle of energy. It's important that no one breaks the circle until the seance is over. Understand?"

She waited until everyone nodded their head before continuing. "I need you to think about a room that is separated into two halves by a thick curtain. On one side of the curtain—or veil—is the living world. On the other side of the veil is where spirits go when they cross over. If it's easier, you can think of it in terms of a transitional plane—or a processing station—before they move on. Where they go when they move on, no one really knows. Heaven? Hell?" She shrugged. "My spirit guide, Henri, remains close to the veil, which is where new spirits linger. The living energy that seeps through from the other side draws them into the veil.

"Older spirits, such as *Llorona*, *El Muerto*, Marguerite, and Yolanda are all spirits that have refused to move on to the next plane. After lingering close to the veil for years, even decades, they have absorbed enough energy to step into our plane of existence and appear before us, temporarily. Seeing them when they appear requires no special ability. Those spirits with lower levels of energy who step into our plane of existence can only be seen by those possessing The Sight."

It sounded like a bunch of mumbo jumbo to Diego, and he had to fight not to scoff out loud.

"If Roy is in the veil, then Henri will find him and, through Henri, we can communicate with him through me using the special link I share with Henri."

"What does that mean?" Sam asked.

"My communication with Henri is like being on a video call with poor reception. I get a few words, but mostly, I get images which we, then, must interpret." She looked at each of them, in turn, while she let her words sink in. After a moment, she nodded. "Good. Let's get started. I know you have questions for Roy. Assuming Henri can find him, what questions or messages do you have for him?"

Sam glanced around the table, stopping briefly on Zelda and then Diego. Her brows furrowed as she raised one shoulder, as much as saying, why not? I'll go first.

"If you contact Roy," she said. "I'd like to know who killed him."

"Of course," Sylvia agreed, nodding in understanding.

Elise looked like she wanted to say something but was too embarrassed or afraid to speak. When her gaze met Diego's, he nodded in encouragement.

"I'd like my father to know that I love him and I'm sorry I didn't spend more time with him while I had the chance," she finally said.

When no one else spoke, Sylvia nodded. "Okay. Let's get started. Join hands."

Elise allowed JoAnn to clasp her right hand before turning to look at Diego. She held her hand out to him and tried to suppress the awareness of him that shot through her when he took her hand in his much larger one. While JoAnn held her hand loosely, impersonally, Diego entwined his fingers with hers, bringing them into much closer contact. She marveled at the rough texture of his palm against hers and couldn't help but wonder how they might feel against other parts of her body.

The slight squeeze of his hand pulled her out of her reverie, and she raised her gaze to meet his. His smile was reassuring, and she was suddenly very glad he was there with her.

"Henri." Sylvia spoke in dulcet tones. "It is I, Sylvia, your humble servant. I seek your help in contacting a dearly departed. Henri, are you there?"

Elise resisted the urge to giggle. Was this woman for real? The temptation to peek at the others, try to gauge their reactions, was too hard to resist.

From where she sat, it was impossible to see JoAnn or Diego without turning her head, but Zelda's eyes were closed, like Sylvia's. Sam's eyes, on the other hand, were open. Her brows were drawn, and her lips pursed. Elise would have loved to know what thoughts were racing through the police chief's head.

Knowing she needed to take the experience seriously, she reined in her wayward thoughts, focused her attention on Sylvia, and waited.

The moment of silence dragged on until Elise wondered if Sylvia had fallen asleep.

The longer the silence ensued, the more convinced she was that this was a bad idea. She should leave. She didn't care if she broke their circle of energy, or whatever the hell it was. All she had to do was get up and walk out the door.

On the verge of doing just that, Diego's warm hand squeezed hers. Gently. Just enough to remind her she wasn't alone. He was with her.

Grateful, she returned his squeeze.

Then, Sylvia started to hum and suddenly there was an eerie presence in the room that made goosebumps appear on Elise's skin. The air seemed thicker, more charged with electricity than before.

The tension in the room was palpable as Sylvia's eyes opened, her face still and tense.

Elise felt a chill run down her spine as Sylvia began to chant strange words that were incomprehensible to her. The candlelight flickered wildly while the temperature plummeted until Elise wanted to rub her arms for warmth, but she didn't let go of the hands she held for fear of breaking the circle. She could hear Diego breathing hard beside her and knew he was nervous, too.

"Henri is here," Sylvia said, a tremor in her voice. "And he has Roy with him. Wait a minute. I'm getting a message." Sylvia's brows furrowed in confusion. "Diego, did you two argue before Roy died?"

Diego sucked in a breath before letting it out slowly. "That morning."

She nodded. "He wants you to know that he's sorry about the argument. I'm getting an image of a young boy; a feeling of love. Okay. Not only is Roy sorry about the argument, but he wants you to know that he loved you like a son."

She inhaled loudly and then released her breath. "Those images are fading, and I'm being shown a hospital room. And the image of a little girl. Elise." Sylvia paused. "I'm being shown an ear. Elise, did you talk to your father while he was still in the hospital?"

"Yes, I did."

Sylvia smiled. "He wants you to know that he heard you. He's showing me an A-plus sign. Okay, he wants you to know he's proud of you." Tears filled Elise's eyes as Sylvia continued.

"Can he tell us who killed him?" Sam interrupted.

"Henri," Sylvia intoned. "Ask Roy if he can identify his killer." A pause. "Hmmmm. This is odd. I see a couple of images trying to form, but they keep changing." The tension in the room was almost physical as they waited for Sylvia to continue. "It's very fuzzy. I'm being shown a horse and rider. Henri, I can't see his face. It's a blur; no wait, there is no face, no head. There's a strong sense of wrongness. Violence. Oh!" Sylvia physically jumped in her chair. "Oh, dear. This can't be right."

"What is it?" Sam asked.

"He was killed by *El Muerto.*"

Elise's stunned gasp wasn't the only one to fill the room.

"Wait," Sylvia continued. "I'm being shown Diego's face. And," she paused. "Oh, dear. Danger. Diego. Danger. Diego. Yes, I'm getting that over and over." Another pause. "I see a question mark. I'm not sure what that means, but it seems to upset Roy. Oh, now the images are fading. Fading... And he's gone."

As the candlelight steadied, everyone released their hands and looked around. Diego couldn't help but feel like everyone was looking at him. What was all that crap about him and danger?

Feeling someone's gaze on him, he looked up to find Sam staring at him. Great. She already thought he was guilty. Nothing they learned tonight from Roy had changed her mind. If anything, tonight had made things worse for him. Hell, even he was starting to think he was guilty. How did he prove his innocence?

Sylvia looked exhausted and worried. "We must be careful about interpreting the messages and not draw the wrong conclusions." She gave Diego an apologetic look.

In other words, Diego thought, they shouldn't assume he killed Roy and was now a danger to Elise.

Sam's gaze narrowed as she pushed away from the table and stood. Zelda took that as her cue and stood as well. Sam looked over at Sylvia. "Would you like help cleaning up?"

"No, dear. I'm fine. Channeling the dead is exhausting work, but after a good night's sleep, I'll be right as rain."

"Okay. Thank you, then, for doing this." She turned her gaze back to Diego. "Don't leave town. Elise, would you like a ride home?"

Diego waited with bated breath for Elise to answer. After hearing Roy's message, would she be too afraid to be alone with him? Not that he would blame her if she was.

"No, thanks. I'll ride with Diego," she replied.

His gaze snapped to hers, and she offered him a slight smile. He could have kissed her. He hadn't realized until that moment how much it meant to him that she still believed in him.

He mentally shook himself. Don't read too much into it, he warned himself. After all, he knew as well as she did that if something happened to her tonight, he'd be the first person the police chief suspected. She was probably safer with him tonight than with anyone else. It didn't mean she believed he was innocent.

"Thank you, Sylvia," Elise said, pushing her chair back so she could stand. "This meant a lot to me."

Sylvia, with some help from JoAnn, also stood, then came around the table to give Elise a hug.

"He loved you so much," she told Elise. "And he was so proud of you. He knew you loved him. Those emotions came through loud and clear."

Elise wiped at the moisture gathering in her eyes and returned Sylvia's hug. "Thank you." Then she turned expectantly to Diego. "You ready?"

He nodded. "Good night, Sylvia. JoAnn." He walked Elise to the front door, reaching it first so he could open it for her. He waited for her to precede him, then followed her onto the front porch, pulling the door closed after them.

The front room where they'd held the seance had been dim, so it didn't take long for their eyes to adjust to the evening's darkness. They walked in silence to the truck, and Diego opened the door so she could climb inside.

The silence continued on the drive home until they'd almost reached the ranch.

"I didn't kill him," he finally said.

"Hmmm?" She turned to him, her blank look telling him he'd interrupted her thoughts. "Oh, I know you didn't."

"You do? How can you be so certain, especially after he basically said I was dangerous?"

She frowned. "That's not what he said."

"Yes, it is. He said it over and over. Diego is dangerous. Diego is dangerous."

"No," she disagreed. "Those were only images that Sylvia saw. We can't know what Dad meant by them – or if it was really even Dad sending them." She paused. "And even if they were legitimate, what if Sylvia got them out of order? Instead of *danger, Diego,* it was *Diego, danger?* Meaning not that you are the source of the danger, but rather you're also in danger?"

He considered it for a minute, not liking the way his heart jumped at her defense of him. "I hadn't thought of that. I like your version better."

They rode the rest of the way to the ranch in silence and when they arrived, Diego stopped the truck in front of the house so he could walk her to the door. He wanted more than anything to take her in his arms and kiss her goodnight, but instead, unlocked the door for her and waited for her to step inside.

"Do you want to stay for a drink?" she asked.

"Believe me, it's tempting, but I can't," he said. "I've got work to do tonight. Rain check?"

"All right."

"We're still on for tomorrow morning, right?"

She nodded. "Six o'clock."

"Okay, then." He hated having to leave. "Sleep well, Elise, and call me if you need anything."

"I will. And Diego? Thanks for going with me tonight."

"Anytime."

Before he could say anything too sappy, he walked back to his truck and got in. He didn't start the engine until he saw her close the door. Then he headed for the barn.

Chapter Eighteen

"WHAT'D YOU THINK?" SAM asked Zelda after they climbed into Sam's truck. "You think *El Muerto* killed Roy?"

"Is it even possible for a ghost to kill a living person?"

Starting the engine, Sam twisted her lips in a frown. "You tell me. You're the expert."

Zelda shook her head. "Wrong field of expertise. It's like asking the eye doctor why your throat is sore."

"Yeah, but don't you read that ghost magazine?"

"Do you mean Mark Allen's *Spirit Guide*?"

"Yeah, that's the one. Doesn't it have articles about ghosts and stuff?"

Zelda replied slowly, drawing out the words. "It does."

"So? Have you read about any ghosts killing people?"

"Nothing comes to mind, but I've kept my old copies plus I have access to the on-line archives. I'll see what I can find."

"Thank you," Sam said, meaning it.

They drove in silence for a bit before Zelda spoke again.

"You know," she said in a sing-song voice that had Sam wanting to cringe because she knew what her friend was about to say. "I could sign you up for your own subscription. It wouldn't hurt the police chief of a haunted town like ours to know a thing or two about ghosts."

"Thank you, but no. I know a thing or two and that's all I care to know."

The silence returned as they neared Zelda's house.

"How's the investigation going?" Zelda finally asked.

"Slowly," Sam admitted. "I've spoken to most of the guests who were at the ranch that night. Most have alibis and no motive. I keep telling myself that eliminating suspects is still progress, but it's feeling like I can't catch a break."

They had reached Zelda's house and Sam had pulled into her driveway. Zelda laid her hand on the door handle but didn't get out of the truck.

"You'll figure it out," she said. "Do you want to come inside? I made cookies. We could hang out for a bit."

At that moment, Sam's phone rang. Giving her friend an apologetic smile and holding up her forefinger in a hang-on-a-moment gesture, Sam answered it, noting that the Caller ID said "Dispatch."

"Sam here," she said into the phone.

"Chief, Dane asked if you could meet him at The Dog House." It was a bar over on Third Street. "Wyatt Henshaw is drunk and breaking stuff. Dane said he could use force to haul him in, but was hoping, with your help, the two of you can persuade him to leave peacefully."

"All right. Tell Dane I'm on my way."

"Will do, Chief."

"Problems?" Zelda asked, opening her door.

"Wyatt's been drinking, again."

Zelda tsked. "One of these days, that drinking's going to get him into trouble."

"Yeah." Sam couldn't help but wonder if maybe it already had. After all, Wyatt still didn't have an alibi for the night Roy was killed, and he had both motive and opportunity. Not to mention poor judgement from being drunk off his ass that night.

"Talk to you later," Sam said, and then waited for Zelda to close the door before backing out of the driveway.

The Dog House was a local hangout, where tourists rarely ventured. When she pushed through the doors, her senses were immediately assaulted by the stench of spilled beer and unwashed bodies. The air was thick with the sound of raucous voices and clacking pool balls, while sports commentators blared from multiple TVs mounted above the bar.

Sam surveyed the room full of boisterous men, fighting the urge to rest her hand on her holstered gun. Some of these men she recognized as hard-working and decent when sober, but she knew all too well how quickly that could change after a few drinks. She had dealt with their chauvinistic behavior before, but right now she had bigger problems to handle and no patience for any additional drama.

She spotted Dane standing near an empty table at the back of the bar and made her way over to him.

"Where's Wyatt?" she asked, scanning the room.

Dane stepped aside and she followed his gaze down to the floor, where she saw a pair of boots. When she crouched down for a closer look, she saw a pair of legs attached to those boots—it was Wyatt.

She stood up and turned to face Dane. "What happened?"

Dane's jaw clenched as he spoke. "I didn't lay a hand on him, if that's what you're thinking." His eyes flicked to the unconscious man slumped on the floor beneath the table. "Not that I wasn't tempted. We were having a civil conversation at the table when he suddenly passed out and slid to the ground like a rag doll. I figured it was as good a place as any to leave him until you arrived."

Sam took in the scene with a sigh. "Well, I suppose we should take him in, let him sleep it off in a jail cell." She scanned the dimly lit bar once more before turning back to Dane. "Any suggestions on how to discreetly remove an unconscious man from a crowded bar?"

A determined glint flashed in Dane's eyes. "If you can help get him up, I can carry him out. I don't think anyone will dare stop us, but we should be prepared for anything."

As they struggled to lift Wyatt's limp body, Sam couldn't help but feel relieved when two men came over to help.

Once Wyatt was in Dane's truck, Dane left while Sam went back in to talk to Tom, the bartender.

"Before he passed out, I understand Wyatt was causing some trouble," she began, watching as he dried a couple of glasses before setting them beneath the counter.

He swung the towel up and over his shoulder as he stepped closer. "Yeah. That boy's got a bad temper, especially after he's been drinking."

"What was he upset about?"

"This time?" He shrugged. "Who the hell knows? I just know I'm tired of him coming in here and tearing up my place."

"You want to press charges?"

"Yeah. I called Matt while you and Dane were carrying Wyatt out of here to see what he wanted to do. Last time this happened, Matt said he'd pay for the damage if I wouldn't press charges. I guess he's reconsidered."

"Last time?"

"Monday night."

"Really," Sam commented, suddenly intrigued. "Tell me about that night."

He shrugged. "Wyatt showed up about nine o'clock, already drunk and spitting nails. He was so mad."

"Do you know why?"

"Sure. Anyone who was here that night knows why because Wyatt wouldn't stop yelling about it. He'd just come from the Richardson place where Roy refused to give him back his job. Said Roy was purposely trying to cause problems between Wyatt and his dad—and for that, Roy needed to pay."

"What did he mean by that?"

Tom pursed his lips. "I didn't ask, and he didn't say. By then, he'd started throwing chairs against the wall and I was afraid someone would get hurt, so I kicked him out."

"Why didn't you call the police?"

"I was going to, but I've known Wyatt's dad a long time. He's helped me out a couple of times when I needed the help, so I owed it to him to call him first."

"And that's when he offered to pay for the damages if you didn't press charges," Sam concluded.

"Yep." He picked up another wet glass and started drying it.

"Any idea where Wyatt went after he left that night?"

"How the hell should I know?"

"You saw him that night. You know what state of mind he was in. Speculate for me."

"The way he was talking, I wouldn't be surprised if he went back to the Richardson place, planning to get his pound of flesh."

That's exactly what Sam was worried about.

"You think he was mad enough to damage private property?"

He scoffed and gestured at the broken furniture piled in the corner. "That boy has no respect for private property."

Sam nodded, silently conceding his point. "Do you think he was mad enough to hurt someone? Maybe even kill someone?"

Tom paused in the act of drying the glass to stare at her. "Shit! I heard about Roy. Was he killed Monday night?" Sam nodded. "And you think it could have been Wyatt?" He looked defeated as he set the glass down and leaned against the counter. "Well, damn. If I'd called you that night, maybe Roy—"

Sam held up her hand to stop that train of thought. "We're just speculating here, Tom. We have no proof that Wyatt went back to the ranch and attacked Roy." At least, she thought, not yet.

"If he did, it would kill Matt," Tom stated.

"Do me a favor and don't share this conversation with anyone. I'll talk to Matt if it becomes necessary."

Tom nodded, a bit reluctantly, Sam thought, and she left the bar, hoping she hadn't been reckless by having that conversation with him.

CHAPTER NINETEEN

ELISE HAD GONE TO bed shortly after she and Diego returned, but her mind wouldn't relax enough for her to sleep. The séance was supposed to have provided answers around the mystery of her father's death. Instead, the few things her father had conveyed only further muddied the waters.

Still uncomfortable, she shifted to her side.

Diego. Danger.

What had her father meant? Was Diego in danger? Or was he the source of the danger?

She immediately rejected the idea, not wanting to believe it was possible. She'd told Diego she believed him, yet, how well did she really know him after being away for so many years?

She rolled to her other side as if she could turn away from the disturbing thoughts. There was no escaping them, she realized, flipping onto her back, and blowing out a frustrated breath.

What she needed was something to take the edge off.

She got out of the bed before making the conscious decision to get up. Dressed only in her nightshirt, she found her shorts discarded on the floor and pulled them on.

A drink and a change of scenery. That's what she needed. Slipping on her tennis shoes, she headed for the kitchenette.

She searched the cabinets until she located where the alcohol was kept and then sorted through the bottles, looking for something to mix with 7-Up or Sprite. She settled on a half-full bottle of peach Crown Royal. When she searched for the 7-Up or Sprite, however, she came up empty.

Not wanting to traipse all the way to the commercial kitchen to look for some, she decided to drink the whiskey straight. She wasn't really a whiskey drinker, preferring sweet, fruity drinks, but this was peach flavored, so how bad could it be?

Taking a highball glass from the cabinet, she filled it with crushed ice and whiskey. About to put the bottle away, she thought better of it. Earlier tonight, she'd talked to her dead father through a spirit guide named Henri; learned that she, herself, was in danger, and the police thought her childhood best friend had killed her father. Oh yeah. It was most definitely a two-glass night.

Sitting on the deck, alone and in the dark while she mulled over these troubling thoughts, appealed to her. With highball glass in one hand and bottle in the other, she headed for the back sliding glass door.

As soon as she stepped outside, she heard voices coming from nearby. She glanced over at the patio behind the dining hall and saw several guests sitting at a table. The presence of beer and wine bottles, visible in the moonlight, suggested they'd been there a while.

Late night socializing, she supposed.

Not wanting to disturb them and, more important, not wanting to join them, she chose a deck chair buried deep in the shadows in which to sit.

Raising the glass to her lips, she took a deep swallow of whiskey. Her eyes teared as the liquid fire burned its way down her throat, into her belly. The warmth spread throughout her body and though it was too soon for the alcohol to have kicked in, she already felt better. The second deep swallow didn't burn as hot and by the third swallow, it hardly burned at all.

She refilled her glass but drank more slowly this time.

Diego. Danger.

Danger. Diego.

The words played in an endless loop in her head as she tried to ferret out their meaning.

Lost in a sea of thoughts, the guests' collective gasps pulled Elise back to reality. She followed the direction of their gazes to the back pasture where a faint glowing light appeared at the top of the ridge. As she watched, the light grew stronger and took on form, revealing the figure of a horse and its headless rider.

El Muerto!

Chills raced down Elise's spine as she remembered tales of this spectral rider from her youth. Tonight, though, there was no excitement or thrill, only a deep sense of dread.

Her pulse raced as she watched the terrifying vision make its slow gallop; imagining she could hear the muted pounding of hooves against the hard ground. She pressed herself deeper into the shadows, hoping to remain unnoticed.

It seemed like an eternity before the headless rider and his horse reached the far side of the pasture. Then they stopped, and the horse reared up on its hind legs, front hooves pawing at the air. And just as suddenly as they had appeared, horse and rider vanished into thin air.

The night was eerily quiet for a few endless moments before one guest exclaimed, "Holy crap!"

"That was absolutely terrifying," another guest said in a shaky voice.

"I can't wait to tell everyone back home," a third person chimed in.

As they drifted away from the table, Elise remained hidden on the deck, watching them return to their bungalows. "I don't know if I'll ever be able to sleep after that," she heard someone say before they disappeared out of earshot.

Elise's heart raced with fear as the guests' reactions to seeing *El Muerto* triggered a vivid memory in her mind. She was transported back to the séance, reliving the chilling moment when Sylvia asked her father's spirit who killed him, and Henri conveyed his haunting reply: *El Muerto.* It had seemed preposterous at the time; the idea of a ghost killing a living person.

Now she wasn't so sure.

She lifted her glass to take another drink, only to find it empty. She couldn't remember finishing the whiskey, but it was working. The anxiety she'd felt moments before was easing. Another glass could only help, she reasoned.

Refilling her glass, she took a drink and let her thoughts circle back to *El Muerto*.

Even if the ghost hadn't attacked her father, it had been there that night. It had shown Diego where her father lay unconscious. What if the ghost had witnessed the attack?

She considered the possibility as she finished her drink and absently poured another. This time, numb to the burning sensation, she downed the entire contents.

She sat there, staring off into the dark, eyes drifting closed as the effects of the alcohol worked their magic.

Then, from out of nowhere, a thought hit her, and her eyes flew open. She could solve this mystery of her father's death. Tonight!

All she had to do was ask *El Muerto*! He could identify her father's killer.

A small internal voice warned her that *El Muerto* might be the killer and confronting the ghost might be dangerous.

She dismissed the warning. If *El Muerto* killed her father, then the ghost, not Elise, needed to be very worried. She would exorcise his ass.

Giddy with excitement and anticipation, she rose from the chair. Stepping off the deck, she almost lost her balance and fell. Righting herself, she stumbled across the lawn toward the back pasture, holding the highball glass in one hand and a nearly empty bottle of whiskey in the other.

She only stopped once to refill her glass with the last of the whiskey. Reaching the back pasture fence, she paused. She needed to get to the other side because that was where *El Muerto* had been, but she didn't want to take the time to walk all the way to the gate.

She had to climb over. It was the only way.

Reaching for a rail to haul herself up, she hesitated, realizing both hands were full.

She gave half a thought to leaving the items behind, but then changed her mind. That would never do.

She looked around, like the answer might appear before her. Then her gaze landed on the patch of level ground on the other side of the fence, visible through the rails.

She smiled as the mental wheels turned. She knew exactly what to do.

Setting the bottle on the ground by her feet, she used her newly freed hand to brace herself as she slipped between the second and third fence rails. Once on the other side, she grabbed the bottle and carried both it and the glass to the patch of ground she'd spied earlier. She had to concentrate and exert extra effort to place the glass and bottle on the ground.

Satisfied they wouldn't topple over, she slipped back through the rails and focused on climbing the fence. It never occurred to her she'd just been on the other side.

When she reached the top rail, she swung her leg over and, unbalanced, fell to the ground.

At first, she lay there; the wind knocked from her lungs. She almost caved to temptation and lay her head down to sleep, but then remembered why she was there. It was time to confront a ghost.

She lifted her head and looked around, feeling like the effort to stand was more than she could muster. Fortunately, her glass of peach whiskey was almost within reach.

She dragged herself forward the few inches needed to close the gap, picked up the glass and drained the contents. Re-energized, she struggled to her feet, wobbled for a moment, then grabbed the empty glass and bottle before trudging to the top of the ridge.

"Elmerko!" She yelled, waving the glass and bottle erratically in the air. "I wanna talk to you."

She turned in circles, shouting the ghost's name, and quickly grew dizzy. Afraid she might throw up, she bent over, resting her forearms against her slightly bent knees.

"Sho-yu-sel, y'cowar!" She muttered in between taking deep breaths. Then, because the ghost was pissing her off, she shouted more loudly, "Elmurdo! I'm taugggin' you, you headless fud!"

"Elise?"

At the sound of her name, she lifted her head and immediately regretted the action.

A short distance away, two figures appeared before her, glowing brilliantly beneath the moonlight. She stared at them, blinking rapidly. As the figures moved toward her, they merged into the single figure of a man—with no head.

El Muerto!

He had come.

"Sta-bak!" She yelled, wobbling as she straightened, brandishing the whiskey bottle in front of her like a sword. When the figure continued to advance, she dropped the empty glass to the ground and reached beneath her shirt for the necklace hanging around her neck. Pulling it out, she fumbled for the tiny cross which she then held out in front of her. "The power uda cross compledes-ewe. Sta-bak"

"Are you drunk?" The ghost asked, coming to a stop in front of her.

"Did-chu kill my fathur?" She wished the ground would stop moving. "Anzor me, damn-it! Did-chu kill my fathur?"

"Elise, calm down."

How dare he tell her to calm down! "I'll banich-u if you don answer my queschun," she threatened.

"Elise. It's me. Diego."

The words and faintly familiar voice surprised and confused her.

"Diego?"

The moonlight reflecting off his shirt was blinding in its intensity, and she released the cross in order to shield her eyes with her hand.

"That's right," the apparition said. "It's Diego." As he moved closer, the features of his shadowed face came into view and she finally recognized him.

Heaving a sigh of relief, she lowered the arm still brandishing the whiskey bottle. "I though-chu were Elmurdo."

She saw one eyebrow arch. "I compel you with the power of the cross?" He mocked. "*El Muerto's* not a vampire, you know." She ignored him. "And what's with the whiskey bottle? Wait." He snatched the bottle from her. "Is that my peach Crown? That bottle was half-full. Don't tell me you drank all of it. Holy hell. Elise. What were you thinking?"

"I havva-talk to Elmurdo."

He sighed. "Why?"

"He killed my dad."

"You think a ghost killed your father?"

She closed her eyes, glad that he finally understood, then quickly opened them again when the world spun around her.

"That's ridiculous," he said.

She'd had the same thought but now resented him for saying it out loud. "No," she started to shake her head but stopped when the world tilted. "He-wuz 'ere. Knows-ewe did-id." It was getting harder for her to think of the right words, much less say them out loud. "I'mma make 'im talk."

He shook his head. "You want *El Muerto*—a headless ghost—to tell you who killed your father?"

"Yez!" Finally, he understood. Why wasn't he more amazed at her brilliant plan?

"The ghost has no head, Elise."

"So?" She shot him a look and would have toppled over if he hadn't put a hand under her arm to steady her.

"No head. No mouth. He's not going to tell you jack."

She didn't like his tone. It sounded indulgent and overly patient. "You-dun undastan," she told him.

"Yeah, I do understand." He raised the empty whiskey bottle and shook it. "You're drunk. Let me take you back to the house." He looked around. "Where's your golf cart?"

"Don-ave one. Walked."

She heard him sigh. "Great. Come on."

She shook her head and immediately regretted it. "I 'ave to..." The words trailed off as she stared at him, having already forgotten what she'd been about to say.

She reached out and dragged a finger down his darkened face, leaving behind a lighter path of skin. "Wuz diz shish on yoo face?"

He muttered an answer, but she didn't understand the words. It felt like there were dense cobwebs filling her brain. The ability to think was further hindered by the world spinning faster and faster around her. Closing her eyes, she tried to focus.

She'd come out there for something. What was it?

Diego was talking to her now; she could see his lips moving, but the ringing in her head was too loud to make out his words. The whiskey had worked; she no longer felt anxious. She felt relaxed and so, so tired. She wanted nothing more than to lie down and go to sleep. So, she did.

Diego's strong arms caught Elise around the waist as her knees buckled, preventing her from tumbling to the ground. The scent of whiskey clung to her like a heavy blanket, masking the floral scent of her new perfume. She was out cold, her body limp and unresponsive.

He couldn't believe it. Prim and proper Elise had gotten drunk on his good whiskey. And now she was out here in the middle of the night, confronting *El Muerto*.

He knew one thing for certain: her timing was incredibly inconvenient. As he looked down at her sleeping face, he briefly considered calling one of the ranch hands for assistance. However, he quickly dismissed the idea. He didn't want anyone to see Elise in this state; it would be embarrassing for her. Plus, there was a part of him that relished the opportunity to take care of her.

Getting her back to the main house was going to be a challenge. Diego was used to carrying heavy bales of hay and sacks of feed without breaking a sweat, but Elise weighed at least twice as much as those objects and their destination was quite a distance away.

He scanned their surroundings, noting that both the back deck and dining hall patio were shrouded in darkness—a good sign that no one was outside. He hoped to keep it that way; they needed to leave the pasture as soon as possible without drawing attention.

Remembering his horse waiting nearby, Diego pursed his lips and let out a sharp whistle. A moment later, he heard the sound of hoofbeats approaching, and soon enough, his beautiful white steed appeared over the ridge, its coat luminescent beneath the moonlight.

There was really no good way to lift Elise's unconscious form onto the horse, but he did the best he could. Scanning the ground, he spotted the empty whiskey bottle and glass. Fortunately, neither had shattered when they hit the ground. Quickly, he looped the saddle latigo around the neck of the bottle, using it as a makeshift holster. Holding the reins in one hand while gripping the highball glass in the other, he led his horse across the pasture towards the gate, praying that Elise would remain unconscious during their journey. The thought of her being jostled as she lay stomach down on the saddle, her head hanging limply, made him wince.

As they reached the barn, he reconsidered taking Elise all the way back to the main house. His temporary bungalow was much closer. Leading his horse to the front of the cozy dwelling, he carefully untied the whiskey bottle and left Elise resting on the horse while he quickly went inside and set the bottle and glass down on the kitchen table. Returning outside with haste, he tugged on her leg and caught her as she slid from the horse.

Normally, he'd do the chivalrous thing and offer her the bed while he took the couch. Tonight hardly counted as "normal" and with Elise unconscious, the gesture would be lost on her. At six feet two inches, he was too tall to stretch out comfortably on the couch. Elise, being shorter, would fit much better.

He carried her over and laid her down on her side, with her back against the back of the couch. He didn't want to have to worry about her suffocating if she threw up while he was putting his horse away.

Pulling off her shoes, he then covered her with an afghan. As an after-thought, he wadded up several paper towels from the kitchen and placed them into the bathroom trash-can, which he then set next to the couch, near her head. Satisfied she would be okay for a while on her own, he left the bungalow.

Out at the barn, Diego washed the sweat and grime from his horse before returning him to his stall. It was warm outside, so he knew the horse would dry within minutes. He put away his tack and then gave his horse an extra helping of grain as reward for the extra work it had done that evening. Then, tugging the water hose around the barn, he checked the water buckets for all the animals and topped off the ones that needed it. Finally finished and feeling exhausted, he returned to his bungalow.

He immediately checked on Elise. As far as he could tell, she hadn't moved. Her breathing was steady, and she hadn't thrown up because the trashcan contained only the dry paper towels he'd put there earlier. She'd have one hell of a hangover in the morning.

Smiling to himself, he went into his bedroom and started to close his door before thinking better of it. He didn't need the privacy and hoped, by leaving the door open, he'd hear her if she got up during the night.

Stripping off his clothes, he tossed them onto the floor at the back of his closet and went to take a shower. A few minutes later, clean, dressed only in his boxer briefs and beyond tired, Diego went to bed.

Several hours later, Elise startled awake, her head throbbing as if a jackhammer was relentlessly pounding against her skull. She groaned, slowly pushing herself into a sitting position, and felt the world spin around her in a disorienting haze. Her body begged her to lie back down, but the urgent need to use the bathroom forced her to stand.

Blinking away a sudden wave of dizziness, she scanned her surroundings, struggling to recognize where she was. This certainly wasn't her bedroom back home. For a brief moment, a wave of panic washed over her as she considered the possibility that she had drunkenly gone home with a stranger. Then she remembered—she was at her father's ranch in Texas, staying in Diego's room. That must explain why everything seemed slightly off and unfamiliar.

She groaned as she recalled how much she must have drunk to feel like this. Before tonight, her limit had always been two drinks, but now, she couldn't even remember how many drinks she had consumed before passing out on the couch.

Feeling embarrassed and grateful that no one had witnessed her drunken state, Elise made a mental note to never drink that much again and stumbled across the room in search of the bathroom. The outside light filtering in through the windows provided enough illumination for her to see, saving her from having to turn on the harsh overhead lights.

Walking through an open doorway, she found herself in the bedroom. To her right was the bathroom, and she hurried inside.

After taking care of business, Elise made her way back to bed. She took a moment to undress before collapsing onto the mattress. Compared to the couch, the bed felt like a cloud, cradling her body with its softness. Pulling up the covers, she closed her eyes, relishing the luxurious warmth enveloping her body. Elise drifted off to sleep, her pounding head momentarily forgotten as a feeling of contentment settled in.

Chapter Twenty

As Diego slowly drifted from sleep, his senses awakened one by one. The first thing he noticed was another body in the bed next to him, a soft and warm form that had not been there when he fell asleep. He shifted slightly, just enough to glimpse ash blond hair resting on his shoulder.

Elise!

Realization dawned on him, followed by a tinge of embarrassment. The softness against his skin was not fabric, but bare flesh. Elise must have slipped into bed with him in the middle of the night after undressing. And he had slept through it all like a fool. He mentally scolded himself for missing such a rare opportunity.

As much as he knew he should leave the bed, something selfish in him held him back. The forbidden pleasure of being in bed with Elise, skin to skin, was too irresistible to pass up. She lay on her side, one arm draped across his chest and her head nestled against his shoulder, her warm breath caressing his skin with every exhale. The feel of her bare breasts pressed against his body made him harden involuntarily. It was only natural for any man to react this way when faced with such an intimate situation, but he worried about how Elise would react if she woke up.

He contemplated quietly slipping out of bed, but the thought quickly dissipated when he heard the change in Elise's breathing, signaling that she was waking up.

"Elise?" With a gentle whisper, he called out her name, freezing when she shifted in the bed.

She rolled away from him and he couldn't believe his luck. Slipping out of bed with careful movements, he gathered his scattered clothes and left the bedroom, quietly closing the door behind him. In the main room, he quickly dressed himself and then made his way out of the bungalow and towards the main house.

Once there, he put on a pot of coffee to brew, filling the air with its rich aroma. As he waited for it to finish, he grabbed a plastic grocery bag and headed to Elise's bedroom. He felt slightly uncomfortable rummaging through her belongings but knew she would forgive him if it meant bringing her back a change of clothes.

Satisfied with the items he had chosen—underwear, jeans, shirt, and socks—he returned to the kitchen and prepared a tray with two plates of scrambled eggs and bacon. As an afterthought, he added a bagel with cream cheese for Elise. Pouring two travel mugs of coffee and fixing one just the way he remembered she liked it, he placed them on the tray and headed back to the bungalow.

Stepping inside, the first thing he noticed was the silence. The bedroom door was still closed the way he'd left it.

Placing the tray of food on the kitchen table, he carried the bag of clothes to the bedroom and pushed open the door.

Elise, now burrowed under the covers, didn't move. They had planned to go riding this morning, but he wasn't sure if she'd feel up to it. He was trying to decide whether to wake her or go without her when he heard her moan.

"Oh, my head."

"You alive under there?"

"No," she groaned and holding the blanket to her chest with one hand, used the other to push herself into a sitting position. She blinked at him several times, like she was trying to clear her vision and then, emitting another soft groan, let her head drop into an upraised hand. "Did you get the license plate number of the bus that ran over me?"

He gave a soft chuckle. "You had a bit to drink last night."

"Don't remind me." Parting the fingers of her right hand, she peeked at him. "What time is it?"

"Almost five-thirty."

She blew out her breath. "I'm supposed to meet you in thirty minutes to go riding."

"Relax. I won't hold you to it," he told her. "I wasn't sure if you'd feel up to it after your bender last night."

He was surprised to hear her hoarse chuckle. "I don't think I've had that much to drink since Robbie Parson's graduation party."

"As I recall, you swore then that you'd never drink again."

"I'm renewing that vow." She rubbed her forehead, no doubt trying to ease the ache.

"How much of last night do you remember?"

She gazed up at him between her fingers. "Not enough, apparently. Did we, um…" She hesitated as her cheeks flushed a bright pink. "Sleep together?"

"No," he told her. "I slept on the couch." He hated lying but he thought the truth might embarrass her.

She lifted the sheet to peak under it. Then lowered it to look at him. "Did you undress me?"

"Nope. You must have done that on your own. I put you to bed fully clothed." That, at least, was the truth. "Do you remember standing out in the pasture yelling for *El Muerto* to show himself?"

Her hand dropped from her face as her eyes rounded with surprise. "Please tell me you're kidding."

"Sadly, no. I believe you tried to compel him with the power of the cross."

She dropped her head and held her hand out to him, palm facing him. "Stop. I don't want to hear any more."

He smiled and held up the grocery bag so she could see it. "I brought you a change of clothes." He walked into the room and set the bag down at the foot of the bed, then gestured to the outer room. "I also have coffee and breakfast, if you feel up to either."

"Thanks. I'll get dressed and see how I feel about breakfast and going for a ride."

"Okay. I'll be in the other room. Holler if you need anything."

"Thanks." Elise remained where she was until the door closed behind him. Then she slapped her hand over her face and slumped back against the pillows.

Oh, my God. How embarrassing.

When she woke up two hours ago, hung over but sober, and realized she was in bed with Diego, wrapped around him like a blanket, she should have slipped out of the bed and returned to the main house. There was no excuse for why she hadn't. At least, no good excuse.

The truth was, she found him extremely attractive and while it surprised the hell out of her to find herself in bed with him, she didn't want to leave. That was new and different for her. Normally, if she even went so far as to sleep with a date, she made sure to do so at his place, so she could wake up early and leave. It was easier to suffer the morning walk of shame than deal with the awkward morning-after breakfast conversation. Elise wasn't interested in long-term relationships because she only had time for her career.

This morning, though, she found herself wishing they'd ended up in bed because they were dating, rather than because she'd mistakenly crawled into bed with him in the middle of the night. Which was why she'd wanted to extend the fantasy a little longer and instead of getting out of bed, had snuggled closer and gone back to sleep.

She pretended to still be asleep when he woke up because it was too embarrassing for her to admit the truth, which was why she appreciated Diego perpetuating the lie for her. It might be the only way she could muster the courage to face him again.

Knowing she couldn't put it off, she climbed out of bed, grabbed the bag of clothes, and headed for the bathroom. A few minutes later, dressed and feeling slightly more alert thanks to the cold water she'd splashed on her face, Elise left the bedroom.

Diego was sitting at the kitchen table, halfway through his breakfast.

"Sorry, I started without you," he told her. "I wasn't sure how long you'd be."

"I'm glad you did." She lowered herself into the chair opposite him and, using both hands, picked up the travel mug of coffee sitting before her. At this point, she didn't care what it tasted like, so long as it was hot and the caffeine kicked in quickly. To her surprise, though, the coffee was fixed just the way she liked it.

"This is really good," she told him. "Thanks."

"You're welcome. How are you feeling?"

"Better."

"Good enough to go for a morning ride?"

"Yeah, actually. I think so." She stared at the plate of food in front of her. "Maybe after I eat?"

"Of course. Take your time."

She considered her options. She wasn't sure she could stomach the scrambled eggs, so she started with the bagel, hoping the bread would settle her stomach.

"Thank you for taking care of me," she finally said.

"I'll always be here for you, Elise."

It was the way he said it, more so than the words, that had her studying his face. It was like he was trying to tell her something and she wasn't sure she was brave enough to figure out what.

"Why don't I go saddle the horses for us while you finish," he offered, breaking the awkward silence that had fallen between them. "When you're done, meet me in the barn. Sound good?"

"Yep, that works. Thanks. I'll be there shortly."

"All right."

After he left, Elise focused on eating the bagel while finishing her coffee. When she was done, she went back to Diego's bathroom and quickly searched the drawers and cabinets until she found a bottle of aspirin. Taking three pills, she washed them down with a glass of water.

Then, she made her way to the barn where Diego was waiting for her by the horse stalls. He smiled warmly at her and gestured towards the saddled horses.

"Shall we?" he asked.

A few minutes later, Elise and Diego were on horseback, headed for the back pasture. The sun was beginning to rise, painting the horizon in soft shades of pink and yellow. The morning air wrapped around them like in a refreshing embrace, offering respite from the sweltering heat that would come later in the day. Elise welcomed the sense of peace that came with riding at this time of day—even if it was only temporary.

They rode in silence, their horses plodding along at a leisurely pace. It was a comfortable silence, one filled with memories and unspoken understanding. As children, they often took these early morning rides together and Elise couldn't help but reminisce about those simpler times as they rode side by side. Sadly, those carefree days seemed long gone.

They approached the rise where *El Muerto* made his ghostly ride. A shiver ran down Elise's spine knowing her father had been attacked just beyond this point.

Her horse came to a stop at the top of the rise, but Diego's horse continued down the other side. He finally noticed her hesitation and turned back to check on her.

"Are you okay?" he asked with concern.

She nodded; her gaze fixed on the view from the top of the ridge. The summer had been harsh and unyielding. "The drought has been rough," she commented, taking in the sight of the mostly barren pasture. In the distance, the cattle were gathered around the tank, resembling a smudge of brown paint on a canvas. "The cattle can't survive off this."

He nodded solemnly. "We've been having to supplement their feed with hay and grain every day. It's been tough on everyone."

She continued to look around, noting how the thicker growth of trees on either side of the pasture shielded them from the nearby highway to the west and the Drake ranch to the east, blocking out any noise or signs of modern civilization. It was easy to imagine being transported back to the simpler days of the old West.

As she prepared to join Diego down the ridge, her gaze caught something unusual in the pasture below. A series of depressions running across the land. She stared at them for several minutes before realizing what she was seeing. "Are those tire tracks?" she asked, pointing them out to Diego.

He spurred his horse back up the rise and came to a stop beside her, confusion evident on his face. "Where?"

"There," she said, gesturing towards the marks in the ground.

Diego studied them. "Damn. I think you're right."

"Why does that surprise you?" she asked, bewildered by his reaction.

"When Rodrigo took over as foreman, I stopped coming out here and while I've been out once or twice over the last couple of days, I hadn't noticed them. Let's take a closer look."

They urged their horses into a slow canter down the ridge and across the pasture. The closer they got, the less obvious the tracks appeared, blending into the dry grass and earth.

When Diego reined his horse to a stop, Elise followed suit. She watched as he scanned the horizon to the east and then the west. "We're about even with the gates on either side." Keeping his gaze fixed on the ground, he changed directions and walked toward the west fence line with Elise following him.

"Look there," he said, coming to a stop about a hundred yards from the fence and pointing at the ground.

Elise peered down and saw what he was pointing at—faint impressions in the ground that could have been made by tires. "We had a big rainstorm about five months ago," Diego explained. "The ground turned to mud. It was a real mess. But look here—you can see where a vehicle drove across the mud." Before she could ask, he answered her unspoken question. "It wasn't us."

They followed the tracks until they disappeared into the trees, at which point, they continued on to the west gate. It was closed and locked, with no signs of forced entry. Maybe they were wrong thinking the tracks were a sign of suspicious activity.

Before she could voice her thoughts, Diego dismounted from his horse and strode towards the gate.

She watched in surprise as he examined the lock closely for a moment before giving a grunt of disgust. With one swift movement, he twisted the base of the lock, and it easily gave way. It hadn't been locked at all! Someone had deliberately turned it to make it appear locked.

Exchanging worried glances, Elise and Diego shared a silent communication before he pulled out a two-way walkie-talkie from his shirt pocket. Pressing a button, he spoke into it in a low voice. "Bunkhouse, come in. Over."

A few seconds later, a voice responded. "Hey, Boss. This is Elliott. Over."

"Have you or any of the other guys gone through the south pasture's west gate recently? Over."

"Not me, but I'll check with the others. Over."

"Thanks, let me know what you find out. Over."

Curiosity getting the better of her, Elise asked Diego once he had put away the walkie-talkie, "What are you thinking?"

He shook his head, looking troubled. "It could be nothing. The unlocked gate might not have anything to do with those tracks we found."

"You suspect otherwise?"

Diego nodded grimly. "I can't shake off the feeling that it's a strong possibility."

Returning to the lock, he carefully realigned the shank with the receiving hole before snapping it shut again. With a quick jerk, he tested to make sure it was secure before mounting his horse again.

"I need to do a headcount of the cattle," he told Elise as they rode away from the gate. "Could you help me?"

"Of course." She could sense the worry in his voice, and she understood why. Cattle rustling was not as prominent as it once was, but it still happened. Instead of men on horseback, rustlers now used trucks and trailers to make off with their stolen livestock.

They reined their horses toward the tank where their herd grazed lazily and urged them into a slow canter. Diego motioned for them to stop once they could distinguish individual cattle from the mass of animals. "Let me know how many you count," he instructed her.

She nodded and focused on the task at hand, silently tallying up the numbers in her head.

Diego finished first and turned to her, raising an eyebrow in question.

"Forty-seven," she reported.

"Same," he confirmed with a nod.

She couldn't help feeling frustrated when he didn't say more. "How many are supposed to be out here?"

"Forty-seven," he replied simply.

A wave of relief washed over her. "Well, that's good then, right? Just means someone forgot to lock the gate."

He shrugged, his expression unreadable. "Maybe. Or it means our cattle weren't the target."

It took her a moment to realize what he meant. "You think JD's place is the target?"

He turned to look at her with a grave expression. "Word around town is that he's training some pretty expensive horses, any one of which could be worth hundreds of thousands of dollars."

"We need to warn him!" she exclaimed, reaching for her phone.

Diego's words stopped her short. "It might already be too late. Who knows how long that gate's been unlocked?" He paused, a frown marring his features. "But that's not our biggest problem. That's our lock on the gate. Only the ranch hands have access to the key."

She didn't like where this was going. "You think one of the Double R hands left it open on purpose?"

His head tilted slightly, indicating that was exactly what he was thinking.

"What do we do?"

"I'll run into town and buy a couple of heavy-duty combination locks to replace the ones on both gates. Then, I'll make sure that only the three of us—you, me, and Rodrigo—know the combination."

"What about JD's horses?"

Diego let out a deep breath. "Let's ride over to the east gate. If we find that lock open like this one, then we'll go talk to JD."

Elise nodded, trying to push down the knot of worry growing in her stomach. When they reached the other gate and found that lock had also been left open, her fears were confirmed.

"We need to warn JD," Elise said urgently, forgetting about their plan to check for campsites. "He's probably awake. Let's go over there."

Diego pointed to a tree, and she saw the No Trespassing sign posted on it. Her eyes scanned the fence line, and she noticed similar signs posted on trees all along it.

"Oh, come on," she groaned, frustration and anxiety bubbling inside her. "How long have these been up?"

Diego's reply was calm and matter-of-fact. "About six months after JD returned home, he put those up."

Elise couldn't help but feel irritated by this new development, but she could also understand their purpose. If anyone wandered onto JD's property and got hurt—or worse, hurt one of his horses—he would be protected from any lawsuits due to these warning signs. Unfortunately, it also meant that even as his neighbor and former girlfriend, she could not enter his land without his permission.

She pulled out her phone and dialed JD's number. When he didn't pick up, she left a brief message explaining their urgent need to speak with him.

"That's all you can do for now. Let's check the back of the pasture for campsites while we wait to hear back," Diego suggested, breaking through Elise's thoughts.

Nodding in agreement, she followed him as they rode further back on the property. When they came upon an abandoned campsite nestled in some trees, her heart sank. She couldn't tell how old it was, but its presence alone confirmed her worst fears— undocumented immigrants had trespassed onto their property. And if they killed her father, finding justice seemed impossible.

As if sensing her thoughts, Diego guided his horse close enough to reach out and lay a reassuring hand on her arm. The warmth of his touch spread through her like a comforting fire in the cold. "This doesn't prove anything," he told her with a gentle squeeze.

Her throat felt too tight to speak, so she simply nodded, grateful for his concern.

Without speaking further, they continued exploring the back of the pasture. The mesquite trees seemed to whisper secrets to each other as they passed. By the time JD returned their call, they had found four more abandoned campsites.

"Elise, it's good to hear from you," JD greeted her warmly over the phone. "Although I can't help but wonder what's so urgent."

"I apologize for leaving such a cryptic message," Elise replied sincerely. "Diego and I are at the east gate. Would it be possible for us to ride over and speak with you in person?"

"Of course," came the easy reply. "You know you don't need my permission to visit me."

"Thank you. I just wanted to be respectful of your *No Trespassing* signs," Elise said gratefully.

"No worries. Meet me in the front barn when you get here," JD instructed.

"Sounds great. We'll see you soon." With that, Elise ended the call and slipped her phone back into her pocket before turning to Diego. "Shall we make our way over now?"

"Yeah," he replied with a slight hesitation in his voice, not sounding very enthusiastic about it at all.

He opened the gate so they could pass through it, then closed it after them. Unlike her father, JD's father had chosen to leave most of the trees standing, creating a peaceful and secluded atmosphere on this side of the fence where the air was thick with the smell of pine and damp earth.

As they rode, Diego pointed at something on the ground ahead of them. "More tire tracks," he said.

"We should follow them and see where they lead," Elise suggested, her curiosity piqued.

For the next five minutes, they followed the tracks as they wound through the woods until they reached a clearing with three barns standing in a row.

"That's new," Elise exclaimed, her gaze fixed on the massive middle barn. Its walls and roof were constructed from corrugated steel, resembling oversized shipping containers. The outside was painted a deep forest green, blending in seamlessly with the surrounding environment. "When did the Drakes build this?"

"Not long after JD returned home," Diego replied absently, his focus still on the tire tracks.

"It must be at least twice the size of our barn," Elise marveled. "It could probably house two dozen horses. Business must really be booming for him."

"Yeah, good for him," Diego muttered unenthusiastically. "He couldn't even stay on a horse in high school."

"Don't be jealous," Elise scolded him playfully. "He's found his true calling in life."

Diego studied the barn intently. "Why wouldn't he install bigger windows, to let in the air? It must get sweltering inside during the summer."

"Maybe not," Elise replied excitedly. "Look up there!" She pointed to the roof of the barn. "There's at least one A/C unit up there, maybe even two. I bet this is where he trains and houses the most expensive horses. It's probably nicer than my apartment."

"Did you notice how the tire tracks stop at the entrance to the barn?" Deigo asked.

"Oh, no. I hope no one has stolen one of his horses. Let's go find JD."

They continued their ride, with Elise confidently leading the way. As they passed the large barn, Diego's eyes caught sight of the security cameras discreetly mounted beneath the roof line and the state-of-the-art security keypad next to what appeared to be the only door. He couldn't help but wonder if JD had installed all these measures because a horse had already been stolen, but he dismissed the notion. JD wouldn't have been able to keep news of a horse theft secret.

Finally reaching the front barn, they dismounted and tied their horses to the sturdy hitching post. This was the second largest of the three barns on the property and boasted spacious stalls lining both sides. In between, there was enough room to ride a horse, which was what JD was doing when they entered.

Spotting them, JD effortlessly changed directions and headed towards them. Diego noticed the easy way JD sat in the saddle; he looked perfectly at home on top of the horse, leaving Diego to think he'd misjudged JD.

Upon reaching them, JD reined in his horse and gracefully dismounted. "Good boy," he purred, stroking the animal's neck affectionately.

"You're up early this morning," commented Elise, stepping forward to stroke the horse's nose in a seemingly friendly manner.

"Well, no rest for the weary," JD chuckled. "I have a handful of horses to train, so I'm usually up at dawn, but it's a bit early for a social visit, isn't it?"

"It is," Elise agreed with a nod, "but this isn't just a social call. Diego and I were out riding this morning and came across something quite disturbing. We thought you should know about it." JD's eyebrows rose in curiosity as he listened intently.

"This morning, we found that the locks on both side gates were deliberately positioned to appear locked, but were actually left unlocked," Elise said.

"We also noticed fresh tire tracks running through our pasture onto yours," Diego added. "We followed them all the way to your large barn; the new one."

"We were concerned that someone may be attempting to steal your valuable horses," Elise finished. "Especially since none of our cattle are missing. And using our pasture is the fastest way to reach the interstate from your property."

JD's frown deepened as he listened to their findings. With a sigh, he reached into his shirt pocket and retrieved his cell phone. "Excuse me a moment," he said before making a call. A second later, Diego heard a male voice answer on the other end. "Check the barns and make sure all the horses and gear are accounted for. Get back to me when you're finished."

Disconnecting the call, JD slipped his phone back into his pocket and turned back to them with a grateful smile.

"Thanks for coming over," he said sincerely. "It's a little troubling to think rustlers have targeted my place, but not entirely unexpected, which is why I've installed extensive security measures. Anyone who's foolish enough to try and steal from me is going to get their picture taken in the act." He chuckled, but his eyes held a glimmer of determination. "Enough about that. I'd love a chance to catch up with you, Elise. Do you have time to stay for a cup of coffee? My mother made some delicious muffins and I know she would be thrilled to see you."

Elise's gaze darted towards Diego, and she must have noticed the look on his face because she thanked JD for his offer but declined. "We really need to get the horses back and see to the guests."

"How about dinner, then?" JD persisted, completely disregarding Diego as he led them towards the front of the barn.

"I'd like that," Elise replied eagerly. "Just let me know when."

"How about tonight?"

"Tonight?" Elise repeated, pausing in her stride. Diego saw her glance his way, but he remained silent and continued walking. The thought of her going out with JD made him want to punch something, but he knew it wasn't his place to stop her. That didn't keep him from silently hoping she would turn JD down.

He reached their horses and untethered them, waiting for Elise who was laughing at something JD said. Diego hated the sound of her laughter directed towards someone who was nothing but an arrogant ass in his eyes.

Luckily, when Elise finally joined him out front, she was alone. He held her horse steady as she mounted before mounting his own. Together, they began their journey back to the east gate.

"So?" Diego finally spoke up after riding in tense silence for some time. "Are you going out with him tonight?" He hated himself for even asking the question, but the curiosity was eating away at him.

"Yes," Elise confirmed without hesitation. "He's picking me up at seven and we're going to Antonio's."

Diego clenched his jaw in frustration as they approached the gate. Antonio's was a charming Italian restaurant known for its delectable food and intimate atmosphere. In high school, it was the go-to spot for a romantic date.

They reached the east gate and Diego made sure to lock it after they rode through.

"Why don't you like him?" she prodded, her voice full of curiosity.

He stole a glance at her, knowing that responding would only lead to trouble, but unable to hold back any longer. "Because he's fooled you into thinking he's this great guy," he said with a heavy sigh. "He's not."

"How can you say that?" Elise challenged. "You hardly spoke to him in high school. Maybe if you had given him a chance…"

"Don't." He turned sharply towards her. "Don't finish that thought. You forgot that I played varsity football with him for two years. Trust me, he's an ass."

She stared at him for a long moment, her eyes searching for some hidden truth. "I think you're jealous of him," she accused, her tone turning icy cold. "And I don't understand why."

"Because he has you," he blurted out before he could stop himself.

The words hung heavy in the air, and he immediately regretted saying them when Elise gave him a sharp look.

"No one has me," she stated firmly, almost defensively.

Before he could try to explain his comment, she urged her horse into a canter, leaving him behind in a cloud of dust.

When he finally reached the barn, Elise was nowhere to be seen and Leo was diligently rubbing down her horse. A pang of misery hit him like a wave as he unsaddled his own horse. He had most likely ruined any chance of rekindling a close relationship with the only woman he had ever loved.

Fucking story of my life—always messing things up when it matters most.

Chapter Twenty-One

As Elise walked back toward the house, she felt upset and confused. JD had been nothing but kind to her, so Diego's attitude upset her. Then there was his comment. *Because he has you.* What had he meant by that? It was like he thought she and JD were romantically involved, even though she hadn't seen the guy since high school. It was ludicrous.

What was more interesting was that he'd sounded jealous over this perceived relationship. What did that mean? He couldn't possibly be interested in her *that* way.

Could he?

There was no question that she found him attractive, but getting romantically involved with him was complicated because, well, because he was like her brother.

Only he wasn't her brother, a distinction she was rapidly growing to notice and appreciate. Especially after waking up that morning to find herself pressed up against him in bed!

A flush of heat spread across her cheeks as she recalled the way she had laid there, fully aware and draped over his strong body. The memory alone was enough to make her knees tremble.

When she reached the house, she made a beeline for the bedroom, eager to wash away the thoughts and emotions that plagued her. Quickly stripping off her clothes, she stepped into the shower and let the hot water cascade over her, hoping it would drown out everything that had happened that morning.

But even the steaming water couldn't keep her in there forever, so she reluctantly shut it off and stepped out. Taking a deep breath, she began to dress for the day ahead. She braided her still-damp hair and applied just a touch of make-up. With eight hours until her date with JD, she needed to figure out how to occupy her time.

Her first call was to Sam Hunter, eager for an update on her father's case.

"I'm glad you called," Sam told her, her voice heavy with concern. The weight of the situation hung in the air between them like thick fog. "I was planning to call you later. Doc performed the autopsy on your father's body. The results confirm that your father died as a result of blunt force head trauma. Additionally, Doc confirmed the rock we found at the site was most likely the murder weapon; the blood and shape of the rock are both matches for your father's blood and the depressions in your father's skull. There was also a lot of internal hemorrhaging due to repeated blows. The bruising became more pronounced, taking on the shape of a fist. All of that confirms our suspicion that your father was murdered." Her words hung heavily in Elise's mind, each one adding another layer of horror to the already tragic situation.

"There are better ways to kill someone than hitting them in the head with a rock," Sam continued, her voice tinged with frustration. "I don't think this was planned. It's more likely this was a crime of opportunity. Your dad was in the wrong place at the wrong time."

"But he was on his own property," Elise pointed out, indignation rising within her at the thought of someone attacking her father at his own home.

"Yeah, I know," Sam replied sympathetically.

"Well, do you have any suspects?" Elise asked, grasping onto any sliver of hope that they might find justice for her father.

"We're checking up on a few," Sam replied cryptically, not offering any further information.

"What about what my father said at the seance?" Elise pressed, unable to shake off the unsettling memory of her father claiming to be attacked by a ghost.

"That *El Muerto* was his killer?" Hearing Sam say it out loud made the notion seem even more ludicrous. She heard Sam sigh before she continued, "I'll be honest. I'm not sure what to make of that. I don't think I can fully discount it, so even if I think it's unlikely, I'm keeping an open mind. Meanwhile, I've started questioning the ranch's staff and hands, as well as the guests. I appreciate you giving your employees time off to speak with me." As she spoke, Elise could sense the weight of responsibility on Sam's shoulders and felt a surge of gratitude for her dedication to finding her father's killer.

"What about the bag of clothes?" She asked. "Carmen said Chad stopped by while I was out to pick it up."

"Yeah, we're checking them. It'll be a while before we know anything."

Elise felt a knot form in her throat as she prepared to ask her next question. "I have to go back to work soon," she began, "but I'd like to bury my father first. Is there any way you could release his body to me?"

Sam's compassionate tone offered comfort as she responded, "Of course, Elise. I'll call Martha and let her know."

Elise thanked Sam for the information and disconnected the call, trying to quell the frustration bubbling in her chest. It seemed the police were no closer to finding her father's killer.

Ten minutes later, Martha, the funeral home director, called with news that she had spoken to Sam and they were ready to schedule her father's funeral. They discussed details of the funeral service, which needed to be held as soon as possible. After considering schedules, they settled on Wednesday morning—just three days away. Martha suggested a closed casket service due to the condition of the body after the autopsy and unexpected delays. Though it pained Elise not to see her father's face one last time, she knew it was for the best.

In a larger city, arranging a funeral on such short notice would have been nearly impossible but in this small town, word would spread quickly and by tomorrow, everyone would know about the upcoming service.

After ending the call, Elise made her way through the sprawling ranch house to find Carmen in the commercial kitchen, where the comforting aroma of herbs and spices lingered in the air.

As they discussed plans for the funeral reception, Elise couldn't help but feel grateful to have such a capable and supportive team at her side. Carmen provided her with options of food to serve and they quickly finalized the menu.

With a cup of steaming coffee in hand, Elise made her way back to the front office, her footsteps echoing through the quiet house. With a few clicks, she logged into work, immersing herself in a sea of emails and projects that demanded her attention.

As she delved deeper into her tasks, her mind drifted off into daydreams about returning to the ranch. The pandemic had shown that many jobs could be done remotely. What if she stayed at the ranch? Worked remotely? That would give her time to explore these feelings she was developing for Diego and perhaps learn if her feelings were reciprocated.

Then she remembered her boss's strict policy against remote work for vice presidents.

She was torn between two strong desires—pursuing a relationship with Diego or advancing her career. The weight of this decision lingered in the back of her mind as she navigated through tasks and emails. And even though she prided herself on being an independent, successful woman who didn't need a man in her life, it didn't mean she didn't want a man in her life.

It was hours later when Elise checked the time and realized she needed to start getting ready for her date with JD. Though earlier she had been eagerly anticipating their dinner plans, now a sense of hesitation lingered in her mind. It wasn't because of JD, who seemed like the same man she had dated in high school, albeit older. Instead, it was because of Diego. What if his feelings towards her were no longer platonic? Was she willing to risk that relationship for a date with a man she had no interest in sexually? Because if she was honest with herself, she wanted Diego, not JD.

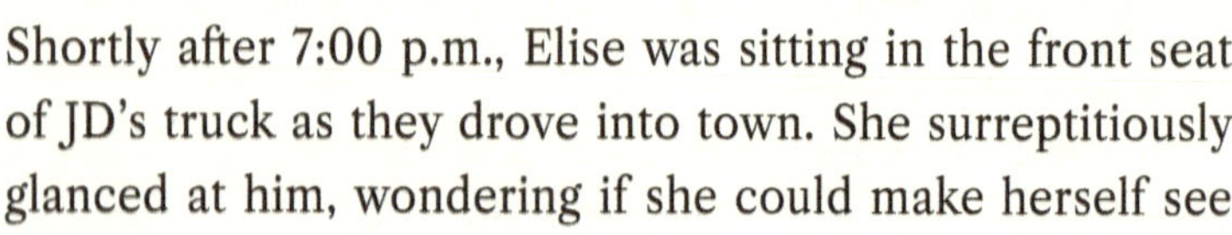

Shortly after 7:00 p.m., Elise was sitting in the front seat of JD's truck as they drove into town. She surreptitiously glanced at him, wondering if she could make herself see him objectively. If so, would she see the JD that Diego saw?

"Everything all right?" He briefly turned his gaze away from the road to look at her, concern etched on his features.

Elise forced a smile. "I'm just tired. It's been a hard couple of days. But being here with you," she gestured towards them both, "brings back happy memories."

JD's smile lit up his face. "Good. I'm glad to hear it. I don't know if I've said this before, but it's wonderful to see you again. I mean it." He paused, his expression turning somber. "I just wish it wasn't under such tragic circumstances."

The mention of her father's death dampened the warmth of their reunion.

"I know. I still can't believe it. How could someone do something so senseless?" Elise let out a heavy sigh. "I don't want to talk about it."

JD nodded understandingly. "Of course, I understand, but Mom asked me to find out if you knew when the funeral would be?"

Elise realized she had meant to call his mother about this. "Oh, sorry about that. Sam has released my father's body, so the funeral service will be held Wednesday morning. And we'll hold the reception afterwards at the ranch."

"I'll make sure to mark it on our calendar and be there," he promised. "And if there's anything I can do to help with arrangements or anything else, let me know."

"Thank you, but I think we have everything under control," Elise said, struggling to keep her voice steady. "I just miss him so much. It's hard to believe he's gone."

"He was a good man."

His words held a hint of distance, as if he were speaking about a stranger rather than someone he had known most of his life. She couldn't help but study him, searching for the cause of this change in tone.

Suddenly, she realized that Diego's words had colored her perception of JD and she scolded herself for allowing it to happen. The truth was, JD wasn't callous at all. In fact, he understood loss more than anyone else, having experienced it firsthand when his own father left him and his mother behind. "I guess you know how I feel, don't you?" she said softly.

JD glanced at her with furrowed brows. "What do you mean?"

"Well, in a sense, you lost your father, too, when he left. I can only imagine how hard it is to run the ranch on your own."

He shrugged nonchalantly. "I'm managing."

His indifference surprised her. She expected him to sound sad or angry, not so unaffected. She wondered if there was more to the story than she knew but decided not to pry. Her past interactions with JD taught her that if he wanted her to know more, he would eventually tell her. Until then, she wouldn't push.

She changed the subject, trying to lighten the mood. "Is this a new truck? It still has that new car smell."

"Yeah," he replied with a small smile. "Got it last month. My old truck finally gave out on me."

"I like it," Elise exclaimed, her eyes lighting up with genuine excitement. The front seat was spacious and luxurious, with a console that resembled a high-tech control center. The large screen displayed a myriad of buttons and apps, making her feel like she was in command of a military vehicle. As they drove through the streets of Las Palomas, she couldn't help but think how completely out-of-place this truck would be in bustling New York City.

"I don't even own a car," she admitted, feeling slightly embarrassed by her lack of ownership. "I guess the good thing about that is I get my daily steps in."

"Well, you're doing something right, that's for damn sure," JD chuckled, his deep voice sending shivers down her spine. "If it's possible, you look better now than you did in high school."

Elise blushed at his compliment and suddenly found it hard to meet his gaze.

The rest of the drive to the restaurant was spent in comfortable silence, the soft hum of the engine filling the air.

JD had made a reservation ahead of time, so when they arrived at the restaurant, they were promptly seated at a small table in a secluded corner. They could still see the other diners around them but were given enough privacy to enjoy their meal.

As the waiter appeared to take their drink orders, JD took charge and ordered a bottle of wine for them. Elise couldn't help but notice the slight raise of the waiter's eyebrows, indicating that JD had chosen one of the more expensive options. She wished he'd asked her before ordering because she would have told him she didn't like wine, but he hadn't, so she bit her lip and decided to make the best of the situation.

Their bottle arrived quickly, along with two glasses. The wine bottle was a rich, dark red, with a label that boasted the name of an expensive vintage. She watched in anticipation as the waiter expertly peeled away the foil from the top of the bottle. However, when he attempted to remove the cork, it proved to be stubborn.

"Give it here," JD barked at him, his voice sharp and demanding as he snatched the bottle from the young man's hands. Clearly embarrassed, the young man released the bottle and laid the corkscrew on the table before scurrying off.

"And bring us some bread!" JD called after him, his tone calmer but still sharp. He picked up the corkscrew and effortlessly removed the cork, pouring generous amounts of the deep red liquid into their glasses, each one glinting in the low light of the restaurant. Only when he handed her one did he notice that she was watching him intently.

"What?" he asked with a hint of annoyance in his voice.

"You were a little harsh with him, don't you think?" Elise said softly, her eyes meeting his.

"Do you think so?" His response held a hint of defensiveness, but then he sighed and softened. "I apologize. I just wanted this night to be perfect. Please, try the wine, Elise. It's one of the best vintages I've ever had."

She lifted the glass to her lips, trying not to grimace as she took a small sip. The wine was dry and tasted like cough syrup, but she forced herself to keep sipping, not wanting to hurt JD's feelings.

"I've never tasted anything like it," she told him diplomatically as she lowered her glass to the table.

His face lit up with pride before taking a drink himself, clearly pleased to have impressed her. "So, tell me about New York," he prompted after setting his glass down.

"I love it," she admitted with genuine enthusiasm. "The constant energy, people rushing around everywhere you look. No matter what time of day, there's always something happening."

He listened intently as she spoke, asking thoughtful questions and showing genuine interest in her life. "I think you'd love it also," she finished with a smile.

Just then, the waiter reappeared with their bread and ready to take their food order. The smell of fresh garlic and herbs wafted from the kitchen, making Elise's stomach growl in anticipation. She was about to order her favorite dish, lasagna, but before she could open her mouth, JD took control, again, and ordered *Rigatoni alla Carbonara* for both of them. He then casually took her menu and handed it to the waiter, dismissing him with a wave of his hand.

Elise suppressed a sigh of irritation and tried to recall if he had always been so domineering. She couldn't quite remember. Perhaps her younger self had mistaken it for confidence. Taking a sip of the dry-as-dust wine, she fought not to grimace and searched for something new to talk about.

"I know you came back to help your folks, but I'm surprised you're still here," she said. "I thought you hated Las Palomas as much as I did."

His expression softened as he replied, "I did, but things have changed. I have my horse training now to keep me busy."

"Tell me more about that," she said. "I was so surprised when I heard that's what you were doing. How did you get into it? You never seemed particularly interested in horses during high school."

"I know. It's crazy, right? A couple of college buddies of mine, from Commerce, were heavily involved in the rodeo scene. They had more money than time and offered to pay me to help train their horses. It started out as a way to earn some extra cash, but soon, word spread, and I found myself with more clients than I could handle." He nonchalantly shrugged, as if his success was no big deal.

"Then what happened?" Elise prompted eagerly.

"Well, after I graduated and started my day job, I continued training horses on the side. When the pandemic hit and I lost my job due to downsizing, I was able to rely on my horse business to make ends meet. It was then that I realized my passion could also be my full-time career. Now, with my clients willing to travel as far as Las Palomas for my services, it only made sense to bring my business back home and use our ranch facilities."

Elise couldn't help but admire his determination and success. "That's truly incredible," she exclaimed, genuinely happy for him.

"I'm pretty proud of how far I've come," he admitted with a smile. "Not only can I afford a brand-new truck, but my watch is a Rolex." He held up his left wrist, revealing a shiny watch.

"It's very nice," she said, mostly because he was expecting her to say something.

"Nice?" He chuckled incredulously. "It's the Taj Mahal of watches!" With a flourish, he lifted his pant leg to reveal the glinting scales of his boot. "These are Lucchese alligator boots. They retail for several thousand dollars."

She couldn't help but gasp in shock at the exorbitant price tag. Who would pay that kind of money for a pair of boots?

She kept her thoughts to herself as she examined the boots more closely. "It looks like you've got a spot of paint or something on them."

Furrowing his brow, he looked down at the chartreuse stain and attempted to rub it off with his thumb. "Must have gotten some paint on it when I was helping Jorge with his science project," he explained.

"Jorge?" She raised an eyebrow in confusion. "I thought you said his name was Andy?"

He gave her a confused look before quickly recovering with a smile. "Yes, Andy. That's what I meant," he mumbled, lowering his foot back to the ground.

And she thought he'd told her it was an art project, but decided not to push it. She was still in shock over the cost of the boots. If she'd spent that much money on a pair of shoes, she wouldn't be nearly as calm if she'd discovered they had paint on them. Something didn't quite add up.

Elise's gaze drifted back to the spot of paint on the toe of his boot. In the dim light of the restaurant, it seemed to glow almost eerily.

JD resumed talking, breaking her train of thought. "That horse I was working with this morning—he's one of the top horses in the country, worth over a hundred thousand dollars."

"He was beautiful," Elise conceded, her mind drifting back to the magnificent animal she had seen earlier.

"I've been working with him for about four months now."

"He looked young. Is he?" she asked curiously.

JD considered her question as he picked up his wineglass and swirled the dark liquid around. "A little over two years. That's when I like to start their training," he replied confidently.

Elise furrowed her brow, remembering how the horse had struggled with its bit that morning. "You prefer using the curbed bit at that age?" she questioned, unable to hide her skepticism.

He let out a hearty laugh, seemingly amused by her innocent question. "As opposed to what?" he joked, brushing off her concern.

Their waiter arrived with their food, saving Elise from having to explain herself. She couldn't believe JD didn't understand the difference between a snaffle bit and a curb bit. Growing up with both her father and Diego's father as trainers, she'd spent countless hours learning about the subtle nuances of horse training. It was common knowledge that most trainers used a snaffle bit during the early stages of training a horse, while a curb bit was reserved for more advanced techniques. Comparing the two was like choosing between a hand shovel and a bulldozer when digging a hole to plant a flower—they served different purposes.

She tried to brush off her doubt, reminding herself that perhaps things had changed in the world of horse training since she had last been involved. After all, she wasn't exactly an expert.

The rest of the meal proceeded pleasantly enough, although the conversation mainly revolved around JD and his accomplishments. By the time she finished her plate, Elise was growing tired of listening to him boast about himself.

When the waiter arrived to take their dessert order, Elise was about to politely decline, but JD, once again, took matters into his own hands. He ordered coffee for them both and a dessert they would "share," which Elise soon realized meant he would periodically offer her a bite from his fork. She couldn't help but feel disgusted by the gesture.

No thank you, she thought, trying to maintain a polite façade as she watched him devour the decadent dessert.

When he'd finished the last bite, he leaned back in his chair and heaved a contented sigh. "Outstanding meal, if I do say so myself."

"Yes, it was very good," she agreed.

He gazed at her for a long moment before leaning forward to gently lift her hand from where it rested against her coffee cup. His touch was warm as he held it in his own, absentmindedly tracing circles on her skin with his thumb. "I know you want to go back to New York City, and I want that for you too," he murmured, gazing deeply into her eyes. "Let me buy the ranch; let me do that for you."

His caring tone left her feeling conflicted. It felt genuine and sincere, not at all like a man trying to manipulate or use her as Diego had accused him of. "The issue is that the decision to sell is not solely my decision to make," she explained with a heavy heart as she extracted her hand from his grip. "The ranch is owned by a trust and both Diego and I are co-trustees. We have to agree to sell it."

He fell silent, his gaze turning inward as he contemplated their situation. After a few moments, he leaned back in his chair. "I understand," he said quietly. "Diego is the obstacle then. He doesn't want to sell, but you do?"

"Yes," she said, more to reassure him than because it was entirely true. She didn't enjoy discussing this topic with JD. It made her uncomfortable, as if she were betraying Diego. "Excuse me for a moment, I need to use the restroom before we leave."

Without waiting for his response, she quickly stood up and grabbed her purse before making a beeline for the restroom. Once out of JD's sight, she pulled out her phone and sent a quick text message to Diego. Then, because the coffee they had just shared seemed to have gone straight through her, she continued on to the ladies' room.

When she reached the bathroom, she was surprised to find it already occupied. In the corner, on the floor, sat a woman, her arms wrapped tightly around her raised knees and her head hung low. At first, Elise feared that the woman was unconscious, but then she saw the slight trembling of her shoulders and heard ragged breathing.

Feeling a twinge of concern, Elise approached the woman slowly. "I'm sorry to intrude, but you don't seem okay. Can I help in any way?" She reached out to place a comforting hand on the woman's shoulder, but her sudden movement caused the woman to startle and jolt upright. As she lifted her tear-stained face, Elise recognized her as Kim Gordon from high school. They had never been close friends, but Elise remembered Kim as being two years younger and a bit socially awkward.

"Hey, Kim. It's me, Elise Richardson. Sorry for startling you," Elise said softly.

Kim quickly wiped her face and looked up at Elise through teary eyes. "I'm fine," she mumbled.

Elise gave her a sympathetic smile. "It's obvious that something has upset you. Do you want to talk about it?"

"No, I don't want to talk about it," Kim snapped, her arms dropping limply to her sides. Elise couldn't help but notice the vertical white scars along the inside of Kim's forearms before she quickly pulled down the sleeves of her blouse to cover them.

"Have you ever despised your life so much that you wished it would just end?" Kim's voice was surprisingly casual, as if discussing the latest fashion trends. Without waiting for Elise to respond, she continued, "I hate it here in Las Palomas. I don't want to be trapped in this small town. I want to live in Austin where there's excitement and opportunity."

Elise was confused. Kim was old enough to make her own choices about where she wanted to live, unless... a dreadful thought crossed her mind. "Is someone forcing you to stay here against your will?" She looked around the bathroom, half-expecting a violent man to burst in and drag Kim away. When nothing happened, Elise realized she may have watched too many thriller movies. She changed tactics. "Is there someone I can call for you?"

Suddenly, Kim's demeanor shifted, and she turned on Elise with intense anger. "I bet you have a perfect life," she sneered loudly. "Don't deny it. You with your flawless face, perfect body... even your hair is perfect." Her voice grew louder with each word. "You have no fucking clue what it's like to be me! So just leave me the hell alone." By now, she was screaming at the top of her lungs. "Get out! Get out!" She grabbed fistfuls of her hair and violently pulled, as if trying to tear it out.

Feeling a rush of fear and helplessness, Elise backed away from Kim as memories flooded back. She felt like an eight-year-old again, watching her mother rant and scream while hitting herself in a fit of rage.

At that moment, the door swung open, jolting Elise free from the memory. Two women rushed in. The older woman went over to Kim and grasped her hands, forcing her to let go of her hair.

"Hush, Kimmie. Everything's okay," the older woman said, her soft words carrying through the air like a gentle lullaby, comforting and reassuring. "You're okay. Hush, baby. It's going to be all right."

"Mommy?"

"Yes, sweetheart. I'm here." The woman stroked Kim's hair, her touch gentle and tender. Slowly, Kim's breathing steadied, and she seemed to relax into her mother's embrace. "I just want to go home now, Mommy."

"Of course, dear." Her mother stood and extended a hand to help Kim up. While this was happening, another woman—younger and closer to Elise's age—stood quietly beside Elise.

"Why don't you take Kim to the car," the woman suggested to the older woman. "I'll be there shortly." She turned to Elise as they left, extending her hand. "Thank you for your help. I'm Dr. Maribeth Gordon. Psychiatrist."

Elise accepted her outstretched hand with a nod. "Kim is your patient?"

Maribeth smiled warmly. "Younger sister, actually. But she's the reason I went into psychiatry."

"I'm Elise—"

"Richardson. I know."

"That's right. Have we met before?"

"Not really," she replied with a gentle shake of her head. "I graduated a couple of years ahead of you, but we were both on the prom planning committee my senior year." Maribeth's smile widened. "You were a freshman, and we didn't really work together, but I noticed you. You were dating JD Drake." She chuckled softly. "And it seems like you're still with him tonight. Are you two married now?"

"No," Elise replied with a shake of her head. "Actually, I haven't seen JD in years. I only came back for," her voice trailed off as the realization of why she was here hit her once again, "for my father's funeral."

"I heard about that. I'm so sorry," Maribeth offered sympathetically.

"Thank you," Elise said, feeling a wave of sympathy for Kim. She hesitated, then asked, "Do you mind me asking what that," she gestured to the corner of the bathroom where Kim had been, "was all about?"

Maribeth's face softened with understanding. "Kim suffers from Borderline Personality Disorder," she explained. "She's on medication, but it only works if she's taking it consistently. The problem is, she starts feeling better and thinks she doesn't need the pills anymore, so she stops taking them." She offered Elise a weak smile. "It's an ongoing cycle, I'm afraid. And it looks like she's stopped taking them again."

Elise couldn't imagine the constant struggle Kim and Maribeth must face and how difficult it must be for them.

"I'm sorry you had to see her like that," Maribeth continued. "When she's on her meds, she's a perfectly lovely person." Clearly, Maribeth cared deeply for her sister.

Elise remembered Kim saying how much she hated living in Las Palomas and wanted to move to Austin. Could that be the root of her struggles? "Maybe if she could live in Austin..." Elise trailed off, knowing it wasn't her place to make suggestions about someone else's life. Seeing Kim reminded her so much of her own mother, who had also hated living in Las Palomas and, as a result, eventually took her own life.

To Elise's surprise, Maribeth didn't seem offended by her suggestion. "The sad thing is," she began with a heavy sigh, "for the past couple of years, Kim has been living in Austin with me." She shook her head. "I got so tired of hearing her complain about how much she hated it, that I finally brought her back here, even though I knew that wasn't really the answer. People who suffer from BPD aren't happy anywhere."

Elise could see the pain and frustration in Maribeth's eyes. "And yet you still tried," she said softly.

Maribeth gave a wry smile and shrugged in a what-can-I-say gesture. "She's my sister."

The memory of her mother's distress came back to Elise in vivid flashes. "My mother used to get upset like that; pulling at her hair and screaming. She killed herself shortly after we moved here. I used to think that if we'd just moved back to the city, maybe she'd still be alive today." She sighed, the guilt weighing heavily on her, especially now after seeing Kim's similar behavior. "I wonder if she might have had Borderline Personality Disorder?"

"She might have," Maribeth conceded. "Sadly, it's one of those mental illnesses that often goes undiagnosed until it's too late."

"Too late?"

"The incident of suicide is higher than normal for people with this illness, which is not only tragic for the afflicted but also for their families because they often blame themselves. I went into psychiatry, hoping to better understand how to help Kim. I thought if I understood it, then I could "fix" her." She used her fingers to make air quotes. "What I learned, instead, is that you can't fix them. There's no cure."

Elise felt a lump rising in her throat as she remembered the day her mother took her own life. "I used to think that if we had never moved here, or if I had been a better daughter..." Her words trailed off as Maribeth shook her head.

"It wouldn't have made a difference," Maribeth assured her. "People with BPD can't control their emotions. It's just part of the illness." She gently withdrew her hand. "Now, if you'll excuse me, I should go help my mother with Kim. It was nice seeing you again." As she walked away, Elise felt overwhelmed by emotion.

For years, she'd blamed her father for her mother's suicide when now it seemed like it wasn't his fault. Because of her anger, she'd wasted so much time that they could have spent together. As tears threatened to fall, Elise couldn't shake the weight of sadness and regret that filled her heart.

CHAPTER TWENTY-TWO

STILL REELING FROM THE shocking revelation from Maribeth, Elise hurried back to the table where JD was waiting for her.

"I'm sorry I kept you waiting," she said, her head still spinning. "You won't believe what just happened. When I got to the bathroom, Kim Gordon was there, and she looked really upset."

JD raised an eyebrow. "Do you know what about?"

"Her sister told me she suffers from Borderline Personality Disorder. Kim was crying and screaming how much she hated it here." She paused, trying to process the information.

JD let out a frustrated sigh and rolled his eyes. "Who can blame her? If it weren't for my family's ranch, I doubt I would have come back either. If Kim doesn't like it here, she should leave."

Elise furrowed her brow in concern. "I don't think it's that simple—"

"Of course it is," he interrupted. "If she wants to leave, then her family should do what they can to help her." He brushed off the topic with a wave of his hand. "Now," he smiled at her. "I've already paid the bill, so if you've finished your coffee, we can leave."

Elise glanced down at her empty cup of coffee and nodded quickly. "I'm ready."

"I thought maybe we could run over to The Waterin' Hole. Kevin said they'd have a live band playing tonight. We could get a drink and maybe do a little dancing?"

She hesitated before responding. "I'm sorry, JD. Maybe some other time? I'm really tired. Would you mind taking me home?"

He looked disappointed but didn't try to coax her into changing her mind. She let out a small sigh of relief.

They didn't talk much on the ride home, and Elise dreaded the moment when they would say goodnight. Not because she hated saying goodbye to JD, but because tonight had revealed that her feelings for him were not as strong as they once were and, more importantly, not as strong as his seemed to be for her.

As they pulled up to her house, she felt a mix of emotions—sadness, disappointment, and a sense of clarity. Going out to dinner with him had been a mistake, and now she couldn't wait for the evening to be over.

"Thank you again for dinner," she told him as he pulled his truck to a stop. The engine's rumbling cast a low hum into the night air. "It was nice catching up with you," she said, trying to keep things casual.

"I enjoyed it, too," he replied with a smile.

Elise felt a twinge of discomfort as she wondered if he was expecting them to continue their evening with more than just conversation. In an effort to avoid any awkward situations, she quickly reached for her door handle.

"I'll walk you to the door," JD said, putting the truck in park.

She couldn't refuse his polite gesture, so she climbed out of the truck and closed the door behind her. By the time she turned back around, he was by her side, placing a hand at the small of her back. She had to resist the impulse to step away from his touch, which, unlike Diego's, was unwelcome.

Her heart began to race as they walked towards her front porch. She hadn't turned on the porch light before leaving, and now, in the darkness, she felt an uncomfortable level of intimacy between them.

"Thank you for tonight," JD said as they reached the front door. "Maybe we could do this again?"

"Maybe so." Elise couldn't bring herself to say yes and saying no would only lead to a confrontation. About to move away, she was stopped when JD's hands were suddenly on her upper arms, pulling her closer.

Panic set in as Elise desperately tried to think of a way to politely decline his advances. Before she could find a solution, however, the porch light suddenly flicked on, momentarily blinding them both.

"What the-?" JD exclaimed, his hands quickly shooting up to shield his eyes from the sudden brightness.

Elise took advantage of the opportunity and stepped away from him as the door opened.

"Hey, I see you're back," Diego drawled as he leaned against the doorjamb, his arms crossed over his chest. "Hope you had a good time. Care to come in for a cup of coffee, JD?"

JD's tone was abrupt as he replied, "Uh, no. Thanks."

"All right, then. I guess we'll see you around." Diego stepped back to give room for Elise to enter.

"Thanks again for dinner, JD," Elise said with a warm smile.

"Sure," JD growled, scowling at Diego but addressing Elise. "I'll call you later."

"Okay." She'd barely finished speaking when Diego shut the door and locked it with a loud click. The sound reverberated through the spacious foyer.

"So," Diego began as he walked towards her. "Have fun tonight?"

"Not as much as I'd hoped I would," she admitted with a sigh. "And thanks for the timely arrival."

"No problem. I came up to the house as soon as I got your text."

"Well, I appreciate it." She wandered into the family room and collapsed onto the couch.

"Did he do something to upset you?" Diego asked, sounding like if she said yes, he'd go out and pummel JD.

"No, he didn't hurt me, if that's what you're asking." She reassured him. "He irritated me. Not once did he ask me what I wanted to drink or eat. He ordered for me. He even bought this really expensive bottle of wine for us."

"I didn't think you liked wine," Diego said with a puzzled expression as he sat down beside her.

She gestured with her hand, acknowledging his point. "I don't, not that he could know that. When we dated, we were too young to drink, but you would think he would at least ask before assuming he knew what I wanted." She paused thoughtfully before changing the subject. "Hey, do you remember Kim Gordon?"

"Of course, we were in the same grade," Diego replied. "Why do you ask?"

Elise told him about her encounter with Kim in the bathroom and the revelation from Maribeth about Kim's illness.

Diego's brow furrowed in concern as he listened. "That's sad." His voice sounded deep and soothing when he finally spoke. "Kim was a nice girl, but even back in high school, she seemed troubled."

Elise's mind raced with questions and doubts. "Diego, do you think my mother had BPD?"

He took a moment before responding, seeming to choose his words carefully. "It would explain a lot," he conceded. "I know your father blamed himself for not doing more to help your mother, but it sounds like, from what Maribeth told you, there's not much more he could have done."

Once again, she felt a pang of guilt for blaming her father all these years. "I blamed him for moving us here," she confessed.

"Did you know that the ranch was your mother's idea?"

Her eyebrows shot up in surprise. "What? No way. She hated the ranch."

He shook his head. "Roy told my dad that you all moved away from Houston because your mother couldn't stand it there anymore. It was her idea to start the ranch here in Las Palomas, to get away from the city and its drugs and crime. She wanted you to grow up in a safe and peaceful environment." He paused for a moment before adding, "Your father agreed with her and made it happen."

Elise sat back against the couch cushions, feeling overwhelmed by this new information about her mother. "Why didn't Dad ever tell me this?" she asked.

Diego shrugged, his expression sympathetic. "My dad told me after your mother passed away, but made me promise not to say anything to you. I think Roy believed it would be better for you to blame him than to think poorly of your mother."

Her mind whirled with conflicting emotions as she digested everything he had just revealed. She felt numb and unsure of how to process it all.

"Are you okay?" Diego asked, gently taking her hand in his. She found solace in the way his larger hand enveloped hers, a sense of safety and comfort that she desperately needed in that moment.

"It's just... a lot to take in," she finally admitted, her voice trembling with emotion. "I feel so guilty for blaming Dad all these years. And angry, too, for all the years I wasted being mad at him when we could have been spending some of that time together."

The weight of all those emotions finally overwhelmed her and tears welled up in her eyes, spilling down her cheeks. Diego immediately wrapped an arm around her and pulled her close, offering a safe haven for her tears.

After what felt like an eternity, the tears subsided and she pulled away from his embrace. "I'm sorry," she mumbled, embarrassed by her emotional outburst.

"No, don't be sorry," he replied, rubbing her back gently. "I should be the one apologizing for upsetting you like that. It wasn't my truth to share, but with Roy gone, I thought you should know."

She nodded, wiping away the remaining tears from her cheeks. "I understand. Just promise me that from now on, we'll always be honest with each other," she said firmly.

"You have my word," Diego affirmed. "And speaking of honesty, I have to tell you...JD is an ass."

Her eyebrows shot up in surprise before a smile tugged at the corners of her mouth. "I don't think that's a fact. I think that's your opinion."

Diego chuckled, giving her a playful side hug. "Then, speaking factually, he's not good enough for you."

"That may still be your opinion," she chuckled, "but thank you."

Diego glanced at his watch and sighed. "I should probably head out and let you get some rest. You must be exhausted after being up half the night last night." His words were considerate, but she could hear the underlying hint of longing.

She knew he was right; she should have been exhausted. However, the mere reminder of the night before flooded her mind with the memory of waking up in bed with him, causing her pulse to quicken with vivid intensity. She was suddenly very conscious of his arm wrapped around her.

"I should probably get going," he repeated, his voice sounding rough and hoarse.

Though he made no move to leave, she couldn't help but fear that it was inevitable. To distract from this thought, she blurted out, "We could watch TV?" Her mind raced for any excuse to keep him here with her. "I think the new Tom Cruise MI movie is on Prime. We could watch that."

Back when they were kids, they always got together to watch movies and eat popcorn. As strongly as she was attracted to him, she wanted to relive that time in her life when everything wasn't so complicated.

"Yeah. That sounds great." She felt a flutter in her stomach as he agreed. "I'll make the popcorn if you want to change clothes."

"That'd be great." She leaned away from him as he stood and then allowed him to pull her to her feet. Their bodies lingered close for a moment longer before reluctantly pulling apart.

With a shy promise that she would return shortly, she hurried off to her room and began rooting through her wardrobe for the perfect outfit. Normally, she would have just thrown on her old T-shirt and shorts, but now she found herself stressing over her appearance. There was a delicate balance between casual and frumpy, and she didn't want to miss it. As she stood debating whether to leave on her bra or not, she realized she was overthinking things. If she wanted to make out with Diego—all she had to do was go out there and kiss him. She couldn't let thoughts of rejection hold her back. Then again, if he didn't feel the same way, kissing him could ruin everything.

In the end, she left her bra on and opted for her comfortable sleeping shirt and shorts. They weren't too revealing, but they were still cute.

Returning to the family room, Elise found Diego already settled on the couch with a bowl of popcorn in hand. He smiled warmly at her as she took a seat beside him and picked up the remote to find the movie.

For the first fifteen minutes, Elise's mind was elsewhere, unable to fully focus on the movie. As a rule, she found Tom Cruise movies entertaining and this one was no exception. She soon relaxed into the familiar plot and characters, enjoying both the film and Diego's company.

By the time the credits rolled, Elise was exhausted and ready for bed. "That was really good," she said as they made their way into the kitchen together, carrying their empty bowls. "Thanks for watching it with me."

"It was fun," he replied with a nostalgic smile. "I can't remember the last time I watched a movie like that," he admitted, setting the bowl in the sink. "It might have been the last time we watched a movie together."

"I'm sorry that earlier I cried all over your shirt," she told him. "But thank you for talking to me. It helped."

He smiled, taking a step closer to her. "You can cry on my shirt any time," he reassured her.

For a long moment, as their gazes met and held, it felt like he was peering into the depths of her soul. Her heart raced as she took in his handsome features, unable to tear her gaze away from his mouth.

And then, without warning, he leaned in and pressed his lips against hers. At first, it was soft and tentative, but as she responded eagerly, he deepened the kiss. It felt like the world disappeared around them, leaving just the two of them lost in this moment. His embrace was strong and comforting, holding her close as if he never wanted to let go. When their tongues intertwined, sending shivers down her spine, she couldn't help but let out a small whimper of pleasure.

Just as suddenly as it began, Diego pulled back with an apologetic look in his eyes. "I'm sorry," he muttered, sounding breathless and overwhelmed. "You've had an emotional evening, and I shouldn't have taken advantage of that."

Her words came out shaky, betraying the nervousness she felt. "I-I wanted to kiss you, too," she stammered, her heart racing as she waited for his response. She couldn't help but hope that he wanted more from her than just a kiss.

"I'm glad," he replied, his voice low and husky. "I'd love to kiss you again, but I know I won't be able to stop."

A rush of excitement and anticipation flooded through her at his admission. She couldn't believe this was happening.

"Then kiss me," she said, emboldened by his honesty.

"I don't want sex to ruin our working relationship," he explained, his voice tinged with concern.

"It won't," she reassured him quickly, earning a smile from him.

"Maybe it won't, but I also don't want our first time making love to be after you've been on a date with JD. I feel like I'm the consolation prize," he admitted, vulnerability lacing his words.

She wanted to argue with him, to tell him that the date with JD meant nothing and that he could never be considered a consolation prize, but she understood how important this was to him, so she simply nodded in understanding.

"Are you going to be okay?" he asked softly.

She nodded, trying to quell the disappointment she felt at not being kissed again. "Yeah, I'll be fine. Thank you for everything."

"My pleasure," he replied genuinely. "I'll be busy tomorrow morning helping out with the guests, but I'm free in the afternoon. How about letting me take you out to a late lunch?" he suggested.

A warm feeling spread through her at his offer. "I'd really like that."

"Great. Then I guess I'll see you tomorrow?" he said, a hint of hesitation in his voice.

She couldn't help but hope that he would give her one last kiss before saying goodbye, but he didn't, and she felt a pang of disappointment as he walked away.

Turning off the lights, she sought the comfort of her bedroom. Crawling under the covers, she lay in bed, replaying their kiss in her mind. The anticipation of a next time made it difficult to drift off to sleep.

Chapter Twenty-Three

The next afternoon, sitting beside Diego in the truck as they drove into town, Elise couldn't help but feel a flutter of nerves in her stomach. Every time she looked at him, she thought about last night's kiss. She had replayed it so many times in her mind that she hardly slept at all. She tried to act nonchalant and "cool" about it, but deep down she was dying to know if it would happen again.

"Do you mind if we stop off at the bookstore first?" Diego's voice interrupted her thoughts. "Katherine called and said the book I special-ordered is finally in."

"Katherine?" Elise asked with curiosity.

"Katherine Hunter. Sam's mom," he explained.

"The kooky hippie?" Elise raised an eyebrow skeptically.

Diego chuckled. "Yeah, but don't let her hear you say that. She's a witch, remember?"

Elise gave him a playful eyeroll. "Being a witch is more acceptable than being a hippie?"

"In Las Palomas, definitely," he replied with a grin.

"Does she wear a pointy hat and carry around a cauldron and broom?" Elise joked.

"No," he laughed. "Think wiccan, not Wizard of Oz. And before you go there, I'm not buying a spell book. The book I ordered is on reloading ammo."

"Why didn't you just order it off Amazon or something?"

"I could have, but I try to support the local economy, when possible," Diego explained, revealing yet another admirable trait.

"Do the witches still gather at night in the game preserve next to Murphy's place?" Elise asked, her voice carrying a slight edge of intrigue.

Diego nodded, his dark eyes glinting with a hint of mischief. "The police chief before Sam was from out-of-town. He considered the group a nuisance and tried to ban them from meeting. All hell broke loose when they stopped. Suddenly, we had all sorts of people coming into town; mostly troublemakers. Crime went up. It was bad." His voice dropped to a conspiratorial whisper. "The story I heard is that Katherine told him that by banning their gatherings, they were unable to reinforce the town's protection spells. And if he wanted things to return to normal, he needed to lift the ban."

Elise couldn't help but be amused by this. "What did he do?"

Diego shrugged nonchalantly. "He lifted the ban."

Her eyes widened in disbelief. "You're kidding?"

He shook his head solemnly. "Not at first, of course, but after another couple of weeks, as things got worse and the entire town was complaining about it, I guess he was willing to try anything. And you know what?"

"What?"

"After the witches started gathering in the woods again, things in town got better." Diego's expression was serious now.

Elise couldn't believe what she was hearing. "And people seriously think those old hippie ladies were responsible?"

"I don't know if they do or not," Diego said with a shrug, "but the police chief decided not to tempt fate. For the rest of his stint as police chief, he let the witches gather whenever and wherever they wanted."

Elise nodded in understanding, her mind still reeling from this revelation. "And Sam?"

"As far as I can tell, she tolerates them," Diego said, pulling the truck into a spot in front of the quaint bookstore.

She stepped out of the truck and took in the sight of the charming Victorian building. Large bookcases lined the front window, blocking any view of the inside. Above the door hung a simple sign that read "Bookstore" in elegant cursive letters.

Inside the store, despite the massive size of the room, Elise and Diego had to navigate through the maze of bookshelves to reach the front counter. There they found Katherine Hunter standing behind the cash register.

"Diego, oh good. You got my message. I have your book here somewhere." She bent down to search the shelves below the counter, her long blonde hair falling over her shoulders. After a few moments of searching, she pulled out a large paperback book and set it on the counter with a thud. Then she looked up and her gaze fell upon Elise.

"Oh, Elise," she gushed. "It's so good to see you." She hurried out from behind the counter and enveloped Elise in a warm hug. "I was so sorry to hear about your father's passing," she told her, holding her at arm's length. "Just so, so sorry for your loss."

"Thank you, Mrs. Hunter."

"Katherine, please. You're an adult now." She finally released Elise after giving her arms a quick pat. True to her hippie image, Katherine wore a brightly patterned brush skirt with a flowing blue peasant top. On her feet were a pair of brown sandals, adorned with colorful beads and feathers. Dozens of bangles jingled on each arm as she moved, and when she turned her head, Elise glimpsed long feathered earrings.

Peering over her shoulder to the back of the quaint shop, Katherine hollered with excitement, "Mom, come quickly! Look who's here!"

Elise couldn't help but worry that they might disturb other customers, but a quick glance around revealed that they were the only ones in the store. It left Elise wondering how Katherine stayed in business with such little foot traffic.

Just then, an elegant older woman appeared from the back room, bearing a striking resemblance to both Katherine and Sam Hunter. She was dressed in a flowing brush skirt, airy blouse, and comfortable sandals—just like her daughter.

"Diego, dear! It's always a delight to see you," she greeted him warmly before turning to Elise. "And my dear Elise. You've grown into such a lovely young woman. It's been far too long since I've seen you. My condolences about your father."

Elise smiled gratefully, relieved that Sam's grandmother remembered her name. "Thank you, Mrs. Stevens. It's good to see you as well."

"Come on back," she urged them with a gentle smile, gesturing for them to follow her down a side hallway. "Let's sit in the break room and catch up over some coffee—it's my special blend."

"We don't want to disrupt your work," Diego protested politely.

Katherine waved her hand dismissively. "Don't worry about it. I have a bell on the door—if someone actually walks in, I'll hear it ring."

Following the two women down the hallway, Diego and Elise entered a cozy break room dominated by a large table at its center. Mrs. Stevens walked over to the side counter, where a full carafe of steaming coffee awaited them. "I just finished brewing a fresh pot," she announced, pouring them each a cup. "Now, tell us all about what you two have been up to."

With a steady hand, she poured thick, dark coffee into two stoneware mugs and carried them over to the table. The rich aroma of roasted beans filled the air as she set them down, gesturing towards the center of the table. "Sugar, sweetener, creamer, and stir sticks are right there. Help yourselves," she said with a smile, before returning to the side to pour two more mugs for herself and her daughter. Together, they joined Elise and Diego at the table, their chairs creaking softly under their weight.

"So, Elise," Katherine began, making idle conversation. "What have you been up to since graduating college? Your father mentioned you're working in New York City."

"Yes, I work in marketing," Elise said, adding sweetener to her coffee. "It's all about helping companies create effective advertising and branding strategies."

"That must be exciting," Katherine commented wistfully. "I wish we had someone with your talents here in Las Palomas. Unfortunately, I doubt we could afford your rates."

"I can imagine it's tough running a successful bookstore in such a small town," Elise sympathized. "Have you ever thought about moving to a bigger city?"

Katherine shook her head firmly. "No, we couldn't do that. Our wiccan group is here in Las Palomas and it's important for us to stay close to Elizabeth."

"Elizabeth?" Elise was now thoroughly confused. "I thought Sam was an only child."

"Oh no," Katherine chuckled. "I'm talking about Elizabeth Parrish—or rather, her ghost."

Elise arched an eyebrow, intrigued by this unexpected turn in conversation. "Ghost? Who is Elizabeth Parrish?"

"She's my great-great-great... well, I'm not sure how many 'greats' grandmother," Katherine laughed. "Anyway, she was accused of being a witch during the Salem witch trials and only escaped being burned because she was pregnant. She left Salem and eventually settled here in Las Palomas, where she continued to practice her witchcraft. She was actually the founder of our wiccan group."

Uncertain of how to respond, Elise gingerly took a sip of her coffee and was pleasantly surprised by the rich and robust flavor that filled her mouth. Her eyes widened in delight as she exclaimed, "Wow! This is truly wonderful coffee." She eagerly took another gulp, savoring the warm liquid that flowed down her throat.

"It's a special blend of my own creation," Mrs. Stevens replied with a smile. "I roast the beans myself and love to experiment. It's a never-ending quest to find the perfect combination. And there's nothing quite like enjoying a good book over a good cup of coffee, don't you agree?"

Elise nodded enthusiastically. "I agree. In fact," she continued, turning to Katherine, "have you ever considered offering a coffee and tea bar in your shop? For a small fee, of course. Not only would it provide an additional source of income, but it could also entice customers to linger longer and potentially increase book sales. After all, it's much harder to put down a book once you've started reading it." Her mind raced with ideas as she spoke. "You could rearrange some shelves to create cozy reading nooks along the walls, with comfortable chairs and floor lamps for ambiance. And perhaps have a few standalone shelves scattered throughout to create private areas where you can place chairs and tables for quiet reading or studying. Complete with free Wi-Fi and tables equipped with electrical outlets."

Katherine's face lit up with excitement as she listened to Elise's suggestions. "Those are fantastic ideas," she said eagerly. Turning towards her mother, she asked, "What do you think, Mother?"

Mrs. Stevens's eyes sparkled with delight as she replied, "Why, that's a marvelous idea. I could sell my special coffee blends."

"Exactly," Elise continued, her voice laced with excitement. "You have so many possibilities here. You could offer a variety of coffees and teas; maybe even some light snacks. Nothing too messy or complicated that could damage the books, of course."

"Maybe I can purchase the snacks from Kathy's Cafe," Katherine chimed in. "That way, Kathy will know we're not trying to compete for her business."

"That's a good idea," Elise agreed, nodding. She glanced over at Diego to see him smiling behind his raised coffee mug and made a mental note to ask him later what was so funny. Right now, her brain was running wild with ideas for the bookstore, and she wanted to share them while they were fresh.

"I would suggest removing the shelves standing in front of the windows and maybe hang some French curtains," Elise said thoughtfully, picturing the cozy ambiance it would create. "Give the store a homey look." She paused, tapping her chin. "And if you're not married to the name of the store, because your store is on the corner, you might change it to something like Katherine's Kozy Korner, with 'Ks'."

Katherine's smile widened, her eyes lighting up at the suggestion. "Oh, I love that name."

"I hope I'm not overstepping," Elise quickly said with a sheepish grin. "I tend to get carried away when I'm brainstorming new ideas."

"No, you're not," Katherine assured her with a wave of her hand. "I love these ideas," she added, her tone filled with appreciation. "You've given us lots to think about."

Just then, the bell above the front door rang, signaling a customer entering the store.

"Sorry, I should go attend to them," Katherine apologized, rising from her seat. "Thank you again, Elise, for all your fantastic suggestions. And Diego, always a pleasure seeing you and I appreciate your business." With a grateful smile, she hurried towards the front of the store to assist the new customer.

"We should get going as well," Diego suggested, standing up from the table.

Elise rose and carried hers and Diego's mugs over to the sink located against the side wall "Mrs. Stevens, can I help you clean up? I'm happy to wash these mugs."

"No, child. I'll take care of it. Gives me something to do," Mrs. Stevens replied with a kindly smile. "You and Diego run along—and thank you. I haven't seen Katherine look this excited in a long time."

"I can't promise these changes will work," Elise admitted with a hint of worry in her voice.

Mrs. Stevens just smiled. "You never know how things will turn out."

Diego and Elise thanked the woman again before leaving and waved goodbye to Katherine as they headed out of the shop. The sultry summer air enveloped them as they stepped onto the sidewalk.

Diego turned to Elise with an apologetic expression. "Would you mind if we walked? It seems like parking in front of the cafe is all taken."

"Sure, sounds great," she replied cheerfully. They started across the street and down the next block, their pace relaxed and unhurried.

"What were you smiling about in there?" she finally asked him, her eyes sparkling with curiosity.

"You," he answered with a grin. "The way your eyes lit up when discussing marketing strategies. You clearly have a passion for it."

"I do," she admitted with a small smile. "I love the creative side; brainstorming new designs and concepts. I don't love the administrative side—all the paperwork and managing other people."

"I can understand that," he said, his voice full of empathy. "What would be your idea of the perfect job?"

"What I did for the ranch," Elise replied, then gestured towards the quaint bookstore they had just left. "And what I did in there just now. Connecting with customers and creating new branding ideas."

Elise fell silent, her thoughts swirling around in her head. She loved the creativity of her work, but loathed the rest of it. Unfortunately, as the newly appointed VP of Marketing, she would have fewer chances to exercise her creativity and would have to wade through more bureaucracy. And she couldn't ignore the cutthroat politics that came with working at a large company. As she contemplated the treacherous path she was about to embark on at *Tinslow and McNeal, Inc.*, her steps slowed until she finally came to a stop. She looked around and realized she was standing in front of a small shop. Elise's gaze settled on the woman standing behind the table out front. It was Zelda.

"Hey there, guys! How are you doing?" Zelda greeted them cheerfully. "Doing a little window shopping?"

"Just taking the scenic route to lunch," Diego replied with a smile.

"Are you having a sidewalk sale?" Elise asked, her eyes scanning over the crystals and herbs laid out on plastic tables in front of the store.

"I'm trying," Zelda said. "Business has been slow lately, so I figured if I couldn't entice people into my store, I'd bring the store outside." She sighed. "It doesn't seem to be working, though. People glance as they walk by, but they don't stay long enough to make a purchase."

"They feel self-conscious about you watching them," Elise explained. "It's like garage sales. People don't like being watched while they browse."

Zelda's face fell in disappointment. "I guess I'm just out of luck."

Elise stepped closer to the open door of Zelda's shop and peered inside. It was narrower and deeper than Katherine's bookstore, but still spacious enough to move around comfortably. Her attention then shifted to the window displays.

"I noticed you don't have any signs advertising your sale," she pointed out.

"No. I figure once they're here, I can tell them all about what's on sale," Zelda said enthusiastically, her eyes lighting up with excitement as she spoke. "You know, establish that one-on-one connection."

"I think one-on-one is great for your established customers," Elise began, "but tourists might not want to get that up-front-and-personal with you. At least, not until they get to know you better," she said, her eyes fixed on Zelda's face with a serious yet gentle expression. "I would put a big, brightly colored sign in the front window to advertise a sale," she said. "I envision jewel tones and sparkles, but no glitter," she added with a smile. "Also, I would display a few of the most popular items in the front window. Inside, I would position the sale items at the back of the store. That way, people interested in the sale items will have to walk past displays of your other products first and might see things they want to purchase."

Zelda grinned with excitement. "I love it! Why didn't I think of that before? Oh, and I already have an idea for the design of the sign."

"Well, I'm glad I could help," Elise replied with a smile. "And since we're here," she continued, "What do you recommend for relieving fatigue and stress?"

Zelda's gaze shifted to the table where various herbal remedies and crystals were displayed. She gestured to a collection of small bamboo plants. "Bamboo is known for its air-purifying properties. It can help create a more peaceful and calming atmosphere." She then moved to the side and picked up a beautiful white quartz crystal. "And this crystal is great for purifying energy. It promotes positive energy and healing while eliminating negative energy." She held it out to Elise, who took it with fascination.

Elise's eyes sparkled with delight. "Great, I'll take one of each," she told Zelda with a smile.

Zelda gestured for her to keep the quartz crystal in her hand as she carefully selected a small bamboo plant and offered it to Elise. "With my compliments," she said, her voice gentle and warm.

"Oh, no, please let me pay for them," Elise insisted.

Zelda simply smiled and shook her head. "Maybe next time. This is my gift to you, for your valuable suggestions. I appreciate it."

Elise held up the plant and crystal in awe. "Thank you so much," she said with genuine gratitude.

"Place them in your bedroom so you can benefit from their healing properties while you sleep," Zelda advised.

After thanking her again, Elise and Diego continued their walk around the Town Park, eventually crossing the street towards Kathy's Cafe.

"Look at you, connecting with the locals," Diego teased with a grin.

"What? Can't I be friendly?" Elise replied with a playful smirk.

He raised an eyebrow, his gaze narrowing slightly. "It was more than that. You enjoyed it."

She pursed her lips momentarily before breaking into a smile. "I did; I enjoyed it."

"That's all I'm saying," Diego said, as they reached Kathy's Cafe. "Now, how about some lunch?"

"Sounds good."

Twenty minutes later, sitting across from Diego in a cozy corner booth, Elise couldn't help but compare this meal to the dinner she'd had with JD. The cafe, with its rustic wooden tables and mismatched chairs, exuded a laid-back charm that reminded her of simpler times. The booth was nestled between two large potted plants, giving them a sense of privacy despite the bustling atmosphere around them. As she sipped on her iced tea, the aroma of fresh-baked pastries and savory soups wafted through the air.

Diego leaned in closer, his warm brown eyes filled with admiration. "I think you really helped Katherine and Zelda with your ideas."

Her cheeks flushed with pleasure. "I hope so."

"You know, there are more small businesses that could use your help, both here and in the neighboring towns. I really think you could start your own business here. You know, if you're interested."

Elise considered his words as she swirled her fingertip absentmindedly across the tabletop. "The idea definitely has some appeal," she admitted.

"All you'd have to do is print up some business cards, set up your website—I could help with that—and maybe get a couple of promotional items, like pens."

She laughed. "Or coffee mugs."

"Exactly! You could call it Richardson Consulting. Or Creative Designs."

"Or, how about Creative Consulting by Elise," she proposed, getting into the game.

"I like it."

They shared a genuine laugh, and Elise marveled at how easy it was to talk to Diego. There wasn't the same underlying tension that had been present with JD.

Feeling relaxed and contented in the charming cafe, Elise allowed her gaze to wander around the space. The building housing the cafe had stood for nearly a hundred years or more, just like many other historic buildings in Las Palomas. Its walls seemed to whisper secrets of the past, and of course, the place was haunted. As a child, Elise and her friends would come here after school, hoping to glimpse ghostly waitstaff delivering food orders to tables.

Today, unfortunately, it looked like none of the deceased wait staff was about, since no dishes could be seen floating through the air.

After their food was delivered, conversation between Elise and Diego shifted from polite acquaintances to that of old friends catching up. They shared stories of their respective college experiences, reminiscing about parties and late-night study sessions. As they talked, Elise couldn't help but notice how attractive Diego was. She remembered what it felt like waking up next to him, his warm body pressed against hers. When he picked up his knife to cut his food, she noticed how large and strong his hands appeared; wondered how they would feel wrapped around her own.

Her gaze fell on his lips as he spoke and she couldn't help remembering how they felt pressed against hers in a passionate kiss. Flustered by her thoughts, she was trying to regain her composure when he suddenly spoke.

"You need to stop looking at me like that." His rough voice sent a shiver down her spine.

"How am I looking at you?" She knew exactly how she'd been looking but wanted to see what he'd say.

He leaned across the table, closing the space between them, and whispered, "Like you want to devour me."

Heat rose to her cheeks at his bold observation, but she couldn't deny its truth. "Is that a bad thing?" she asked, trying to ignore the way her heart raced, and her face flushed.

"Not at all," he replied with a sly grin. "But it's putting ideas into my head."

Elise couldn't believe they were flirting like this in public. It took her out of her comfort zone, but she couldn't resist playing along. "Care to share?" she challenged with a raised eyebrow.

Lowering his voice, he said, "Stripping you naked and taking you to bed comes to mind."

The image his words created in her mind was so vivid that she had to lower her gaze in embarrassment. She pressed her legs together tightly, trying to quell the delicious tension building deep in her abdomen. It took a few moments of steady breathing for her to rein in her emotions and remember that they were sitting in a public restaurant.

As Elise looked up, she found Diego's warm gaze fixed on her. His lips curved upwards in a knowing smile, as if he could read the thoughts running through her mind. Before she could say anything, their waitress arrived to drop off their check, saving her from any further awkwardness.

Elise couldn't help but wonder what would have happened if they had gone back home together at that moment. The air between them was charged with electricity, their flirtatious banter lingering like an unspoken invitation, but then fate intervened. Shortly after they left the café, she received a call from the funeral home, asking her to stop by to finalize arrangements. Any lingering flirtation between her and Diego dissipated during the somber errand.

"Do you want to come inside?" Elise asked when they arrived back at the house, hoping he would say yes.

"I do want to," he said, a hint of regret in his voice, "but I think I'd better pass. There are some things I need to take care of in the barn. Can I take a rain check?"

"Of course," she said with a small smile, trying to hide her disappointment. As she watched him drive off, she couldn't help but feel bereft without him around. With a sigh, she went inside and booted up her computer, resigned to spending a long and lonely afternoon working. If it wasn't as fun or rewarding as the time she'd spent with Katherine or Zelda, well, that was just the way it was.

CHAPTER TWENTY-FOUR

THE NEXT DAY, ELISE woke feeling a heavy weight on her chest. After Diego had dropped her off the previous day, she hadn't seen him again, despite their flirtation over lunch. It left her feeling disappointed and confused. She tried to push these thoughts aside, reminding herself that keeping things platonic with Diego was probably for the best. After all, she would eventually have to return to her life in New York City.

The house felt emptier without her father's presence, and as she sat down for breakfast alone, her mood became even more desolate. The empty chair across from her seemed to mock her loneliness. To make matters worse, tomorrow was her father's funeral. The thought of it only added to her already somber state, especially when she realized she had nothing appropriate to wear. She would have to go into town today and buy something. While she wasn't a fan of shopping, it would be better than sitting around feeling sorry for herself.

After washing her dishes, she had just made her way to the bedroom when her phone rang. For a moment, she felt a surge of excitement, thinking it might be Diego. As soon as she saw the caller's name on the screen, her heart sank and she had to force a cheerful tone into her voice as she answered.

"Hi, Bob."

"Hi, Elise. I'm sorry to bother you, but I was wondering if you know when you'll be coming back to work? The Johnston group is getting anxious and wants to meet first thing Friday morning to review our latest ideas. If you can't make it back in time, Sean has offered to lead the meeting."

Of course he has. He's like a vulture waiting for an injured animal to die before ripping into its flesh.

"No, Bob. That won't be necessary." She knew damn well that the Johnston account was crucial to their business, and she couldn't afford to mess it up. If Sean met with the Johnston group, she'd end up losing the account—and possibly even her promotion. "I can be there. My father's funeral is tomorrow, so I can fly back Thursday."

"That's excellent news, Elise. I don't have to remind you how important the Johnston account is to our business. We want to be sure to keep them happy."

Her stomach churned with nerves as they spoke for a few more minutes before ending the call. She disconnected, feeling even more depressed than before. The weight of her boss's thinly veiled threat hung over her like a dark cloud, and she resented it even more than she resented Sean.

With a sigh, Elise retreated to the study and booted up her computer. She needed to book a flight back to New York

City for Thursday, and she also called a car service to pick her up and take her to the airport. As she finished these tasks, tears threatened to spill from her eyes. Going back to the city meant putting an abrupt end to whatever was developing between her and Diego. She tried to convince herself that it was for the best, but deep down, she knew she didn't want it to end.

Feeling restless and overwhelmed, Elise grabbed the keys to her father's truck and left the house. She drove into town, seeking some distraction from her thoughts. The first shop she came across was a small clothing boutique, and she hesitated before entering. Thinking no small-town store could compare to the big-name brands she was used to in New York City, she didn't have high expectations. To her surprise and delight, she found several outfits that caught her eye.

After hours of browsing and making purchases, Elise made her way back to the truck with arms full of shopping bags. Taking a detour through Town Park, she found an empty bench and sat down, taking a few minutes to clear her mind and enjoy the peaceful surroundings.

The park was quiet and serene, with only a few people milling about. The trees provided a canopy overhead, filtering the sunlight into delicate patterns on the ground. As she sat and watched the world go by, Elise couldn't help but feel a sense of calm wash over her. She closed her eyes, trying to block out the rest of the world and be fully present in this moment, but just like everything else lately, even "the moment" couldn't last as the oppressive heat eventually forced her to stand up, intent on returning to her truck.

As she turned to leave, something caught her eye in the opposite direction. There was a woman sitting a couple of benches away who looked familiar. Without consciously deciding to do so, Elise walked towards her.

It wasn't until she was practically standing in front of the woman that Elise recognized JD's mother, Beth Drake.

"Mrs. Drake, how are you?" Elise greeted her. She was met with a confused expression as the older woman blinked up at her.

"Elise Richardson," Elise said, gesturing to herself.

Mrs. Drake's eyebrows shot up in recognition, and she smiled politely. "Elise. How nice to see you! I didn't know you were in town." At first, Elise wasn't sure how to respond. Had JD not mentioned their date?

Feeling slightly uncomfortable under Mrs. Drake's gaze, Elise explained, "I came home to take care of my father's funeral arrangements." Based on the look of shock on Mrs. Drake's face, this was news to her. Her hand flew to her throat in surprise as she asked, "Oh dear, when did he pass?"

How was it possible that Mrs. Drake hadn't heard about what happened to Elise's father? Unless maybe the woman was experiencing early onset of Alzheimer's?

A sense of unease settled over Elise and she hesitated before responding, "He passed last week." She left out the fact that he'd been murdered—it was probably better not to mention it.

"I'm so sorry. He was such a sweet man and a good friend to me and Howard." Mrs. Drake's eyes watered as she spoke, and she took a deep breath to steady herself. "I lost Howard recently."

Elise hesitated before responding.

"I'm so sorry," she said sincerely. "I know that must have been hard on you and JD."

"It was," Mrs. Drake agreed, wiping at her eye as she looked away.

Feeling awkward and unsure of what else to say, Elise decided it was best to leave, but as she turned to go, concern tugged at her heart for the woman who seemed to be drifting in and out of reality.

"Are you waiting for someone?" she asked gently.

Mrs. Drake turned to face her once more, her expression clouded with worry. "JD is coming to pick me up."

Elise couldn't help but worry for the woman's safety, especially if she wasn't fully aware of her surroundings. "Maybe I'll wait here with you until he arrives," she offered, taking a seat next to Mrs. Drake on the bench. "That way I can say hello to him and you don't have to wait alone."

Mrs. Drake shook her head, insisting that it wasn't necessary. Elise stayed anyway, trying to make small talk despite the older woman's disinterest in conversation.

After ten minutes of waiting in the scorching heat, Elise was starting to feel uncomfortable, and she wondered how Mrs. Drake was faring. She couldn't imagine waiting for hours in this weather.

"What time did JD say he'd be here?" she finally asked.

"He said he'd pick me up at noon," Mrs. Drake replied with a worried look.

Elise glanced at her Apple watch. "It's already after two," she pointed out.

Mrs. Drake's brows furrowed in concern as she looked down at her own watch. "He's just running a little late," she said, though Elise could see the worry in her eyes.

Elise noticed the beads of sweat forming on the older woman's forehead. "Why don't I call him?" Without waiting for a response, she pulled out her phone and dialed JD's number. It rang several times before going to voicemail, prompting Elise to send a text instead.

> *Hey, in town and ran into your mom. She looks like she's struggling in this heat. Just wanted to let you know I'll give her a ride home. It's no trouble, your house is on my way.*

"He didn't answer," she explained to Mrs. Drake as she put her phone away. "He must still be busy. I told him I'd take you home. Let me help you with those." Elise reached for the handles of several shopping bags, some of which seemed quite heavy.

"I'm in Dad's truck," she said, gesturing. "Just across the street."

Mrs. Drake hesitated before reluctantly standing up from the bench. Her eyes darted around nervously as she spoke, "If—if you're sure?"

"It's no trouble at all," Elise reassured her as they started walking together. "I'm sure JD is just busy, or he would have been here. This way he won't have to make an extra trip into town."

As they made their way to the truck, Elise tried to keep the conversation light and distract Mrs. Drake from her worries. "Looks like you had a good time in town," she commented, gesturing towards the various shopping bags.

She continued her idle chatter as she drove Mrs. Drake home, noting how much the woman had changed since she had last seen her. Once friendly and self-assured, now Mrs. Drake seemed frail and burdened by her husband's betrayal.

The Drake family's main house, like the Double R ranch, was nestled a good distance from the road. Elise had barely parked in the circle drive in front of the house before Mrs. Drake had her door open and was gathering up her shopping bags.

"I'll be right back to get the others," she told Elise before scurrying inside.

Elise debated waiting in the truck, but she didn't want to burden the older woman with all those heavy bags. So she grabbed the remaining bags from the back seat and followed Mrs. Drake into the house.

It was like stepping back in time for Elise. She had spent many days as a teenager inside this house and not much had changed since then. The house still maintained its old Texas-rustic ranch style, with well-loved leather furniture scattered around the spacious rooms. Above the fireplace hung a set of Longhorn cattle horns, a symbol of Texas pride, and a cowhide lay on the floor as an area rug.

As Elise made her way through the foyer and into the great room, she noticed it was empty. She continued walking until she reached the dining room, where she found Mrs. Drake standing at the dining table.

The older woman didn't seem to notice that Elise was there. Her attention was on the other side of the kitchen, where a hallway led to the various bedrooms. As Elise set the shopping bags on the table, she finally heard the raised voice that had captured Mrs. Drake's attention.

"Shit happens." Elise heard JD shout, his words exploding like shrapnel, angry and sharp. "I don't care if you think it's too risky," he continued, his tone dripping with disdain. "This fuck-up is your fault." A chair scraped against the floor followed by the sound of footsteps, heavy and purposeful. "My client doesn't give a damn about your opinions. We're doing this my way from now on—Sunday night, not Monday." He let out a loud, frustrated breath. "And now I have to fly up to Dallas Friday afternoon to clean up your mess, which means I probably won't get back until Saturday. No, it doesn't leave me much time to get ready for Sunday, but you don't need to worry about that. Just make sure you're there Sunday night." The sound of his hands slamming against the table punctuated his words. "Don't fuck this up again!" His voice echoed harshly off the walls, filling the room with tension and frustration. "My client is not as forgiving as I am."

A loud crash was followed by the tinkling of broken glass. In a split-second, Mrs. Drake's panicked whisper broke through the chaos. "You need to leave—now!" Her urgency was palpable. "If he finds you here—" The sudden sound of a door opening and approaching footsteps cut off her warning.

Then JD walked into the kitchen, his face contorted in anger and his eyes blazing with fury.

He stopped as soon as he spotted Elise, his tense eyebrows furrowing and his gaze flickering with an emotion she couldn't quite decipher. Was it anger or alarm? She couldn't tell. In the next moment, his expression shifted, and he was all smiles.

"Elise! What a pleasant surprise! What brings you here?" His voice was warm and welcoming, but Elise couldn't shake off the uneasiness from his initial reaction.

"Just giving your mom a ride home," she replied, trying to keep her tone light. "I ran into her in town. I tried texting you, but it must not have gone through."

JD turned to his mother, his tone taking on a sharper edge. "Mom, you know I was coming to get you. You shouldn't have bothered Elise."

Mrs. Drake's face paled at the accusation and Elise quickly interjected, "I didn't really give her a choice. I was headed home, and your place is on the way."

"I appreciate it," JD said politely, his tone shifting back to pleasantness. "It's good to see you again. I'm sorry I wasn't here when you arrived. I had a business call. Did you have to wait long?"

Wait? Did he think she had come all this way just to see him?

"I helped your mom bring in these packages," Elise gestured towards the shopping bags on the table. "But I'm glad I ran into you. Thank you again for dinner the other night. It was lovely."

Elise couldn't quite put her finger on it, but there was something about JD's smile that made her uneasy. It didn't reach his eyes, and she could feel them watching her closely, like an entomologist studying a fly.

"You were eavesdropping," he accused, taking a step closer to her. His size and presence were meant to intimidate her, but Elise refused to let it affect her.

"Eavesdropping? Seriously?" She scoffed, pushing herself up to her full height. "First off, you were shouting and second, I could care less about your horse-training business. Trust me, I have enough on my plate already. The only reason I'm here is because it's sweltering outside, and I didn't want your mother to suffer in this heat because you left her waiting." Her words dripped with censure.

His demeanor immediately softened, and he hung his head in shame. "I'm sorry, Elise. I've been under a lot of stress lately and it's made me paranoid." He raised his head to meet her gaze, his own gaze beseeching her to understand. "Can you please forgive me?"

She closed her eyes for a moment, taking deep breaths to steady herself before meeting his gaze again. "I apologize for snapping at you, JD. It's been a tough week for me, too. My father's funeral is tomorrow and then I have to go back to New York on Thursday. Diego and I haven't even decided what to do with the ranch yet."

JD stepped closer and wrapped his arms around her, attempting to comfort her. She couldn't help but feel uneasy in his embrace, fighting the urge to pull away.

Luckily, he released her after a brief moment. "We're both on edge," he said, his voice filled with understanding and remorse.

"I should go," she told him with a small smile. "I have some things to take care of before the funeral tomorrow."

She turned to Mrs. Drake, who was standing nearby. "Bye, Mrs. Drake. It was nice to see you again."

She started for the door, aware of JD following her. He escorted her all the way to her truck, opening the door for her while she climbed in.

"I'm here for you, Elise," he offered, holding open the door to talk to her. "If you need anything, just let me know."

"Thanks." She leaned forward to start the engine. "I appreciate it."

He looked like he wanted to say more, but she reached for the door handle to pull it closed and he obediently stepped out of the way.

She gave him a half-wave after putting the truck in gear and then drove off.

She drove the rest of the way home in a mental fog and parked her truck. Thinking back over the whole encounter with JD and his mother—from Mrs. Drake's initial fear of accepting a ride home to JD's accusation of eavesdropping—it all felt so surreal.

Before she could fully process her thoughts, there was a knock on her driver's side window that made her jump in surprise.

"Elise?" Diego's muffled voice came through the glass. "Open the door."

She pressed the button to unlock the doors, and Diego opened it for her. Concern etched his features as he asked, "Are you alright? You were just sitting here."

Her response sounded hollow even to her own ears as she said, "I'm okay."

"I'm not buying it," he said, pinning her beneath his stare.

She forced a smile and tried, unsuccessfully, to push away the lingering unease from her encounter with JD and his mother. "I was just over at the Drake house, and it was—strange," she finally admitted.

"Let's go inside and you can tell me all about it."

She let him help her from the truck and, after gathering up her shopping bags and closing the driver's side door, they went into the house. Diego steered her into the family room, where he sat beside her on the couch.

"Now tell me what happened."

She shook her head, now feeling embarrassed because they were making too big a deal out of it. "It was nothing, really."

"Let me be the judge of that, okay?" Diego sat beside her on the couch, his presence calming her nerves. "What happened?" he asked, his voice full of concern.

She told him about running into JD's mother in town, the older woman's strange behavior when she'd offered her a ride home and JD's bizarre, almost hostile, reaction at seeing her in his house. "What do you make of it?" she asked when she'd finished.

Diego shrugged. "Same thing I thought before. The guy's a jerk. Probably treats his own mother like crap, which would explain her behavior."

At first, she wanted to defend JD, but then she realized Diego was probably right. His harsh words somehow comforted her. She was making something out of nothing. Feeling better, she finally noticed the faint strains of music floating from the backyard.

"What's going on outside?"

Diego fished his phone out of his pocket and checked the time. "It's just past five, so I'd say Carmen and the staff are getting ready to start up the grill. Tonight, we're having hamburgers and hot-dogs."

"Are you serious? You're not serving Beef Wellington with stuffed mushrooms or some other extravagant dish for the guests?" She joked.

He chuckled in response. "It's all your fault. The hamburgers and hot dogs were such a big hit that the guests requested we have them again tonight. If you're hungry, we could go outside and grab an early dinner."

"Yes, please." Her stomach rumbled at the thought of a juicy burger.

She wanted to tell Diego about her impending return to New York, but the words stuck in her throat. Just thinking about leaving this paradise was too depressing, and she didn't want to spoil their time together this evening.

"Great." He stood up and offered her a hand, which she gladly took. His hand was warm as he led her outside, and she didn't mind at all when he continued to hold it.

CHAPTER TWENTY-FIVE

SAM SAT IN HER office at the police station, surrounded by stacks of paperwork and files. The fluorescent lights hummed above her, casting a harsh glow on her worn desk and computer screen.

Matt Henshaw had refused to post bail for his son, so Wyatt had been in their custody since his arrest on Saturday. With no memory of where he was Monday night and with motive but no alibi, Wyatt was rapidly becoming Sam's number one suspect in Roy's death.

But she needed solid evidence to make an arrest for murder, and that was the one thing she didn't have.

The sound of the front door chime pulled Sam from her thoughts, and she looked up to see Kelly Palmer enter the station. Kelly, a waitress from Kathy's Cafe, was delivering food for their prisoner.

For a split second, Sam expected to see Chad hurry to meet Kelly since the two were dating, but then remembered he was out patrolling. Instead, Steve, one of her other officers, rose from his desk in the bullpen to take the bag of food from her before disappearing through the door leading to the holding cells.

Instead of leaving, Kelly surveyed the bustling bullpen until her gaze landed on Dane sitting at his desk. She swiftly made her way over to him.

Sam's second-in-command appeared surprised to see the waitress, but his expression changed a moment later as they spoke. The two of them then left the station together.

Curiosity piqued, Sam wondered what that interaction was all about.

Just then, a slender man with dark hair walked into the station. He wore a Double R work shirt paired with faded jeans and looked vaguely familiar. Like Kelly before him, he scanned the bustling bullpen before his gaze landed on Sam. He made his way towards her, stopping in the open doorway of her office.

"Chief Hunter? I'm sorry to just show up like this, but I was hoping for a chance to talk to you. In private."

Recognizing Leo Stoddart, Sam gestured for him to come in. "What can I do for you, Mr. Stoddart?"

He shifted uncomfortably and glanced at her open door. "Would you mind if I closed your door? I don't want anyone to know I'm here talking to you."

Intrigued now, Sam nodded, and he closed the door before taking a seat in front of her desk. She couldn't help but notice the sweat on his brow and the way he fidgeted with his hands.

"Thank you," he said, offering her an awkward smile. "This is difficult for me."

"I understand. Would you like something to drink? Coffee? Or maybe some water?" She hoped it would help him relax.

"No, thanks. I'm fine."

She patiently waited for him to continue, but it was clear he was struggling to tell her why he had come. Maybe if she could get him talking about himself first, he would loosen up.

"How long have you been working at the Double R? I don't remember seeing you there before the other day," she asked.

"I've been there for almost two years now," he said quietly. "I used to work in San Antonio before that."

"Do you enjoy working at the ranch?"

"Yeah. I suppose."

She observed his darting gaze and sensed his unease. "Mr. Stoddart, was there something specific you wanted to discuss with me?" She prodded gently.

He furrowed his brow, and after a long moment of uncertainty, finally spoke up. "The thing is... I have information about Diego Juarez that I think you need to know."

"Okay," Sam replied evenly. "What information is that, exactly?"

"I overheard you telling Elliott that Diego claimed to have returned to the ranch after one in the morning on the night Roy was killed."

"That's right," Sam said, wondering where he was going with this.

"Well, he's lying."

That was unexpected. "How do you know?"

Leo reached into the front pocket of his shirt, his fingers deftly grasping a small notebook. The leather cover was worn and creased, evidence of its constant use. He flipped it open to reveal pages filled with neat handwriting and scribbled notes. "I have ADHD," he explained, as if sensing Sam's curiosity. "I have trouble remembering things, so I write everything down."

Leo skimmed through the pages as if they were ingrained in his memory. Finally, he stopped on one page and glanced up at Sam. "Here it is," he said confidently. "Diego got back to the ranch at 11:37 p.m."

"You saw him?" Sam asked, her heart racing with excitement.

"Yes ma'am," Leo replied proudly. "With my own eyes. I just returned one of the golf carts and plugged it in to charge. I was about to head back to the bunkhouse when I saw him come walking down the driveway."

Sam couldn't believe her luck. This could be a breakthrough in their investigation. "Did you talk to him?" she pressed, hoping for more information.

Leo snorted. "Hell no. It was my day off, and I didn't want him to catch me taking out one of the golf carts for personal use. We're only supposed to use them for ranch work. After Evie—Evelyn McNamara, that is—after she left, I invited one of the other female guests for a little drive around the property, just being friendly and all. She wanted to be back in time to see *El Muerto* ride, so after I dropped her off at her bungalow, I returned the golf cart to the garage. I made sure to write down the time when I plugged it in because it takes a couple of hours before it's fully charged and if it wasn't ready by morning, I didn't want nobody blaming me for it. That's when I saw Diego."

"Did you see where he went?" Sam asked, her brow furrowed in concern.

"Not exactly," Leo said, his voice low and hesitant. "He looked like he was headed for the main house. He lives there with Roy, you know." His gaze flickered around nervously before continuing. "Anyway, as soon as I was sure he wouldn't notice me, I slipped out."

Sam's mind raced with possibilities as she processed this information. "Was there anything else?" she asked, unable to shake off the feeling that something was amiss.

"That's all, but I thought you should know," Leo said, scratching his arm anxiously.

"I appreciate you coming by," Sam replied smoothly, masking her thoughts behind a polite smile. She hated the possibility that Diego, whom she considered a personal friend, had lied to her. Of course, it was possible that Leo was nothing more than a disgruntled employee out to make trouble for his boss. "Knowing that the penalty for perjury involves jail time, would you be willing to swear to this in court if necessary?"

Leo shifted uncomfortably under her gaze but nodded resolutely. "If I need to, I will."

"Okay." Sam stood up, signaling an end to their conversation, and waited for him to stand before shaking his hand. "Thank you for coming by. I'll show you out."

She walked him to the station door and said goodbye. As she headed back to her office, she couldn't help but feel a sense of unease settle over her. Dane was still gone and now she had this new information to process. The case had just taken a disturbing turn, and she wasn't sure how she felt about it.

Sinking into her chair, she let out a heavy sigh. She needed to clear her head and figure out what steps to take next.

Closing her eyes, she focused on taking a couple of deep breaths. When it didn't help ease her growing headache, she reached into her desk drawer for a bottle of aspirin.

She'd just finished taking a couple of pills when Bev buzzed her phone.

"Call for you on line one," she said after Sam picked up. "It's the manager at the Grand Hyatt San Antonio River Walk, returning your call." Sam's heart raced as she gripped the phone tightly, bracing herself for whatever news awaited her.

"Thanks, Bev," Sam said before pushing the button for line one. "This is Chief Hunter."

"Hello, Chief Hunter," the woman said in a smooth, professional voice. "This is Teresa. We spoke earlier?"

"Ah yes, Teresa," Sam recalled. "Thank you for returning my call."

"As I mentioned before, we typically don't share information about our guests, but I spoke with Mr. McNamara, and he asked that I provide you with whatever information you requested."

"That's great news," Sam responded, eager for any lead in her investigation. "Do you have a record of when he checked in?"

"I do," Teresa confirmed. "It looks like he checked in at 11:52 p.m. on Monday evening."

"And what about video footage? I'd like to confirm that your Tom McNamara and mine are the same."

"Absolutely," she replied without hesitation. "I'll send that over to you right away."

After providing her email address, Sam thanked the manager and ended the call. Her mind was racing as she waited for the footage to arrive in her inbox. When it finally did, she carefully studied the image and compared it to the photo on McNamara's driver's license. With a sigh, she mentally ruled him out as a suspect. It would have been impossible for McNamara, in San Antonio at 11:52 p.m., to have driven back to Las Palomas and killed Roy shortly after midnight. Her list of suspects was rapidly shrinking and she didn't like the names remaining on the list: Wyatt, Diego and *El Muerto*.

Great – the town drunk, a close friend or a ghost.

Sam was staring off into space, silently mulling over her suspect list when Dane entered her office, his usually cheerful expression replaced with a somber one. The fluorescent lights cast an eerie glow on his features as he approached her desk.

"Looks like Wyatt might have an alibi for the night Roy was killed," he informed her gravely.

"Kelly?" Sam raised an eyebrow in question. Dane nodded solemnly. "She was with him?"

"Not in the way you think, but yeah." His voice was low and cautious.

Sam felt a twinge of irritation. "Then why didn't Wyatt tell us earlier? We could have crossed him off our suspect list."

"Because he doesn't know," Dane answered, taking a step back to survey the bustling bullpen before stepping all the way into Sam's office and closing the door behind him. "He was passed out."

Sam leaned forward, her curiosity piqued. "Passed out? Where?"

"In his truck, parked in front of his house, a block over from Lou Taylor's house," Dane said, taking a seat across from Sam at her desk. "Apparently, Kelly saw him on her way to Lou's after her shift Monday night. The two of them are having an affair, which is why she kept quiet about it. She doesn't want Chad to find out."

Poor Chad, Sam couldn't help but think. "Did you tell Kelly that we might not be able to keep her affair a secret?"

Dane nodded. "I told her that Roy's death is still under investigation, and it might be necessary for her to make a formal statement."

"And what did she say?"

"She wasn't happy about it, but she agreed to do it."

Sam let out a sigh. "Alright, so tell me more about this alibi."

"The cafe closes at ten. Kelly said she headed over to Lou's about twenty minutes later, after cleaning up. Because she doesn't want anyone seeing her car parked at Lou's house, she parks on the next block and walks. That night, she had just parked her car when she noticed Wyatt's truck parked on the opposite side, a couple of houses up."

Sam nodded in understanding, letting Dane continue.

"As she walked past the truck, she noticed Wyatt in the front seat. She got worried he might say something to Chad about seeing her, so she went over to ask him not to. When she got up to the truck, though, she found Wyatt passed out in the front seat. The doors were unlocked, so she opened the driver's door and tried to wake him, but he was out cold. The inside of the truck reeked of alcohol, and she thought about calling 9-1-1 to report him, but then she'd have to explain what she was doing there and Chad would find out."

"So, she left Wyatt there? How do we know he didn't wake up and drive over to Roy's house after she left?"

"Kelly said the keys were still in the ignition and because she didn't want him driving drunk, she turned the car on just long enough to crack the windows, then shut it off and locked the doors with Wyatt still inside. She took the keys with her to Lou's house and made him promise to return them to Wyatt the next day. When she left Lou's later, Wyatt was still passed out in the front seat."

"What time was that?"

"Shortly after three in the morning."

"She's positive?"

He nodded, a serious expression on his face. "She had to work the morning shift at the cafe, so she set her alarm for three, to make sure she had enough time to get home, shower and change clothes before heading into work." He paused, his gaze drifting towards the window as he thought. "Wyatt said he found his keys behind the screen door later that morning, so I'm guessing Lou's the one who left them there."

Sam nodded, feeling like they were finally piecing some things together. "Would you call Lou and confirm that? And when you talk to him, ask if he saw Wyatt still sleeping it off in his truck."

"Will do," Dane replied with a small nod.

As they spoke, Sam's stomach growled loudly, reminding her it was dinnertime. "I think I'm going to head over to The Waterin' Hole for a bite before I tackle this paperwork. Care to join me?" she asked, hoping dinner would take her mind off of the case for a little while.

Dane's lips curled into a smile. "Sure, that'd be great."

As they made their way out of the station and towards their cars, Sam couldn't help but reflect on her relationship with Dane. They had dated briefly during high school before realizing they were better off as friends. Even after she was promoted to chief over him, there were no hard feelings between them. In fact, Dane had been nothing but supportive and dedicated as her second-in-command. On top of that, he was one hell of a good officer.

Fifteen minutes later, they were sitting at a booth inside The Waterin' Hole. The rustic wooden walls and dim lighting created a warm atmosphere, which was only enhanced by the scent of sizzling burgers and fried onions wafting from the kitchen. Despite her desire for a stiff drink, Sam opted for soda.

"Before you came into my office," she began, after the waitress left, "I spoke with the hotel manager in San Antonio. They have video evidence placing McNamara in their lobby at eleven-fifty-two that evening."

"So, he couldn't have killed Roy," Dane concluded.

"Exactly. What about those campsites on the Richardson property that Diego called us about?"

Dane let out a frustrated sigh. "I checked them out yesterday morning. The sites look like they've been there for at least two weeks, maybe longer." His brow furrowed. "And the closest one is still a good distance from where Roy's body was found. If he had encountered illegal campers, it would've been deeper into the pasture where the campsites were."

Sam's voice was measured, but her eyes were sharp as she spoke. "I agree. I don't think we can completely rule out the possibility, but illegal campers aren't at the top of our list of suspects."

Dane furrowed his brow in confusion. "That sounds like there's still a list," he remarked.

Sam sighed and set her cup down on the table. "Diego's name is still on the list," she told him, leaning forward. "Leo Stoddart came in to see me while you were out talking to Kelly. He claims to have seen Diego returning to the ranch around eleven-thirty."

Dane's face contorted in frustration. "Shit," he swore, running a hand through his hair. "That would mean he was there when Roy was killed."

Sam nodded grimly. "Yep."

"No, I don't believe it," Dane protested, shaking his head. "Diego wouldn't hurt Roy. They were friends."

"I don't like it any more than you do," Sam agreed. "But I don't think we can cross him off the list without finding out the truth."

"Leo could be lying."

"One of them is lying and we need to find out who and why."

Dane let out a frustrated sigh and leaned back in his chair. "If only Dwayne had installed those damn security cameras."

Sam's mind raced as she tried to come up with a solution. Suddenly, it hit her like a bolt of lightning, and she smacked her hand down on the table with a smile spreading across her face. "You're a genius," she exclaimed, looking at Dane.

He looked at her, confused. "I am?"

Sam quickly explained her idea. "It took the town so long to install those traffic cameras, I forgot all about them," she said eagerly. "They should all be up and running by now, right? God, I hope we're backing up all the images." Excitement filled her as she realized this could be the breakthrough they needed. "The only entrance into Dwayne's is on Second Street," she continued. "After we finish eating, let's see what time Diego really dropped off his truck."

CHAPTER TWENTY-SIX

As the sun rose on Wednesday morning, it cast a warm, golden light across the bedroom, but for Elise, the day was anything but peaceful and serene. Today was the day she would bury her father, and it felt like the end of the world.

Thankfully, Diego had offered to join her on the ride to the funeral home. As he arrived to pick her up, he complimented her appearance. "You look lovely," he said, noticing her new dress.

"Thank you," she replied, feeling grateful for his kind words.

He walked her to his truck and opened the passenger door for her. She hesitated, realizing her dress was too tight to climb into the seat gracefully. Without hesitation, he placed his hands at her waist and lifted her effortlessly into the truck. The gesture should have made her feel small and childlike, but his intense gaze made her feel cherished and cared for.

"Thank you," she mumbled shyly, flustered by the direction of her thoughts. She watched as Diego closed her door and hurried around to the driver's side, taking in how handsome he looked in his charcoal suit.

"You look very handsome in your suit," she complimented him as he settled behind the wheel. A part of her wished they were going on a date instead of attending a funeral.

As they entered the church fifteen minutes later, Diego guided Elise to the front pew and sat beside her. Despite her efforts, Elise found it difficult to focus on the service. Her mind was a jumble of memories and emotions. When it came time for her to read one of her father's favorite poems, she gave Reverend Edington their prearranged signal to let him know she couldn't do it.

"Now I'd like to read a poem, which I understand was one of Roy's favorites," Reverend Edington said solemnly, his voice filling the space. His gaze swept over all those who had come to pay their last respects.

As he recited the poem, Elise turned to Diego. In his familiar eyes, she found comfort and understanding. Somewhere in the past, there may have been moments when she resented his close relationship with her father, but now, in this moment of grief and loss, she was grateful to have someone to share it with.

The reception at the ranch was a somber affair, with guests dressed in dark colors and subdued voices filling the space. Sam and Dane made their way through the crowd, paying their respects and noting who had come to honor the deceased. It was not uncommon for a murderer to attend the funeral of their victim, but Dane held little hope that they could identify Roy's killer among their friends and neighbors.

As they stood slightly apart from the others, Dane turned to Elise and offered his condolences once again. "I'm sorry for what happened to your father," he said softly.

Elise nodded; her eyes glassy with unshed tears. "Do you have any leads on catching his killer?"

Dane's heart sank at the question. Despite their best efforts, they had made little progress in the investigation. "The truth is, it's been harder than we expected," he admitted. "But we've made some progress."

"Anything you can share?"

He shook his head sadly. "No, not at this time." He could see the frustration and sadness in her expression, and he felt guilty for not being able to offer her any closure.

She let out a heavy sigh and looked away, her gaze landing on Diego across the deck. "It's just so difficult. Finding Dad's killer wouldn't bring him back, but it would make going back to New York a little easier."

"So, you're going back?" Dane thought Elise had grown into a beautiful woman and there was a part of him that had hoped she would stay in Las Palomas long enough for him to get to know her better. He followed the direction of her gaze, realizing that ship had sailed. It was obvious to him that she only had eyes for Diego. Of course, her feelings might change if it turned out Diego had killed her father. A part of him was tempted to warn her, but he decided against it. "When do you leave?"

"Tomorrow, actually."

"Wow. That soon." He wondered how Diego felt about that.

"Yeah." She leaned in close and whispered. "Please don't say anything to Diego. I haven't told him yet."

As if on cue, Diego broke away from the group he was with and began making his way towards them. "Thanks for coming, Dane," he said sincerely upon reaching them and shaking Dane's hand.

"Of course," Dane replied, smiling softly. "It was a nice service. I think Roy would have appreciated it."

At that moment, Sam approached their group.

"Elise, Diego," she greeted them both. "I just wanted to express again how sorry I am for your loss." Then, turning to Dane, she added, "Ready to go?"

Dane nodded and let out a heavy sigh. "Yeah, we really should get back to the station."

They said their goodbyes and walked in silence towards Sam's truck.

"Elise is flying back to New York tomorrow," Dane informed Sam once they were on the road. "It's feeling like Roy's killer is going to get away with it." He couldn't shake off the feeling of helplessness, knowing that time was running out and justice may never be served for Roy's death.

"I know—and I hate it. We're missing a piece of the puzzle, but damn if I know what it is."

They fell silent, each lost in his or her thoughts, the only sound coming from the occasional car passing by and their own breathing. As they were almost to the station, their phones dinged simultaneously, indicating they'd both received a text.

Dane reached for his phone, his fingers tapping quickly on the screen as he read the message. "It's Bev," he told Sam. "Looks like Matt had a change of heart. He's paid the bail for Wyatt and is headed to the station to pick him up."

"Call Bev and tell her not to release Wyatt just yet," Sam instructed urgently. "I want to have another talk with him." She glanced over at him and added, "Care to join me?"

Twenty minutes later, Sam watched as Dane led Wyatt into the interrogation room. The fluorescent lights overhead cast a harsh glare on the metal table and chairs, making the room feel colder than it already was. Wyatt took a seat on the opposite side, eyeing them suspiciously, but Sam kept her expression neutral.

She waited until Dane took the chair beside her, letting the silence hang between them for a few moments before she spoke.

"You've made bail and we're going to let you go, but first, I want to ask you a few questions about Monday night."

"I already told you about that night," Wyatt complained, his words slightly aggressive.

"I know," Sam acknowledged calmly. "But you've had a couple of days to sober up, so I'd like to see if there's anything new you can add."

He huffed out a breath, frustration evident on his face. "I don't remember what happened after I left the ranch. It's a big, fucking black hole."

"I understand." Sam leaned back in her chair, studying him carefully. She thought about telling him that Kelly had provided him with an alibi, but held off for now. "What were you hoping to gain by going out to the ranch that night?"

"You know, this whole thing's my dad's fault," Wyatt ranted, his voice growing louder and more agitated.

"How's that?" Dane asked, raising an eyebrow in curiosity.

Wyatt's sharp gaze narrowed as he scrutinized Sam, then turned to Dane with a hint of disdain. "He never should have convinced Roy to give me a job. I hate waking up early and mucking out stalls. And those guests—they're never satisfied. Always demanding this and that, expecting to be waited on hand and foot."

"If you hated it so much, why didn't you quit?" Sam questioned.

"Because I'm good with horses," Wyatt boasted proudly. "And I like riding. If you ask me, I made the best *El Muerto* of anyone at the ranch."

"There are other jobs that involve riding," Dane suggested. "Why not take one of them?"

Sam was still thinking about Wyatt's last statement. "Wait, what do you mean you were the best *El Muerto*?"

"The headless horseman," Wyatt clarified.

"I know who it is. What made you the best?" Sam pressed.

"Roy wasn't satisfied with the real *El Muerto* only appearing once a month, so he paid some of us to dress up like the ghost and ride across the pasture at night. You know? To entertain the guests," he explained.

"What" Sam exchanged a stunned look with Dane. "Who all knows about this?"

"Roy and Diego, of course. Plus about half of the ranch hands," Wyatt replied casually.

Sam was incredulous. She thought back to the last time she had witnessed *El Muerto*'s midnight ride at the ranch. "How long has this been going on?"

Wyatt shrugged nonchalantly. "Beats me."

Dane leaned forward, clearly intrigued. "So, Roy was paying you to impersonate a ghost?"

"Well, not at first. Not until I figured out what they were doing."

"How'd you find out?" Sam asked, curious.

"Roy made an agreement with my dad that I wasn't allowed to drink while I was on ranch property. One night, when no one was around, I snuck out of the bunkhouse with a six-pack and went out into the back pasture to drink it. Just happened to be a night *El Muerto* rode. I waited until he finished before heading back in, but then I heard a noise near the barn and decided to investigate. That's when I saw *El Muerto*, giving his horse a bath."

He paused for dramatic effect before locking eyes first with Sam, and then Dane. "At least, that's what it looked like. I figured I drank that six-pack too fast and needed to sleep it off. But then I heard *El Muerto* talking to his horse. Something didn't add up. I mean, he ain't got no head, right? So, how's he talking to his horse?" "

There was a moment of silence before he continued. "Anyways, I stuck around and watched Elliott, all dressed up in a costume, black, washing glow-in-the-dark paint off his horse. When I confronted him about it, he swore me to secrecy and told me I'd have to sign an NDA. Then he put me on the schedule."

"Is that how they kept it a secret?" Dane asked. "Roy had everyone sign an NDA?"

"Not everyone," Wyatt said. "Just those of us doing the impersonations. If anyone broke the agreement by talking about the impersonations, not only would they be fired, but Roy could sue for damages."

"Aren't you worried about getting sued?" Sam asked him.

Wyatt simply shrugged and gave her a nonchalant smile. "Naw. Roy fired me before I could sign the damn thing."

A heavy silence fell over the room as Sam struggled to process this new information. During the seance, Roy had claimed that *El Muerto* had killed him. She had dismissed it as impossible. Now she realized it was very possible, if *El Muerto* was someone in disguise. But who?

"You mentioned a schedule?" she asked, her voice barely above a whisper.

"Yeah, I have it on my phone," Wyatt replied, pulling out his phone. He scrolled through several screens before handing it to Sam. "Here it is."

The screen displayed a list of dates with the names beside them. Her heart skipped a beat when she reached Monday's date and saw the name beside it.

Diego!

CHAPTER TWENTY-SEVEN

DANE LEANED BACK IN his chair, the dimly lit office casting shadows across his face. Sam sat across from him, listening to the sound of the clock on the wall ticking ominously, a reminder of time slipping away. The weight of the case hung heavy in the air, weighing down her thoughts.

Matt Henshaw had just picked up his son from the station and outside Sam's office, the bullpen was relatively quiet. All of her officers were either at home or on night patrol, leaving her and Dane alone to process the bombshell Wyatt had dropped on them.

"If Diego got into town around eleven-thirty, like Leo said," Dane spoke up, breaking the silence, "then he'd have time to dress up as *El Muerto* and kill Roy."

Sam leaned back in her chair, tapping her fingers against the armrest as she processed his words. "We really need to check that traffic cam footage," she said finally. "Have you received those images from the city office?"

"Not yet, but I should have them soon," Dane said, remaining rooted to his seat. His eyes were clouded with disbelief. "I just can't wrap my head around Diego being the killer."

"Anyone can become a killer with the right motivation," Sam replied, her mind racing a mile a minute. "Let's say, for the sake of argument, someone dressed up like *El Muerto* killed Roy. There's no way they could have escaped without getting dirt and blood all over the costume."

Dane furrowed his brow in confusion. "Yeah... so?"

"So how come no one else at the ranch reported seeing dirt or blood on the costume? They all loved Roy. I highly doubt they would let his killer walk away unscathed."

"Right..." he trailed off like he was trying to connect the dots.

"So, we have two possibilities here," she began, her thoughts moving faster than her tongue could keep up with, ideas sparking and merging like a puzzle slowly coming together. "Either no one has worn the *El Muerto* costume since Roy's murder..."

"Or?" Dane prompted eagerly.

"Or the killer kept the bloodied costume and replaced it with a clean one," she finished, a triumphant smile forming on her lips.

Dane nodded slowly. "That makes sense, but how do we find out which it is?"

Sam frowned, her mind following the thread of an idea like a mouse following a trail of breadcrumbs. She felt her heart beat faster with excitement as she pulled out her phone and made a call.

A second later, Elise answered, sounding breathless. "Hi Sam."

"Hi, Elise. I hope I'm not disturbing you."

"No, not at all. Do you have any new information on the case?"

"Not yet, but I do have a question for you. Have you seen *El Muerto* since you've been back in town?"

There was a moment's hesitation before Elise answered. "Actually, he made his ride Saturday night, after the seance. Why do you ask?"

"Just curious," Sam replied coyly. "Thanks for your help, Elise." She ended the call and turned to meet Dane's questioning gaze. "Saturday night."

"So, if it wasn't the real *El Muerto*, it had to be Diego or one of the ranch hands. You'd think they'd say something if they went to put on the costume and found it covered in blood."

"Unless they wore a replacement costume," Sam said thoughtfully. "Now the question is, where is the bloodied costume?"

Dane shrugged. "If one of the ranch hands killed Roy—or if it was Diego—then my money's on the ranch, somewhere."

"I agree. And I can probably get a search warrant from Judge Adams." She rocked back and forth in her chair, staring at him but not really seeing him, lost in thought. "Where do you suppose someone goes to get an *El Muerto* costume?"

He furrowed his brow in thought for a moment before responding. "That wouldn't be something you could just buy off Amazon. At least, I don't think you could. You'd have to commission someone to make it."

She smiled at him. "Exactly what I was thinking. You go check to see if you've received the traffic camera footage, and I'll make a call to our local seamstress."

She waited until Dane left before dialing JoAnn Bolland's number.

"I would love nothing more than to give you the information you're looking for," JoAnn began after Sam asked if she had made any *El Muerto* costumes and for whom. "However, I have all my clients sign non-disclosure agreements. It's to protect my pricing, but some customers prefer to keep their projects private."

"When you made that elegant dress for me, I didn't sign anything," Sam protested.

"No, you're right, but that was almost three years ago. I only started doing this recently—about two years ago, maybe?—after one of my customers made me sign one for him," she explained.

"Would that client have been Roy Richardson?"

There was a pause. "Actually, yes," JoAnn admitted.

"Did he ask you to make an *El Muerto* costume?"

"Sam. I can't tell you that. If it gets out that I don't take the NDA seriously, neither will my clients."

"I don't suppose you can tell me if anyone recently asked you to make a new *El Muerto* costume?" Silence greeted her question and she huffed out a breath. "All right. I understand."

"Thank you."

"Sure. Talk to you later."

Sam disconnected the call, feeling disappointed but not deterred. She quickly made another call and when she finished, she booted up her computer and set to work. An hour later, paperwork in hand, she left her office.

"I'm headed out," she announced to Dane, who was sitting at his desk. I've got an appointment to see Judge Adams."

Elise sat alone at a table on the back deck, her fingers tracing the rim of her glass as she nursed a drink. The night air was warm and filled with the distant sounds of crickets and frogs. Her mind was consumed with thoughts of the strange conversation she had just had with Sam about *El Muerto*. Why was she asking about it? Having ruled out other possibilities, was the ghost now her number one suspect?

The back door to the house opened and Diego stepped onto the deck. A tumbler of whiskey glinted in his hand as he made his way over to sit across from her at the table. His dark hair glistened under the moonlight and his strong jawline caught the shadows, giving him an almost otherworldly appearance.

"The last of our guests checked out this afternoon," he informed her, taking a sip of his drink before placing it down on the table. "Carmen and the girls are cleaning up before they leave. We'll have some peace and quiet until Friday, when the next wave of guests arrives." He kept his gaze fixed on her, concern etched into his features. "How are you holding up?"

His gentle tone warmed her heart. "I'm... I don't know. I guess I'm okay," she replied uncertainly. "I just thought that everything would be settled by now, but today we buried Dad, and nothing has changed. His killer is still out there somewhere. And you and I haven't even discussed what will happen to the ranch. And if I don't go back to New York City tomorrow, not only will I lose my promotion, but maybe even my job." The words slipped out before she could stop them, and she instantly regretted it.

"What?" His surprise and hurt were evident in his voice.

Her heart twisted with guilt as she rushed to apologize. "I'm sorry. I meant to tell you earlier, but with the funeral and everything that's going on, I honestly forgot." She paused to take a deep breath before continuing. "My boss called Tuesday morning and basically threatened me with loss of my new position if I wasn't back by Friday. I know everything's crazy right now, but I worked so hard to get this promotion."

Diego shook his head, his expression a mix of disappointment and understanding. He let out a heavy sigh before speaking. "I get it. Of course, you have to go back," he said, surprising her with his level-headed response. "I can manage the ranch until we decide what to do."

"Thank you, Diego. I can't tell you how much I appreciate your understanding," she said, feeling a lump form in her throat for reasons she couldn't quite pinpoint. "Once I finish up the new campaign for our client, I should be able to get away for a couple of days. I'll come back down then."

"How long do you think the campaign will take?" Diego asked, concern lacing his voice.

"A couple of weeks," she replied. *If the client is reasonable.* "Of course, we don't have to wait until I'm back to discuss the ranch. We could have regular video calls."

"I don't want you to go," he said simply.

"But..." she trailed off, unsure how to continue.

He held up his hand to stop her protest. The faint light coming from inside the house highlighted the soft lines of his face as he leaned forward, taking her hands in his. The warmth of his touch sent a shiver up her spine.

"I know how important your job is to you," he said. "I would never suggest that you give it up."

Their fingers intertwined, creating an unbreakable bond between them.

"I've been waiting for the perfect moment to tell you this," he continued, "but it seems like we don't have that kind of time. So, I'll just say it." He took a deep breath and held her gaze with his intense brown eyes. "I love you, Elise. Not as a friend or a brother, but as something more."

Her heart skipped a beat at his words.

"I've loved you for as long as I can remember," he went on. "I don't expect you to feel the same way, at least not right away, but these last few days have given me reason to believe there's something between us."

"There is," she agreed. As quickly as her heart had soared, it now sank. "What about the distance? Long-distance relationships are hard enough when they're established. How can we possibly make this work?"

His thumb traced circles on the back of her hand in a soothing motion. "We don't have to solve that problem right now, Elise. We'll figure it out together as we go along."

She couldn't help but feel reassured by his words and the gentle touch of his hand.

"And besides," he added, "planes fly both ways. When you can't come to me, I'll come to you."

A sense of relief washed over her. She didn't have to leave everything behind to be with him.

"Do you need to go pack?" he asked.

Shaking her head, she replied, "No, I just need my purse and laptop. I'll leave my new clothes here, so I have something to wear when I come back."

"Excellent," he exclaimed with a smile. "Then, if you don't mind, I'd just as soon not spend the last couple of hours we have together tonight sitting out here talking." He gracefully rose from his seat and circled the table, pulling out her chair as she, too, stood up.

"What do you have in mind?" she asked curiously.

"It's time for bed," he declared playfully, a mischievous glint in his gaze.

"Tired?" she teased back, leaning in closer.

"Not in the least." His warm hand reached out to take hers and together, they made their way inside, heading to their bedroom, eager for the night ahead.

Chapter Twenty-Eight

THE MORNING SUNLIGHT STREAMED through the windows, casting a golden glow over Elise and Diego as they lay tangled in each other's arms. Elise sighed and nuzzled her head into the crook of his neck, not wanting to leave the warmth and comfort of their shared embrace.

"I wish I didn't have to go back today," she murmured, not for the first time. Diego tightened his hold on her, offering reassurance as he had done every time before. "It's okay," he said, his voice low and soothing. "I know how important your job is to you. I would never want to be the reason you lost it."

Elise pulled away slightly so she could look at him, needing to see the understanding in his eyes. "This is not me choosing my job over you," she clarified earnestly. "You understand that, right? Because I love you. I think I always have."

Diego leaned up and captured her lips in a gentle kiss. "I know you're not choosing your job over me," he whispered against her mouth. "The most important thing is that I know you love me and you know how much I love you—and the rest of it, we'll figure out as we go along."

With a small smile, Elise snuggled back into his arms, resting her head once again against his chest. Closing her eyes, she let herself get lost in the steady rhythm of his heartbeat, allowing it to lull her back to sleep.

All too soon, Diego roused her from her peaceful slumber. "If we stay in bed any longer, you're going to miss your flight," he reminded her with a playful nudge. He hugged her close and pressed a kiss to the top of her head before pulling back slightly to meet her gaze.

Without hesitation, he pulled her closer until their lips met in a tender kiss. It was several minutes before they finally pulled away, both breathless and reluctant to let go.

"I think I might hate your boss," Diego groaned, his arms still wrapped tightly around her. "Yes, I'm sure of it. I think he's a dick for making you go back."

Elise couldn't help but chuckle at his words, though she couldn't argue with his sentiment. "Right now, I'm not so fond of him either," she admitted with a slight pout. "But it's not personal with him."

Diego nodded in understanding as he released her from their embrace, though his gaze remained intense and un-wavering. "I know," he said softly. "It's all about business."

Reluctantly, she pushed herself up into a sitting position and ran her fingers through her tousled hair, letting out a deep sigh. She knew she had to get up if she wanted to eat breakfast with him before hitting the road. After climbing out of bed, she quickly found clean clothes to put on, stealing appreciative glances at Diego as he pulled on his clothes.

As she finished dressing, she asked him the question that had been on her mind since they woke up. "How soon do you think you could get away and come see me?" Her voice was hesitant, hoping for a positive answer.

He sat on the edge of the bed, pulling on his boots with practiced ease. As he slipped the final boot on, he stood up and smiled at her. "Would next week be too soon? I'll need a couple of days to tie up loose ends here, but then I can fly up to see you. Carmen and Rodrigo can handle things while I'm away."

"Good." A sense of contentment washed over her at the thought of seeing him again. Knowing he would visit made leaving just a little easier.

"How about some breakfast?" he asked, coming to stand beside her.

"That sounds great." She grabbed her purse and looked around the room with bittersweet nostalgia. "Oh, wait," she said suddenly, remembering that this wasn't her room anymore. "I can move my clothes into Dad's room."

"No," he interrupted, placing a gentle hand on her shoulder. "I'll enjoy having them here as a reminder that you'll be back."

"Okay, if you're sure." She smiled gratefully at him, feeling comforted by his words.

Hand in hand, they left the room together. Elise paused when they reached the foyer. "I just need to grab my laptop from the study," she told him, gesturing towards the door.

"You go do that while I start breakfast." Diego walked off towards the kitchen, leaving Elise to gather her belongings before joining him for their last breakfast together.

As she entered the bright and inviting kitchen, Elise was greeted by the mouth-watering aroma of bacon sizzling in a cast-iron skillet. She couldn't help but smile as she poured herself a cup of freshly brewed coffee and settled in at the small wooden table, watching Diego expertly crack eggs into a bowl and whisk them together.

The eggs cooked quickly and soon Elise was digging into a hearty breakfast with Diego across from her. The warmth spreading through her body made her feel content and at peace, although the absence of her father lingered in her mind, keeping this from being the most perfect moment of her life.

When the doorbell rang just moments later, both Elise and Diego exchanged worried looks, knowing that no one would call this early unless there was trouble.

Together, they made their way to the front door and a feeling of unease washed over Elise when she saw Sam Hunter standing on their doorstep, accompanied by several officers.

Diego spoke first. "Sam? What's going on?"

"Diego. Elise." Sam held out a folded piece of paper towards them. "I have a warrant to search the premises and grounds, including the barn, the bunkhouse and guest housing."

Elise's heart skipped a beat as she watched Diego read over the paper with a furrowed brow before handing it to her. Her eyes scanned the words, feeling like a weight was pressing down on her chest. They were looking for bloodied clothing.

Diego stepped back to let Sam enter the house, grumbling under his breath. "We would have let you search without the warrant," he said tersely. "All you had to do was ask."

"I appreciate that," Sam assured them, her voice firm and professional. "I think, for everyone's sake, it's best if, moving forward, we keep things formal." She met Diego's gaze, her eyes steely and unwavering. "I would also appreciate it if you informed your staff to cooperate fully with our search and refrain from any actions that may result in their arrest."

Turning to her team, Sam gave out instructions. "Two of you will search the main house, two will take the bunkhouse, and two will search the barn." She waited for all but Dane to nod and walk off before turning back to Diego. "How many guests are currently staying on the property?"

Diego let out a breath, his shoulders slumping slightly. "None at the moment," he replied. "The bungalows are unlocked and awaiting cleaning."

Sam exchanged a knowing look with Dane, who silently nodded in agreement before walking away, leaving Sam alone with Elise and Diego.

"I need you both to remain on the premises while we conduct our search," Sam spoke firmly but politely.

Elise was taken aback, her stuttering attempts at a response revealing her surprise. "B-but I have a flight back to New York today," she protested. "I could lose my job if I'm not back in the office tomorrow."

"I understand," Sam replied sympathetically. "What time is your flight?"

"One o'clock, leaving from McAllen," Elise answered, panic creeping into her voice. "I was just about to head out."

Sam glanced at her watch. "We will do our best to expedite the search, but it may be wise to see if there is a later flight you can take."

Elise swore under her breath, resenting the inconvenience. The only thing she hated worse was thinking one of the staff had killed her father. Because that's what Sam thought, wasn't it? If she was searching the premises for bloodied clothing.

"Let's sit down and talk while my team conducts their search," Sam suggested.

"Come on in," Diego invited, stepping back to allow her room to enter. "We can sit at the dining table."

Elise shot him a worried glance. Even if Sam had allowed her to leave, she wouldn't have felt comfortable leaving Diego alone to deal with everything.

Diego reached for her hand and gave it a reassuring squeeze. "I'll put on a pot of fresh coffee. Why don't you call the car service, then change your flight to a later time?"

She nodded and, after she and Sam sat at the table, she pulled out her laptop.

As the coffee brewed, Elise searched for flights to New York on her laptop while Diego busied himself cleaning up their unfinished breakfast plates. As he scraped the food into the trash before rinsing and stacking the plates, she couldn't help but feel unnerved by the tense atmosphere in the room.

When the coffee was done, Diego prepared three mugs and carried them to the table. By that time, Elise had changed her ticket to take a later flight and called the car service to change her pick-up time.

"Help yourself to sweetener and creamer," Diego said quietly to Sam, gesturing towards the center of the table.

After everyone had fixed their drinks, Diego finally addressed the elephant in the room. "You think Roy's killer is someone working for the ranch?"

Sam was silent for a moment as she studied each of their faces. "Yes. I think the killer was wearing an *El Muerto* costume when he killed Roy and it's somewhere on this ranch."

Elise's eyes widened in disbelief. "The what?" She quickly glanced at Diego, who was not nearly as surprised as she apparently was.

Sam noticed and pinned him under her gaze. "You know what I'm talking about, don't you, Diego?"

Time seemed to stand still, and then Diego slowly nodded, his expression guarded. A million thoughts raced through his mind, wondering how she'd discovered their secret.

"I do," he finally spoke up, trying to regain control of the situation.

Sam looked like she wasn't planning to say more, but then shrugged nonchalantly. "What the hell," she muttered. "I know the ranch has an *El Muerto* costume that you use to impersonate the ghost. The night Roy was killed, *El Muerto* was seen making his ride across the pasture. Only it wasn't the real *El Muerto*, was it, Diego?"

"What is she talking about?" Elise asked, sounding confused.

Diego cursed under his breath, feeling Elise's intense gaze on him as she waited for an explanation. He wished he had told her about the impersonations in private, but there had never been a good time. That wasn't a valid excuse, he knew, turning to meet her questioning gaze.

"Your dad came up with the idea a couple of years ago," he began tentatively, hoping to smooth things over. "He noticed that the guests who were here when *El Muerto* made his ride often booked return trips. And after they shared their experience with friends, those friends would come and stay as well. The problem was that *El Muerto* only rides once a month, if that often, so Roy came up with the idea of increasing the number of rides by impersonating the ghost. Once a month, at first. Then, more recently, to twice a month."

Elise's jaw dropped in disbelief. "But...how?"

Diego sighed. "It was easier than you'd think. I worked with JoAnn on a costume." He turned to Sam; his tone slightly accusatory. "I'm guessing she told you?"

Sam shook her head. "No. I found out about the impersonations from someone else. When I asked JoAnn about the costume, she refused to say anything. I had to get a court order to search her records."

"I guess it's nice to know she didn't sell us out. Anyway, we keep the costume in the barn. Inside the metal storage closet in the tack room. I have a key and so does Rodrigo," Diego said.

Sam tapped the radio pinned to her shirt collar and conveyed the location of the costume to Dane.

"The other night... was that the real *El Muerto* I saw?" Elise asked.

He shook his head. "No, it was me."

"Why didn't you tell me?"

He gave her a raised eyebrow look. "You weren't quite yourself that night, if you remember?"

"Yeah, point taken." She sighed. "How could you make a costume that looked so... real?" she asked, still sounding dazed.

He was reluctant to answer, feeling like he was digging a hole deeper and deeper with each word he spoke. "We coated the cowboy costume in glow-in-the-dark paint and used black grease paint on our faces to create the illusion of a headless rider. We also paint a horse in the same glow-in-the-dark paint. At night, from a distance, the effect is pretty convincing."

"What I want to know," Sam interjected, "is how you avoided running into the real *El Muerto*?"

Diego shrugged nonchalantly. "That was easy. We wait until midnight. If *El Muerto* hasn't shown up by then, it means he's not coming." He hesitated before adding, "Impersonating a ghost isn't against the law, is it?"

Sam's frown deepened. "It's a little late to be asking that question, don't you think? But no, as far as I know, impersonating a ghost is not illegal. However, committing murder certainly is. You remember at the seance? Roy told us *El Muerto* attacked him. At the time, it didn't make sense to me. Now it does."

A sudden jolt of alarm raced through Diego. "You think one of the ranch hands killed Roy while dressed as *El Muerto*?"

"No," Sam said. "I think you killed Roy. Your name was on the schedule to ride that night and I have a witness placing you at the ranch at eleven-thirty."

Elise gasped at the accusation, but Diego barely heard her over the ringing in his ears.

"They're mistaken. I told you. My truck broke down—."

"I don't think so," Sam interrupted, pulling out her phone. She thumbed through several screens before holding her phone out to both him and Elise. What he saw on the screen sent a chill down his spine—a picture of him driving his truck. "This was taken on Second Street, just a block from Dwayne's. Note the time stamp of ten-forty-five? With a thirty-minute walk from Dwayne's place to here, that puts you here close to eleven-thirty."

Elise leaned in closer to the screen and then turned to him with a questioning look. "Diego?"

He felt his heart sinking as his shoulders slumped in defeat. "I lied about what time I got back because I didn't want anyone to suspect me of impersonating *El Muerto*." Then he realized what he had admitted and hurried to explain. "It's not like that. I didn't kill Roy. I got back to the ranch and went out to the barn to get ready to ride. Then I saw what I assumed was the real *El Muerto*, so I snuck back up to the main house. I was exhausted from being out in the blistering sun all afternoon and ended up falling asleep. When I woke up, it was after one. That's when I noticed Roy wasn't in his room and went looking for him."

As he finished his explanation, the back door to the house swung open and Dane walked in with Chad close behind, both carrying clear large plastic bags filled with evidence.

"We found something," Dane announced, holding up one bag containing a bright, yellowish-white cloth. "This is the costume we found hanging up in the barn. Looks fairly new."

"That's probably the newest costume JoAnn made," Sam commented.

Dane gestured to Chad holding another bag containing fabric that was clearly soiled. "And we found a second costume. This one is covered in dirt and what looks like dried blood. And," he paused, reaching into his pocket to pull out a smaller clear bag containing a scrap of fabric. "There's a piece missing that matches this one we found at the crime scene."

"Where did you find it?" Sam inquired, her voice laced with suspicion.

Dane's gaze met hers. "It was stuffed into the back of the closet of Bungalow #9."

"What?" Diego demanded, feeling shocked. "No way."

"Why?" Sam's gaze narrowed on Diego. "Who's staying in Bungalow #9?"

Diego's jaw tightened as he met her glare. "I am, but I did not put that costume there. I didn't even know there was a second costume," he insisted, his voice firm and resolute.

Sam let out a heavy sigh and slowly pushed away from the table, her hand instinctively going to the butt of her holstered weapon. "Diego, I'm placing you under arrest on suspicion of murdering Roy Richardson," she announced sternly, her gaze locked on him. "Stand up and don't try anything."

Stunned by the sudden turn of events, Diego slowly rose to his feet, his mind reeling with shock and fear.

"Cuff him," Sam instructed Chad, motioning towards Diego with a nod.

Elise sat unmoving at the table, her expression reflecting her shock. Diego wanted to reassure her but the cold metal clamping around his wrist left him too stunned to speak.

"I know you have a plane to catch," Sam said calmly, turning to face Elise. "I'll be in touch."

Elise shook her head defiantly, getting to her feet. "I'm not going anywhere," she stated firmly as she walked over to stand by Diego's side.

She placed a gentle hand on his cheek and looked up at him with unwavering support. "I know you didn't do this," she said, her voice full of conviction. "I'll call a lawyer and we will fight this together."

Diego's gaze softened as he leaned down to rest his forehead against hers. "Thank you," he whispered gratefully.

Then, with one last fleeting glance at her, they led him away. It was a slight comfort knowing that she believed in his innocence. However, considering what he was being accused of, it was not enough to ease the heavy weight of dread crushing him.

CHAPTER TWENTY-NINE

Elise's mind was in a state of shock as she watched Chad lead Diego away, his hands cuffed behind his back. The weight of the situation settled heavily on her shoulders as she stood alone, surrounded by the fading presence of Sam and the other police officers who had left after finding what they were looking for.

Taking a deep breath, Elise gathered her composure and immediately called Mr. Barientos. She explained the events that had just unfolded, and he agreed to represent Diego, at least for the time being.

"I specialize in business law, not criminal defense," he informed her with a heavy sigh. "But I'll do what I can to help."

"I don't know any criminal attorneys," she told him. "Can you recommend someone?"

"Unfortunately, you'll have to look outside our small town," he informed her. "I'll start reaching out to my contacts in bigger cities to see if I can come up with a recommendation or two."

"Thank you," Elise sighed gratefully. "In the meantime, what do we do?"

"I'll head over to the police station and see if I can speak with Diego," Mr. Barientos offered. "Our courts aren't exactly overflowing with cases, so we should be able to schedule an arraignment for tomorrow. He can plead not guilty and bail will be set." He paused before asking, "Do you have enough money to cover his bail? It could be quite costly—several thousand dollars. I'm afraid the Trust can't pay for it."

Elise hesitated for a moment before confidently responding, "Yes, I have enough to cover his bail."

"Very well then," Mr. Barientos said. "I'll call you once I know more."

She thanked him and hung up the phone, her mind racing with Maddie's words from earlier—to use some of the money she had been saving for something she wanted. Well, now she knew exactly what she wanted—to get Diego out of jail and clear his name. It was now her top priority, and she would do whatever it took to make it happen.

Elise's heart was heavy as she grappled with the idea that Diego may have been her father's killer. She shuddered at the thought of trusting, sleeping with, and worse, falling in love with, a murderer. The logical part of her brain argued that she hadn't seen him in years and couldn't truly know him, but her heart told her otherwise.

She took a deep breath and pushed those thoughts aside. She refused to let her world fall apart without a fight. Seeking Rodrigo, she found him hard at work in the barn with several ranch hands. Despite the shock of recent events, Rodrigo assured her he would take care of the animals. Feeling better that the ranch wouldn't fall apart while she was preoccupied with helping Diego, she returned to the house and cancelled her flight and ride to the airport.

The search conducted by Sam's officers had left a trail of disarray throughout every room of the house. To keep her mind occupied while waiting for news from Mr. Barrientos, Elise set to work cleaning and organizing each space.

As she finished tidying up, she glanced at her phone and saw that it was well past 6:00 p.m. She had missed her flight back to New York, but it didn't matter to her now. She checked her phone once more for any missed calls from Mr. Barrientos and felt disappointed.

Feeling anxious and restless, Elise dialed Mr. Barrientos' number, only to hang up when it went straight to voicemail. The thought of Diego potentially being locked away in prison among hardened criminals made her stomach churn.

Needing a distraction from her worrying thoughts, Elise turned on the television and mindlessly flipped through channels.

An hour passed before Mr. Barrientos finally called back.

"What took you so long?" Elise snapped as she answered the call. Immediately regretting her tone, she quickly added, "I'm sorry, Mr. Barientos. That was rude. It's just hard not knowing what's going on."

"I understand," he replied graciously. "Bureaucracy, even in small towns, takes time. The arraignment is set for tomorrow morning at ten o'clock."

"Do you think there's any chance the judge will dismiss the case?"

"It's unlikely," he responded grimly. "The evidence against Diego is mostly circumstantial, but it doesn't paint a favorable picture."

They spoke for a few more minutes before Elise thanked him for calling and hung up. No longer interested in the mindless chatter on television, she shut it off and retreated to her bedroom. Her head was throbbing with worry, so she took two nighttime pain tablets to ensure she could fall asleep and climbed into bed. As she lay in the darkness, the faint scent of Diego lingered on the sheets, triggering memories and longing within her that made his absence even more painful.

As the sun peeked through the curtains the next morning, Elise slowly opened her eyes and groggily sat up in bed. The previous night's tears had left her eyes swollen and red, and she struggled to shake off her brain fog. Glancing at the clock, she saw it was already past 8:00 a.m. With a sense of urgency, she quickly showered and dressed before making her way to the kitchen for a much-needed cup of coffee.

As she waited for the pot to finish brewing, a sudden knock sounded. Startled, Elise turned to see Carmen standing in the open doorway.

"Sorry to interrupt," she apologized.

"No, you're fine," Elise said with a tight smile. "What's up?"

"I just wanted to tell you we heard from the guests who were supposed to check in today. They've canceled their reservations."

Elise let out a heavy sigh. "Good news travels fast," she said sarcastically. It seemed like everything was falling apart at once. "Thanks for letting me know, Carmen. How are you doing? And the rest of the staff?"

"We're worried," Carmen admitted. "Not for us, but for Diego."

"He didn't kill my father," Elise defended him fiercely.

"I know that. We all do," Carmen said with a nod. "We're worried he won't get a fair trial if he has to rely on the public defender's office. The staff and I took up a collection to help pay for his legal fees." As she spoke, she held out a sealed envelope towards Elise. "It's a couple thousand dollars."

Elise hesitated for a moment before reluctantly taking the envelope. She knew the staff couldn't afford to part with their hard-earned money, but their kind gesture touched her deeply. "Thank you," she said, silently vowing to find a way to repay them in the future. "Please thank everyone for trying to help. Diego will be touched when I tell him what you did. I'm going to find Diego the very best legal counsel I can."

"Thank you," she replied with a warm smile.

Elise's expression softened. "As for the ranch staff, please give them the next couple of days off, with full pay, of course," she quickly added when she noticed Carmen's worried expression.

Carmen thanked her profusely. "The girls and I have already prepared some meals for Rodrigo and the ranch hands, but there's plenty left for you, too, if you get hungry. And I also made some cookies and there's a pitcher of fresh tea in the fridge."

Elise's heart swelled with gratitude for Carmen's thoughtfulness. "Thank you so much, Carmen. That means a lot to me." She hesitated for a moment before asking another question. "Have you told Diego's parents about his arrest yet?"

Carmen shook her head, looking uncertain. "I wasn't sure how to tell them."

"Diego's arraignment is this morning, and I'm hoping he'll be released on bail," Elise explained. "Perhaps we should wait and let him talk to his parents?"

Carmen nodded in agreement before they exchanged goodbyes and parted ways.

As Elise watched Carmen leave, a faint memory stirred within her. She felt a small twinge of worry at its elusiveness, but she couldn't seem to grasp it no matter how hard she tried. Eventually, she gave up and let the memory slip away.

Glancing at the clock, Elise finished her coffee and rinsed out her mug before heading out of the cozy kitchen and towards the garage. Her father's old truck was parked outside the garage. As she made her way towards it, a familiar rumbling sound caught her attention and she turned to see JD's sturdy red truck coming up the drive from the barn.

Her curiosity piqued, she waited for him to pull up alongside her before stepping up to the open driver's side window.

"JD, what brings you here?" she asked, surprised to see him.

"I wanted to check on you," he replied, getting out of his truck. "I knocked on the front door, but when you didn't answer, I thought you might be in the barn, so I drove down there. I heard about the arrest. Is there anything I can do to help?"

Her smile faltered slightly at the mention of Diego's arrest, but she quickly composed herself.

"No, but th—" She paused, considering his offer. "Well, actually. Maybe there is something you can do. Would you happen to know the name of a good criminal attorney? I need to hire one for Diego." Her frustration spilled out as she spoke. "This charge against him is absolutely ludicrous."

JD held up a finger for her to wait a moment as he hurried back to his truck. Reaching inside, he pulled out a leather-bound notebook and pen. Opening the notebook, he wrote something down and then tore out the page.

"These guys are based in Dallas and from what I hear, they're pretty good," he said with a reassuring tone as he handed her the page.

Elise thanked him profusely as she took it from him, only briefly glancing at the names before slipping it into her pocket.

"I wish I could stay and chat, but I have to get to the courthouse," she said, already making her way to the driver's side door of her father's truck.

"Sure, I understand," JD replied, opening the door for her and holding it while she climbed in. "Good luck, Elise."

"Thanks," she said with a grateful smile before starting the engine. Driving off, her mind raced with thoughts of what lay ahead for Diego.

Her heart was pounding in her chest and her mind was buzzing with worry when she walked into the courthouse a few minutes later. She had completely forgotten to call her boss and let him know why she wouldn't be in the office today. As she entered the courtroom, a bright "Silence Your Cellphones" sign caught her eye, reminding her of her mistake. When she took out her phone to silence it, she saw the notifications for two missed calls from him. That couldn't be good.

Making a mental note to call him at her first opportunity, she took a deep breath and tried to compose herself as she looked around the room. Her gaze fell upon Mr. Barientos, sitting at the defendant's table. Sitting at the prosecutor's table was Sam and, beside her, a lawyer from the state attorney general's office who'd most likely driven in that morning from one of the bigger cities. He looked exhausted, but also incredibly competent. Elise reminded herself that this wasn't a trial yet, just an arraignment.

As a side door opened, all eyes turned towards it and Elise saw Diego being escorted in by guards, his hands cuffed together. As he approached the defendant's table, his eyes scanned the courtroom until they landed on her. She raised a hand in greeting and offered him a reassuring smile.

She could see the worry etched on his face, but there was a brief glimmer of relief when he spotted her, letting her know he was glad she was there.

As if I would have stayed away, she thought. *Not a chance.*

The courtroom was hushed as Judge Adams entered and the arraignment began. His robes rustled as he took his seat, his expression stern and unwavering. The judge read out the charges against Diego—murder in the first degree—after which Diego plead "not guilty." Elise sat quietly in her seat, trying to maintain a calm façade despite the turmoil churning inside her.

When the time came to set bail, Judge Adams called Sam and both attorneys to the bench for discussions too quiet for Elise to hear. She anxiously watched them, her heart racing with anticipation and fear. After what felt like an eternity, they finished, and Sam and the attorneys returned to their seats, their faces unreadable. Judge Adams then addressed Diego directly.

"It is the opinion of the court that you do not pose a flight risk," he announced, his voice booming through the courtroom. "Therefore, I'm setting bail at $500,000." He rapped his gavel against the top of the judge's bench to render his decision final.

As soon as the judge left the bench, Diego was led off by guards and Elise hurriedly made her way to the local bail bondsman. Her hands shook as she filled out the paperwork, her mind reeling from everything that had happened in such a short span of time.

Posting bail took longer than expected and while she waited for Diego's release to be processed, she nervously called her boss.

"Elise?" Bob's voice sounded stern and impatient. "I thought you were coming into the office today."

"I was," she told him with a heavy sigh, bracing herself for what she knew was coming next. "But I ran into problems yesterday and wasn't able to make my flight."

"Elise, what the hell is going on? I had the Johnston executives here today. They waited hours for you to show up and you didn't even have the decency to call to let me know you weren't coming. How do you think that makes us look?"

"I'm so sorry, Bob. It wasn't intentional," she said, her voice trembling with emotion. "My father's death wasn't an accident," she revealed, unable to contain the truth any longer. "He was murdered, and yesterday, my..." *Lover? Best friend?* "father's foreman was arrested for it." Her words hung in the air, heavy with grief and disbelief.

"I'm sorry, Elise," he said, sounding more sympathetic.

"I needed to be here for the arraignment," she hurried to explain. "I don't believe he's guilty, so I'll need to help him hire an attorney. And on top of that, I have to figure out what to do about the ranch. I can't manage it from New York, and he certainly can't manage it from jail."

Bob let out a sigh. "I don't want to seem unsympathetic, Elise. Take all the time you need to sort things out there. Use as much of your PTO as necessary and if you need more time, we can work something out without pay."

"Thank you so much for understanding." She breathed a sigh of relief.

"And when you return, we'll have a position open for you as a marketing consultant."

"A marketing consultant?" Elise repeated in surprise.

"Yes, Elise. I don't want to lose someone as talented as you in the marketing department. However, I need my VP of Marketing to be here in the office. While I sympathize with everything you're going through, I can't afford to lose a major client over it. That's why I've appointed Sean as the new VP and he will take over the Johnston account. I'll fill

him in on your situation, but after today, you'll be report-
ing directly to him."

Elise sat in stunned silence, her heart sinking as she
heard the words she had been dreading. She had poured
years of hard work and determination into achieving the
VP position, only to have it snatched away from her in an
instant. A flicker of hope crossed her mind, wondering
if she could persuade him to reconsider if she promised
to be back on Monday morning. Then Diego appeared
in the doorway leading to the back of the police station,
and everything changed.

As he walked towards her, Elise knew that her life
was taking a different turn than she had expected. The
hustle and bustle of New York City seemed like a distant
memory now.

"Bob, I understand," she managed to say, keeping her
emotions in check. "I need to go now, but I'll be in touch."

Diego stepped into the cool, sterile lobby of the police
station, and his heart raced as he scanned the room.
His gaze immediately landed on Elise, who was talking
on her phone by the reception desk. He couldn't read
her expression from this distance and worried she might
harbor anger or resentment towards him.

The memory of last night flooded back to him; sitting
alone in a cramped cell, unable to even speak to Elise. It
had been the darkest and most helpless night of his life. Yet,
just the night before, he and Elise had been tangled together
in passionate lovemaking until dawn. The contrast between

those two nights was striking, and it made him realize how fragile happiness could be.

Elise spotted him and quickly ended her call, rushing over with open arms. Diego held her tightly, relieved beyond words that he hadn't lost her completely.

As much as he wanted to stand there and never let go, they were being watched by Dane and Sam, both of whom he could feel judging him. He wanted to protect Elise from their scrutiny as much as possible.

"Let's get out of here," he whispered softly, gently pulling away but keeping their hands entwined because he needed to feel connected to her.

They left the station hand-in-hand, walking in sync as they made their way to the truck. Diego took the keys from Elise when they reached the vehicle, feeling a sense of normalcy returning as he slid into the driver's seat with her at his side. Despite everything hanging over them—the murder charge looming like a dark cloud—he couldn't help but feel content driving back to the ranch with Elise by his side.

"I was so worried about you," she confessed, breaking the comfortable silence that had settled between them.

"Everything will be okay," he said, hoping he sounded more confident than he felt. "Before we reach the ranch, we need to discuss how much to tell the staff and the guests."

"The staff already know everything, and no one believes you killed my father," Elise replied. Her hand found its way into his, offering comfort and support.

"I'm relieved to hear that," Diego said, feeling a small weight lift from his shoulders.

"As for the guests, there aren't any. The ones scheduled to arrive today canceled their reservations."

"News of my arrest must have spread quickly," Diego sighed. "I'm truly sorry, Elise."

"Don't blame yourself," she scolded gently. "This is not your fault, but there are important matters we need to discuss."

"Could they possibly wait until I've had a chance to freshen up? Spending the night in the Las Palomas jail has left me feeling rather grimy."

"Of course," she agreed, giving his hand a gentle squeeze. They rode the rest of the way home in silence, each lost in their own thoughts.

"Are you hungry?" Elise asked as they entered the house a few minutes later.

"Now that you mention it, I am," he admitted. "I was too nervous this morning to eat breakfast."

"Go shower and change while I prepare lunch," she said, shooing him away. "And by 'prepare', I mean I'll heat the food Carmen and the girls left us."

Diego couldn't resist pulling her close and holding her as he replied, "Or... you could shower with me."

Elise let out a soft laugh, which felt like balm for his wounded soul. He expected her to protest, but she surprised him.

"Lead the way," she said with a mischievous glint in her eye.

Chapter Thirty

As the steamy water cascaded over their bodies, their passion rose to a peak and then slowly ebbed. Reluctantly, they left the soothing embrace of the shower and got dressed. Their stomachs growled in unison, signaling their hunger. Heading towards the commercial kitchen, they discovered containers of grilled chicken and mac-n-cheese in the refrigerator. Placing heaping portions onto their plates and returning to the main house, they settled at the kitchen table.

With a silent understanding, they kept their conversation light as they ate. After finishing his meal, Diego noticed Elise's gaze fixed on him.

"What?" he asked curiously.

"We need to talk," she said in a serious tone.

He nodded in agreement, knowing she was right. "Why don't you make some coffee while I do the dishes?"

As they sat back down with steaming mugs of coffee, Diego couldn't help but study Elise's expression. It was clear she was struggling with her thoughts. A sudden sense of unease washed over him as he waited for her to speak.

"Are you breaking up with me? Not that I would blame you," he blurted out anxiously.

Elise shot him a shocked look. "Why would you ask that? Especially after what we just did in the shower."

"You look so serious. I got worried," he explained sheepishly.

She didn't laugh like he had hoped. "I'm not breaking up with you, but there are so many things we need to talk about. I don't even know where to start." She paused to study his face before continuing. "Let's start with your *El Muerto* impersonations. Is it even legal?" Her incredulous tone conveyed her disbelief.

His voice laced with nostalgic amusement and using a Russian accent, he quoted a line from a favorite movie, *Cutting Edge*. "Legano. Illegano. Is grey area." She simply frowned at him, prompting him to raise his hands in surrender. "Okay, okay. You heard Sam. It's not illegal."

"But it's not ethical," she countered firmly.

"Are you sure? Remember how every Halloween, the high school puts on a haunted house? And how much fun we had going through it? Remember when the zombie shot out of the grave, or the vampire reached for you out of the fog?"

She nodded slowly, understanding his point, but still feeling uneasy.

"It's not that different, Elise," he continued. "People come here hoping to see a ghost, even though they're not sure they exist. When they leave our ranch, some might realize what they saw was just a performance, while others will swear they saw the real thing. And in some cases, they did. But what they'll all agree on is that they had a good time—and that's why we do it. So, you may not think our impersonations are ethical, but everyone enjoys them. Which is why your father started them." He paused, studying her face with a hint of regret. "And I'm sorry he didn't tell you, but in his defense, you stopped showing any interest in the ranch and what goes on here."

She furrowed her brow in thought. "Okay, I guess I can understand how the impersonations came about. So that was you I saw Saturday night after the seance, not the real *El Muerto?*" She couldn't hide her surprise and slight disappointment.

He gave a small smile and nodded. "Yep, just me in costume and black face paint. I was out behind the barn, washing the paint off my horse, when I heard you yelling in the pasture and went to investigate."

"The costume you wore must have been the one they found in the barn, right? I mean, you would have noticed if it was covered in blood." He nodded. "So, the ranch purchased two costumes?" she asked.

Diego frowned. "Actually, now that you mention it, no. We only purchased one."

"So, where did that second one come from?" she pressed.

"JoAnn Bollard," Diego replied. "Mr. Barientos told me that Sam found in JoAnn's records that a second costume had been ordered last Tuesday."

"That's the day after my father was killed."

Diego nodded. "Sam's theory is that when I realized the first costume had blood all over it, I ordered a second costume after tossing the ruined one into my closet."

"But Diego, that doesn't make any sense. Remember on the night of the seance when JoAnn told you she had a pickup order ready? What if that was for the second costume?"

He shrugged. "It probably was."

"When we left the seance, JoAnn was still at Sylvia's. There wouldn't have been time for you to pick up the costume before wearing it that night." Elise's tone was incredulous.

"You're right," he admitted, sounding stunned.

"Which means..." Elise trailed off, her mind racing with possibilities.

"There's a third costume?" He asked, his voice thick with urgency.

Elise's eyes widened in realization. "We need to talk to JoAnn," she said firmly.

Diego pulled out his phone and dialed JoAnn's number, putting it on speaker so Elise could hear. The air fairly crackled with tension as they waited for her to answer.

"Diego? Oh, my goodness, I am so sorry," JoAnn's distressed voice came through the speaker. "I didn't want to show Sam my records, but she had a court order."

"It's okay, JoAnn. You did nothing wrong," Diego reassured her. "I have you on speaker. Elise is here with me, and we were hoping you could share some information with us."

There was a hesitant pause before JoAnn's voice came back on the line. "What did you want to know?"

"How many *El Muerto* costumes have you made altogether?" Diego questioned.

After a few moments of typing on her keyboard, JoAnn replied, "Since the ranch is the only customer to order that costume, I can share that information. According to my file, I made the first costume two years ago. You picked up that order. Then ten months ago, I made a second one and last Tuesday, I got the order for the third one which I finished on Saturday."

"Who placed the orders for the second and third costumes?" Diego asked.

"Both times it was Leo Stoddart," JoAnn confirmed.

Diego's jaw clenched in frustration. "Did he also pick up the costumes?"

"The second one, yes. He paid cash for it. The third one is still here," JoAnn revealed.

Diego and Elise exchanged a meaningful glance, both understanding the significance of this information. "Okay, JoAnn, thank you for your help," he said with forced calmness, before ending the call.

"The only reason to pay cash for the costumes would be to keep you and my dad from knowing about it," Elise surmised, her blue eyes narrowing in suspicion. "But why even order a third costume if he'd already replaced the one that was ruined?"

"All good questions," Diego agreed. "That only Leo can answer."

Elise shifted beside him, clearly wanting action to be taken. "Are you going to call him?"

Diego hesitated before deciding. "No. I don't want to give him a chance to disappear on us. Let me call Rodrigo to see where he's got Leo working." He picked up his phone again and placed the call.

"Hello?"

Elise recognized Rodrigo's voice and watched Diego's expression change from concern to relief. "Hey, Rodrigo, how's it going?"

"Diego, man. It's good to hear from you," Rodrigo replied. "Things are okay. Work is light right now, considering we have no guests. How about you, though? You doing okay? Where are you calling from?"

"I'm calling from the main house."

"Seriously?" Rodrigo sounded pleasantly surprised. "That's great."

"Yeah. I'm out on bail. Listen, are you in the barn?"

"Yeah."

"Any chance Leo's there with you?"

"Naw. He texted me this morning that he wasn't feeling well and wanted to take the day off. Since it was slow, I told him no problem."

"Have you talked to him since then?"

"No, I haven't heard from him. I can try to track him down for you."

"That won't be necessary, but thanks." Diego ended the call and turned to Elise.

"I guess we're headed to the bunkhouse?"

Without a word, he nodded, and they both pushed their chairs back from the table. Once outside, they took a golf cart to the bunkhouse. The once bustling ranch now seemed eerily silent with no guests around.

A few minutes later, they arrived at the bunkhouse. As they entered and looked around, Elise couldn't shake off the feeling of heaviness that seemed to permeate the air. "It's so quiet," she remarked, her voice breaking through the stillness.

Diego nodded in agreement. "Let's go check his room."

They walked down the hallway until they reached a door with Leo's name on it. Diego knocked twice, waiting patiently for a response. When none came, he tried again.

"Leo? It's Diego and Elise. Can we talk?" he called out, his voice echoing in the hallway.

"I don't think he's here," Elise spoke up after a moment of waiting. "Maybe he went out somewhere. Try calling him."

"More likely, he lied about being sick and went off to have fun," Diego muttered under his breath as he pulled out his phone to make the call. Moments later, they heard ringing coming from behind Leo's closed door.

"I don't like this," Elise voiced her unease.

Diego shared her sentiment as he knocked on the door once more. "Leo, are you in there?" Still no response. He tried the handle and found it unlocked. With a deep breath, he slowly pushed open the door and called out again. "Leo? I'm coming in."

Elise looked like she wanted to object but said nothing as he pushed the door open far enough to peer inside.

The first thing he noticed was the bed, neatly made. As he stepped further into the room, his gaze fell upon a pair of men's cowboy boots sticking out from the far side of the bed.

"Stay there," he commanded Elise, stepping cautiously into the room and moving toward the bed. Then he saw Leo lying on the floor, his body unnaturally still and lifeless. Foamy spittle dribbled from his slightly parted lips, and his complexion had turned a sickly gray. His eyes were wide open, staring blankly at the ceiling.

Feeling a sense of dread settle over him, Diego quickly knelt beside Leo's body and placed two fingers against his neck, searching for any sign of life.

"Is he alive?" Elise whispered from behind him, having followed him into the room.

Diego shook his head slowly. "No."

Elise's hand fluttered to her throat as she tried to make sense of the gruesome scene. The air was thick with an eerie stillness that seemed to permeate every corner of the room. It wasn't just the fact that Leo was dead that bothered her—there was something else, something unsettling and unnerving.

"I saw him just the other day," she said in disbelief. "He didn't seem sick to me."

"I don't think he was," Diego replied, gesturing towards the rubber band wrapped loosely around Leo's right arm and the spent syringe and needle lying close by. "I think he overdosed."

Her gaze flicked to the syringe and then back to Diego, who had pulled out his phone and was dialing a number.

"What are you doing?" she asked, her voice trembling slightly.

"Calling the police," he replied calmly.

As he spoke on the phone, Elise scanned the room for any clues or signs of what had happened. It all felt like a terrible nightmare that she couldn't wake up from.

"No," she heard Diego say into the phone. "I'm positive he's dead. He's already stiff as a board." A shiver ran down her spine at his words. "Yeah, of course. We won't touch anything. Fine. We'll wait for you outside the bunkhouse."

After hanging up, Diego motioned for Elise to follow him out of the room. Her legs shook as she tried to process everything that had happened. They made their way to the kitchen, where Diego reached under the sink and pulled out a pair of latex gloves.

"Put these on," he instructed, holding them out to her.

Confused and still in shock, Elise hesitantly put on the gloves. "What are these for?"

"I want to look around before the police arrive," Diego explained, putting on his own pair of gloves.

"But they said not to touch anything," Elise protested, already feeling guilty.

"So?" Diego replied with a shrug.

"What if we leave fingerprints?"

He held up his gloved hands in response. "Hence, the gloves."

Diego led them back to Leo's room, and Elise reluctantly followed, stopping in the doorway. She watched as he pulled out his phone and began taking pictures of the room from different angles.

"Okay," he said after a few minutes, satisfied with the photos he had taken. "Let's see what we can find."

Elise's voice was hesitant as she looked down at her shoes. "Wait! Shouldn't we cover our shoes?"

Diego shrugged, not bothering to look at her. "No need. The police already know we were in the room. It's how we discovered the body." He moved towards the body and took several more pictures before putting his phone away. Then he knelt beside the body again.

"Now, what are you doing?" she asked, bewildered.

"I want to see what's in his pockets." He glanced up at her. "Make yourself useful. Go check his desk."

Feeling a sense of urgency from Diego's tone, Elise quickly walked over to the desk and eyed its contents uncertainly. "What am I looking for?"

"I'm not sure," he admitted. "Just anything that seems out of place. Hurry, we don't have much time."

She quickly did as he requested, hoping she knew what she was looking for as she opened the top drawer. Moving items around, she found nothing that stood out as suspicious. With a frustrated sigh, she closed the drawer and moved on to the next one. This time, she found a stack of bank envelopes tucked against the side. Had Leo been old-fashioned and preferred paper bank statements?

Taking out her phone, she opened one and hurriedly snapped a picture of it before placing it back where it came from and selecting another. She'd just taken a picture of the fifth statement when she heard the distant wail of sirens approaching.

"Time's up," Diego said urgently.

A quick glance around the rest of the drawers revealed nothing of note, so Elise joined Diego in their retreat to the kitchen. He took her gloves and, along with his own, buried them in the bottom of the trash can before leading her outside to wait for the police.

CHAPTER THIRTY-ONE

"OKAY, LET'S TAKE IT from the top," Sam said in a no-non-sense tone. "Tell me what happened."

Diego and Elise recounted their story again, leaving nothing out except for their impromptu search of Leo's room. The three of them were sitting in the main room of the bunkhouse while Doc Niven and Dane were in Leo's room.

"Why did you want to talk to him?" Sam asked, her gaze shifting between the two of them.

"We talked to JoAnn earlier, and she told us she'd made three *El Muerto* costumes," Diego explained. "That's two more than I knew about, so I asked her who ordered them."

"Leo?" Sam asked with a knowing look.

Diego nodded solemnly. "Yes. Not only that, but he paid cash for them, and he was the one to pick up the second costume, which was about ten months ago. The third costume is still at JoAnn's."

"So, you decided to ask Leo about them." She said.

"Yeah. Rodrigo said Leo called in sick, so we went to the bunkhouse to talk to him. When we knocked on the door and got no answer, I called him," Diego explained.

"That's when we heard his phone ringing inside the room," Elise chimed in.

"We got worried and tried the door. It was unlocked, so I opened it." He paused. "We found Leo on the floor. I checked for a pulse but it was pretty obvious he was dead. That's when I called you."

Sam closed her notebook with a snap and looked thoughtful, like she was trying to piece together a puzzle. "Okay. I'll call you later if I have any more questions. Meanwhile, I'd like to question your staff."

"I can call Rodrigo and have everyone come to the bunkhouse," Diego offered.

Sam shook her head. "No. Ask them to meet me in the barn." Her expression was serious as she added, "For now, you two should head back to the house. We'll tape Leo's door shut when we finish, and I'd appreciate it if you'd tell your staff not to go into his room until I've released the scene."

Diego couldn't help but feel a sense of unease settle in his stomach at her words. He and Elise exchanged worried glances before standing up.

Sam's voice stopped them as they headed for the door. "Leo's death looks accidental, but I find the timing suspect. Don't leave town."

"You can't seriously think either of us killed Leo," Diego protested.

"There have been two deaths at the Double R in less than a week's time," Sam pointed out, her expression unreadable. "Of course you're a suspect. Both of you are."

Elise followed Diego into the house, her footsteps heavy with the weight of all that had transpired. When they reached the comfort of the family room, she sank onto the couch, feeling utterly drained. Diego sat beside her, his warmth a welcome presence as he slipped an arm around her shoulder and pulled her close.

As she leaned into him, Elise couldn't help but feel like everything that had happened was too surreal to comprehend. Her father murdered, her boyfriend arrested for it, and now Leo's sudden death. It was all too much for her mind to wrap around.

"Did you know about Leo's drug use?" she finally asked, turning to meet Diego's steady gaze.

Diego shook his head, his expression grave. "No. I didn't work with him as closely as the other guys, but if they knew something, I think one of them would have said something to me. Roy didn't tolerate that kind of behavior." He paused before adding, "But I don't think Leo was using drugs."

Confused, Elise furrowed her brows. "What do you mean? The needle was practically sticking out of his arm."

"I know," said Diego, his voice dropping lower. "But when I searched his pockets, I got a close look at his arms. They were clean. No track marks on either arm. Not even any old scars."

She considered this for a moment. "He could have injected himself somewhere less obvious, like between his toes."

"Yes," agreed Diego with a nod. "But why change to his arm now? And if he really was an addict, wouldn't we have seen some signs or evidence before this?"

Elise pondered this for a moment before looking back at Diego. "So maybe he wasn't a hardcore addict. Maybe he was just starting to experiment with drugs?"

Diego's eyes narrowed in contemplation. "I don't think so. Did you notice which arm the rubber band was wrapped around?"

Elise nodded, a sense of unease creeping over her. "His left arm."

"Exactly," said Diego with a raised eyebrow. "Which is interesting because Leo was left-handed."

Elise furrowed her brow, trying to recall if she had ever seen Leo write anything down. Then it hit her—the afternoon they spent drawing with the kids. He had pulled out his notebook and jotted down notes while she asked him to purchase a metal trough in town. She remembered how he held the notebook in his right hand but wrote with his left. The realization of Diego's implication hit her like a ton of bricks. "He couldn't have injected himself in the arm using his non-dominant hand, especially if he wasn't a regular drug user. Oh, my God!" The gravity of the situation dawned on her. "Leo was murdered!"

Diego's expression grew somber as he nodded slowly. "At first, I thought maybe because Leo ordered that third costume, that meant he killed your father," he mused. "Now, I'm wondering if your father's killer might be someone else and Leo knew who it was. Maybe he even knew why your father was killed, and because of that, he became a liability to the killer. "

"If only we had gotten the chance to talk to him," Elise lamented. Then a thought dawned on her. "Leo's notebook."

"Pardon me?"

"He had ADHD, so he had trouble remembering things. That's why he always carried around a notebook—to jot everything down. I'm sure he must have made notes about ordering those costumes. Maybe he even mentioned who they were for. We just have to find that notebook."

"Excellent idea," Diego said, nodding in agreement. "Did you see it when you searched his desk?"

She shook her head. "No, but he usually kept it in his front shirt pocket. You didn't find it when you checked his pockets?"

Diego shook his head sadly. "No, I didn't."

"That's odd. I don't think he'd go far without it," Elise murmured, her mind racing with possibilities. "Maybe it was on his dresser or nightstand?"

"I don't remember seeing a notebook, but let me check the pictures," Diego said, adjusting his position so he could pull his phone from his back pocket. Elise leaned in close, her scent of lavender and vanilla filling his senses. He tapped on the screen and navigated to his photos, flipping through several until he found a picture showing the nightstands. He enlarged the photo and they both peered at it closely.

"No notebook," Diego confirmed with a frown.

Next, he scrolled through more pictures until he came across the one of the dresser. Once again, he enlarged the photo, and they searched for any sign of the missing notebook.

There was no trace of it.

"I can't believe it's not there," Elise said with frustration. "Maybe the police will find it when they search his room."

Diego quickly retrieved Sam's contact information from his phone and placed the call. Elise listened intently as Diego asked Sam if they had found Leo's notebook.

"Hang on," Diego said into the phone before pressing the speaker icon. "Elise, tell Sam what the notebook looks like."

Focusing on her memories of that earlier day when she had spoken to Leo, Elise began describing the notebook. As she spoke, a feeling of unease settled over her. She couldn't shake the nagging thought that she had seen the notebook more recently.

That troubling thought consumed her so much that when Diego took the phone off speaker and continued talking to Sam, she'd stopped paying attention.

When did I see that notebook?

She closed her eyes and tried to summon the details. She'd seen it twice, and both times she remembered someone had torn a page out and given it to her.

The flash of memory struck Elise like a bolt of lightning, jolting her back to reality. She stood and reached into her back pockets, feeling around. They were empty. She switched to the front pockets and from the right pocket, pulled out a folded piece of paper.

With bated breath, she unfolded it and saw the familiar drawing of a hula dancer; the one from Leo's stop-motion film. The implication hit her like a punch in the gut.

Desperate to share her revelation, she smacked Diego's arm repeatedly until he turned to look at her with annoyance. Ignoring his irritation, she motioned for him to get off the phone.

Once he ended the call and gave her his full attention, she showed him the drawing.

"Cute," he remarked casually.

"No, I mean, yes, it's cute, but the point is, Leo drew this," Elise said urgently.

"Okay," Diego responded with confusion.

She frantically shook her head as she flipped the page to the other side. Then she held it out to him. "That's JD's writing."

"Okay," he repeated slowly. "Why are you supposed to call these people?"

She waved her hand dismissively. "They're criminal attorneys, but that's not the point," she explained, with a hint of frustration in her voice. "This morning, when I left the house to drive into town, I ran into JD. He said he came over to see how I was doing. I told him I needed to hire a good criminal attorney, and he said he knew of a couple of lawyers in Dallas. This notebook was in his truck. At the time, I thought the notebook looked familiar, but I was in a hurry and blew it off. It looked familiar because it was Leo's notebook. I can prove it. Hang on a second."

Elise jumped up from the couch and raced into the bedroom. Frantically, she searched for Leo's note, praying she hadn't absentmindedly thrown it away.

Finally, her gaze fell upon her drawing pad on the nightstand. She quickly flipped through the pages until she found the slip of paper with Leo's drawing. With determination in her stride, she took it back to Diego.

"Look," she demanded, holding out the note for him to see. Diego carefully compared it to the page JD had given her earlier. The size of the pages matched exactly, along with the color and spacing of each line. And most damning of all, the drawings of the hula dancer were undeniably similar, only able to have been drawn by one person.

The realization settled over Diego's face like a dark storm cloud brewing on the horizon. "What the hell was JD doing with Leo's notebook?" He turned his gaze on her. "Tell me again when you saw JD?"

"This morning. He was driving up the road from the barn."

"The same road that leads to the bunkhouse," Diego pointed out. She nodded, her thoughts spiraling in a direction she didn't like. "What was he doing? Did he say?"

"Well, he said he came over to see me and when I didn't answer his knock at the door, he thought I might be in the barn, so he went to see if I was there."

She fell silent; her gaze alternating between Diego's expression and the two pages, held side by side.

"There must be a logical reason JD had Leo's notebook," she finally said, trying to quell the uneasy feeling growing in her gut. "Maybe Leo dropped it on the road and JD found it?"

"Or maybe..." Diego trailed off, momentarily deep in thought. "JD took the notebook after killing Leo."

"What?!" The statement knocked the breath out of her and sent shivers down her spine. "Just because he was here this morning doesn't make him the killer. Why kill Leo?"

"Because JD killed your dad and Leo knew it."

Elise shook her head, refusing to believe it. "That's ridiculous. JD might be an ass, but he wouldn't kill anyone. I mean, why would he?"

"Yeah, you're right," Diego agreed, sounding confused. "It doesn't add up." He let out a heavy sigh. "Maybe Leo's death really was just an accidental overdose. Still, we should tell Sam that JD has Leo's notebook."

Elise's answer was the rumbling growl of her stomach, reminding her that it had been hours since they ate a late lunch. She looked over at Diego, who seemed lost in thought. "Are you hungry? I can make us a couple of plates of food," she offered.

"Yeah. Yeah, that'd be great," he replied absently. Then his expression changed as he remembered something. "Wait, did you take any pictures while we were in Leo's room?"

Elise reached down to the coffee table where she had set her phone earlier. "I found some bank statements in the desk drawer. There wasn't time to study them, so I took pictures of them." She activated her screen and went to her photos app. She found the first picture she had taken and handed the phone to Diego. "They start here."

"Do you mind if I stay here?" He asked. "I'll call Sam and then I'd like to look through these pictures while you work on food."

"Not at all," Elise replied with a smile before heading to the commercial kitchen to heat some leftovers in the microwave. When she returned to the main house with two steaming plates of food and two sodas, she was surprised to find Diego already sitting at the dining table with an odd look on his face.

"Is everything okay?" she asked, setting one plate in front of him.

Diego hesitated before responding. "Not sure," he admitted. "These bank statements show Leo has been making regular cash deposits for almost a year now. Two and three thousand dollars each time."

Elise raised an eyebrow. "Could it be his paycheck?"

"No," Diego replied firmly. "We do direct deposit."

She shrugged nonchalantly. "Still doesn't mean anything."

"True," Diego conceded. "But cash deposits suggest whoever is giving him the money doesn't want to leave a paper trail."

Elise took her time chewing her food, lost in thought as she considered Diego's words. "That doesn't necessarily mean JD gave him the cash," she pointed out after swallowing a mouthful.

Diego tilted his head in concession. "I called Sam," he said. "I asked if they had a time of death for Leo. She said she was okay telling me because Doc put it sometime between last night or early this morning, which means I have an alibi since I was in police custody during that time. So, I told her about JD being here and having Leo's notebook. She's going over there to talk to him."

Elise nodded and then they both fell into a comfortable silence, each lost in their own contemplations.

Their dinner was almost finished when Sam's call came through to Diego's phone. He answered, putting it on speaker for Elise to hear.

"Hey, Sam. You're on speaker," Diego greeted. "Elise is here with me. Did you talk to JD?"

"No, I went over there, but Beth said he left earlier this afternoon, headed over to San Antonio for business, and won't be back until tomorrow. Remind me again why this notebook is so important."

"Leo was meticulous about keeping notes in those notebooks," Elise stated with certainty. "He told me himself. We believe that whoever wanted those costumes must have been involved in my father's death and Leo may have written their name in his notebook."

Diego added in a low, grave tone, "We don't believe his death was accidental. Leo was left-handed."

There was a long pause on the other end of the line as Sam processed their words. The silence was finally broken by an audible sigh. "Elise, did you happen to ask JD how he got his hands on the notebook when you saw him this morning?" Sam's tone was calm, but urgent.

"No. At the time, I didn't realize it belonged to Leo," Elise admitted regretfully.

"I've asked Beth to let me know when JD returns," Sam said. "I appreciate you letting me know about the notebook, but from now on, I need you two to stay out of this investigation. You already have enough problems to deal with."

"That was underwhelming," Elise commented once the call ended.

Diego sighed, and Elise couldn't help but notice the weariness in his expression. It seemed like disappointment was becoming all too familiar for him.

"Do you want to watch TV for a while?" she asked after they'd finished their meal and taken care of the dishes. She was desperate for any distraction from their current situation.

"I'm pretty exhausted," he confessed wearily. "I didn't sleep much last night. Those cells aren't exactly built for comfort."

She went to him, slipping her arms around his waist. "I could be persuaded to go to bed," she purred, waggling her eyebrows suggestively.

He closed his arms around her, pulling her even closer, but a somber expression crossed his features as he looked down at her.

Then he bent his head and pressed his lips against hers, fanning the flame of her desire. When the tip of his tongue traced the seam of her lips, she eagerly opened for him, their tongues tangling in an enticing and erotic dance.

Lost in the moment, she hoped it would never end, but just as things were heating up, he suddenly pulled away and took a step back.

"I should go," he said quietly, releasing her from his embrace.

Her heart sank at his words, but she tried to hide the pain. "I thought maybe you could stay here tonight. With me."

His face grew serious and he shook his head. "Not tonight, Elise. There's a lot going on and I think it would be better for you if we kept some distance between us."

Before she could protest and remind him that she was a capable adult who could make her own decisions, he had turned and walked away, leaving her standing alone with a heavy heart.

Chapter Thirty-Two

Walking away from Elise after that kiss was one of the hardest things Diego had ever done. The kiss they shared was electric, igniting a fire within him that threatened to consume him whole. Imagining her lying beneath him, her eyes sparkling with desire, nearly caused him to stumble.

Damn it.

But turning back was not an option. He had a mission tonight, and he couldn't let his desires get in the way. Tonight would be his only opportunity, so he continued on, making his way to the garage where he borrowed a golf cart. He drove it to his bungalow and left it parked out front, knowing he would need it later.

Going inside, he booted up his laptop, thinking JD should have spent a little less money on his truck, watch and clothes, and a little more money on his home security. It took Diego only moments to hack into JD's system, granting him access to all the camera feeds. For the next few hours, he studied each camera carefully, memorizing their positions and angles. Most focused on the newly built barn with its high-tech keypad entry system.

Something about this setup piqued Diego's curiosity. Was JD really making all his money from training horses? Or was there something else going on in that barn? Something that led JD to murder Leo, because Diego had little doubt it was JD who'd killed the ranch hand.

He waited until ten o'clock, then opened a recording app and started recording the feeds from each of the cameras. He captured several minutes of no activity from each camera and then he set the digital recordings to run on a continuous loop.

Time was of the essence, and there was no room for elaborate plans. He could only hope that whoever monitored the camera feeds would be too disinterested to notice any discrepancies in the timestamp. As an added precaution, he synced the camera feeds to his phone so he could keep a close eye on them.

Slipping into his bedroom, he hastily changed into dark clothing, hoping to blend into the shadows. As he did, his mind raced with questions about JD's ranch hands. He had seen no sign of them on the cameras, but from his previous visit with Elise, he knew there were at least two men working for JD. Did they live on the property? Or did they live in town? The last thing he needed while snooping around was to run into someone patrolling the property.

Even as adrenaline surged through his veins, Diego couldn't ignore the danger involved in this mission. If Sam's intel proved to be wrong and JD returned home unexpectedly, things could go south quickly. It was a risk he was willing to take, especially now that Elise was a suspect in Leo's death. Leaving the bungalow, he hopped into the golf cart, making his way towards the back pasture under the cover of darkness.

Elise sat in her golf cart and watched Diego driving away. What was he up to? She couldn't shake off the unease that had been plaguing her since he'd left earlier. Too many questions had kept her awake. She had tried to distract herself with a book, but even that failed.

Fueled by a desperate need for answers, she had put on jeans and shoes. Then, because she was wearing a thin nightshirt, she threw a navy-blue hoody on over it. Commandeering the remaining golf cart, she had started toward Diego's bungalow, grateful for the faint glow of outdoor lights and the soft beams of moonlight lighting her path so she hadn't needed to turn on the headlights.

Her stomach was twisted in knots and with each passing second, doubts crept into her mind. She refused to let them get the best of her. If Diego's feelings for her had changed, she needed to know.

She had driven halfway to his bungalow when she spotted Diego leaving. Her heart had quickened with hope, thinking he had changed his mind and was coming back to her, but as she watched him drive off in the opposite direction, all hope disappeared, replaced by a mix of hurt and anger.

She watched as Diego's golf cart trundled along the dirt drive toward the barn and assumed he was going to check on the horses. Only he didn't stop. When he continued past the bunkhouse, her curiosity spiked. Instead of returning home like she should, she followed him all the way to the back pasture.

When she reached the gate, Diego was already disappearing over the top of the ridge. She waited, letting him completely disappear before following him, wondering if he was checking the locks on the side gates, worried about potential horse thieves.

With each passing minute, her curiosity grew, and she quickened her pace up the ridge. When she finally reached the top, Diego was nowhere to be seen. She strained her ears for the sound of his golf cart's engine but heard nothing over the sound of her own racing heart.

Deciding to check the east gate first, Elise made her way there slowly. The rough terrain and minimal moonlight made it difficult to navigate without headlights, but she didn't want Diego to know she was following him.

Arriving at the gate, she found Diego's abandoned cart with its keys still in the ignition, but there was no sign of Diego. Suddenly, a rustling of twigs caught her attention from somewhere off to her left. Her heart skipped a beat as she realized Diego was sneaking onto JD's property.

Parking her cart next to his, she deftly removed the loose padlock and carefully unwrapped the heavy chain so she could slip through the gate. The metal links clinked against each other, creating a soft symphony that seemed overly loud in the night's stillness. After re-wrapping the chain to its original position, she placed the padlock back in place without locking it.

As she turned around, her gaze fell on the No Trespassing sign. There was no logical reason for Diego to be sneaking onto JD's property in the middle of the night, and the sign was a reminder of the danger they were in.

Using the flashlight on her phone, she cautiously followed the familiar path through the dense trees that she and Diego had ridden on before. As she neared the edge of the wooded area, she quickly shut off the light, not wanting to attract any unwanted attention.

In complete darkness now, Elise relied on her other senses to guide her as she moved forward. She could feel Diego's presence nearby; could hear his quiet footsteps. With the trees blocking the moonlight, there was nothing but an all-consuming blackness that engulfed her.

A chill ran down her spine as she closed her eyes and took a few deep breaths, trying to steady her nerves. She knew she needed to give her eyes time to adjust to the dark surroundings.

When she opened them again, her vision was slightly better. She could make out faint shapes of trees and a lighter patch of ground ahead—most likely the clearing with the barns. She remembered from the other day that the trail came out between the big new barn and an older, smaller one.

Moving to the edge of the clearing, she scanned the older barn, taking in every detail. The faint glow of a lone lightbulb illuminated the front entrance but cast deep shadows over the rest of the structure. She strained her eyes, trying to make out any movement in the darkness.

And then, she saw it—a slight shifting of shapes to her left. She focused her gaze on the spot, straining her eyes to distinguish the figure from the shadows. The more she stared, the more convinced she became it was Diego.

She debated calling out to him, but the eerie stillness of the night made her hesitate. Any sound, even a loud whisper, seemed too loud in the peaceful darkness. Instead, she braved the open clearing and hurried towards the side of the barn.

Staying close to the wall, where she could remain hidden, Elise crept closer until she could finally make out Diego's form. When she was near enough, she reached out and tapped his shoulder.

In an instant, she went from standing behind Diego to flat on her back with all the air knocked out of her lungs, a foot pressed against her throat, cutting off her oxygen supply, and a hand twisting her arm at such an awkward angle, searing pain shot through her shoulder. Tears sprang to her eyes from a combination of physical agony, fear—and rage.

"Elise?" Diego's voice sounded far away as he looked down at her.

Did he really expect her to answer with his foot crushing her windpipe?

Fury surged within her, overriding her fear as she weakly pushed against his foot with her one free hand.

He lifted his foot and released her arm, leaving it limp and throbbing on the ground. She gasped for air, still glaring up at him in defiance and anger.

He leaned over her, and she felt the intensity of his gaze like a physical weight on her skin. She heard him mutter a curse under his breath as his features twisted in frustration or maybe anger.

He was mad at her?

The realization only fueled her own anger. Wincing in pain from her injured arm, she pushed herself into a sitting position with a burst of determination. When Diego reached out a hand to help her stand, she swatted it away with irritation. She didn't want his damn help.

With a supreme effort, she pushed herself off the ground and onto her feet, relieved when her trembling legs held her upright. Glaring at him, she rubbed her injured shoulder, trying to ease the persistent ache.

"What the hell?" she demanded in a loud whisper, unable to contain her anger.

"I'm sorry," his voice dropped lower with contrition, slightly lessening her irritation. "Are you okay?"

"Yeah, no thanks to you," she retorted petulantly.

"You shouldn't be here," he told her firmly.

"No shit. Neither should you."

His lips pursed together in a tight line, as if he was struggling to control his temper. "Go back home. Now."

"First, tell me what you're doing here," she challenged him.

"I think JD's story about training horses is crap. There's something else going on here, and it's related to why JD killed Leo. I want to know what it is."

"Okay," Elise nodded, understanding why he was there despite her annoyance. "I've thought about it and I'm staying." When he opened his mouth to argue with her once more, she raised her hand to stop him. "Two sets of eyes are better than one, and we're wasting time."

Diego let out a heavy sigh. "Fine, but stay close and keep your eyes peeled. I don't know if any of JD's ranch hands are lurking around," he warned, heading for the back of the barn.

The structure once housed cattle and had walls on three sides with an open entrance on the fourth side where the animals could enter and seek shelter from the elements. However, it had been years since the Drake ranch had any livestock, leaving the barn abandoned and falling into disrepair. Diego was curious to see if it was still being used for anything.

As they rounded the corner, he stopped in his tracks, his interest piqued.

Well, well. This was unexpected.

In the moonlight, he could just make out a line of sleek golf carts parked side by side at the back of the barn. Each one looked brand new, purchased within the past year or so. And there was a key in each ignition, with a slow-trickle battery charger attached to keep them charged.

Diego cautiously stepped inside the shelter, passing by the row of golf carts as he tried to peer beyond them into the darkness. Realizing it was too dark to see anything, he pulled out his phone and turned on the flashlight to give him a better view of what lay beyond, knowing the barn's walls would keep light from escaping.

"What's with the mini trailers?" Elise pointed to the small trailers hitched to each of the carts. "You think they use these to run hay to the horses?" Her tone suggested skepticism, and he couldn't blame her. If there were only a couple of horses on the property, there was no need for so many carts and trailers.

Diego moved closer to inspect one of the trailers, noting that there was no dried grass inside. Confused but not concerned, he was about to leave when Elise stopped him.

"Wait," she whispered, pulling him towards the corner. "There's something over there."

In the dim light, he could just make out three 55-gallon containers standing in the corner. Diego pushed on them. One was full and wouldn't budge, but the other two felt empty. He ran the beam of his light down the side of one, spotted the stamped lettering and read aloud. "Acetone. Hazardous. Use caution."

Elise gave a soft huff of laughter. "That's a lot of fingernail polish remover." Diego gave her a questioning look, and she waved off her own comment. "I'm kidding. You know as well as I do that JD's not operating a beauty salon out here. But seriously, why would he need that much acetone?" Her voice sounded full of curiosity.

Diego had a guess, but he hoped he was wrong. Until he had more proof, he kept his thoughts to himself and merely shrugged.

"Let's keep looking," he suggested.

They moved cautiously through the dimly lit corners of the barn, their footsteps echoing off the metal walls. In one corner, they stumbled upon a pair of tall, narrow cylinders made of cold, unyielding metal.

"Gas tanks," Diego said, whispering. "No labels," he added after checking them.

They continued on, passing the rows of golf carts before reaching the outside of the barn.

"What now?" Elise asked uncertainly.

"Let's check out the new barn," he replied, his voice low and serious.

"Aren't there security cameras?" she questioned nervously.

He pulled out his phone and checked the feeds, relieved to see that his recorded footage was still playing. "They won't be a problem," he assured her.

Ignoring her curious look, he led the way towards the new barn. As they approached, he noticed that there was no rear entrance—a red flag in itself. Continuing to the front, he saw there was only a single front door with dimensions similar to those of a typical house door. It was definitely too narrow to accommodate livestock.

"Do you know the code?" Elise whispered, staring at the numeric keypad.

He scowled in frustration. Maybe with enough time, he could hack through the security system—but that was not an option right now.

"Let's try the windows," he said instead, gesturing to the row of five narrow side windows positioned along the top of the wall. They were specifically designed to let in light and air, but not to allow anyone or anything else inside.

Elise looked up at them skeptically before turning back to Diego. "And how do we get up there?"

He smiled mischievously and linked his fingers together, extending his arms downwards. "I'll give you a boost."

The corners of Elise's mouth dropped in disbelief. "You've got to be kidding?" she blurted out, staring at him with a mix of shock and amusement. She knew he wasn't teasing her, but she still searched his face for any signs of deceit. This wouldn't be the first time he'd boosted her up so they could spy through someone's window—ah, misspent youth—but not only were they both older, they were also taller and, if she fell, the ground was a long way down.

Still, she was as curious as he was about what might be in that barn. Ignoring the breadth of Diego's shoulders and the strength beneath her hands, she grabbed onto him and placed her right foot on his interlaced hands.

As he lifted her, she wobbled for a moment, but he steadied her until she found her balance. Slowly, she released him and, pressing her palms against the side of the barn, stood tall. Then she peered through the window into a room illuminated by dim lights. The unexpected sight surprised her. The inside was filled with strange equipment that she couldn't immediately identify. Then it hit her. She was looking at a chemistry lab.

Slowly reaching into her back pocket, she retrieved her phone and activated the video app with one hand while using the other for support. She held the device up to the window, hoping to capture some clear images for later analysis.

After a few minutes of recording, she turned off the video and stowed her phone back in her pocket. Now came another challenge.

"How do I get down?" she asked nervously. The ground looked so far away.

"Right hand against the barn and left hand on my head. Hang on."

Following his instructions, she steadied herself as he lowered her until she could easily jump to the ground.

"What'd you see?" he asked once she was standing beside him.

She shook her head, still slightly dizzy from the height. "I don't know, but I took a video of the inside. We can review it later. Can we go now?"

"Not yet," he said, looking around. "I want a quick look in the front barn. Plus, I noticed some horse trailers parked off to the side and I want to see what's inside."

She felt a surge of fear at the thought of getting caught. "Are you crazy? Those trailers are too close to the main house. Someone could see us."

"Except no one's home, remember?"

"Except Mrs. Drake—"

"Who is sound asleep and won't hear a thing." His confidence was both reassuring and terrifying.

"What if she does and calls the police?" she argued.

"You're right," he conceded. "No point in both of us getting caught. Stay here and keep watch."

She stared after him in shock as he took off for the first barn. "Oh, hell no." With every step plagued with misgivings, she followed after him.

The night air was warm and heavy with the scent of hay and manure. As they approached the first barn, she realized that someone had left both the front and rear barn doors slightly open for ventilation.

Taking advantage of the rear opening, they slipped inside quietly. A horse whinnied in greeting from somewhere in the darkness, but otherwise the barn was silent except for their soft footsteps on the dirt floor.

Diego and Elise moved cautiously along the sides of the barn, staying in the shadows where the orange glow from the dusk-to-dawn lamp out front couldn't quite reach. As they inspected each stall and room, they counted four horses nestled inside, while eight stalls stood empty. The feed room was well-stocked with bundles of fragrant hay and bags of grain, while the tack room held an array of gleaming harnesses, bridles, and saddles, along with brushes and combs for grooming.

As they approached the ladder leading to the second level, Diego motioned for Elise to stay below while he climbed up. She shifted nervously as she waited for him to return. Every sound seemed amplified in the darkness. In the distance, a dog barked, and she could hear the faint rustling of mice somewhere above.

When Diego finally descended from the ladder, Elise looked at him hopefully, but he only shook his head, signaling that everything seemed normal upstairs. He motioned for her to follow him to the back of the barn, where they slipped out through the rear entrance.

Once outside, Diego pulled Elise close and whispered in her ear. "The trailers are parked over there." He pointed discreetly to the side of the barn.

They crept to the corner and peered around it, spotting six horse trailers parked a short distance away. Diego took Elise's hand firmly in his.

"Ready?" he asked quietly. She nodded, feeling a surge of courage at his touch. "Let's go."

Keeping low to avoid detection, they sprinted across a small clearing towards the parked trailers, their footsteps muffled by soft grass underfoot.

They stopped behind the last trailer, peering cautiously around for any signs of movement or alarms. When none were present, Elise let out a tense breath of relief. She followed Diego as he moved to stand between the last two trailers, his focus shifting to the windows of each one. Elise kept watch on the nearby house, her senses on high alert.

Diego touched her arm and gestured for them to move to the next set of trailers. They repeated the process, with him checking the trailers while she kept watch for any potential threats.

As they made their way up the row of trailers, everything went smoothly until they reached the second one. It was larger than the others, with enough space for four horses to ride comfortably inside. There were no open windows to peek through, making it difficult to see what was inside.

Elise suggested moving on to the next trailer, but Diego shook his head determinedly. He cast a quick glance at the house before moving to the back of the trailer. With bated breath, Elise watched as he expertly undid the back gate latches and slowly lowered the trailer door to the ground. Before she could protest or stop him, he ran up the ramp and disappeared inside.

Her stomach clenched with fear as she turned back to keep watch on the house. Then she froze, her eyes widening in panic as twin lights appeared around the side of the house.

Headlights? Surely not. Sam had said JD wouldn't be returning until tomorrow and Mrs. Drake would never go out alone and return this late at night.

Elise's heart raced as the sound of tires grew louder, her mind racing with potential scenarios. "Diego!" She hissed urgently. "Someone's coming."

Time seemed to slow down as the sound of tires crunching on gravel grew louder and louder. Anxiety clenched at her stomach—they were running out of time to get away unnoticed.

Crouching behind one of the trailers, she peered around its side and watched in horror as the vehicle passed by the main house and continued down the long driveway towards the barns. It wasn't until it came to a stop beneath the glowing dusk-to-dawn lamp that she recognized the truck. When the door opened, JD climbed out.

From her hidden vantage point, Elise watched as JD stood in the open doorway of his truck, his silhouette outlined by the glow from inside. His broad frame and confident stance gave off an air of authority as he peered across the clearing, to the darkened area where the trailers were parked. Then he pulled his phone from his pocket and placed a call.

Elise strained to hear his voice as he spoke into the phone, the sound carrying easily across the distance.

"Hey. I just got home." A pause. "Yeah, I know, but I got done early. Where are you?" Another pause. "I thought I heard something. Get over here and help me check it out."

For a long while, JD continued to stare at the trailer after putting his phone back in his pocket. Then he reached into his truck and when he turned around again, he was holding a gun.

Elise's mind raced in panic at the sight of the weapon. If JD found Diego snooping around in his trailer, there was no telling what he would do. She couldn't let that happen.

Her mind quickly searched for a way out of this situation. She could step forward and pretend she was alone, try to distract JD with small talk or flirtation while Diego made his escape. As she played out each scenario in her head, they all seemed unrealistic and unlikely to work.

Desperate for a solution, her gaze fell to the ground, where she spotted several rocks scattered about. A memory from her childhood came rushing back—a trick she used to play when she and Diego played Hide-n-Seek.

Elise's hand darted out and quickly selected a small, strawberry-sized rock from the ground. She threw it as hard as she could at the barn. The noise it made when it hit echoed loudly.

Immediately, JD took off in that direction and Elise whirled around, her heart racing. She almost collided with Diego as he came up behind her in a hurry.

"We have to leave," he growled urgently.

"Thank you, Captain Obvious!" she snapped sarcastically.

When he started to head towards the barn, she grabbed his arm and shook her head. "JD is over there," she whispered urgently. "Follow me."

Without waiting for a response, she took off in the opposite direction, as if being chased by hounds from Hell. Her destination was an old shed on the property used to store tractors back when JD's grandfather leased the neighboring property for hay farming. The Drake family had left it behind when they stopped leasing the property, and over time, it had fallen into disrepair. During their teenage years, Elise and JD had often snuck away to make out in that very shed.

Now, as she dodged trees and felt sticker bushes snagging at her pants legs, she prayed that JD's father had never gotten around to tearing down the shed. With her heart pounding in her ears, it was difficult to hear anything else. Fear drove her forward at an even faster pace as she raced towards their hiding spot, hoping that in the darkness of night, she was heading in the right direction.

Sprinting through the sparse forest, her feet pounded against the uneven ground. She couldn't tell how long she had been running or how far they had gone, but her lungs were burning, and she had to slow to a walk. As she caught her breath, she looked around for any sign of the shed she was searching for. Panic started to set in as they continued on and still she saw no sign of it.

Then, as they burst through a grouping of trees, the dilapidated shed loomed in front of them. The sight of it brought them both to a stop, and they listened intently for any sound of JD running after them. If they'd made a clean escape, they could simply follow the fence line to the very back of the property and then cut over to their side.

Then the sound of someone coming through the brush filtered to them and they both moved toward the shed. As they approached, Elise noticed that the front double doors were now padlocked, a recent addition.

She led Diego around to the side of the shed, where there was a smaller door. She grasped the knob and turned it, relieved when it moved easily, but when she pushed on the door, it only opened a few inches before stopping. Something inside was blocking it. Behind her, she heard Diego's frustrated sigh. Then, he stepped forward to help.

Bracing themselves against the door, the pushed with all their strength, but it stubbornly refused to budge any further. "Looks like we'll have to make a run for it," Diego muttered.

Elise refused to give up that easily. "Maybe not."

With her heart racing, she hoped that whoever placed the padlock on the door hadn't remembered about the loose metal panel on the side. Praying that it hadn't been fixed or secured, she made her way to the corner of the shed. As she reached for the panel, she couldn't help but remember how she and JD had discovered it while making out one afternoon.

With a hopeful glance at Diego, she pulled on the panel and was relieved when it gave way easily. She motioned for him to follow as she crawled inside, grateful for their stroke of luck.

With moonlight streaming in past the broken pane of glass in the side window, the inside of the shed was dark but not pitch black. As her eyes adjusted, Elise began to make out shapes.

To her surprise, the once empty shed now held a sleek, dark-colored car parked inside. Whoever had brought it here had carefully backed in with just enough room for the driver to exit. This explained why they couldn't open the side door from the outside. JD wouldn't be able to open it either, so unless he remembered the loose paneling, JD would have to open the front double doors to see inside, and hopefully, he didn't carry around the key to the padlock.

Elise resigned herself to waiting and was glad for Diego's company, especially when she heard a hissing noise.

She froze. "What was that?" Images of snakes slithering below filled her thoughts.

Diego didn't answer, but instead used the light from his phone to search the ground by their feet. After a moment, he dropped to his knees and carefully reached under the car.

"Here kitty, kitty," he called out in a soft voice. "There's a good kitty, kitty."

Elise watched in amazement as he stretched out his arm and gently retrieved a cat from underneath the car. She took the feline into her arms, worried it might protest, but it settled comfortably and purred softly as she stroked its fur.

She turned to Diego with a smile, only to find him preoccupied with studying the car.

"What's the matter?" she asked.

"I've seen this car before," he replied, his gaze never leaving the vehicle. "Howard Drake drove a car like this."

Elise's brow furrowed in confusion. "Are you sure? JD said his father left town."

Diego's expression was clouded with uncertainty. "Unless he didn't." His words hung in the air, lingering like a question that had yet to be answered.

Just then, a sudden gust of wind blew across her neck, causing her to shiver. The cat in her arms hissed and leaped from her grasp, landing gracefully on the trunk of the car. Its back arched and its fur stood on end as it stared intently at something on the vehicle's surface. Elise reached out to retrieve the cat but froze when she noticed a fresh rub mark in the dust coating the car.

"Diego!" she whispered urgently, grabbing his arm and pointing towards the mark.

Together, they tried to step back, only to realize there was nowhere to go—they were already standing against the wall of the shed.

Mesmerized by what was happening before their eyes, they watched as new rub marks appeared on the dusty surface and letters began to take shape.

O

P

E

N

"What the—?!" Elise exclaimed, taken aback by what she was witnessing.

"Ghost," Diego stated matter-of-factly, reminding Elise that she had been away from their haunted town for too long. "The question is, whose ghost?"

She continued to watch with wide-eyed fascination as he slipped around to the driver's side of the car until he could reach the door.

"Wait," Elise whispered as he started to open the door. She bent down to retrieve the cat, then she nodded for him to proceed.

With a gentle tug, he opened the door and reached inside.

Elise couldn't help but jump when she heard the snick of the trunk lid coming unlatched. A minute later, Diego rejoined her behind the car and lifted the lid.

The reeking stench of death wafted through the air, causing them to double up, heaving and coughing. Desperately regaining their composure, they anxiously leaned closer, struggling to see into the murky darkness. Diego hastily pulled out his phone, tapping frantically on the flashlight app.

At first, Elise was perplexed by what she saw. From beneath a mass of plastic sheeting, a ghastly brown liquid oozed out. Beneath it lay something that sent shivers down her spine.

The cat meowed in her arms, sensing her fear, and nearly escaped. Lurching forward to grab it, Elise bumped the rear of the car, jostling its contents and sending a chunk of plastic sliding away. An object rolled out from between the folds.

Elise stared at it for what felt like an eternity before reality hit her; they had stumbled upon something far worse than they could have imagined.

Chapter Thirty-Three

ELISE'S HEART JOLTED IN terror, her eyes locked on the withered human forearm and hand that had slipped out of the plastic sheeting. In her panic, she collided with a precariously balanced wall shelf, sending it crashing to the ground along with several cans of paint.

"Who's there?" JD's voice boomed from outside the shed, causing Elise and Diego to freeze. They had been so consumed with the gruesome discovery that they hadn't heard him approach.

With her heart pounding in her chest, Elise turned to Diego for guidance. He gestured for her to move to the side, away from the window. As JD's heavy footsteps drew closer, Diego grabbed a dried mud dauber's nest from the shelf.

Through the broken windowpane, Elise watched JD step into the moonlit clearing, his gun gleaming in one hand as he used his phone's flashlight app to guide his way.

"I know someone's in there," he shouted. "Leave now and I won't call the police. *Vete y no llamaré a la policía.*" His use of Spanish told Elise he thought illegals were taking refuge for the night in his shed. Not an uncommon occurrence this far south. "Last chance," he growled, moving closer. "*Sal de aquí.*" Get out of here.

With a swift movement, Diego hurled the dried nest through the broken windowpane. It landed, making a small noise in the woods. The second JD turned, Diego grabbed the cat from Elise and shoved it out the window.

The feline let out a piercing yowl as it landed on the ground below, causing Elise to fear for its safety. Before she could even process her concern, JD cursed under his breath.

"Damn cat," he grumbled, before retreating into the shadows.

Elise and Diego remained frozen in terror, afraid that he would return any moment and discover their deception.

Finally, after what felt like an eternity, it seemed JD had fallen for their ruse with the cat and was now searching for them elsewhere.

Diego's voice was barely audible as he cautiously whispered, "I think he's gone. We should go."

Elise nodded in agreement, but her eyes were drawn to the gruesome sight within the trunk of the car. "What do we do about that?" she asked nervously.

Diego let out a resigned sigh. "What can we do? We shouldn't even be here."

"We can't just leave it," Elise persisted.

After a moment of tense silence, Diego raised his phone. "I'll take pictures. Maybe we can send them to Sam anonymously."

As he started snapping photos of the decaying body inside, Elise's eyes fixated on the ugly, yellow-faced wristwatch still clinging to the withered arm by a strand of dried tissue. A chill ran down her spine as she realized where she had seen it before. Her heart nearly skipped a beat as she grabbed Diego's arm and pointed at the watch, her voice barely above a whisper. "That's Howard Drake's watch."

He leaned closer to get a better look, his expression grim. Then he nodded, confirming her suspicions. Howard Drake had not abandoned his wife, nor had he left town. Someone had murdered him.

"We need to tell JD what we found," she said, her voice trembling.

Diego turned; his expression unreadable. "Do you honestly think JD doesn't know his father's body is in this shed?"

Her heart raced. "You can't possibly believe he killed his own father."

"That's exactly what I believe," Diego replied, his voice cold and calculated. "How many people do you think know about this shed?"

She opened her mouth to argue, but he placed his hand on her arm to stop her. "Can we discuss this after we're back at our place?" He peered out the window and then, apparently satisfied that JD was no longer out there, waiting for them, he guided her over to the back panel and held it while she slipped through. Then she held it for him as he followed her.

"Let's go." He took her hand and they started walking, heading toward the back of the property. They'd only taken a couple of steps when they heard someone shout.

"Over here!"

"Damn it," JD shouted from further away. "Stop them."

Elise's mind raced as they broke into a run.

The sound of gunfire shattered the night air and propelled them forward even faster. The realization that they were being hunted like animals filled Elise with rage and terror. How could JD do this? How could he shoot at them without hesitation?

Then another thought entered her mind—if JD could kill his own father, then he was capable of anything.

With a renewed sense of urgency and fear, she ran alongside Diego towards safety, hoping against hope that they would make it out alive.

Diego's hand clasped hers tightly as they raced through the dense underbrush, tearing through bushes and branches that clawed at their skin. Gunshots echoed through the air, causing Elise to flinch with each deafening blast. She could feel her heart pounding in her chest, expecting at any moment to be struck by a bullet or see Diego crumple beside her.

They kept running until finally reaching the end of JD's fenced property. With a swift motion, Diego pulled apart two strands of barbed wire and Elise crawled through. As soon as she was on the other side, she mimicked his stance and held the strands apart for him.

Both of them were gasping for breath and her arm stung where a tree limb or bramble had scratched her. Ignoring the discomfort, Elise followed Diego over the slight rise in the land until they were on the other side. Then they slowed to a walk.

"We're safe now," Diego panted. "This is state property, but we can't let our guard down. We'll keeping walking until we're behind Double R property."

Elise's mind raced with fear and adrenaline as she followed Diego, her legs burning from exertion and her wounded arm throbbing with pain. She couldn't shake the thought of JD waiting for them, gun in hand.

"Do you think he knows it was us?" she asked, trying to keep her voice steady.

"I don't know," Diego replied grimly. "But I made sure there would be no evidence on his security cameras. And he never got a clear look at us. All he knows is that two trespassers tried to spend the night in his shed."

"If JD goes into the shed, he'll know someone discovered the body." The realization hit Elise like a freight train, causing her to feel nauseous and weak. "What if he moves it before we can tell someone?"

Diego shook his head. "If he thinks we're illegals, he'll know the last thing we'd do is go to the police. He won't risk moving the body unnecessarily."

She couldn't argue with his logic, yet it offered little comfort. They continued walking, Elise's body trembling with every step. Every muscle screamed in protest, begging for rest and safety.

Finally, Diego stopped and turned to her. His face was grim and determined as he spoke. "I'm going to see where we are," he told her, his voice low and urgent. "Stay here. If you hear shooting, call the police."

Elise nodded, unable to form words as he disappeared into the darkness. Every second felt like an eternity as she stood alone, listening to the eerie silence broken only by her own heavy breathing. Then, just when she thought she couldn't take it anymore, she heard approaching footsteps. Her body tensed instinctively, but relief washed over her when Diego reappeared.

"All clear," he announced, his voice barely above a whisper. "Let's go." He reached out to take her upper arm, intending to assist her, but she cried out in pain.

"You're hurt!" he exclaimed, releasing her arm, concern etched on his face.

"It's nothing," she dismissed, trying to brush off his worry. "I think a tree limb scratched me. We'll clean it up at the house."

He didn't look convinced, but perhaps realizing now was not the time to discuss it, he gestured for her to follow him. Just as they had when leaving JD's property, when they reached the Double R fence, Diego held strands of the barbed wire apart for her to crawl through, then followed her when she did the same for him.

They walked for several minutes until they reached the tank where the cattle stood in a loose group, with heads down, resting for the night. Diego led Elise through the center of the group, their silhouettes blending in with the shadows of the animals. The rustling of grass and the occasional lowing of a cow filled the air as they made their way across the pasture.

"Can you drive?" Diego asked when they finally reached the waiting golf carts. Elise nodded silently, her heart pounding with nerves and adrenaline. "You go on to the house," he continued, his hand gently guiding her towards the cart. "I'm going to lock the gate and then I'm right behind you."

The trip to the house passed in a blur for Elise. Fear still pulsed through her veins as she worried about getting shot during the drive through the pasture. She only felt safe once she was on the path that led past the bungalows.

Finally reaching the garage, she parked the golf cart and shut off the engine. Exhausted from the events of the night, she closed her eyes and leaned forward in the seat, allowing herself a moment to rest.

Before she knew it, Diego was standing beside her, gently shaking her awake. "Come on, Elise," he said softly. "Let's get inside."

Feeling grateful for his presence and support, she took his offered hand and let him help her out of the cart. As they walked towards the house, his arm slipped around her waist, providing a sense of comfort and protection. She was relieved when he locked the door behind them upon entering the main house. It may have been unlikely for JD to come after them, but this added security brought some peace of mind.

Diego carefully guided her through the darkened halls of the house, his hand warm and reassuring on her back. As they reached the bathroom attached to her bedroom, he flicked on the light switch. As she caught sight of her reflection in the large mirror above the sink, she noticed a dark stain on the right sleeve of her hoody. Her heart raced as she pulled at the fabric to inspect the rip made by the tree branch, only to find it wet with something warm and sticky.

Blood.

"I guess the tree limb got me worse than I thought," she said weakly, trying to downplay her injury. She went to remove her hoody, but as she raised her right arm to grip the hem, a sharp pain shot through her and she let it drop back down at her side.

"Let me help," Diego offered, taking hold of the cuff of her left sleeve. "Let's start with this arm."

Diego helped her out of her hoody and gently probed the wound on her arm with his fingertips. "A tree branch didn't do this," he said, his voice grim. "A bullet did."

Her heart skipped a beat. "What?" She was sure she had misheard him.

"One of those bullets grazed you," Diego said somberly, pointing to the nasty gash across the outside of her upper arm that had bled so profusely it had stained her entire arm red.

The sight of her own blood, combined with the realization of how close she'd come to dying, made her light-headed.

Elise's vision tunneled and vertigo hit, causing her to sway unsteadily. "God. I think I'm going to faint or puke. Or maybe both."

As her knees began to buckle, Diego caught her and lowered her gently to the floor. She barely registered the soft towel he placed beneath her right arm, or the rolled up one he put under her feet. The room swirled in her peripheral vision as she struggled to stay conscious. She had never considered herself squeamish, but she'd never seen so much of her own blood.

Closing her eyes tightly, Elise focused on staying awake. With her legs elevated and the blood rushing back to her head, she started feeling better.

After a few minutes, she heard Diego moving about near her. She felt him gently lifting her arm and running a warm washcloth across her skin, careful to avoid the wound. Then he placed her arm back on the floor and stood.

The sound of running water reached her ears, and she knew he was rinsing the cloth. He returned to her side and continued wiping away the blood with gentle strokes.

Finally feeling stable enough, Elise opened her eyes. The first thing she saw was Diego's intense expression—his brow furrowed, and jaw clenched with anger. His gaze shifted from the wound on her arm to meet hers.

"If this had been a few more inches to the left..." his words trailed off, the unsaid meaning hanging heavy in the air.

Elise could see how upset he was and reached up with her left hand to stroke his cheek in reassurance.

"Diego," she murmured softly. "I'm fine."

He shook his head, his expression still fierce. "No, Elise. You've been shot."

The words echoed in her mind, but it was hard to process their meaning. Shot? It all seemed so unreal.

"That Motherfucker shot you," Diego growled, his anger bubbling over. "I'll fucking kill him."

Taking a deep breath, she reminded herself that the worst was over. She was alive and relatively unharmed, all things considered. The shock of what had happened hit her in waves, each one more overwhelming than the last. Her heart raced and her hands shook as she tried to steady herself.

"JD didn't know who he was shooting at," she said weakly.

Diego shot her a sharp look. His jaw clenched. "That doesn't make it okay," he growled.

He was right, but they had more pressing matters to worry about now. Images of Howard Drake's decomposing corpse filled her head, making her stomach churn.

"We have to tell Sam about Howard," she moaned.

"I know," he agreed. "But first, I need to take care of this wound. I should probably take you to the hospital."

"No," she protested. "If they recognize it as a gunshot wound, they'll have to report it. Just do the best you can."

"Okay," he said with a nod. "Let me grab the first aid kit from the kitchen. I'll be back in a second."

"That's fine," she sighed. "I'm not going anywhere."

She must have drifted off for a moment because Diego returned before she knew it, holding a small red box in his hands.

"How are you feeling?" he asked gently.

"Better," she whispered.

"Good," he replied with a smile. "Do you think you can stand long enough to take a shower? It'll be the quickest way to wash away all the blood and clean your wound."

She closed her eyes, considering his words. The rush of adrenaline that had propelled her across JD's property was gone now, leaving behind an overwhelming sense of exhaustion. Diego was right—she would feel much better if she could just get clean. So, she opened her eyes and nodded.

"I think I can." Her voice was barely above a whisper.

"Good. Let me help you." Slipping a hand beneath her back, he helped raise her into a sitting position. She gave herself a moment to adjust to sitting and make sure she didn't feel dizzy. When Diego offered her a hand, she took it and allowed him to help her stand.

As he turned the shower on for her, she attempted to remove her night shirt, but the pain in her injured arm was too great. She winced as she struggled with the fabric, feeling helpless and frustrated.

"Can you please help me take these clothes off?" she asked, turning to face him.

"Of-of course." Something in his tone drew her gaze to his face. His expression told her nothing, but he couldn't hide the longing in his eyes or the way his gaze traveled down her body, staring at her unbound breasts pushing against the thin fabric of the cotton T-shirt. Warm desire spread through her, causing her nipples to harden. When she saw the slight widening of his eyes, she knew he'd noticed.

He cleared his throat as he fingered the hem of her shirt. "I think this shirt is ruined." Before she could reply, he ripped the shirt up the front. For a moment, he simply stared at her, standing exposed before him. Then he swallowed hard and eased the torn pieces of shirt down her arms.

"It's easier to get off like that," he mumbled, dropping the remnants to the floor. She toed off her shoes and kicked them to the side. Then, with trembling hands, Diego carefully removed her jeans and underwear. As she stepped free of them, she met his gaze and the heat she saw there made her insides warm and liquid. When he started for the door, she realized how much she didn't want him to leave.

"Will you stay?" she asked, surprising herself.

He paused for a moment before nodding slowly. "If you want me, too."

She nodded in response and then stepped into the shower. The warm water felt like bliss against her skin as she stood beneath the spray, letting the water cascade over her body, washing away the blood and dirt. Then the shower door opened and Diego, nude and magnificent, stepped inside.

Diego was gentle but efficient as he washed her body with slow, circular motions, starting with her shoulders and working his way downward. His touch made it difficult for Elise to focus on anything other than how good it felt to be so close to him. She closed her eyes and just enjoyed the moment until he reached the wound in her arm.

"This is going to hurt a bit," he said softly before cleaning it gently with soap and water. Even though his movements were careful, Elise winced when he touched it but soon enough, he was done.

Once she was clean, she stood and watched unabashedly as Diego washed himself, unable to resist running her hand across his soapy chest. She sighed, amazed that she could feel this content under the circumstances.

When they finished, Diego got out first and wrapped a towel around his waist. Then he helped her dry off and when they were done, he helped her to the bed, where he used the first aid kit to treat and bandage her wound.

"Will you stay with me tonight?" She asked, running her hands through his hair before cupping his face and pressing a soft kiss to his lips.

He responded eagerly, deepening the kiss until they were both panting for air. Joining her in bed, he rolled them so that she was on top of him and then lifted her off just enough to slide into her. She gasped at the sensation of him filling her completely before starting a slow rocking motion that made them both groan in pleasure. Together, they moved with increasing intensity as their passion built.

"I love you," he murmured just before they exploded in ecstasy.

Afterwards, they lay tangled in each other's arms until both of their breaths slowed.

"I love you, too," Elise whispered to him. His arms momentarily tightened around her, letting her know he'd heard.

Seconds later, they slipped into a deep sleep, exhausted from the night's events but content in the knowledge that no matter what the future may bring, they would always have this moment of perfect bliss.

Chapter Thirty-Four

THE SUN PEEKED THROUGH the window the next morning as Elise and Diego sat at the kitchen table, savoring a breakfast of crispy bacon and fluffy pancakes. Diego was watching the video she'd taken when he suddenly paused it, his eyes going wide in shock.

"Look at this," he said, pointing at the two large metal cylinders with connecting tubes.

"What in the world?" she asked, staring at the photo. "It looks like the set of *Breaking Bad*."

"That might be closer to the truth than you think."

"What do you mean?"

"You remember the barrels of acetone we found in the back barn? You wondered what JD used them for? One use is the manufacturing of drugs."

Elise took the phone from him and stared at the picture on the screen. Then she handed the phone back to him. "No." She shook her head. "It's ridiculous." Diego said nothing, continuing to study the pictures. "Diego?"

"I don't know, Elise. It would explain a lot."

"Like what?"

"For starters, it explains why he needs all that security at his place. I noticed he gets a lot of horse trailers showing up at his place, but never seems to have more horses. It would make sense if those trailers were delivering the raw materials he needs to manufacture drugs. Plus, no one would suspect the former high school star quarterback of manufacturing drugs at his ranch, so it's a perfect cover."

Elise didn't want to consider the possibility, but now he had her thinking about it. "I guess it would also explain how he has the money to spend on a new truck, a Rolex and those fourteen-thousand dollar boots he's so proud of." It was making more sense to her. "And why he doesn't know the difference between a snaffle bit and a curbed bit for training horses."

Diego nodded his agreement. "And now I think I understand why he has all those golf carts and why there are tire tracks across our pasture."

Elise furrowed her brow. "What do you mean?"

"It's risky for him to transport the drugs through town, but why should he when the main road out of town is just on the other side of our property?"

"You think he's loading drugs into those trailers behind the golf carts and driving them across our pasture to waiting transport vehicles on the main road?"

He nodded. "I do."

"Wouldn't someone have noticed him doing that?"

"Not if he did it while *El Muerto* was making his ride."

"But the timing. How would they know?"

He huffed out a breath. "Same way we do. Because he's *El Muerto*."

Understanding dawned. "The second costume that Leo ordered. It was for JD."

"It fits, doesn't it? He, or someone working for him, wears the costume and impersonates *El Muerto*. It's the perfect distraction. While everyone's attention is on *El Muerto*, his men slip across the pasture unnoticed."

Elise thought about it and had to agree it made sense. Then she remembered something else. "And *El Muerto* rode the night my father was killed."

"Sam assumed it was me because I was scheduled to ride that night, but I didn't because the real *El Muerto* showed up. Only, it wasn't the real *El Muerto*. It was JD, or one of his men."

"That would explain why he needed a new costume," she barely managed to say past her growing horror. "Crap!" She just remembered something else from her date night with JD. "He had a drop of paint on his boot that glowed in the dark. I saw the same type of glow-in-the-dark substance on Dad's clothes."

"That would make sense. We used glow in the dark paint on our costume. Leo would have known that and could have told JD."

Another memory snapped into place. "Carmen saw JD purchasing cans of glow-in-the-dark paint at the store. He told her it was for a boy named Andy, whom he was helping with a school project. The other night at dinner, though, when I pointed out the paint to him, he gave me the same story but said it was to help a boy named Jorge, not Andy.

I think he'd forgotten what name he'd used the first time, which makes me think the story is a cover for why he needed so much paint."

She sighed. JD was looking more and more guilty with each piece of the puzzle that fit into place. No longer hungry, Elise pushed her plate of food away. She waited until Diego finished his breakfast before bringing up the next subject.

"We haven't talked about the body we discovered."

"Howard Drake's body," Diego said.

"You think JD killed his father." It wasn't a question and, God help her, considering everything they'd discussed, she was starting to think so, too.

Overwhelmed, she blew out a breath and dropped her head into her arms on top of the table. "What are we going to do?" She moaned aloud.

Before Diego could respond, there was a loud knock at the front door. Startled, they looked at one another and then, together, went to open the door.

Sam and Dane stood on the front porch.

Diego shifted his gaze from one to the other, scrutinizing their expressions.

"I take it this is not a friendly visit," he eventually concluded.

"JD called the station this morning to report he had seen trespassers on his property last night. Know anything about that?"

"Not a thing," Diego answered.

Dane shot him a skeptical look. "Where were you last night, Diego?"

"I was here, with Elise."

Sam's brow furrowed as she looked at the pair of them suspiciously. "I can't think of any good reason for you to have been over at the Drake place in the middle of the night, and I'd better not find out otherwise. You're already in enough trouble as it is." To Dane, she said, "Let's go."

They walked away, and Diego started to close the door when Elise grabbed his arm. He faced her and noticed her troubled gaze.

"Maybe we should tell them," she suggested. "They could help."

Telling them the truth was not without risk, he knew, but they were running out of options, fast.

Pulling open the door, he stepped out. "Sam! Dane! Wait up."

They stopped and, after exchanging a quick glance with one another, started back toward the house.

"What's up?" Sam asked when they were close enough.

"You have time for coffee? Elise and I have something we want to share with you."

A few minutes later, everyone was gathered at the table, except Elise. She ignored Sam's and Dane's watchful gaze as she put another pot of coffee on to brew. Soon, the comforting aroma of freshly brewed coffee filled the kitchen, mingling with the sweet scent of the pancakes they'd cooked earlier that morning.

"What's all this about?" Dane finally asked, breaking the tense silence.

Diego held up a hand in a gesture for patience. "In a minute. How do you take your coffee?" he asked, pushing a small tray of sweetener and creamer towards them.

Elise joined them at the table, carrying two steaming mugs of coffee, then refilled her and Diego's mugs.

"Now then," Diego said, pulling out his phone and scrolling through until he found the pictures he wanted to share. "I have to warn you, these pictures are not pleasant," he said somberly before handing his phone to Sam.

She took it cautiously and studied the images for a long moment before passing it to Dane. She turned her attention back to Diego, a questioning look in her eyes.

"Why do you have pictures of a decomposing body on your phone?" she finally asked him.

Diego met her gaze steadily. "Do you recognize who it is?"

Sam shook her head. "Of course not—" she began.

"What about you Dane?" Diego interrupted her. "Recognize that watch?"

Dane looked up at him in surprise before taking another look at the picture. He enlarged it to get a better view and a few seconds later exclaimed, "Holy shit! That's Howard Drake's watch."

Sam took the phone from him, studying the image again. "How do you know?" she asked curiously.

"Howard was our seven-on-seven coach in high school," Dane explained, a look of disbelief on his face. "That watch had a stopwatch feature he used to time us. He was always shoving it in our faces when we weren't meeting his expectations." A grimace crossed his features. "Damn it. That body looks like it's been dead for quite some time."

"Yeah, about six months, don't you think?" Diego interjected. "That's around the same time JD told us Howard ran off with another woman. At the time, I didn't think it sounded like something Howard would do."

"Where did you find the body?" Sam asked, her voice holding a mix of horror and suspicion.

Diego stared at her, debating what to say. "In a shed on JD's property," he finally replied in a low tone.

Sam shook her head in obvious exasperation. "Damn it, Diego. That *was* you last night."

Elise leaned forward, refusing to let him take all the blame. "It was both of us." She raised her sleeve, revealing a bandaged arm. "And this is where JD, or one of his men, shot me last night for trespassing."

"What?!" Sam exclaimed, clearly shocked.

"Yeah," Elise said with disgust. "Didn't he mention he shot at his trespassers?"

Sam grimaced, obviously appalled by JD's actions. "Must have slipped his mind."

"Before you charge us with trespassing," Diego interjected, desperation creeping into his voice. "Hear us out. Howard's body isn't the only thing we discovered."

He gestured to Elise, who scrolled through her phone until she found the video. She handed the phone to Sam and then waited as Sam and Dane watched it. Then Elise and Diego shared their suspicions about JD using the *El Muerto* costume as a distraction while transporting drugs across the Richardson property.

"I think it's possible that JD tried to transport drugs Monday night and Roy caught him," Diego concluded, his voice strained with emotion. "They fought, and he killed Roy. Then JD used Leo to order another costume and probably killed him because he knew too much."

"Oh, my God," Elise exclaimed suddenly.

"What?" Diego asked.

"At dinner with JD. He asked me again about buying the Double R. I didn't feel like explaining the entire situation, so I sort of..." She looked apologetically at Diego. "I might have suggested you were the reason I couldn't sell the ranch."

"That's okay," he said, clearly not understanding.

"No, it's not. He saw you as an obstacle," she explained. "I bet he paid Leo to put the bloodied costume in your closet, so you'd be arrested. If you were convicted of murdering my dad, then you'd be out of the way."

"And then you'd be free to sell him the ranch," Diego concluded.

"Holy hell," Dane swore, looking stunned by the revelations.

Sam rubbed her temples. "I suddenly have a horrible headache."

"So, you believe us?" Elise asked, holding her breath.

Sam frowned; her expression conflicted. After a moment, she let out a heavy sigh. "Yeah, I do."

"Great," Elise said with relief. "Then you can arrest JD for murdering Howard, my dad, and Leo, and drop the charges against Diego."

"It's not that simple," Dane cut in, his tone serious.

"Why not?" Elise demanded.

"We need concrete proof," Sam explained patiently.

Elise's shoulders slumped in defeat, the weight of their situation bearing down on her. "But your proof is right there," she protested with growing desperation, gesturing to the incriminating photos on Diego's phone.

"You mean the photos and video you took while trespassing on JD's property?" Sam asked, her voice thick with skepticism. "It wouldn't take a good attorney long to find a way to discredit those."

"And if JD finds out we suspect him and destroys the lab and removes the body," Dane added, "we'll have no evidence to arrest him with. We need to catch him in the act."

Sam let out a derisive snort. "Sure. I'll call him now and ask when he's planning to make his next delivery."

Then Elise remembered the conversation she had overheard when she dropped off JD's mother. "Sunday night." She smiled at the stunned faces staring at her from around the table. "His next drug run is going to be Sunday night."

CHAPTER THIRTY-FIVE

Sunday night was cloaked in a thick silence, save for the hushed whispers between Elise and Diego. They were crouched near the fence that separated the Double R from the Drake property, dressed all in black to blend into the darkness. The faint glow of their watches revealed it was close to eleven o'clock.

"Do you think this will work?" Elise's voice trembled with a mix of fear and determination.

"If what you overheard JD say on the phone was about moving a shipment of drugs, then there's a good chance it will," Diego replied, his voice sounding taut with anticipation.

As they sat at the base of the ridge, shrouded in darkness away from the moonlight, she was reminded of *El Muerto's* nightly rides along this very path.

Earlier that evening, Sam had tried to talk them into staying indoors but eventually gave up after Elise and Diego made it clear they refused to be pawns in the stakeout at their own home.

Earlier preparations had been made to guarantee a flawless operation. No Trespassing signs had been placed along the fence by ranch hands earlier that day as added legal insurance. Diego had pulled the security cameras from around the ranch house and set them up in the pasture at strategic locations designed to capture JD and his team as they came onto the property. Finally, Rodrigo and Diego had scouted the pasture under the pretense of checking the cattle to identify the locations where Sam and her officers could set up that evening as they waited for JD to make his appearance.

Then Elise and Rodrigo had driven separately into town to pick up Sam and her officers to avoid alerting JD to their plans by having police cars showing up at their residence.

The atmosphere during dinner had been somber, everyone aware of the high stakes involved tonight. If they were wrong about what Elise overheard at JD's house, then all their efforts would be for nothing. But if she was right...

Elise's hand instinctively went to her upper arm, where her skin was still raw from the bullet that grazed her during their last encounter with JD and his men. She pushed away thoughts of all the ways this evening could go horribly wrong, steeling herself for what lay ahead.

Just thirty minutes ago, Bev, the Las Palomas police dispatcher, had frantically sent out a false alarm over the radio, calling all available officers to a location on the opposite side of town. In case JD or one of his men were monitoring the police radio, they would now think the police were occupied elsewhere.

Elise shifted her position, the hard, rocky ground beneath her only adding to her discomfort. Every second felt like an eternity as she waited for JD's next move. Some things did not get better with anticipation.

Several yards away, Sam crouched beside the fence, her heart pounding with a mixture of fear and excitement. She was well aware that this stake-out could turn deadly in an instant. Next to her, Chad's hands were shaking as he gripped his gun tightly, ready for action.

She imagined Dane and Steve, crouched on the other side of the pasture, also feeling on edge as their eyes scanned the surroundings for any sign of movement. This was uncharted territory for the Las Palomas police force, but they were determined to put a stop to JD's drug operation.

Sam knew her team was prepared for this scenario, but the lack of real-world experience made her uneasy. They had only each other and their training to rely on.

The tension in the air was suffocating as they waited for JD to appear. Various outcomes played out in Sam's mind and she had to force herself to focus on the plan: wait until JD reached the middle of the pasture and then close in from both sides.

Her gaze flickered to where Elise and Diego were stationed, against her better judgment. They refused to sit back at the house and wait, so she reluctantly allowed them to wait in the pasture—under strict orders not to get involved.

Suddenly, the sound of crunching grass broke through the stillness, and Sam's hand shot out to touch Chad's arm. He turned to her, his eyes wide with anticipation. Silently, she motioned for him to be quiet and pointed towards the east gate. The sound of hoofbeats grew louder, accompanied by the whine of electric engines. Sam's blood ran cold as she realized what it meant: everything Elise and Diego suspected was about to be proved true.

With a surge of adrenaline, Sam and Chad simultaneously drew their guns from their holsters. This was it. This was the moment they had been waiting for. The tension in the air was palpable as they braced themselves for the impending confrontation. It was about to go down, and there was no turning back.

Diego pulled Elise further into the darkness as a shadowy figure on horseback rode past them, sending chills down Diego's spine. His eyes had adjusted to the dark after hours of waiting and he could see the rider urging his horse forward, heading towards the ridge on the other side of the pasture. Diego waited for Sam and her team to make their move, but nothing happened.

The rider halted at the top of the ridge; the night growing eerily quiet as he waited. For what, Diego didn't know.

Then he heard it—the low rumble of golf cart engines. It was happening. JD was moving the drugs across the pasture.

A flash of light caught his attention and when he turned back to the rider, *El Muerto* was there, perched atop his horse.

No. Not *El Muerto*, he corrected himself. JD, or one of his men, dressed in a costume rigged with lights to impersonate the ghost.

Beside him, Elise gasped and reached for his hand. Diego squeezed it in return, trying to offer some comfort in this terrifying moment. They only had a moment to process what they were seeing before the rider started galloping towards them along the ridge.

Diego watched in anticipation as *El Muerto* drew closer and then, suddenly, gunshots rang out from further back in the pasture. Even *El Muerto* seemed startled by them and abruptly reined his horse to a stop.

Now Sam's voice could be heard shouting, identifying themselves as police officers. More chaos ensued, with shouts and gunfire echoing throughout the night.

The lone rider, perched on the ridge, hadn't moved. Diego's heart raced as he watched the figure, knowing that if he didn't act quickly, the rider would escape.

With a surge of determination, he was up and running toward the horse, barely aware of Elise following him.

"Go back!" he shouted at her, but she was stubborn and didn't heed his warning.

As he neared the rider, Diego made a split-second decision and threw himself in front of the horse, hoping to startle it into throwing off its rider. The animal reared up in surprise, its powerful hooves flailing through the air.

In the chaos, Diego misjudged his distance and took a glancing blow to the head from the horse's hoof. Dazed and disoriented, he dropped to his knees as everything around him spun.

He heard Elise shouting his name but couldn't seem to make sense of her words. His body felt heavy and sluggish, refusing to obey his commands.

As he struggled to clear his head, the sound of hooves fading into the distance only added to his growing panic. The rider was getting away.

Finally regaining control of himself, Diego looked around for Elise, but she was nowhere to be seen. Panic gripped him as he heard her voice growing fainter in the distance.

Then he realized *El Muerto* had taken Elise!

Dread settled over him like a suffocating blanket as he realized the danger she was facing alone.

El Muerto grasped Elise tightly as she fought and screamed, the pounding of her fists against his solid form reverberating through the air. Not a ghost, as they had suspected. He was a man, but who?

It didn't matter now. What mattered was escaping from this dangerous predator.

With all her strength, Elise grabbed onto the man's waist and used her knees to push against the horse's side, shifting their weight until they both tumbled to the ground with a bone-jarring impact.

The horse galloped away, leaving Elise alone with *El Muerto*.

Before she could catch her breath, a powerful hand gripped her arm and yanked her to her feet.

Instinctively, Elise fought back, using all her force to push away from her captor. Her hand snaked up to grab hold of the dark hood of his costume, pulling it down and revealing his identity.

"I wish you hadn't done that, Elise," JD growled, pulling a gun from between the folds of the costume and aiming it at her. His eyes scanned the area before landing on the golf cart she and Diego had used earlier.

He dragged her across the field towards it. Further back in the pasture, the sounds of gunshots and shouts echoed. The police had their hands full and Elise knew there would be no help coming for her. She was on her own. The realization sent icy tendrils of fear snaking through her body, threatening to freeze her in place.

"Get in," JD ordered when they reached the cart, shoving her. "You're driving."

Knowing she had no choice but to comply, with trembling hands, she turned on the ignition and sped away. Fear coursed through her as she tried to come up with a plan.

"I'm truly sorry it has come to this, Elise," JD said, his voice as calm and smooth as if they were sitting on the back deck, reminiscing like old friends. "You have to understand, if Sam arrests me and throws me in jail, it's a death sentence. The cartel has eyes and ears everywhere. You don't want me to die, do you? I'm not a bad guy."

Elise's blood boiled at his audacity. "You killed my father!"

"Jesus, Elise! You can't possibly think I did it on purpose. It was an accident. Your father caught us driving through his pasture and demanded to know what we were up to. I offered him a cut of the profits for using his land, but he refused and threatened to call the police. I had no choice."

He glanced at her, but she was no longer listening.

Jesus! That was it.

She looked around, trying to recognize where they were. The landscape of the pasture looked so different at night. She hoped she wouldn't miss it.

Then she saw it—the cactus shaped like Buddy Christ silhouetted against the starlit sky. The ditch, where she'd crash the cart, lay between her and Buddy Christ.

Without hesitation, Elise slammed her foot down on the accelerator, causing the cart to jolt forward with increasing speed as she headed toward the cactus. Gripping the steering wheel tightly, she braced her other foot against the front of the cart.

JD sat next to her, gun pointed at her side, his attention darting behind them for any pursuers.

As they neared the dip in the pasture, Elise held on for dear life as the cart jerked and bounced violently. Beside her, JD's weight shifted with every bounce.

Then everything changed. The impact of the cart against the side of the ditch was like an electric shock jolting her body. Her mouth snapped shut and she tasted blood.

The windshield in front of them gave way, the plastic tearing from its hinges as JD's body flew into it, and then hit the ground with a sickening thud.

Ignoring the throbbing ache caused by her impact with the steering wheel, Elise levered herself out of the cart. She didn't even bother to check on JD but began a limping-run back the way they had come. Every step was agony, but her focus was on one thing: Diego. She prayed he was still alive.

She'd only gone a few feet when she heard heavy footsteps pounding after her. A second later, JD tackled her, pinning her down with his weight. Flipping her onto her back, he sneered down at her with pure malice in his eyes as he wrapped his fingers around her throat.

"You should have gone back to New York," he taunted.

"It's over, JD," Elise struggled to say between gasps.

He shook his head, his grip tightening. "For you, it is. You're about to be the second tragic death at the hands of Diego Juarez." With each word, he squeezed harder, cutting off her oxygen supply.

Elise fought with all her might, struggling against his hold on her, but he was too heavy, and her energy quickly faded. Her vision began to tunnel as she felt her life slipping away.

It seemed so unfair, facing death like this.

As she lay there helplessly under JD's grasp, her final thoughts were of Diego and how much she loved him. Then the weight on her chest disappeared.

She gasped for air, her mind consumed with fear and anger. She didn't care about JD's fate at that moment. All she could focus on was survival.

As her vision returned, she heard the sounds of a brutal fight nearby. Struggling to stand, she stumbled towards the noise until she saw two men locked in combat. Her heart stopped as she recognized one of them as Diego, his face covered in blood. She knew he couldn't defeat JD alone. With determination burning within her, she grabbed a rock and staggered forward.

JD's back was to her and, without hesitation, she swung the heavy rock down on his head with all her might. It wasn't enough to kill him, but it gave Diego the opening he needed to break free from JD's hold.

"We have to get out of here." Elise gripped Diego's arm, half pulling him, half supporting him. That he let her, told her how seriously he was injured.

"Stop! Or I'll shoot!"

They froze and turned around to see JD standing there. He'd retrieved his gun and now aimed it at them. His hand was surprisingly steady as he held the weapon, ready to take their lives without hesitation.

"Don't do it, JD," Diego told him. "It's over. The police have your men in custody. They know about the drugs and your father. Killing us only makes it worse."

JD's expression twisted into a mask of rage. "You've ruined everything!" he roared, spittle flying from his mouth.

Panic filled her as she faced him. There was no reasoning with him—and no stopping him. He was a man teetering on the edge of sanity; a man with nothing to lose.

With a shaky hand, he pointed the gun at her and pulled the trigger.

Elise flinched, expecting to hear the deafening roar of gunshot, anticipating the burning stab of pain in her chest.

Neither occurred as the gun gave an impotent click.

For a moment, confusion clouded her mind until she saw him pull the trigger again and nothing happened.

Tossing the gun aside, JD charged towards them, his face twisted into a grotesque mask of fury. Before they could react, he stumbled to a halt, his gaze fixed on something behind them.

A shiver of fear shot up Elise's spine as she followed JD's gaze to see what had caught his attention. There he was. *El Muerto.* Riding towards them with an unearthly aura radiating from his headless form. This was no human impersonator; this was a supernatural being, returned from the dead.

Elise clutched Diego's arm as the spectral figure rode toward them—and then passed them as if they weren't there. When it reached JD, however, it lifted him into the air with an invisible grasp.

Frozen in shock and terror, Elise and Diego watched as *El Muerto* carried JD off into the night; then disappeared into thin air. The only remains of their encounter were JD's anguished cries lingering in the stillness before they, too, faded away completely.

Chapter Thirty-Six

Panic and chaos erupted as the shrill wail of sirens pierced through the silence of the night. Dane's urgent shout snapped Diego out of his frozen state.

"Diego!"

"I'm here!" Diego called back, trying to remain calm.

"What's your status?"

"We're okay," he replied, trying to catch his breath. "But JD—"

Dane didn't let him finish before cutting in. "I radioed for medics. They're on their way. I need you to direct them to us. Sam's been shot."

Elise gasped in shock. "I'll go see if I can help," she said, starting to walk away.

Diego grabbed her arm. "No, you go meet the medics. If Sam's injured, Dane might need my help with the prisoners."

Elise nodded and set off across the pasture towards the front while Diego sprinted across the pasture in the opposite direction.

The next sixty minutes passed in a blur.

Despite wearing a bulletproof vest, Sam had been shot in the abdomen by one of the drug runners. For the second time in a week, air transport was called to the Double R. The man who'd shot Sam was dead; her aim had been better than his.

The rest of the drug runners had surrendered and were hauled off in handcuffs to the Las Palomas jail.

After dinner, as the moon cast a pale glow over the dusty ranch, Elise, Diego, and Dane stood outside in the front driveway. The night was finally still and quiet, save for the occasional rustle in the bushes or the distant hoot of an owl. Chad sat nearby in his truck, waiting to take Dane back into town.

"It sucks that JD got away," Dane said, looking around as if JD might suddenly appear around the corner of the house.

Elise exchanged a worried look with Diego before speaking up. "He didn't exactly get away," she said softly. Then she told Dane about their confrontation with JD and his subsequent confession that he'd killed her father. When she told him about the real *El Muerto* carrying off JD, he stared at her in disbelief. She couldn't blame him. She was still struggling to believe it herself.

"I don't know what that means for JD," Dane admitted. "I guess, for now, we'll stake out JD's ranch in case he comes back. By morning, we'll have a warrant to search the entire premises."

Elise's mind whirled with thoughts of what they might find and how dangerous it could be. She took a deep breath and asked, "What about his mother?"

"She'll be questioned, and then we'll see," Dane replied.

Elise didn't believe that JD's mother was involved in her son's criminal operations, but until they had more information, she knew they would have to treat her as a suspect. "I understand," she said with a nod.

Diego turned to Dane. "Do you want coffee to take with you?"

Diego shook his head. "No thanks, I think we'll pass. Oh, I almost forgot," he said, turning to Diego. "When I called Judge Adams for the search warrant, I let him know you're no longer considered a suspect. All the charges against you have been dropped."

Relief flooded through Diego at these words. He extended his hand to shake Dane's. "Thanks. Please be sure to let us know how Sam's doing."

"Definitely," Dane promised before climbing into the truck.

Diego and Elise stood in the darkness, their bodies rigid with tension as they watched the taillights of the truck disappear from sight. The sound of the engine slowly faded into the distance, leaving them alone in a quiet stillness. The silence that enveloped them was heavy with emotions as they both tried to process the events of the night. Exhaustion seeped through their bodies, weighing them down as they made their way back into the house. Then, with a soft click, Diego locked the front door, shutting out the rest of the world.

His arms enveloped her in a warm embrace, pulling her close to his solid chest. His touch was comforting and reassuring, his concern etched on his handsome face. "Are you okay?" he murmured against her hair.

Elise shook her head, feeling overwhelmed and uncertain about everything. "I don't know...I just...don't know."

"It's okay," he whispered, his breath tickling her ear. He held her tighter, providing a sense of safety and calm.

"Are you tired?" he asked after a moment, noticing the tension in her body.

Elise considered for a moment before responding. "Not really... I feel wired."

A playful smile spread across his lips as he took her hand and led her down the hallway towards their bedroom. "Well then, lucky for you, I know just the cure for wired nerves."

She raised an eyebrow and let him guide her into their cozy bedroom, where he closed the door behind them.

Leading her to bed, he wasted no time fulfilling his promise. As their bodies became intertwined and their breathing became deeper and more relaxed, Elise couldn't help but forget about all her worries and be completely present in the moment. This was exactly what she needed—to be lost in passion and pleasure with the man who loved her unconditionally, their bodies moving together in a symphony of love and desire. The world outside may have been chaotic, but here in each other's arms, they found peace and solace.

It was noon the next day when rays of sunlight, filtering through the curtains, finally roused Elise from her sleep. Though tempted to stay nestled in bed a little longer, she roused Diego with a tender kiss that quickly led to lovemaking that left her breathless and satisfied.

After a late lunch, Diego set off to the barn to speak with Rodrigo and the other ranch hands who had spent the previous evening in town. They deserved to know about JD and the events that had taken place while they were away.

Meanwhile, Elise went back into the bedroom and dialed Maddie's number, eager to fill her in on all that had transpired.

"Oh my goodness," Maddie exclaimed upon hearing the news. "I can't believe so much has happened in such a short amount of time."

Elise let out a small laugh. "I know. It's been a wild ride."

"So, what now?" Maddie asked, curiosity lacing her tone. "When are you planning on coming back up here?"

Elise hesitated, knowing that her answer might sound crazy. "Actually, I was thinking of staying down here and helping Diego run the ranch."

She could almost hear Maddie's jaw dropping through the phone. "Are you serious? Well, I mean, I get it. That's your childhood home, and it's all you have left of your father."

"It's not just that," Elise admitted. "I've realized how much I enjoy interacting with the guests and being a part of this town."

There was a long pause before Maddie responded with a heavy sigh. "Elise, you worked so hard for the VP position.

Even though Bob gave it to Sean, we both know he'll mess it up eventually and you'll be able to reclaim it."

"I know, but this past week has taught me something about myself," Elise said thoughtfully. "I love marketing, and I love working directly with clients. What I don't love is all the bureaucracy and politics that come with the vice president position." She paused before adding, "And I've discovered that there's something I love even more than marketing. Or rather, someone."

Maddie's voice softened. "And does this someone feel the same way about you?"

Elise couldn't help but smile. "He does."

A small sigh escaped Maddie. "I'm so happy for you, Elise. And sad as hell for me because I'm going to miss having you around."

"About that..." Elise hesitated before continuing, "How would you feel about moving to Texas?"

The women talked for another twenty minutes before Maddie put Elise's call through to Sean.

"Hi, Sean," Elise greeted him warmly when he answered the phone. "Congratulations on securing the vice president's position."

"Thanks, Elise. I was worried you might be upset and working together could become awkward."

"That's actually what I wanted to discuss with you."

It was early evening when Elise heard Diego come back into the house. She was standing in the kitchen, studying the contents of the refrigerator, and trying to decide what to make for dinner. Her thoughts were interrupted by Diego's footsteps, and she turned to greet him, only to see that he wasn't alone. Dane was with him, his usually sharp features etched with exhaustion. The man looked as if he'd aged ten years overnight.

"Hey there," Elise greeted him, gesturing for them to take a seat at the table.

"Dane came by to update us," Diego explained.

Elise glanced at Dane and immediately felt sympathy for him. "If you don't mind my saying so, you look like you could use a cup of coffee."

Dane managed a small smile. "That would be nice. Thanks."

As she started a pot of coffee, Elise remembered a bag of cookies in the pantry and set it on the table for them. She retrieved some mugs from the cupboard and soon they were all seated around the table, each with a steaming cup of coffee.

They waited patiently as Dane took a few sips before setting his mug back down with a satisfied sigh.

"That hit the spot," he said gratefully.

"How's Sam?" Elise asked, concerned.

"It was touch and go." Dane's voice trailed off before he took a deep breath and continued. "The bullet caused some internal damage. She actually coded on the flight to McAllen and then again during surgery, but she's tough and it looks like she's going to pull through. Katherine is with her right now, insisting on taking her somewhere peaceful, like Destin, to recover once she's released," Dane continued. "In the meantime, I've been appointed as acting chief of police."

"Congratulations," Diego said sincerely.

"Thanks," Dane replied, but it was clear he wasn't thrilled about the promotion.

"And JD?" Elise asked, her voice tense.

"Still no sign of him," Dane admitted with a heavy sigh. "We can't afford to relax yet. The cartel knows we've dismantled their operation and they'll be looking for revenge. If they find JD before we do, he might disappear without a trace."

Diego's brow furrowed in thought. "So, our suspicions were correct? He was involved in making drugs?"

Dane nodded grimly. "Oh yeah. That middle barn was essentially a high-tech meth lab. Exactly as you suspected. It seems JD was having the raw materials brought in on horse trailers."

"Isn't that risky?" Elise asked.

Dane took a sip of coffee before responding, his expression grim. "He had everyone in town fooled. Running a horse training business was the perfect cover for his actual operation. And technically, there's nothing illegal about transporting those raw materials." He shook his head in disbelief. "A meth lab, right here in Las Palomas."

A shiver ran down Elise's spine as she pictured the hidden lab and its dangerous contents.

"I had to bring in the Feds," Dane said, taking another drink of coffee. "You might see some activity over there for a while."

Elise nodded, feeling a mix of relief and apprehension. She couldn't believe this was happening in their quiet little town.

Dane's expression grew even more serious as he spoke again. "We also retrieved Howard's body from the car in the shed where you found it."

Elise and Diego exchanged glances but kept quiet.

"I guess JD didn't have time to move it," Dane continued. "I asked Beth about it. Turns out she was there when it happened."

Elise's heart dropped at the mention of Beth, wondering what her involvement had been with JD and his dangerous game.

"Apparently, Howard found out about the drugs and got into a fight with JD, who lost his temper and killed Howard," Dane explained with a shake of his head. "And Beth was too scared to say anything because she knew JD would kill her, too."

The room fell silent as they processed the information, the weight of it heavy on their shoulders.

"That JD is a real son-of-a-bitch," Dane swore, his voice filled with anger and disgust. "If we catch him, he'll go away for a long time. One of his guys has already made a deal in exchange for providing information about JD's operations." Dane paused, then looked over at Elise. "He confirmed JD attacked and killed your father that night."

Tears welled up in her eyes as she thought about her father's final moments.

Dane looked over at Diego. "Sorry about the arrest. I hope there are no hard feelings."

Diego shook his head, a small smile on his face. "No. You were just doing your job."

Dane took a last swallow of coffee before pushing away from the table. "I wanted to let you know the latest, but if you'll excuse me now, I'm going home to sleep."

They all rose from the table, their movements synchronized as they walked Dane to the front door. The night air was balmy and carried the gentle scent of wildflowers. Diego slipped his arm around Elise's waist, a protective gesture that she welcomed gratefully.

"Thanks for stopping by," he said, his voice sincere and warm. "We appreciate it."

Dane's eyes lingered on the way Diego held onto Elise, a small smile tugging at the corners of his lips. "You bet. I guess I'll be seeing you *both* around."

He opened the door, but before they could close it behind him, he poked his head back through. "Just a word of caution. Stay alert. We know now that JD was working with one of the Mexican cartels. They're the ones who funded both the construction of the barn, but also his operations. They're not going to be happy about his operation getting shut down."

Elise's heart skipped a beat at the mention of danger. "Do you think we're in danger from the cartel?" she asked, her voice trembling slightly.

Dane shook his head. "No, I don't think they'll bother you," he reassured her. "They want JD. And I don't know where he went, but he'd be crazy to go to Mexico. He may look for a place to hide out here."

Diego nodded understandingly as Dane left, closing the door behind him. He locked the door and, turning back to Elise, must have noticed how worried she was.

"We'll keep our eyes open," he promised her, pulling her into a comforting embrace.

She nodded and let him lead her back into the cozy family room. Exhaustion washed over her as she collapsed onto the soft couch, her mind racing with everything that had happened.

"I can't believe it's finally over," she murmured, as a sense of relief washed over her.

Diego's expression was pensive as he sat beside her. She could see the weight of their recent events reflecting in his eyes.

"What are you thinking?" she finally asked, breaking the silence between them.

He hesitated before answering. "I'm wondering when you'll be heading back to New York."

Elise nodded, realizing she hadn't mentioned losing her vice president position yet. "Soon," she replied, feeling anxious. "Come with me," she said softly.

He shook his head, his eyes searching hers before he responded. "You know I can't. Someone has to run the ranch. Maybe, in a couple of weeks, I could fly up for a visit."

It was her turn to shake her head. "That won't work."

He turned to her in alarm. "Why not?"

"Because I'm only flying back long enough to pack my things and return my work laptop."

He looked at her with surprise written all over his face. "What?"

A small smile tugged at her lips now as she continued. "I can't keep wearing these same two pairs of jeans," she joked lightly. "I'll need the rest of my clothes, even though I won't have much use for my business suits here on the ranch. Maybe I could wear them when I meet with new clients in town."

"Elise, I'm feeling lost," he admitted, confusion etched on his features as he searched her face for answers. "Are you telling me you're going to stay here and help me run the ranch?"

She smiled, relieved that he finally understood. "That's what I'm telling you."

Relief flooded his expression as a grin spread across his face. "Oh, thank God," he exclaimed. "What can I do to help? I'll move my stuff out of the house. I can stay in the foreman's house and let you have your old room back, if that's what you want."

Shaking her head, she reached out to cup his cheek gently. "No, you moving out is not what I want."

"Then what do you want?" he asked, his voice sounding gruff.

Her gaze never faltered as she answered with unshakable determination, "You, Diego. I want you." He stared at her in disbelief as she continued, fueled by newfound courage. "I love you. Maybe I always have and just didn't realize it, but I do now. I'll stay and be your business partner, if that's all you want, but I'm telling you that I want more. I want it all and I need to know if that's what you want, too. If it is, then please ask me what you need to ask me. I'm ready to give you an answer. Just please, don't make me wait any longer."

Almost afraid he'd misunderstood her, Diego took her hands in his and slowly lowered himself down to one knee. "Elise," he began, looking into her teary eyes with all the love he felt for her. "You are my best friend and the love of my life. Will you do me the honor of marrying me?"

Tears streamed down Elise's face and in that moment, Diego saw the love she held in her heart for him. "Yes, Diego," she cried, her voice trembling with emotion. "My best friend and the love of my life, I will marry you!"

Diego stood up and pulled her into his arms, their lips meeting in a kiss that spoke volumes about their love for one another. In that moment, all doubts and fears vanished as they held each other tightly. Theirs was an unbreakable bond, one that would only grow stronger with time.

CHAPTER THIRTY-SEVEN

THE PIERCING BLARE OF the alarm jolted Elise out of her deep slumber. She reluctantly opened one eye, only to be met with darkness enveloping her room. With a groan, she reached out to silence the shrill sound emanating from her phone. It took several fumbling swipes at her phone screen before she was successful, but the resulting silence was like music to her ears.

She had stayed up way too late the night before, pouring over today's presentation until the wee hours of the morning. Now, all she wanted was to sink back into the welcoming embrace of sleep. But as her heavy eyelids drooped closed again, she jolted herself awake. Today was not a day for giving in to temptation.

With a resigned sigh, she pushed the covers aside and swung her legs over the side of the bed. Just as she was about to stand up, a strong male arm snaked around her waist and pulled her back onto the mattress.

"Where are you going in such a hurry?" Diego groaned, still half asleep.

Elise chuckled and snuggled into his warm embrace, making no further move to get out of bed. "I promised Kathy I'd come over this morning and show her my ideas for her cafe."

"Can't it wait?" He pressed his lips against her skin in a tender kiss, sending tingles racing down her spine. She closed her eyes, savoring the sensation of his hot breath brushing across her neck each time he exhaled. The warmth and comfort of their shared bed beckoned to her, tempting her to stay nestled in his arms instead of facing the challenges of the day ahead.

She had spent the past month working tirelessly to launch her new marketing business in Las Palomas, and this presentation for Kathy's Cafe was crucial to her success, but if there was one thing she had learned over the past couple of weeks, it was that some things were more important than work.

A smile spread across her face as she nuzzled into Diego's chest, feeling his steady heartbeat against her cheek. "Yeah," she said with contentment in her voice. "It can definitely wait."

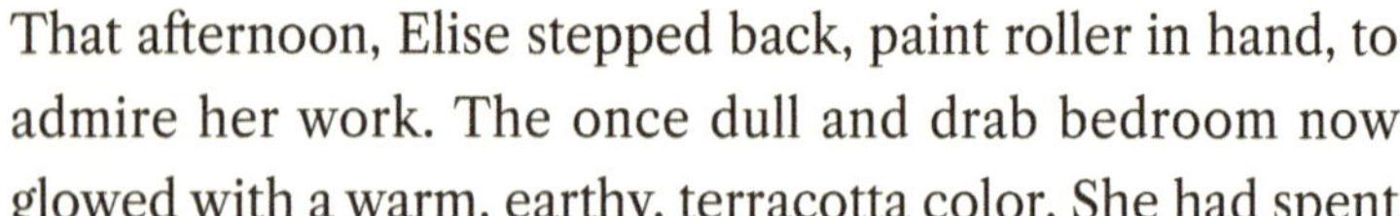

That afternoon, Elise stepped back, paint roller in hand, to admire her work. The once dull and drab bedroom now glowed with a warm, earthy, terracotta color. She had spent hours carefully painting each wall, her determination fueled by the rapid approach of their wedding day.

Diego's eyes scanned the room, taking in the transformation. "I like it," he admitted. "At first, I thought it would be too dark, but it's not."

Elise smiled, relieved that he approved of the change. It no longer looked like her father's bedroom; they had donated all of his old furniture to the local church and had a new master bedroom set on order. It was scheduled to arrive two days before their wedding, perfect timing for Diego's parents, who would stay in their old bedroom.

So much had happened in the past month since their encounter with JD and his men. The Feds had swooped in and dismantled the meth lab at the Drake farm. Howard Drake's remains had been laid to rest at a funeral attended by Elise, Diego, and most of the town.

Just last week, Beth Drake left Las Palomas for good and moved to Pennsylvania to be with her sister. Before she left, she signed over ownership of the farm to Elise and Diego, who had purchased it with plans for expanding the Dude ranch into a more family-friendly destination—adding a pool, jungle gym, and riding trails.

"Oh, I forgot to tell you." She turned to face him, a bright smile spreading across her face. "I finally talked to Maddie this morning."

"And?" Diego asked, a playful glint in his dark eyes.

Elise's laughter filled the room as she replied, "She can't stand working for Sean and is excited to move down here and become our new event planner. I promised we'd put her up in one of the guest bungalows until she finds her own place."

Diego shook his head. "I hope we haven't bitten off more than we can chew."

She smiled, already picturing the possibilities. "It'll be great," she reassured him. "We can turn JD's meth lab into a reception hall and once you've built the gazebo, we can cater weddings as well as host conferences. And with Maddie's help, I can expand my creative consulting business, too."

A soft smile spread across his face as he took in her enthusiasm. "You sound happy," he observed.

"I couldn't be happier," she replied, leaning in to kiss him.

"Good." His eyes scanned the room she had just finished painting. "Are you done in here?"

"For now," she confirmed with a nod. "I'll let this dry and come back to do the bathroom later." She grabbed several paper towels from the roll and used them to protect her hand as she removed the paint roller. She tossed it into the nearby trash bag.

"Dane called earlier. He should be here soon. Do you have time to talk with him?"

She pulled her phone from her pocket to check the time. "Sure, so long as I'm done by five. I have a call with a potential new client."

"Here, let me get that." He used a hammer to secure the top on the can half full of paint while Elise tossed the empty ones into the trash bag. "Who's the new client?"

"Potential client," she corrected. "Believe it or not, it's Hank Wells."

"Why does the president of the First Bank and Loan need creative consulting?"

"Zelda told him I was redoing her website, and he wants to talk to me about redoing the bank's website. He thinks it could be more user friendly. I told him I work with a very talented IT guy with affordable rates."

"Well, we definitely have the talent for that," he said with a grin. "But just to clarify, you didn't tell him I work for favors instead of actual payment?"

"Of course not," she giggled.

His lips captured hers in a tender kiss before pulling away. "Speaking of which, I finished those updates on Zelda's site. How about we go negotiate my fee in the bedroom?"

A playful sparkle danced in her eyes as she considered his proposition. "Very tempting," she began before being interrupted by the doorbell ringing. "That must be Dane."

"I'll get the door," Diego offered.

"Thanks, I'll wash up and then join you," Elise said as she headed towards the bathroom.

Making her way back, a short time later, to the family room where Dane and Diego were now engaged in conversation, she greeted them with a welcoming smile.

"Hi, Elise," Dane said in his deep, rumbling voice.

"Hey there. Can I get you something to drink? I have iced tea or a cold beer," she offered.

Dane shook his head. "No, thanks. I won't be here long. Wanted to let you know we found JD."

Elise's heart skipped a beat at the mention of JD's name. No one had seen or heard from him after that fateful night. "He's in custody?"

Dane shook his head, causing his short blonde hair to ruffle slightly. "Not exactly." He paused for a moment before continuing. "He's dead."

"Oh!" The news was shocking, but not entirely unexpected, given JD's involvement with the cartel.

"The cartel?" Elise asked, voicing her thoughts.

Dane hesitated before answering. "We don't know for sure. His body was found a couple of miles from here. We had to use his fingerprints to make a positive ID because..." he trailed off, looking hesitant.

"Because?" Diego prompted.

"Because his head was missing," Dane replied bluntly.

Elise felt her stomach churn at the gruesome image. "What?" she exclaimed, unable to believe what she was hearing.

"Yeah," Dane confirmed with a slight shrug. "Anyway, as far as Las Palomas police are concerned, the case is closed. I thought I'd stop by and let you know."

"Thanks for telling us," Diego said sincerely as they started toward the front door.

"How's Sam doing?" Elise asked. "Have you heard from her since she and her mother went to Destin?"

"She's good," Dane answered with a small smile. "Katherine has her sitting around all day and she's going stir crazy. The doctor said he won't release her to return to work for a couple more weeks, so they're staying there. I think she'd like a break from her mother hovering over her, but with the bookstore undergoing renovations, I don't see that happening. Zelda might fly out to spend some time with her, though."

"That's good to hear," Elise said with relief.

"Yeah. I'll be glad when she's back," Dane admitted with a chuckle. "Being chief comes with too much paperwork for me." He opened the front door, but before leaving, he turned back to them. "Oh, before I forget, I don't think I congratulated you on being engaged. I'm happy for you both."

Diego grinned and pulled Elise closer to his side, pride and love evident in his voice. "Thanks, man. We really appreciate it. And we hope to see you at the wedding?"

Dane nodded. "Absolutely. I wouldn't miss it."

After dinner, as the sun sank beyond the horizon, the sky turned a brilliant shade of orange and pink. Elise and Diego sat on their back porch, surrounded by the sounds of crickets and the gentle lowing of cattle in the back pasture. The air was warm and inviting, perfect for enjoying a quiet evening together.

Diego let out a contented sigh, rubbing his slightly bloated stomach. "I really need to tell Carmen to stop experimenting with menu ideas," he said. "I've put on at least five pounds since she started."

Elise chuckled, her eyes sparkling with amusement. "She's just following her passion for cooking. And judging by how quickly our ranch hands devour her meals, I know our guests will love her new recipes."

"Speaking of work," Diego said. "How did your call with Hank go?"

"Really well," she replied with a smile. "I told him I would present some ideas next week."

"That's great news." Then he added, "Oh, I have something for you."

"What is it?" she asked, curious.

He reached down and picked up a small box that she hadn't noticed before. With one hand, he held it out to her. "I wanted to give you this."

Her heart fluttered as she took the box from him, eagerly anticipating what could be inside.

"Before you open it, I want to tell you how happy I've been this past month with you," he said with genuine affection. "I love you, Elise, more than words can express."

Tears welled up in her eyes as she gazed at him lovingly. "I love you too," she whispered. "If you had told me just two months ago, I would live on the Double R with you and be this happy, I would have never believed it. Now though, I have everything I never knew I wanted."

She leaned in to kiss him, but he pulled back gently. "Not yet. I want you to open your gift." His eyes sparkled.

A warm smile spread across her face as she looked down at the box. The flaps weren't sealed, so she easily peeled them back to reveal a layer of delicate tissue paper. Carefully removing it, she couldn't contain her excitement as she caught sight of a chartreuse mug nestled inside. With anticipation building, she pulled out the mug and read the bright blue letters imprinted on the front: "Creative Consulting with Elise."

"My first company mug!" she exclaimed, turning to him. "I love it. I'll drink my morning coffee from it."

"Look inside the mug."

Curious, she removed the tissue filling the inside to discover a small ring box resting at the bottom. Confusion fluttered in her chest as she looked up at Diego for an explanation. "What's this?"

With a wide grin on his face, he took the mug from her hand and gently removed the box. Placing the now empty mug on a nearby table, he turned to face her with a mixture of nerves and hope in his eyes.

"I know we agreed to put most of our money towards purchasing the Drake farm instead of having an extravagant wedding," he began nervously. "And I'm truly happy with that decision. But, I couldn't resist getting you this."

Her heart skipped a beat as he opened the box to reveal a dazzling diamond ring glistening in the soft porch light. She gasped in awe as he slid it onto her finger—it fit perfectly.

Overwhelmed with emotion, Elise leaned in close and wrapped her arms around him in a loving embrace. "I love it," she breathed, feeling tears of joy streaming down her cheeks. "And I love you."

Diego's eyes sparkled with happiness as he pulled her closer. "Why don't we take this celebration inside?" he suggested with a mischievous glint in his eye.

Her heart racing, Elise nodded eagerly. "An excellent idea, but first, may I have a few moments to freshen up?"

"Of course," he replied with a playful wink. "It'll give me time to finish my beer."

He watched as she carefully carried the new mug across the deck, stopping every few steps to admire the ring. After she disappeared inside, he turned his gaze back to staring out into the night. With a contented sigh, he raised his beer to his lips, about to take a drink, when movement out in the field made him stop.

Curious, he stood and moved to the edge of the deck, peering out into the darkness. The full moon cast a silver glow over the land, and he could just make out the silhouette of a horse approaching. As it drew closer, he saw its rider was missing a head.

El Muerto.

The hairs on Diego's arms stood on end as the horse passed through fences and trees, coming to a stop just a few feet away from him.

Diego dared not move as the ghostly figure simply stood there, emanating an eerie presence. Then, with a small shift in the horse's stance, Diego's attention was drawn to an object hanging from the saddle horn.

It was JD's severed head.

Barely recognizable in death, his lifeless eyes were opened wide in terror and his skin had taken on a sickly pale hue.

Maybe he should have felt fear, or sympathy, but Diego felt neither for the man who had killed three men, one of whom was Elise's father and Diego's closest friend.

"In death, *El Muerto* serves swift and brutal justice upon criminals," he whispered, remembering the tales he had heard about this vengeful spirit.

As if in acknowledgement of the words, the horse gave a ghostly whinny, and then, as suddenly as it appeared, *El Muerto* turned his horse and disappeared into thin air, leaving behind only the echo of a maniacal laugh.

Shaking off the unsettling encounter, Diego returned indoors to find Elise waiting for him. He discarded his clothes and climbed into bed with her, seeking comfort and release from the chilling experience. As they made love under the covers, Diego knew he would never speak of what he had witnessed. Some things were best left unsaid and kept secret in this mysterious land filled with ghosts and spirits.

9 781961 835016